Works

MAC Detective Agency Mysteries

This Angel Has No Wings

This Angel Doesn't Like Chocolate

This Angel's Halo is Crooked

This Angel Isn't Funny

Non-fiction

Seeing Beyond the Wrinkles:
Stories of Ageless Courage, Humor, and Faith

Study Guide (Seeing Beyond the Wrinkles)

The Enduring Human Spirit:
Thought-provoking Stories of Caring for our Elders

This Angel Isn't Funny

A MAC Detective Agency Mystery

CHARLES TINDELL

HILLIARD HARRIS

HILLIARD HARRIS

P.O. Box 275
Boonsboro, Maryland 21713-0275

This novel is a work of fiction. Names, characters, places and incidents
either are the product of the author's imagination or are used
fictitiously. Any resemblance to actual persons, living or dead, events,
or locales is entirely coincidental.

This Angel Isn't Funny Copyright © 2008
By Charles Tindell

First Edition-August 2008
ISBN 1-59133-270-2
978-1-59133-270-1

Book Design: S. A. Reilly
Cover Illustration © S. A. Reilly
Manufactured/Printed in the United States of America
2008

Dedicated to: Mom

Acknowledgements

Acknowledgement must be made to those whose reading and critiquing of my manuscript proved invaluable.

Special acknowledgement goes to Helen L. Montgomery for her many constructive suggestions while editing the manuscript. Ms. Montgomery, an author herself (*The Osecca Option*—Mundania Press), has a unique eye for editing and I feel fortunate to have had the benefit of her expertise.

I wish to express my gratitude to my publisher, Stephanie Reilly, and to my editor-in-chief, Shawn Reilly. Their support has been appreciated.

I wish also to thank my wife, Carol, for her support and encouragement. Thanks also go to my sons, Scott, Andrew, and Robert.

Finally, appreciation is given to my readers. Thank you for your readership and continued interest in the series.

Chapter 1

The downstairs door slammed shut and the wooden stairs leading up to Howie Cummins' office began to creak. He knew by the footsteps that it was Hershel Kass, the owner of the corner drugstore below his apartment. Kass also owned the building in which Howie lived. Two years ago, Kass had rented the apartment to him at a price far below the going rates for 1966, even remodeling the living room into an office. The agreement was that Howie, in lieu of paying the full rent, would work behind the soda fountain from time to time. But their agreement didn't stop Kass from paying him a small salary. Howie protested, saying it didn't seem right. Kass, however, had replied with a good-natured grin, "I'm the boss and I don't want any arguments." Howie hadn't given him anymore.

Working as a soda jerk didn't fit Howie's image of a private detective, but the extra money came in handy whenever the cash flow got a little tight. He could make it without working at the drugstore, but he continued to dish ice cream as a favor to Kass.

Listening to Kass' footsteps on the stairs, Howie took a sip of his morning coffee, having spiked it with a shot of bourbon. He wondered what Kass wanted to see him about.

Within moments the office door opened and Kass walked in. Although Howie nodded a friendly hello, the somber look on his friend's face told him this wasn't a social call.

"What's up?" Howie asked after Kass settled in one of the two worn leather chairs in front of the desk. He moved his coffee cup away from Kass.

"I have client for you."

Howie took out his notepad and rummaged through a desk drawer for a pen. A new client meant money. Perhaps now some dough could be put away until he saved enough to replace the lumpy couch pushed up against the wall opposite his desk. After the couch, he would work on replacing the floor lamp, getting one where all the light sockets worked. His four drawer metal file cabinet had a few dings and dents, but served its purposes. Adam, one of his partners, had called the office Spartan, but Howie preferred to think of it as uncluttered.

"Okay. Go ahead," Howie said, flipping open his notepad.

Kass hesitated. "Can I ask you a question first?"

"Sure, no problem," Howie replied, concerned about the worried look on his friend's face.

"You still handle all kinds of cases, don't you?" Kass asked in a tone as sober as the look in his eyes.

"Sure we do." Howie studied Kass for a moment, curious about what kind of client he had for them this time. "It's not a little kid and his lost cat again, is it?"

"No."

"So what kind of case is it?"

"A very unusual one."

Chapter 2

"A totem pole!" Howie nearly choked on the sip of coffee he had just taken. "Did I hear you right?"

Kass nodded. "I'm afraid so."

"Why in the world would anyone want to steal a totem pole?"

"Wish I knew." Kass scratched the top of his bald head. With only a fringe of baby-thin, light-brown hair encircling his dome, he often joked that he could pass as a monk, although it would have to be one with Jewish roots. "All I know is that my friend desperately wants it back. He considers it his good luck charm."

"Did he report it to the cops?"

"Oh, yes, right away."

"And?"

"They took the report and said they'd investigate it, but..." Kass shrugged, throwing his hands into the air as if to say that one shouldn't expect too much. "Well, you know how busy the police are." He folded his arms and rested them on a stomach that had been the recipient of too many of the banana splits served at the soda fountain of his drugstore. "What would that police detective friend of yours say? What was his name again?"

"Jim Davidson."

"That's right. Now I remember. I'm sure Detective Davidson would tell you that the police aren't going to spend a lot of time looking for a stolen totem pole."

Howie visualized Davidson's gray-blue eyes going ice cold if he was ever asked to spend his time looking for some totem pole when he could be working on the latest bank robbery or homicide.

"You're not going to get any argument on that from me," Howie said. "He's been busy with that string of gas station robberies on Washington Avenue."

"Yes, I've heard about them. Terrible. Just terrible. I hope they catch whoever's responsible. It gives the area a bad name." Kass paused for a moment. "But couldn't you get some information from Detective Davidson?" he asked, his eyes expressing hopeful expectation. "Wouldn't he be happy to do that for you?"

"I'm sure he would."

Jim Davidson had one of the finest reputations on the North Side for ridding the streets of bad guys. Police departments throughout the Twin City area had deep respect for the man's tenacity at sticking with a case to its end, often calling upon him for consultation on the most difficult ones. Howie had met him through a mutual acquaintance at a party. They had hit it off immediately. After Howie shared his plans of starting up a detective agency with the help of two friends, Davidson, an eighteen-year veteran of the police force, slapped him on the back.

"That's great," the detective had said. "We need people like you to fight the gutter scum. Give me a call if you ever need any help."

"I just might do that, Detective Davidson," Howie had replied, adding with a hint of bravado, "And the same goes for you. I'm here if you should ever need my assistance."

Davidson laughed out loud and took a swig of beer.

"You know something, kid?"

"What's that?"

"You remind me of myself when I was just starting out."

"Yeah? In what way?"

"You're just as cocky as I was. Hell, maybe even more. Howie Cummins, I like your style. So why don't you call me JD? All my friends do." Davidson saluted him with his beer and finished it off.

From his very first case, however, Howie had only sparingly sought JD's help and almost always at the insistence of his partners. While his partners were happy to have a seasoned detective's expertise as a resource, Howie was determined to handle the work on his own. The tougher the case the better. Davidson could call it cockiness, but he called it determination...and perhaps a competitive desire to demonstrate a one-upsmanship on the local cops.

Now, as Kass sat in front of him with the offer of a case, Howie tried to decide whether or not to take it. Locating a missing totem pole wouldn't be much of a test for his detective skills. On the other hand, it would provide him and his partners added exposure in the community and additional cash.

"So, Kass, what you're saying is that your friend doesn't think the cops are going to make this a high priority and that's why you came to me."

"Exactly."

"I see. Give me a minute to think this through."

Why not take the case? His partners would welcome something routine for a change. Kass wouldn't have come to him for help if it hadn't been important. Yet, for reasons Howie couldn't explain he had an uneasy feeling about the case. But hey, what could it hurt, right? He'd take the client as a favor to Kass. He turned to a blank page in his notepad and wrote *Totem Pole* at the top. Next he jotted down the time, date, and who he was talking with, a practice he had done since opening the agency.

"Who is this guy anyway?"

"His name is Stuart W Hatchaway."

4

"And what does this Mr. Hatchaway do?"

"He owns Yesterday's Treasures. It's an antique shop up on Oliver and Broadway." Kass waited while Howie jotted down the information. "Hatchaway's a very nice man." He cleared his throat. "And Howie, he prefers to be referred to as Stuart W. It has something to do with him being named after his grandfather."

"Is this totem pole worth a lot of dough?"

"I don't think so. It's been out in front of his store in all kinds of weather. Stuart W wouldn't have done that if it was valuable."

"And you say that he considers this thing his good luck piece?"

"I know that may sound a little strange, but you'd understand if you knew him." Kass' face broke into a broad smile. With a twinkle in his eyes he looked every bit the image of Santa Clause (with the rotund figure, but minus the beard). "Stuart W has been my friend for nearly twenty-five years."

"How old of a man is he?"

"Oh..." Kass stoked his chin. "I'd say he must be in his early seventies, but he's got a young spirit. A great guy, but a little on the superstitious side."

"Superstitious? In what way?"

"When he opened his business back in June of '63, he stood the totem pole outside his store as a promotional. It worked wonders."

"You mean, it brought people in?"

"Oh, yes. Each year his business did better than the year before. Next month will be the five year anniversary of his store's opening and he wants the totem pole back to continue on with his good luck." Kass turned and pointed to the framed movie poster on the wall behind him. "It's like your Bogart poster. How would you feel if somebody stole it?"

Howie eyed his poster—Humphrey Bogart and Mary Astor starring in The Maltese Falcon. Bogart had been his role model ever since high school when he decided to become a detective. The poster, his prized possession, hung on the wall opposite the door so that it would be the first thing people saw when they entered the office.

"Yeah, I see what you mean."

"You know, Howie, you remind me of Bogart."

"Well, it can't be in the looks department," Howie said. With reddish-blond hair cut short on the sides and top, a couple of dimples that appeared whenever he smiled, he had looked more like a choir cherub than a detective when he first got into the business. "The only thing we share in common is that we're about the same height, although he's a little taller."

"Height doesn't matter." Kass glanced back at the poster. "What counts is how tall you are on the inside." He pointed his finger at Howie. "And in the past couple of years you have grown tall."

"Thanks." The past couple of years, however, had also added some hard lines, and Howie hoped that in the years to come he would have that hardened, no nonsense expression that Bogart had. He was resolved to

5

prove that he had what it took to make it as a detective and to be as tough as Bogart appeared on the screen. "I better get a description of this totem pole."

"Does that mean you'll take the case?" Kass asked, his eyes reflecting the hopefulness in his voice.

Howie nodded. "Do you have Hatchaway's phone number and address?"

"I sure do." Kass gave him the information, waiting for a moment while his friend wrote it in his notepad. "You can always reach him at the antique shop."

"How about after hours? Does he live in the area?"

"Oh, no. He's like you."

"What do you mean?"

Kass smiled. "He lives in the back of the place in a small apartment."

The ringing of the telephone interrupted their conversation. Howie picked up the phone, motioning for Kass to keep his seat.

"MAC Detective Agency. Howie Cummins speaking."

"Hey, this is Margo." The deep male voice sounded like a foghorn with a cold. "You remember me?"

"Of course. How could I forget a guy like you?" Margo owned and operated a beer joint on upper Hennepin Avenue in downtown Minneapolis. The Watering Hole, as Margo so proudly named it, catered to a clientele that included some of the more colorful characters inhabiting the downtown area. "What can I do for you, Margo?"

"I've got to talk to you."

"Let me call you back. I'm with somebody right now. What's your number?" Customers in the background yelled for another round of beer as the jukebox belted out some country western tune about someone's cheating heart. The Watering Hole was the kind of place that made a lasting impression. Howie could picture the dingy atmosphere, and remembered the odor of spilled beer and the lingering cigarette smoke that hung like a stubborn morning haze.

"Get rid of whoever the hell you're with fast." Margo gave him the number, sounding like a man who expected people to do as he demanded. And people usually did, since the guy looked like he had been a pro wrestler in a former life. "Call me back as soon as you can. It's damn urgent, and I don't like waiting. It makes me crazy."

"Don't worry. I'll get back to you in a few minutes." Howie hung up the phone and turned his attention back to Kass. "Looks like I might have another client."

"That's good…that's good." Kass shook his finger at Howie. "See, what did I tell you? Your fame is spreading. Soon, you'll be as well known as Bogart."

"Don't hold your breath." Howie confirmed the information Kass had given him. "I'll get in touch with Hatchaway as soon as I can."

6

"Thanks. I really appreciate you doing this." Kass got up and walked toward the door, stopping at the poster. "Bogie, you've got good competition here in that young man." He waved good-bye to Bogart's competitor and left.

Howie leaned back in his chair and laced his fingers behind his head as he stared at the poster. Bogart no doubt would have crossed paths with a character like Margo, and he would have been right at home in Margo's place. While working on their last case, Howie visited the bar to check out a lead and almost made a fatal mistake when he asked the burly six-foot-plus bartender in bib overalls if he could speak to Margo if *she* was around.

"I'm Margo!" the bartender had shot back, scowling as if his honor had just been trampled upon. "Have you got a problem with my name?"

He'd had to think fast to get out of that one. He must have said the right thing, though, to have the guy call him now like they were old buddies. But what could be so urgent for a guy like Margo? Well, he would soon find out.

Chapter 3

After Kass left, Howie picked up the phone and dialed Margo's number. While the phone rang, he wondered if Margo still had that sign, *The Watering Hole - Where All the Animals Go,* posted behind the bar. He was just about to hang up when a recognizable gruff-sounding voice answered.

"Yeah?" the voice growled.

"Margo, it's me, Howie Cummins calling back." The same country western song played in the background. "So what's going on?"

"My whole damn life is falling apart! That's what the hell's going on!"

"Sorry to hear that." Howie wondered if the guy perhaps needed a priest or a shrink or maybe even an animal tamer. "Are you sure you want me?"

"Damn it! Why in hell do you think I'm calling you?"

"I don't—"

"I need a detective!"

"Okay. Okay. Calm down." Howie pictured Margo's nostrils flaring like a bull about ready to charge. He felt sorry for anyone who had the misfortune of getting in the way. "So, what's the problem?"

"It's about…hang on, will you? Just wait a damn second, Charlie, and I'll get you your beer!" Howie heard Margo let go a string of expletives as several other customers yelled for their drinks. Margo came back on the line. "Look, I don't even have time to take a piss now. The place is crazy with customers."

"Should I call back?"

"Hell, no!"

"I don't understand. If—"

"I want you to get your ass down here!"

"What?"

"I need to see you."

"When?"

"Today."

"Today?" That would conflict with his plans to see Hatchaway. "Look, Margo, I don't know if I—"

"Make the time, damn it!"

Howie didn't like being ordered around, but the guy sounded like he wouldn't take no for an answer. That was okay. This could be a good opportunity to get the MAC Detective Agency known beyond the North Side. "Okay. What time do you want me there?"

"Be here in—Charlie, shut your big trap, will you? Didn't I tell you I'd get you your damn beer?" The bull snorted. Charlie and the other customers better clear a path. "Are you still on the line?"

"Yeah."

"Be here in an hour. By then, the crowd will have thinned out."

"Okay. I'll see you then." As soon as Howie hung up, he called Mick Brunner, one of his partners, but got no answer. He dialed his other partner, Adam Trexler. "Hey, what are you doing right now?"

"I'm struggling with a school assignment." Frustration filled Adam's voice. "The professor wants a five page paper."

"On what?"

"On what it means to put faith into action in today's world." Adam grew silent for a moment as if waiting for a snide comment on God and religion. "I'm having a hard time writing it."

"How long have you been working on it?"

"A couple of hours. Why?"

Howie suspected that Adam's struggle didn't have anything to do with writing the paper; he had always been an excellent student. His partner's struggle had to do with trying to decide whether the ministry was the best place for him. Adam had shared with him that he sometimes thought he would make a better detective than a minister. "I want you to come over," Howie said. "We need to go see a client."

"We've got a client?"

"Actually, we've got two. I'll tell you all about them when you get here."

"How soon do you want me there?"

"In twenty minutes." He heard Adam sigh. "Come on. Take a break. You're due for one, aren't you?"

The line grew silent for several long moments.

"Sure, why not?" Adam finally said. "I guess the paper can wait."

The door downstairs slammed shut. Howie could tell by sounds of the footsteps on the wooden stairs that it was Adam. At six feet, with dark-brown hair that fell over his forehead and brooding bedroom eyes, Howie thought Adam should give modeling a try. With his good looks and athletic build, he would be a natural.

Although Adam's moralistic approach to detective work irked Howie, for now, he was glad to have him onboard. In time, he counted on the harsh realities of the work putting a rougher edge on his partner. When Adam had first had misgivings about coming on as a detective, Howie had argued that being a detective is no different than being a preacher. "Instead of telling the bad guys they're going to hell, you just tell them they're going to prison." His logic had won him over.

Within moments the office door opened and Adam walked in. He made himself comfortable in one of the chairs in front of Howie's desk and got straight to the point.

"So what kind of cases are we dealing with?"

"I haven't met our first client yet, but let me tell you about him." Howie summarized his meeting with Kass about Hatchaway and the missing totem pole.

"I remember that totem pole," Adam said. "It has to be seven or eight feet tall. Did you get a description of it?"

"No, but I'll be going to see Hatchaway tomorrow. I'll get one then. Hopefully, even a picture."

"So who's the client we're going to see now?"

"A guy by the name of Margo. He owns a beer joint called The Watering Hole on Hennepin Avenue, just on the fringe of downtown."

A thoughtful look flashed through Adam's eyes.

"Didn't you visit that place while working on our last case?"

"That's right."

"And didn't you say this Margo was a beefy giant of a guy who wore bib overalls and had a face that only a mother rhino could love?"

"That's the man, all right."

"Why does he want to hire us?"

"I don't know. He wouldn't tell me over the phone." Howie got up from his chair. "What do you say we go find out what we're getting ourselves into?" He offered Adam a half-smirk. "Who knows? Maybe it'll give you some ideas for that paper you're writing."

Chapter 4

Stuart W Hatchaway immediately sensed that the man storming into his place of business with the gruff scowl on his face wasn't interested in antiques. He could always tell those who loved antiques. As soon as they entered his store, their faces lit up with excitement at the prospect of finding another treasure to add to a life already filled with treasures of the past.

Because most people began browsing as soon as they came in, Stuart W had his checkout counter in the middle of the store. From this, the center of his universe, he sat in his rocking chair and sipped hot lemon tea as he watched his customers' delight grow as they strolled back into history.

This man, however, ignored the collection of pocket watches, the old kerosene lanterns, even the copper bathtub dating back to the 1880's. He strode past the table of collectable salt-and-pepper shakers without so much as a sideways glance. Stuart W wondered if he was some husband who felt that his wife spent too much money on "junk" and he was coming to complain. Well, he would soon learn that Stuart W Hatchaway never sold junk and always priced his items at a fair market value. That's why he had so many repeat customers! And if those who came into his store didn't have a smile on their faces when they entered, why smiles would soon appear as they stopped to rummage among tables, bins, and floor-to-ceiling shelves teeming with artifacts of bygone days.

"May I help you?" Stuart W asked, offering the man a friendly smile.

"Where is it?" the man demanded in a harsh voice.

"Where is what, sir?"

"The totem pole that was outside!" The man glared around as though expecting to see it somewhere in the store.

Stuart W set his mug of tea on the counter and stood up on arthritic knees that ached more today than yesterday. He prided himself on never getting upset, even when customers thought he was charging too much for an item—which he would never dream of doing. He started in the antique business in his early twenties and in nearly fifty years had never taken advantage of a customer, and never expected to get rich. He loved dealing in antiques because it was a way of preserving history.

"You ask what happened to that totem pole," he said. "I'd like to know that myself."

"What are you talking about?" the man asked, his sullen tone as unfriendly as his coal-black eyes.

"Someone stole it."

The man swore under his breath.

"When did that happen?"

"Two days ago. Sometime during the night." Stuart W peered over his glasses and brushed back a shock of white hair that had fallen over his forehead. "May I ask why you're inquiring about it?"

"Because I wanted to buy it."

"Oh, my, my, I'm afraid that wouldn't have been possible anyway."

The man's eyes narrowed.

"What do you mean? I've got money." He spit the words out as though the old man deserved his indignation.

"I didn't mean to imply that you didn't have the means to purchase it. The fact of the matter is that the totem pole wasn't for sale. Never has been. And, if I ever get it back, never will be." He was about to suggest that he would be happy to check with the other antique dealers in the area to see if they had any totem poles in their possession when the man turned on his heels and stormed out. Well, that was the problem with the younger generation now days—too much in a rush.

Stuart W picked up his mug of tea and settled back down in his rocking chair. Over the years he had learned to enjoy each moment. Whoever that man was, he needed to learn to take life easier. Life was too short to be as angry as he seemed to be.

Chapter 5

Howie parked the car. He and Adam got out and headed toward Margo's bar. Pleased that he had persuaded Adam to come with him, he hoped that working on a case would give his partner a chance to forget his struggles for a while. Why Adam brooded so much about whether he should become a minister was beyond him.

Howie didn't have any time for God, not since his mother had died back when he was in grade school. In the past ten years he had only been in church twice: once for his father's funeral, and last year for Mick's wedding.

Adam had the makings of a good detective if only he would shed some of the moralistic teachings he had been brainwashed with at the seminary. Ethical standards and high-sounding platitudes might be okay for preachers and the stained glass churches they lived in, but trying to adhere to such codes out in the streets wouldn't help you solve cases and could get you hurt or even killed.

"Are you sure you should be going into a place like this?" he asked, wondering if Adam caught the hint of needling in his tone.

"What do you mean?"

"You being almost a preacher and all that." Howie couldn't resist the little digs he gave his partner from time to time. Adam needed to lighten up; his brooding personality got a little tiring. "Wouldn't those professors at seminary have a fit?"

"Larson wouldn't."

"Who's he?"

"He teaches practical theology."

"Is that so? I didn't think any theology was practical."

Adam gave Howie a sideways glance as they approached the bar.

"Larson would argue that as long as I have a good reason going into a place like this, then there's nothing wrong with being here."

"So does that mean if you didn't have a good reason for coming here, you'd be afraid of people judging you?"

"People want to judge me, that's their problem." Adam pointed to the sign and shot Howie a quizzical look. "Isn't The Watering Hole an odd name for a bar? What kinds of people come here?"

13

"The motto of this joint is 'Where All the Animals Go.' That should give you a clue." Howie opened the door and led his partner into the dimly-lit bar.

"Oh, man, is it ever smoky in here!" Adam rubbed his eyes. "Don't they have any windows to air it out?"

"I don't think this place has ever breathed fresh air," Howie said as someone in the back booth yelled for another beer. "That's what draws the animals here. It's like a cave where they can come and get away from the rest of the world." He nudged Adam with his elbow. "If your Professor Larson spent a couple of evenings here he just might learn some real life practical theology."

To the right were half dozen booths. Three of them were filled. The bar was to the left. In the back near the jukebox a guy wearing a cowboy hat and denim had his arm around a dark-haired woman wearing the same. They swayed to the sounds of country western as they sipped beer from bottles. At the far end of the bar, two shaggy-bearded men rolled dice from a cup. They paused, turning their heads at the loud conversation from another booth where two men were engaged in a heated argument about who should buy the next round of drinks for their lady friends. The ladies sat giggling, enjoying the attention.

"Charming atmosphere," Adam whispered.

"If you want charm, wait until you meet the owner."

"Hey, Cummins!" yelled the man behind the bar. "Over here!"

"Let me guess." Adam nodded toward the barrel-chested giant wearing bib overalls. "That's Margo."

"You got it. Come on. Let's go see what's troubling the big guy." They moved to the bar and slid onto stools.

"Get you guys a beer?" Margo asked. "It's on the house."

"Not for me," Adam said.

"Me, either," Howie added.

Margo hadn't changed much from the last time they'd seen each other. His black curly hair was a bit longer and just as unruly as Howie remembered. He had the look of a prize fighter who had fought one too many rounds. His eyes curious, he scanned Adam.

"This is Adam Trexler, one of my partners," Howie said. "I brought him along to show him your place."

Margo gave a gap-toothed smile.

"So what do you think of it?"

Adam took an uneasy look around and cleared his throat. "It's got a style all its own."

"Damn right it does." Margo braced his hands on the bar counter and leaned toward Howie. "Does your partner here know?"

"Ah...know what?"

"What we share in common."

"I'm not sure what you're—" Then he recalled the first time he'd visited The Watering Hole. He'd lied about his middle name being Margo,

14

justifying it in his mind because it got him out of the corner he had painted himself in when he mistakenly assumed Margo to be a woman's name. "Nah, it's just between us," he said, ignoring the puzzled look Adam gave him.

"Cool." Margo poured a glass of beer for himself and guzzled it, wiping his mouth with the back of his hand when he was done. "Damn. I needed that."

"So what's so urgent?" Howie wanted to get straight to the matter. The noise and cigarette smoke were giving him a headache.

"It's about Donna Mae."

"Who's she?"

"My woman! At least, I thought she was." Margo slammed his fist on the counter hard enough that a nearby ashtray jumped. His eyes filled with anger. "Damn it to hell. I think she's cheating on me. I want you guys to follow her and find out what the hell is going on. I want to know who she's dating."

Howie gave Adam a sideward glance, wondering what kind of practical theology lesson he was learning so far.

Adam looked unhappy about the idea of following people around. It was an invasion of privacy.

"You want us to spy on her?" he asked.

"Yeah, don't detectives do that kind of shit?"

"We'll see what we can do," Howie said. He took out his notepad and plucked a pen from his shirt pocket. "Why don't you give us her name and address, and one of us will track her for a week or so."

"Then what?"

"Then we'll give you a report of where she goes and who she's meeting." Howie paused, and when Margo didn't respond, gave him a questioning look. "Does that work for you?"

"Works for me fine. And don't worry about money. I'll pay you guys the going rate plus expenses. This place doesn't look like much, but it's a gold mine." Margo poured himself another beer and gave Howie the information he wanted. "Man, I've been so good to Donna Mae. I can't believe she's doing this to me! She knows she can come down here any time and have all the drinks she wants on the house."

"Guess she doesn't know a good thing when she sees it," Howie said, maintaining a straight face. He slipped his notepad back into his pocket. "You hang in there, Margo. We'll be in touch."

Howie and Adam returned to the office to find Squirrel, a one-time street bookie who had helped them with their last case, waiting for them. The little guy was leaning back in Howie's chair with his feet up on the desk and his hands clasped behind his head, as if he hadn't a care in the world. As soon as he saw the two detectives, he jumped up, nearly tipping the chair over.

"Hi, guys," he stammered. "I just wanted to see if this thing was as comfortable as it looked." He gave the chair a spin, looking like he had just been caught with a fifth ace up his sleeve. "Man, it's weird you have this dentist chair. Makes me think of getting my teeth filled." He rubbed the side of his jaw. "I hate going to the dentist."

Howie walked past Squirrel and sat down. The warm seat made him wonder just how long the wannabe detective had been sitting there. He liked the idea of having a converted dentist chair. It made a great conversation piece. Besides, it had come with the place. "So what are you up to?"

"Just seeing what you guys are up to."

Squirrel made himself comfortable in another chair. His high-pitched voice, pea-size black eyes that constantly darted back and forth, and his thick dark-brown unruly hair caused others to joke about him living in a tree and gathering nuts in the fall. That he was barely five feet tall and had front teeth too large for his mouth to conceal only added fuel to the jokes about him. No one knew his given name (not even his last name) or anything about his background. Some said he came from a wealthy family. Others thought he was raised in an orphanage. Still others heard that he'd served time in prison. Howie would solve the mystery one day but meanwhile, the word on the street that he was a reformed bookie with dreams of becoming a private eye only added to his legend.

"Come on, Squirrel, what are you really here for?" Adam asked.

"Just checking to see if you guys can use my services. I told you I'd work for the experience." His nose twitched as he sucked air through his front teeth. "And where else can I get better experience than rubbing shoulders with the best detectives on the North Side? You guys are the greatest. Why, the bad guys don't stand a—"

"Squirrel!" Howie put up his hand to stop the flow of words.

"What?"

"Don't lay it on too thick. Okay?"

"Sure enough. I can dig that." His upper two front teeth overlapped his lower lip when he grinned. "So how can I help?"

"I don't know if we—"

"Don't forget I know a lot of people on the North Side. I've got a deck full of connections. If anything is going on around Broadway, Old Squirrel will find out about it." The little guy studied his forefinger for a moment before chewing off and spitting out a hangnail.

Howie rocked in his chair for several seconds, pondering the offer.

"Okay. Maybe we can use you." He liked Squirrel in spite of the guy's quirky personality and his annoying habits. "Tell you what. I have something right up your alley. You might just save us some legwork."

"Great!" Squirrel rubbed his hands together as though he had just swept a big pot in a high stakes poker game. "Boss, just tell me what you want me to do. I'm your man. You won't regret it."

Adam shifted in his chair. "Howie?"

"What?"

"Are you sure about, ah…" He gestured toward Squirrel.

16

"Very sure." Howie turned to Squirrel, irritated. Adam should save his judgmental attitude for the pulpit. "Squirrel, ask around and see if you can get any information on a certain missing item we've been hired to locate."

Squirrel's eyes doubled in size. "No sweat. I can handle that." He inched forward in his chair. "What is it? Stolen diamonds?"

Howie shook his head.

"Loot from some bank heist!"

"That's not it either. It's—"

"I know. I know," Squirrel blurted, his high-pitched voice rising in crescendo with every syllable. "It's a hot car! That's it, isn't it? I've heard there's been a rash of car heists around here lately." A look of indignation appeared on his face as he folded his arms across his chest. "You just can't trust nobody on the North Side."

"Hang on there for a minute," Howie said, amused by the little guy's enthusiasm. "It's none of those things."

"It isn't?" Squirrel sagged back into his chair. "Man, I would've laid you ten-to-one that it was."

"I thought you were done making bets," Adam said, shooting a quick *I told you so* look at Howie.

"You're right, preacher. It was a slip of the tongue." Squirrel sat up straight. In dramatic fashion, he placed his hand over his heart and held his head high. "I swear on a royal flush that I'll stop making bets." He laughed and turned his attention back to Howie, his eyes flashing with curiosity. "So, tell me. What are you looking for?"

"A totem pole."

"What?" Squirrel glanced from Howie to Adam and back to Howie. "Is this some kind of joke?"

"Nope. The totem pole stood out in front of Yesterday's Treasures, an antique shop up on Oliver and Broadway."

Squirrel scratched the side of his head.

"Oh, yeah. Now that you mentioned it, I do remember seeing that thing in front of the store." He dug in his ear for a couple of seconds and then flicked away whatever wax he had mined. "Old man Hatchaway runs that place, doesn't he?"

"That's right." Howie folded his hands on the desk. "Somebody took the totem pole the other night and he wants it back. It's as simple as that. I thought with all the connections you say you have, you just might turn up a lead or two. What do you say? Still want to give it a try?"

"Sure." Squirrel flashed a toothy grin. "And I'll give you seven-to-three odds that..." His eyes darted toward Adam for a moment. "Sorry, I forgot." He slapped his mouth as though reprimanding himself for the slip. "Trust me. I'll come up with a lead within a couple of days."

Howie grinned. Squirrel's exuberant spirit more than made up for Adam's dark moodiness.

"Good deal. Remember, if you're going to be working with us, you can't go around trying to get people to bet no matter what kind of odds you give them. Do you understand?" He glanced at Adam and added, "We've got a reputation to maintain."

"Don't forget that you've supposedly turned over a new leaf," Adam said in a tone more suited for a Sunday morning church service.

"Yeah, yeah, Preacher, I know." Squirrel shrugged. "Can I help it if I backslide? Isn't that what you preachers call it? And wasn't there some guy in the bible who kept slipping back to his old ways and complained of a sliver in his finger?"

Adam shook his head as he let out an audible sigh. "No, that was the Apostle Paul...and it was a thorn in his side."

"See, I know my bible. That guy's got his thorn and I've got my sliver. We're dealing from the same deck." Squirrel stood and gave Howie a mock salute. "I'll get on this right away. You don't have to worry about a thing."

After Squirrel left, Howie leaned back in his chair and chuckled to himself. The reformed street hustler would be more than happy to sit down with Adam and his professor over drinks and clue them in as to what they needed to know to reach the lost souls who roam the streets and back alleys of the North Side. A couple of beers with Squirrel, and Adam and his professor's practical theology would be turned upside down. Howie would give ten-to-one odds on that.

Chapter 6

He'd be here any minute.

Donna Mae LaBelle looked forward to it. He'd made it a practice to come over every Tuesday evening, a night that Margo always worked late. She had only known him for a couple of months, but she had fallen for him by the second date. He was sensitive and caring, and took her to concerts and was always interested in her as a person. Oh, Margo had been fun, but his idea of a good time involved bowling, a pizza, and a few beers at his bar. On the other hand, her new love took her dining at some of the finest restaurants in the Twin Cities, places Margo and his friends had never even heard of. The only thing unusual about him was that he rarely smiled or laughed. That he was so serious seemed odd considering his other interest outside of his regular job.

The doorbell rang. She hurried to answer it.

"Hi, I've been expecting you," she said, hoping he liked her new perfume. "You're early, but that's nice. Come on in." She took his hand and led him to the couch in the living room. They would go out to dinner, come back to her place, and head for the bedroom.

He took her hand and caressed it, tracing each finger up and down.

"Donna Mae, I've been meaning to ask you a question."

Donna Mae caught her breath, hoping that this might be the big question she was hoping he would ask. She composed herself.

"And what is it that you want to ask me?"

"Didn't you have a brother by the name of Johnny?"

Her mouth dropped open.

"Ah…yes, but he died five years ago."

"I know…that's what I thought."

Mention of her brother made her nervous. She glanced around for her cigarettes, but knew he didn't like her smoking.

"Did you know my brother?"

"Let's say we shared a mutual interest."

"Really? What?"

"Johnny liked to collect unusual items, didn't he?"

"Yes, I have a few of them in my house." She sighed. "It makes me sad that he died so young."

He continued to caress her hand.

"It makes me sad too, but for a different reason."

"How well did you know Johnny?"

"Well enough to know that he wanted a glamorous life style so much that he decided to make a career change."

"You..." A cold chill went through Donna Mae. "You were one of his partners?"

"Too bad Johnny died before we could split our profits."

Donna Mae gasped. Her brother told her about his partners, particularly the one who seldom smiled. Johnny had said that the guy was a psychotic killer.

"That case is still open and—" She jumped up and began backing away. "You're going to have to leave."

"I will as soon as you tell me about the key."

"Key! What key? I don't know what you're talking about."

He studied her for several long moments.

"Why, Donna Mae. How did I know you'd say that?" He reached in his pocket, took out a pair of white gloves. "Time for us to go."

"Go?" she cried, nearly hysterical, her eyes on the gloves. "What are you talking about? Where are we going?"

"To your car. It's in your garage, isn't it?"

"Ye...yes, but where are we going?"

"*You're* going on a long trip."

Tears filled her eyes as she fought back panic. If she could make it to her bedroom, she could lock the door.

"I'll go pack," she said, her voice quivering.

"That won't be necessary," he said as he slipped on the gloves.

Chapter 7

Howie wiped his brow, ready for a break from dishing up ice cream, serving cherry phosphates, and cleaning up the messes people made. It had been busier than usual at the drugstore. The soda fountain had gotten more than its share of customers who, while stopping to pick up the evening newspaper or a carton of cigarettes, decided to treat themselves.

You do what you have to do he kept telling himself as he wiped the counter. But he looked forward to the day when he and his partners were so swamped with cases that he would have to tell Kass that he was turning in his apron. Of course, he would pitch in behind the counter occasionally as a favor to Kass; he owed him that much. His goal, however, was to become a top-notch detective and to have the best detective agency not only on the North Side, but in the Twin City area.

JD, his detective friend at the police department, told him to be patient. "It's going to take several years to build a reputation and get the word out that you're a good detective," JD had said. He would be patient all right, but being a good detective wouldn't be enough. He aimed for being the first phone call people made when they needed a private detective.

After cleaning up after a group of teenagers, Howie took off his apron, walked out from behind the counter and plopped down on the end stool. If he was upstairs in his office right now, he would relax with a cup of coffee with a shot or two of bourbon. Or maybe just the bourbon. He ran his tongue over his bottom lip, thinking. Perhaps next time he'd bring a shot and slip it into a Coke.

The cowbell over the front entrance clanged and he glanced up to see who was coming in. His jaw dropped when he saw who it was.

"Hello, Margo," he said as the big guy walked up to him. The owner of The Watering Hole looked like he hadn't slept for days. Whatever his problem, it was a cinch that he wasn't coming in for a dish of ice cream. Howie noted his client's bloodshot eyes, furrowed brow, and the snarled, twisted mouth revealing teeth stained with tobacco. He smelled beer on Margo's breath, and his clothes reeked of cigarettes. "What's wrong?"

"Donna Mae's dead!"

"What?" Howie said, uncertain he'd heard correctly. Kass shot them a glance from the other end of the counter where he was talking with a

21

customer. His boss was accustomed to the colorful characters of Broadway, but this brute dressed in cowboy boots, bib overalls, and a flannel shirt cut off at the shoulders had a look about him that spelled danger. Howie quickly mouthed "it's okay" and turned his attention back to Margo. "What do you mean, dead? What happened?"

"She was..." Margo eyes glistened and for a second, it looked like tears might come. That he could have such a tender side surprised Howie. Then anger flashed and he snarled, "She was found early this morning in her car in the garage."

"Oh, man. I'm sorry."

"The motor was running and the garage door was shut."

"Margo, that's awful."

"You don't have to tell me that." Margo ground his fist into the palm of a hand that looked as if it could crush rocks. "By the time the cops arrived, they figured that she'd been dead somewhere between eight and twelve hours."

"Why don't you sit down?" Margo declined but then changed his mind and nearly collapsed onto the stool. Howie went behind the counter and poured him a glass of water. "Who found her?" he asked as he set the glass in front of Margo.

"A newsboy delivering the morning paper heard the car running in the garage."

Howie flashed back to his own childhood when he saw his mother lying in a coffin. It had left an indelible image in his mind. "He found her?" he asked, feeling sympathy for the kid.

"Naw. He ran next door and got the neighbor out of bed. The guy came over and rang the doorbell, but got no answer." Margo massaged the back of his thick neck. "The neighbor tried to open the garage door but couldn't, so he called the cops." He eyed the glass of water and looked behind Howie with searching eyes. "Don't you have anything stronger than this? I just use that shit for washing."

"I can get you a Coke or something."

"Don't bother unless you've got some bourbon to go with it." Margo buried his face in his massive hands for several seconds. He took a couple of deep breaths, his overalls barely able to contain the heaving of his barrel-like chest.

"What did the police say?" Howie asked, wondering if JD was involved in the investigation.

"Coppers are a bunch of shitheads."

Although Howie generally agreed with Margo's assessment, he still found himself asking, "Why do you say that?"

"Hell, they called it a suicide." Margo's jaw muscles tightened as he said the word.

"How did they come up with that?"

"Damn if I know."

"Come on, Margo, there had to be something."

"Well, I guess there was a note." Margo's thick lips curled into a sneer. "Damn cops wouldn't let me look at it."

"Why not?"

"Because I'm not family," Margo said, spitting the words out as though they were dirt. He ran his hand through his unruly hair a couple of times. "I know my Donna Mae wouldn't do something like that. Hell, she had too much to live for."

Kass glanced at them again. Catching Howie's eye, he gestured with a nod toward a customer who was staring at them. Howie nodded at Kass to let him know he understood. He lowered his voice. "Margo, are you saying the cops are wrong?"

"You damn right they are." Margo's nostrils flared and his bloodshot eyes turned fiery-red. "And I want you to get whoever the hell did it and I don't give a shit how long it takes as long as we get the bastard."

Kass glanced at them once more, his annoyance showing.

"Keep it down, Margo, will you? What do you say that we go up to my office? We'll have more privacy there." Howie okayed it with Kass, and he and Margo headed up to the office. While Margo settled in one of the leather chairs, Howie poured a glass of bourbon and set it front of the big guy. "Here you go. Try this."

Margo picked up the glass, took a sniff, and gulped it down. "That's some damn good stuff," he said, setting the glass on the desk. He spotted a letter opener and picked it up.

"That's made from solid steel," Howie said. "It was a gift."

"It's pretty damn sharp," Margo noted as he touched the point of it. "You could do some serious damage with this." He set the opener back down. Although he spoke in a quiet tone, his eyes glared with rage. "I don't care how long it takes or how much it costs me," he said, his voice rising. "I want you to get the guy who killed her."

Howie wasn't about to point out that maybe the police were right about it being a suicide. Given Margo's emotional state, it wasn't the time to express that. He took out a notepad and pen from his shirt pocket. "Did she have any family?"

"Yeah. Her parents live up north in International Falls. Dad works for some paper mill." Margo hesitated, and then continued as though feeling the need to explain. "I know because one night she talked about him retiring from the mill in the next couple of years."

"How about brothers or sisters? Does she have any?"

Margo shook his head. He lowered his eyes until he seemed fixated on the letter opener. "She didn't talk much about her family." He kept his head down as though ashamed he didn't know more.

"Do you have any idea who'd want to kill her?"

"Damn right I do." Margo placed his hands on the desk and looked at Howie with eyes filled with wrath. His hands formed enormous fists, causing Howie to wonder if he could have been a boxer at one time, and if he had been, how many men he had knocked out, or killed. "I bet if you find

23

out who the hell Donna Mae was seeing behind my back, you'd have your damn answers. And I know why he murdered her, too."

"Keep talking," Howie said. "I'm listening."

"She must have realized how good she had it with me. She decided to ditch him and come back to me, and the creep got jealous."

"That's a possibility." Howie figured it sounded more convincing to Margo than it did to him. His bets were with the cops. People commit suicide for many reasons. According to JD, suicide was more frequent than most people realize. "Do you have any idea who this guy she was dating might be?"

"Damn it, if I did I wouldn't be here," Margo snapped. "The creep would be lying dead in some alley by now." No doubt he could easily kill a man and then go have a beer and a smoke without giving what he had done a second thought.

"If you don't know who she was dating, is there someone else who might know?"

Margo nodded. "Yeah, she's got a couple of girlfriends who could know something." He dug into the pocket of his overalls and pulled out a slip of paper. "Here are their names and phone numbers. I would've gotten in touch with them, but they don't like me for some reason."

"Any other friends she might have?"

"No. These two were the ones she hung around with mainly. If anybody knows, they'd know who the guy might be."

Howie took the slip of paper, glanced at it, and slipped it in his shirt pocket. "Okay, I'll tell you what. We'll get in touch with them and see what kind of leads we get."

"You're going to stay on the case, then?" Margo asked.

"Sure, you can count on me." Murder or not, it would be good experience. It would also be more exciting than looking for a missing totem pole. "I'll fill my partners in tomorrow and we'll get right on it. I'll give you a call when we find out anything."

Margo got up to leave. "Just one more thing."

"What's that?"

"I want you to keep me in the know about this."

"No problem. We always keep our clients informed."

"But I want to know everything no matter how little of a detail it is." Margo's eyes hardened. "I've got to know everything. Have you got that?"

"Sure."

"Keep in touch then, you hear?"

Howie watched Margo leave. If Donna Mae had been murdered, his partners, especially Adam, would want to bring the person responsible to justice. To keep Margo fully informed, however, just might lead to a North Side form of back alley justice. His partners wouldn't care for that outcome, but Howie could care less. After all, it would be one less bad guy that wouldn't ever get out on parole. Maybe Mick and Adam couldn't live with that kind of street retribution, but Howie could.

Chapter 8

Mick grimaced. "Are you saying that Margo's case has turned into a possible murder case?"

"That's right," Howie said, suspecting that Mick was thinking about their last case. It had been six months since Damien escaped. It would be only a matter of time before he turned up again. Not tomorrow, or the next day, but one day...

"Let me get this straight," Adam said, a note of skepticism in his voice. "The police aren't considering her death as foul play, but Margo does?"

"You've got it." Howie leaned back in his chair. "And I know you both think that tracing down a missing totem pole is just the kind of easy case we need for a change."

"That's for sure," Mick said. He cracked his knuckles.

"Wait a minute," Adam said. "Let's think this through. All we have is Margo's assertion that she was murdered. Isn't that right?"

"For now it is."

Adam stood up, walked over to the window, and gazed out at the street for a minute. Of the three of them, he was the most cautious, always wanting to carefully think through something before moving ahead. His approach to detective work, though, prevented him from taking the risks Howie felt you needed to take.

"Has it ever occurred to you that Margo might be just overreacting?" Adam asked.

"He could be," Howie replied, suddenly deciding to give the owner of The Watering Hole the benefit of a doubt.

"Does he have any evidence that Donna Mae was murdered?" Mick asked.

"Not at this point." Howie took out his notepad and flipped to the page when he had jotted down some things from his conversation with Margo. "He said that the cops didn't volunteer any information since he wasn't a member of the immediate family, but they made it clear that they were ruling it a suicide. As far as they're concerned, the case is closed."

Adam walked over and sat down. "Call JD and see if he can give us anything on it."

"I guess I can do that," Howie said, not surprised that Adam would bring up Davidson's name. Adam was always ready to run to JD. "I'll give him a call later. We got anything else to discuss?"

Mick cleared his throat. "Yeah, I do."

One look in Mick's eyes, and Howie knew trouble was brewing. The last time Mick had committed them to helping the grandmother of one of his eighth grade students. He and Mick agreed on many things, but his partner had too much of a soft spot for little old ladies and kids. "Okay, let's hear it," Howie urged.

When Mick cleared his throat again, Howie knew it wasn't a good sign. "Come on. Out with it," he said, preparing himself for the worst.

"Ah...guess who I ran into the other day?"

Adam looked at Howie, but only received a shrug in return. "We have no idea," Adam said to Mick. "So, who was it?"

"Bernadine McGuire."

"You mean *Saint Bernadine*?" Howie rolled his eyes.

"What's the matter?" Mick asked.

"She was the one girl in our senior class who refused to date throughout her high school years because she thought guys only wanted to score with her."

Adam frowned at Howie. "At least she had morals."

Howie turned his attention to Mick. "Please tell me she's turned into a wild, luscious babe."

Mick rubbed the hump on his nose, a souvenir of his high school football days when his nose had been broken twice in three years. "Bernadine isn't a babe by any standards, but...ah..." He offered his partners a half smile. "She's attractive in a sisterly sort of way. If you know what I mean."

"Yeah, I know what you mean. She's still got that mousy-brown straight hair."

Mick nodded. "Well, but it's short and I, ah, I think it looks nice." His eyes dodged Howie's for a second. "And...she's put on a little weight, but hey! She's got a nice personality."

"A nice personality?" Howie nearly laughed out loud. The kiss of death. He turned to a blank page in his notepad and printed *Saint Bernadine* at the top and drew a halo above the name. "So what's going on with her? Did she turn into a nun or something?"

"Oh, no. Nothing like that."

"What then?"

Mick shifted uneasily in his chair. "Well, when we ran into each other at the grocery store we had a few minutes to talk. When she found out about our detective agency, she asked if she could come up and talk to us."

"You told her we have a detective agency?" Howie blew out a breath. He had a feeling he was about to get a headache. "Talk to us about what?"

"About her brother, Les."

27

"Wasn't he one of the hoods in school?" Adam asked.

"I guess he thought he was cool wearing that black leather jacket."

"He also had a ducktail," Howie added.

Mick nodded. "I know, but we were all a little crazy in those days."

Adam reached over and tapped Mick on the arm. "And wasn't he part of some gang called the Black Knights or something like that?"

"Yeah, and he was always getting in trouble."

"Look, we don't have time for this," Howie said. "I hope you told her—" The downstairs entrance door slammed shut and the stairs creaked as someone started up. He cocked his head to one side but didn't recognize the footsteps. "Who's that now?"

Mick offered Howie a weak smile. "I bet that's her now. I told her it was okay to come up around four."

"You what!" Howie buried his face in his hands.

"Hey, what else could I do?" Mick looked pleadingly at his boss. "After all, she was a classmate of ours."

"So?"

Adam jumped up from his chair. "Sorry to miss the reunion. You're going to have to tell me all about it tomorrow."

"And just where do you think you're going?" Howie snapped.

"I'm still working on that paper I didn't finish because of that trip we took to The Watering Hole." Just as Adam got to the door, it opened and in walked a woman dressed in a brown skirt and a white turtleneck sweater. A small golden cross hanging from a necklace was her only jewelry.

"Hello, Bernadine," Adam said, his eyes on the cross. "Do you remember me?"

"Of course, I do. You're Adam Trexler."

He pulled his eyes up to hers. "Wow. You've got a good memory."

"Thank you. I remember you being such a loner in school. All the girls wanted to date you because you seemed so mysterious." She offered a hint of a smile as she adjusted her glasses. "So you're a detective now?"

"Only part-time. I'm going to school." Adam glanced at Howie and cleared his throat. "In fact, I've got a paper to finish so I'm afraid I won't be able to stay."

"He's going to be a preacher," Howie said. Those black horned-rimmed glasses she was wearing were the same ones she wore in high school.

Bernadine's eyes widened. "That's simply wonderful. I'm pleased that God has shown you the way." She cast a sideways glance toward Howie and smiled back at Adam. "Miracles do happen, don't they?"

Adam nodded. "They sure do. Well, I've got to be going. Nice seeing you," he said to Bernadine. "See you guys tomorrow."

"Bernadine, how are you?" Howie said as he rose from his chair and offered his hand. "It's been a long time."

"Nearly nine years." The smile she had given Adam had already disappeared. "The last time I saw you, Howard, was on the night of graduation. Do you remember?"

"How can I forget?" On graduation night, he'd celebrated by lighting up a cigar. He'd offered a puff to Bernadine and received a fifteen-minute lecture on the evils of smoking. Good thing she hadn't known about the pint of whiskey he'd out in the car. Besides, she was the only classmate who called him Howard.

"Why don't you sit down?" he said, shifting his offer of a handshake to an offer of a seat. "And then you can tell us why you wanted to see us." He waited until she sat down. "Now, Bernadine, what's the reason for the visit?" he asked, amused at how she tugged at her skirt to make sure it covered her knees.

"I have come here to engage your services. I wish to hire you, Howard."

Howie wanted to bury his face in his hands. Better yet, he could really use a stiff shot of bourbon. "Are you in trouble?"

"Of course not," Bernadine replied sharply. "This is about my brother, Lester."

"What about him?"

"He's taken up smoking again." She turned up her nose as though to say she would never indulge in such a disgusting habit. "He had quit for nearly six months—"

Howie swallowed a smirk. "That's hardly worth hiring a detect—"

"Don't interrupt me, Howard! I'm not finished!" Bernadine's eyes flashed, reminding him of graduation night and how she had admonished him. "Last week when I visited my brother to invite him to a prayer meeting, he looked like he'd been in a fight."

"Did you ask him about it?"

His former classmate scowled. "Of course, I did."

"So what did he say?" he asked, keeping his tone mild.

"He said it was nothing. He didn't want to talk about it."

Good for him Howie thought.

"But I just know he's in some kind of trouble." She leaned closer, her face grim. "And I want you to find out what's going on."

"Well, I don't know. We're pretty booked right now..."

"I was told that you would take the case."

Howie shot a look at Mick.

Mick gulped. "I guess I forgot to mention that part."

"I guess you did," Howie replied through gritted teeth. He turned to Bernadine. "Well," he said through a forced smile, "I guess that means we'll take you on."

"Thank you."

"No thanks needed," he said with a sigh. "My partners would tell you that I'm always happy to do a favor for a former classmate."

Chapter 9

"Where's Adam?" Mick Brunner settled into his favorite chair in Howie's office. Howie had called him earlier and asked him to come up as soon as he finished his teaching duties at school.

"He's over at the seminary," Howie said.

"What's he doing there?"

"Working on some paper he needs to finish by tonight." Howie took a notepad out of his shirt pocket, opened it, and laid it aside. "I'm glad you could make it, though." He glanced at the notepad as he drummed his fingers on the desk. "How did school go today?"

"Same as usual at this time of the year." Mick loosened his tie. He loved teaching, but he hated the tie. "It's spring and the kids are anxious to get out for summer break."

"You teachers are ready for it as well, huh?"

"Oh, sure." Mick stretched out his legs and folded his arms across his chest. "But you didn't ask me to drop by to chitty-chat about the trials and tribulations of being a teacher." He eyed Howie suspiciously. "You've got that look about you."

"What are you talking about? What look?"

"Don't play innocent with me. We've known each other too long." Mick pointed to Howie's notepad. "What have you got going on?"

"Just trying to keep up with our cases. After we're done here, I'm going to pay a visit to Hatchaway. I want to get a description of that totem pole." Howie offered a winsome smile. "Can't find something if we don't know what it looks like, now can we?"

Mick cleared his throat while swallowing a smirk. Whenever Howie flashed that engaging grin of his, he wanted something.

"And where do I fit into all this?" Mick asked.

"I need someone to follow up with those two girlfriends of Donna Mae's." Howie flipped a page in his notepad. He looked up, a trace of the winsome smile still lingering. "I tried to contact them earlier today, but they weren't home."

"And with Adam at school, that leaves me, right?"

"I know this is short notice, but would you handle it for me?"

Mick ran a hand back through his curly black hair. "You mean before I go home to the delicious supper I know my wife is going to fix for me?"

"Look. Margo wants us to get on this thing about Donna Mae as soon as possible." Mick heard a hint of exasperation in Howie's voice. "He's already called me a couple of times today asking what we've done so far."

"And what did you tell him?"

"That I'd call him later this evening."

"You don't think it was a mistake to take him on, do you?"

"Oh, no. Not in the least. But to keep him off my back, I promised that we'd have something for him by tonight." Howie shrugged as if to say that there was nothing else he could've done. "I know it means you missing supper, but I'd like to have something to tell Margo when I call him later. So, what do you say? Will you do it?"

Mick hesitated. He was worn out from a day of controlling kids with spring fever, but Howie also looked exhausted. Right from the beginning of the agency, Howie had put in long hours to make sure their detective business succeeded. "Sure, why not. I figured you might be asking me to do something like this anyway."

Howie's eyebrows rose. "You did?"

"That's right." Mick leaned forward. He offered Howie a half smile. "Listen, buddy, I know you better than you realize."

Howie pushed the phone toward Mick. "Do you want to call Mary and tell her to hold off on supper?"

"That's not necessary." Mick stretched his back; an old football injury from his high school days still plagued him. "Mary and I talked just before I left school. I told her that you wanted to see me."

"And what did she say?"

"That it probably meant I wouldn't be home for supper."

"You have a pretty smart wife."

"I think so. She knows with me being in this line of work that it means missing supper some evenings, but she's always been supportive of what we do." When he had told Mary that he hoped he wouldn't be too late, she had given him a hug. "You and Howie and Adam are there to help people when they need it. We know first hand what that means, don't we?" she'd said.

"So, you got those names and addresses for me?" Mick asked Howie. He enjoyed the interviewing aspect of detective work because it gave him the opportunity to meet people from all walks of life. While Adam was more of a loner, Mick had always been told that one of his best traits was being a people person. "I might as well get going on this. The sooner I start, the sooner I can get home."

Howie tore a page from his notepad and handed it to him. "And don't worry about returning that. I've copied their addresses onto another page."

Mick studied the information. "I'll start with Cindy Higgins since she lives south."

"That's what I'd do. That way, the visit with the Johnson woman brings you back to the North Side and you'll miss the rush hour traffic." Howie leaned back in his chair, a satisfied look upon his face. No doubt, he felt that his winsome smile had worked its charm again. "Be sure to give me a call later to let me know what you found out. Okay?"

"Don't worry, I will."

"Sorry again about you having to miss supper with your wife."

"No you're not, but Mary understands." Mick stood and gave Howie his own version of a winsome smile. "Besides, it goes with the territory." He slipped the paper into his pocket, and stood there unmoving with a thoughtful expression.

"What's the matter?" Howie asked.

"All of a sudden it seems like we've got our hands full with cases."

"That's the detective business. Feast or famine."

"Don't get me wrong. I'm not complaining." He thought about mentioning Mary's suspicion that she might be pregnant, but no. It was too soon to share that. "Let's just say the extra money coming from this job will come in handy for a down payment on a house."

Howie stood and slipped on his sports coat. "I keep forgetting that you and Mary grew up in a house. You two aren't accustomed to apartment living like me and Adam. You don't know what you're missing." He took out his car keys. "Well, I've got to get going. Anything else?"

"How about Bernadine's brother?"

"What about him?"

"What are you going to do about him?" Mick felt an obligation to Bernadine. After all, he'd promised her they would help. And although he and Howie agreed on many things and had a similar attitude toward detective work, Mick, like Adam, had a higher degree of compassion for people than their boss. "She seemed pretty anxious when she was up here yesterday."

"I know, but she's the type to get upset over nothing. I wouldn't worry about it."

"Yeah, but it sounds like her brother could be in trouble."

"Wouldn't be the first time."

"Yeah, but—"

"Mick, don't worry. I'm not going to forget her." Howie rounded the desk and walked with him to the door. "I'll have Adam check on it tomorrow. Maybe he can help Saint Bernadine save her brother's soul."

The drive to Cindy Higgins' took less than twenty-five minutes. She lived a couple of blocks from one of the city's lakes on a residential street lined with oak trees that were just beginning to bud. Most of the houses in the neighborhood had unattached single garages. Mick parked the car, and double-checked the address on the rambler-style house against the one Howie gave him. Even though he wasn't on the North Side, he automatically locked the car when he got out. He walked to the front door and rang the buzzer. As he waited he glanced around the neighborhood. Two young girls played hopscotch across the street while an elderly woman with a broad-brim straw hat attended the flower garden in her front yard. He was about to ring the bell again when the door opened and a woman dressed in tan slacks and a light-blue sweater answered.

"Yes, can I help you?"

"I hope so. My name is Mick Brunner and I work for the MAC Detective Agency." He gave her his card. "I'd like to speak to Cindy Higgins."

"That's me." The woman offered a smile. Long hair, bleached blond, hazel eyes, modestly attractive. She appeared to be in her mid-forties. "And oh my, you say you're a detective?"

Mick nodded.

"How exciting." She slipped his card into the pocket of her slacks. "I guess I'll have quite a story to tell the girls of the bowling league tomorrow night, won't I?" A twinkle appeared in her eyes. "Unless you've come to take me in for questioning...have you?"

"No, ma'am, only the police do that." Howie had told him that there were women who were attracted to detectives, and if he came across any he should refer the gorgeous ones to him. "I wonder if I could have a few minutes of your time?" Mick asked, deciding his boss wouldn't be interested in a woman old enough to be his mother.

"Of course. Please come in." She lead Mick into the living room, offered him a chair, and went over to turn the television off just as a female contestant was about to spin the wheel to win a prize. Cindy hesitated just long enough to see the wheel's arrow stop on a mink coat. "I just knew she was going to win that," she said and turned the television off. "May I get you a cup of coffee?"

"No, thank you." Mick sat down across from her, placed his left hand on his knee, twisting the wedding band on his finger. Disappointment flickered in her eyes.

"Well, just what is it that you wish to see me about?"

"About the death of Donna Mae Labelle."

At the mention of Donna Mae's name, Cindy's lighthearted tone disappeared. "That was so tragic. I just don't know what could've been so terrible in her life that would make the poor woman want to do that."

"Then you're aware of the circumstances surrounding her death?"

"Oh, yes. I read about it in the paper." Cindy folded her hands on her lap. "Why would she do something like that?"

"That's what I'm here to find out. I hope you can be of some help." Mick spoke in a practiced tone that was meant to signal he would be attentive to her every word. This interest in others was a technique he developed as a teacher dealing with students. The intention was to make each student feel special. Howie used the same technique in dealing with people. The difference between them was that unlike Howie, his interest was always sincere. "How well did you know her?"

"Not that well, I'm afraid." Cindy gazed at her folded hands for several moments. "We'd known each other for a couple of years, but we weren't exactly close friends. It was more like we shared a mutual friend."

"And who would that be?"

"Her name is Bea Johnson. She and I have been close for years. I met Donna Mae through her. The three of us would do things together. She knew Donna Mae much better than I did."

"Were you surprised that Donna Mae took her own life?"

"I was stunned when I heard about it." Cindy's eyes still revealed her shock. "She always struck me as being such a positive, upbeat person. As I remember, she even talked about going to a business college in the fall."

"She mentioned that to you?"

"Oh, yes."

"And what was she going to take?"

"I think court reporting or something like that." Cindy brushed back a lock of blond hair that had fallen into her eyes. "She really wanted to make something of her life. I believe she was determined to."

Mick listened with interest. He'd been skeptical when Howie first told he and Adam that they'd been hired to investigate Donna Mae's death as a possible murder. Adam had argued that if the police concluded that her death had been a suicide, it had to be an open and shut case. But the more Cindy talked, the more suspicious Mick grew. "I understand she was dating a man by the name of Margo."

"She was, but Bea told me that she kind of lost interest in him when she began to date some other guy."

"And who was that?"

"I don't know. She was pretty secretive about him. If anybody would know, it would be Bea."

"Is there anything else you could tell me about Donna Mae?"

"Not really." A questioning look crossed Cindy's face. "Why are you investigating this? The paper said that the police had already closed the case."

"We've been hired by an insurance company to do some work on it. They're very careful on matters such as these," Mick explained.

"I see." Cindy leaned forward and lowered her voice. "I've heard that when people do these things, insurance companies don't pay out the full amount." Her eyes grew large as though she was expecting her guest to share secrets of the insurance industry. "Is that really true?"

"I'm sorry, but I'm sure that whatever the insurance company pays or doesn't pay is confidential. We don't have access to that information."

"I understand," Cindy said although her eyes reflected her disappointment.

"I'd appreciate it if you'd keep this visit between us."

"Don't worry, I will."

Mick had a feeling, however, that the girls on Cindy's bowling team would get an earful tomorrow night about how a private detective came to visit her. The whole bowling league would be abuzz with it before the end of the first game. He stood to leave. "Thank you for your time."

"Are you sure you don't have time for coffee?" she asked. "I'd love to hear more about your work…it's got to be so exciting."

"Perhaps another time, but I really must be going." Mick said good-bye, left, and walked out to his car. As he drove away, he glanced back at Cindy's house in the rearview mirror. After his visit with her, he was convinced they were investigating a murder case.

Chapter 10

Howie wasn't sure what to expect when he approached Yesterday's Treasures, Hatchaway's antique store. Although he had driven by the store many times, he'd never been inside and only vaguely remembered the totem pole in front of it.

When he opened the door to the place, he was nearly run over by two women who, themselves, could have passed for antiques. The older of the two ladies cradled in her arms an object that appeared to be nothing more than a slab of corrugated tin framed on three sides by wood. As they brushed by him, he overheard the one carrying the item say excitedly to the other, "I remember one of these in my grandmother's kitchen."

"And my mother used one all the time," replied her friend.

After the door closed behind Howie, he stood there for several moments taking in the scene before him. An elderly man, sporting a handlebar mustache and wavy white hair parted down the middle, occupied a rocking chair about halfway down the aisle directly ahead of Howie. He poured himself a cup of tea from a floral-design porcelain teapot and returned it to a hotplate on the counter beside him. Dressed in dark slacks, a plaid light-blue shirt, and a bulky navy-blue cardigan sweater, the distinguished-looking gentleman appeared as though he could have been transported into the 1960's from an earlier century. As Howie glanced around the store, however, it seemed like *he* was the one who had stepped into the past.

"May I help you?" the man asked.

"I'm looking for Stuart Hatchaway." The aroma of lemon tea permeated the air as he approached the man.

"That would be me." Hatchaway put his cup on the counter, rose from his seat, and extended his hand. His grip was surprising strong for as frail as he appeared. "And it's Stuart W," he announced as he stroked the end of his mustache and then picked up his cup. "May I offer you a cup of tea? I've just brewed it." He held the cup under his nose, closed his eyes, and breathed in the aroma. "This is the best lemon tea, bar none, on the North Side. My own special blend."

"It smells good, but no thanks."

"I'm glad you can smell it because with this head cold, I surely can't." Hatchaway frowned. "And with my taste buds nearly shut down, I can barely taste it." He noticed Howie eyeing a large fan standing next to the potbelly stove. "You're looking for the electric cord, aren't you? Young man, that there is what is known as a candle-powered fan."

"A candle what?"

"A fan run from heated air." Hatchaway stroked his mustache again, this time twisting the end of it. "You light the candle under that cylinder head there." He pointed a bony finger toward the fan. "Do you see it?"

Howie nodded even though he had no idea what Hatchaway was talking about, but he let the old guy ramble on for a few minutes to get a sense of his character.

"The cold air taken in expands when heated by the cylinder walls. When that happens it forces the piston out for another charge of cold air to repeat the process." A look of satisfaction swept over Hatchaway's face like that of a teacher who had just shared his knowledge with one of his students. "When it comes right down to it, it's just a simple law of physics."

"Well, I have to confess that science wasn't one of my best subjects," Howie said.

"Air expands when heated, and contracts when cooled. That particular fan goes back to the 1890's." He scratched his chin and his eyes brightened. "You're not going to find another like it. If you're interested in it, I'll give you a good price."

"No, I don't think so. I've—"

"Then how about this little gadget?" Hatchaway reached into a shoe-size wooden box on the counter and took out what looked like a pair of pliers. "Do you know what this is?" he asked, holding it up for Howie to examine.

"I'm afraid not."

"What you're looking at is a genuine barber tooth extractor."

"I thought only dentists pulled teeth."

Hatchaway gave Howie a look that told him he was about to be given another history lesson. "In the mid-to-late eighteen hundreds, barbers not only cut hair, they also pulled teeth, lanced boils, and bled folks that felt dizzy. Did you know that?"

"No. My barber only cuts hair."

"Let me ask you a question, then." Hatchaway offered an impish smile. "What color is a barber's pole?"

Howie felt like he was back in school being called upon by one of his teachers. "They are... ah...red and white."

"And do you know what those colors stand for?"

"No idea."

"Take a guess."

"Candy canes?" Howie's childhood barber had handed them out to kids who sat still while getting a haircut.

37

"No, sir! They represented red blood and white bandages." Hatchaway laid the tooth extractor on the counter. "People think that antiques are nothing but junk, but let me tell you..." He gestured around the store with a wide sweep of his hand. "All the things you see around here are history lessons. In the back room, I've got a couple devices that were used at one time to bleed people. I could give you a good..."

Hatchaway seemed like he could go on forever. Perhaps some other time Howie would have a cup of tea with the gentleman and discuss antiques, but for now... "Listen, I'm not here to buy anything," he blurted out. "My name is Howie Cummins. I run the MAC Detective Agency down on the corner of Third and Broadway."

"Third and Broadway?" Hatchaway grinned, revealing a gold tooth. "Why, that must be right above my friend Kass' drugstore."

"Yes, sir. He talked to me about what happened to you. I'm here about the totem pole that was taken. I understand that you might be interested in hiring us."

"I sure am. Kass told me you'd be coming." When Hatchaway frowned, his eyebrows nearly touched at the bridge of his nose. "My anniversary sale is coming up next month and I just know it'll be a flop if I don't get Charlie back."

"Charlie?"

"That's the name I gave the totem pole. The carving at its base reminded me of my Uncle Charlie."

Howie didn't know much about totem poles. He once saw a wooden Indian standing in front of a tobacco shop in downtown Minneapolis, but he didn't think that qualified as a totem pole. "So this thing is made up of several carvings?" he asked as he took out his notepad and a pen.

"Oh, yes. The carvings represent the family history of a clan." Hatchaway's eyebrows rose a bit and a twinkle appeared in his eyes. "You've heard the expression low man on the totem pole?"

Howie nodded.

"Most people think it means someone who is least important." Hatchaway's voice revealed the obvious pride he took in having such knowledge. "On totem poles, though, the most important figure is placed at the bottom."

"How big is this thing?" Howie asked, hoping to avoid a mini history lecture on totem pole carvings.

"It's only seven feet tall."

"Only?" Howie looked up from writing in his notepad.

"Oh, that's quite short. Charlie's just a replica of a much taller totem pole. And Charlie has a thunderbird at the top."

Howie jotted the name in his notepad. "And a thunderbird is..."

"In American Indian mythology, the thunderbird is a powerful winged creature." Hatchaway's eyes flickered with excitement. "According to legend, the bird is said to make thunder roll from its great wing beat and lightning flash from its blinking eyes." He paused, thinking. "Would you like to see a picture of it?"

"A thunderbird?"

"No, the totem pole."

"Oh! Yes, that would be helpful."

"Just a minute." Hatchaway stepped behind the counter by the cash register and stooped down. "Here it is," he said as he stood up groaning and clutching at his back. "My darn old arthritis is acting up again. Son, don't ever get old," he advised as he handed the picture to Howie.

The black and white photograph showed Hatchaway standing next to the totem pole in front of the store. "May I hang on to this for a while?"

"Certainly, and don't worry about returning it. I have several others. They were taken when I first opened the store five years ago come next month."

Howie slipped the photograph into his pocket. "Do you have any idea who could've taken the totem pole?"

Hatchaway shook his head. "I wish I did."

"How about any of your competitors?" Howie couldn't remember if there were other antique dealers on the North Side. "Would any of them have taken it as a joke, or to throw a monkey wrench into your anniversary sale?"

"Absolutely not!" Hatchaway cried as though Howie had uttered blasphemy. "There's only one other antique shop."

"And where would that be?"

"Over on Lowry Avenue. Theodore Shaw owns it. He and I've known each other for years." Hatchaway gave Howie a stern look. "Theodore's a good person. He would never think of doing anything like this."

"Are you sure?" Howie asked, not having the faith in the innate goodness of his fellow man that Hatchaway seemed to have.

"Of course, I'm sure." Hatchaway pinched the end of his mustache. "Why, we're practically partners. When I don't have a certain item, I'll send the customer over to him and he does the same for me. We've even talked about combining our stores and opening up one big one." He paused to take a sip of tea. "Young man, I'm anxious to get Charlie back. When will you start your investigation?"

Howie grinned. "I already have."

"That's good." Hatchaway nodded approvingly. "I admire that get-up-and-go in young folks today. Have you got any leads?"

"Ah...we're working on a couple now," Howie replied, thinking of Squirrel's promise that he'd check with his contacts. He hoped that Hatchaway wouldn't inquire further since he didn't think anything would come out of Squirrel's involvement. "What's that object there? Is that some kind of eye chart?"

Hatchaway chuckled. "Hardly. That's a stereoscope. It was all the rage in the early part of this century. Do you know what it does?"

39

"No."

"Let me get you a chair so you can sit down. Have a mug of tea with me. I'll tell you all about it and even show you how it works."

Howie didn't want to risk offending Hatchaway. But he was curious, and after all, the guy was a paying client. "Sure. I have a few minutes."

"Excellent." Hatchaway looked lovingly around his store. "Son, I tell you, you're surrounded by history…"

Chapter 11

While Howie got another history lesson from Stuart W Hatchaway, Mick was knocking on the second floor apartment door of Beatrice Johnson. Within a few moments, the door opened and a heavyset woman in her early forties wearing tan slacks and a bright-orange sweater appeared. Her auburn hair was cut short and looked frizzy, as though she had recently stuck her finger into an electrical socket. She appeared to be the type of person who wouldn't be intimidated by a detective, or anybody else, appearing at her door. From her apartment the aroma of freshly baking pie drifted into the hallway.

"Hello, I'm Mick Brunner with the MAC Detective Agency. Are you Beatrice Johnson?"

"Yes, but for goodness sakes call me Bea." She had a deep voice, the type that would be easily heard in a room crowded with people. "I'm still upset with my mother for naming me Beatrice—it's so old fashioned."

"Oh, I wouldn't say that." Mick wanted to get on her good side. Howie had advised him and Adam to always butter up people, especially women, whenever interviewing them. "I know a lot of young women with that name. It's a very pretty name," he added for good measure.

"That may be, but all the kids in school used to tease me about it. My mother named me after my grandmother on my father's side. While I was growing up they'd never call me Bea, they said it wasn't my birth name. Can you imagine that? I just hated—" The woman put her hand to her mouth as a hint of blush appeared on her already rosy cheeks. "Oh, excuse me. I don't mean to go on like that. You're not here to hear about my family history, are you? Where did you say you're from?"

"The MAC Detective Agency here on the North Side."

"Oh, yes. I know where that is, above the drugstore." She ran her eyes over him. "So you're a detective, huh? I have a cousin who was a cop. You should hear some of the stories he has to tell. And what is it that you want from me?"

"If I could, I'd like a few minutes of your time."

"Why not? Come on in." Bea led him through the living room into the kitchen. "I hope you don't mind talking in here. We can sit at the table."

She glanced at her stove. "There's an apple pie that I need to watch. It should be ready to come out of the oven any minute."

"It smells delicious," Mick replied as the fruity aroma filled the small kitchen. He hoped his stomach wouldn't start growling. "How do you happen to know about our agency?" he asked as he sat down.

"I go to Kass' Drugstore a lot. I've seen the sign next to the side entrance to the apartment building."

Mick nodded. "That's us."

She moved over to the oven door and opened it just enough to peek in, allowing the aroma to fill the room. Mick's taste buds turned somersaults as the mouth-watering smell encircled him. Hot apple pie, a scoop of vanilla ice cream...

"Another few minutes," she announced, eyeing him with a knowing grin. "Now, let's see...what was I saying?" She sat down again opposite him.

"You mentioned our sign."

"Oh, yes." A look of puzzlement appeared on her face. "Wasn't there a dentist office above the drugstore at one time?"

"That's right. The guy who runs our detective agency turned the space into a combination office and living quarters."

"How convenient. I had an aunt and uncle who owned a small grocery. They lived in the back of the place." Bea wrinkled her nose. "I don't think I'd like that because then you're always at work. They didn't seem to mind it, though. So, what can I do for you?"

Mick got right to the point. "Ma'am, I'm here to ask you about Donna Mae LaBelle. I understand that the two of you were close friends."

"We were. I was devastated when I heard of her death." Bea shook her head as though trying to make some sense of the tragedy. "That poor girl. I just can't believe Donna Mae committed suicide." She paused for a moment, putting two and two together. "So that's why you're here."

"Yes, we're looking into her death."

"Really? Who hired you?"

"I'm sorry, but I can't reveal that information," Mick said, although he might if she bribed him with a piece of pie. "It's a matter of confidentiality."

"Of course. It was silly of me to even have asked. How can I be of help?"

"I talked with a friend of yours. Cindy Higgins. She said you knew Donna Mae quite well."

"Yes. We were very good friends."

"Do you know who she was dating?"

"I know she was dating a guy named Margo. He owns *The Watering Hole* on Hennepin Avenue." Bea rolled her eyes. "I've been there a couple of times. It's not exactly high class, but neither is Margo. She dated him because he made her laugh and he treated her nice. She liked him but it wasn't serious."

"Did she date anyone else?"

"You mean before Margo?"

"No, during the time she was going out with him."

"Well, there *was* this one guy. Excuse me for a minute." Bea got up, walked over to the counter, and opened a drawer. She took out a pair of oven mitts, closed the drawer, and came back and sat down. "Donna Mae started dating him a couple months ago."

"And who was that?"

"I don't know his name," she said, slipping on the mitts. "In fact, I never even met the guy. Donna Mae was pretty secretive about him. All she told me was that he was a clown."

"A clown? You mean he liked to goof around?"

"Oh, no. Nothing like that." Bea snickered. "The man works as a clown from time to time. From what Donna Mae told me it isn't a full-time job, but something he does as a hobby with a couple of other guys. She thought it was great."

"And she never mentioned his name?"

"Not that I recall." Bea paused for a moment. "Wait a minute. Now that I think about it, she did give me one of his business cards. I guess she wanted to drum up some work for him and his partners."

"Do you still have it?"

"I think it's on my dresser."

"May I see it?"

"Of course." Bea got up, walked over to the oven and opened the door. "Let me get this pie out first." She set the pie on the counter, then slipped off the mitts and turned off the oven. "I'll be right back."

Steam rose from the hot apple filling that bubbled through the slits. Mick waited, his eyes on the pie, and wondered what his wife had prepared for supper. Maybe he would stop and pick up a pie and some ice cream for dessert.

"I found it." Bea handed the business card to him.

Brightly colored balloons formed a boarder around the front of the card. *3 Clowns and Oscar* was printed in bold-red lettering in the center of the card. Underneath the lettering was a phone number. Mick turned the card over. *Available for small and large parties. If you want to have lots of fun—3 Clowns and Oscar will supply the laughs.* "May I take this? I'll see to it that you get it back."

"You can keep it."

"Thank you." Mick got up to leave and Beatrice walked him to the door. He stood at the door for a moment and breathed in one last whiff of the pie. For sure, he would stop at the grocery store before going home. "Thanks again for the card. By any chance do you know who this Oscar is?"

"I've no idea, but Donna Mae always told me that I'd be surprised if I ever met him."

Chapter 12

"Who's Oscar? Is he a clown, too?"

Howie looked over the business card Mick had gotten from Bea Johnson. Mick and Adam had stopped at the office for an early morning meeting and breakfast. He had fed them scrambled eggs and toast, and they now all sat in the office area drinking coffee. Howie wished he could have slipped some bourbon into his coffee without his partners taking notice. Besides the bottle of bourbon he kept in the kitchen, he now kept an extra one in the bottom drawer of his desk.

"Bea didn't know." Mick took the card and handed it to Adam.

"Maybe Oscar's a ventriloquist dummy like Charlie McCarthy," Adam said, laying the card on the desk. "That would be a different way of putting on a clown act."

Mick shot a questioning look at Adam. "I don't think a clown is supposed to talk, is he? Isn't that against clown rules or something?"

"I don't know, but if the clown was a ventriloquist, then technically he wouldn't be talking. He'd just be throwing his voice, wouldn't he?" Adam looked at Howie as though expecting support of his argument, but none came.

"Clowns doing ventriloquism?" Mick gently punched Adam in the arm. "Isn't that stretching it a little?"

"You got a better idea?"

Mick nodded. "Yeah. As a matter of fact, I do. My guess is that Oscar's a trained dog that's dressed up as a clown." A twinkle appeared in his eyes. "The mutt probably does tricks. I've seen it on one of those television variety shows." He looked at Howie. "What do you think?"

"I think we shouldn't be wasting our time guessing." Howie picked up the phone and dialed the number listed on the card. "We'll find out who this Oscar is right now." He liked getting to the core of the matter whenever there was opportunity. The longer he did this kind of work, the more action-orientated he became. The phone rang several times before being answered.

"Three Clowns and Oscar," a man's voice chimed. "I hope your morning is starting out with laughter. If not, let me help you."

Before Howie could reply, three blasts of what sounded like a bicycle horn came across the phone followed by the shrill of a whistle. He jerked the phone away from his ear as Mick and Adam gave him a puzzled look. When he figured the sound effects were at an end, he asked, "Ah...who am I speaking to?"

"Edward Squires, II." Three more honks on the bicycle horn. "Better known as...Squirts the Clown!" The man's baritone voice made him sound as though he could be a radio announcer. Even though sounding cheery, a certain hollowness in his voice could be detected. "And may I ask to whom I've the pleasure of conversing with at nine o'clock on a bright sunny Tuesday morning?"

"The name is Howie Cummins." He wondered if he was talking to some guy in a clown suit. "I'm with the MAC Detective Agency."

"You're a detective?"

"That's right."

"My, my, with the kind of things you get involved with, you must be in the market for some laughs." Squires gave a forced laugh. "Today is your day because you've certainly called the right group of clowns to make you laugh. We'll even give a crime fighter like you a discount."

"That's mighty nice of you, but this isn't a request for your services." Howie waited for a reaction but none came. "My partners and I are investigating a case that involves the death of Donna Mae LaBelle."

"Who?"

"Donna Mae LaBelle."

"And what has this person's death got to do with me?"

"You don't know her?" Howie noted that Squires' tone had become sober and business-like. He now pictured Squirts the Clown dressed in a three-piece gray-flannel suit.

"I've never heard of the woman before."

"Is that so?" Howie drummed his fingers on the desk. "We have reason to believe that she was dating one of the members of your clown group. If it wasn't you, then it was probably one of your partners. Perhaps I should speak to one of them."

"Neither is here right now."

Howie picked up the business card. "What about Oscar?"

"Ah...yeah, Oscar. Oscar's with one of my partners."

"Then I'd like to come over and talk with you."

"I'm rather busy. Can't we talk over the phone?"

"No, it's important that we meet." Howie always preferred talking to people in person. When you talked face-to-face so much more could be learned from body language, facial expressions, and even the things people surround themselves with in their office or home. Besides, if this guy were giving him the run-a-round, he would be able to see it in his eyes. "Do you have some time today?"

"I don't—"

"You can understand it's important."

"Well, if you insist, you could come before noon," Squires replied, sounding as though it would be a great inconvenience. "I'd be available for no more than a half hour. Otherwise, we're booked for a program this afternoon at a nursing home and this early evening we're doing a children's birthday party."

"I'll be there by eleven. What's the address?" Howie took out his notepad and jotted down the information Squires gave him. The address placed Squires in Edina, a southern suburb, about twenty minutes away. He hung up the phone and recapped the conversation for Mick and Adam.

"How did he sound when you mentioned Donna Mae's name?" Mick asked.

"He's a very smooth operator. He didn't miss a beat when he said he'd never heard of her."

"How can that be when she was dating one of his partners?" Adam asked. "Don't they talk to each other?"

Howie slipped his notepad into his shirt pocket. "Maybe whichever of his partners was dating Donna Mae wanted to keep it hush-hush. Or maybe the guy was lying. Who knows?" He leaned forward and pointed his finger at his partners. "But let me tell you this. We're going to find out. He and his partners aren't going to hide behind their clown makeup."

The downstairs entrance door banged shut and the wooden steps began to creak. "Are you expecting someone?" Adam asked.

"No, but it sounds like Squirrel." Howie prided himself in being right more than half the time as to who could be coming up the stairs. His degree of accuracy depended whether how many times the person had previously come up to his office. For first time visitors, he often could guess the gender of the person, their weight within ten pounds, and occasionally even their mood. Squirrel was easy to guess. A shade less than a hundred and twenty pounds, the little guy always scampered up the stairs pausing only on the top landing for a moment before making his grand entrance into the office. His mood was easy to predict because the guy was always upbeat.

Within seconds the office door flew open and Squirrel came bouncing in. His tiny-black eyes alive and alert, and for once, his bushy hair appeared reasonably combed.

"How're you guys doing?" Squirrel stopped at Howie's movie poster, eyed it for a moment, and then moved the left side up a little. "There you go, Bogie, you're on the level now." He walked to the window, used the sill for a seat, and folded his arms across his chest. "What's up?" His eyes darted from detective to detective. "Did you guys have any luck finding that totem pole yet?"

"Nothing so far," Howie said. "How about you?"

Squirrel huffed on his fingernails a couple of times, and buffed them on the front of his shirt. "I'm working on it."

"Well, keep at it." Howie had grown to like Squirrel, even though the guy had the habit of showing up at his office at any time of the day or night. At times, the little guy's quirky traits became annoying, but they offset Adam's moodiness.

Adam stood up and stretched. "I've got to run."

46

"What's up?" Mick asked. "Have you got studying to do?"

"Yeah, and then this afternoon I'm going over to check on Les McGuire. Maybe he'll give me a few answers about what's going on in his life."

"And if not?" Howie asked.

"At least, Bernadine will be reassured that we're following up on her brother. That should ease her mind some."

"I've got to be going too." Mick got up from his chair.

"Where are you going?" Howie asked.

"Mary wants me to go shopping with her and then have lunch. We haven't done that for a while."

"So, neither of you guys want to come with me?" Out of the corner of his eye Howie saw Squirrel's eyebrows rise.

"Why don't you take Squirrel?" Adam said.

"Yeah," Mick said. "You could demonstrate your interviewing techniques."

"Oh, I'm sure he's busy. I—"

"No, I'm not." Squirrel moved over to Howie's desk. "I've got all day." He clapped his hands together and vigorously rubbed them back and forth. "So, where are we going? Have you got a hot tip?"

"Maybe," Howie replied, resigned to Squirrel's coming with him.

"Who are we going to see?"

"Squirts the Clown."

"What!" Squirrel's eyes widened. "You're joking, aren't you?"

"Come on. I'll explain in the car."

47

Chapter 13

Howie wasn't sure what to expect when he and Squirrel arrived at the address for Edward Squires, II, but he wasn't expecting such a stylish two-story office building. The white-stucco structure sat in the middle of the block on France Avenue in Edina, a suburb of Minneapolis that oozed wealth. The upscale building with its expensive landscaping looked more like a place for appointments with a medical specialist or a stockbroker than a place where you'd hire a clown act.

"The clowning business must pay pretty good dough," Squirrel quipped as he and Howie walked up to the double-entrance doors. "You've got to be paying a hefty chunk of change to rent space in this joint."

"I won't argue with that." Howie wondered if he and his partners would ever office their detective agency in a place like this. Probably not. He wanted to stay on the North Side, and there was nothing this fancy on Broadway. And even if there were, his cash flow wouldn't support the rent.

Squirrel opened the door and he and Howie walked into the marble-floored lobby. "How do you think they can afford this?" Squirrel asked.

"I don't know. Your guess is as good as mine." Howie located the glass-enclosed room directory. *Three Clowns and Oscar - Suite 214A.* They took the elevator to the second floor. "It's this way," Howie said when the elevator doors opened. He pointed to the arrow indicating the suite was to the right.

"Man, just feel this rug under your feet." Squirrel let out a low whistle. "It's like walking on clouds. You should get some in your office."

"I'll think about it." Within moments he and Squirrel stood in front of Suite 214A. A *Please Knock* sign was posted on the door.

"Do you think he'll be wearing his clown get-up?" Squirrel asked after Howie knocked. "I'll lay you five-to-one odds he is. And two-to-one that he'll give us a red balloon," he added, sounding like a kid about to see his first circus.

"You're not going to start with that betting stuff again, are you?" Howie whispered just as the door opened. A tall, distinguished-looking gentleman with wavy salt-and-pepper hair stood before them. With neatly-pressed dark trousers, polished black shoes, long-sleeve white shirt with gold cufflinks, and gray tie, he looked more like a banker or a lawyer than a clown.

"Yes, may I help you?" the gentleman asked.

"I'm Howie Cummins of the MAC Detective Agency." He felt Squirrel tugging at his sleeve. "And this is...ah, my associate."

"Name's Squirrel," the little guy said, hunching up his shoulders as though that would add a few inches to his height.

The sardonic raise of an eyebrow was the man's only reply.

"We're here to see Edward Squires," Howie said. "I spoke to him earlier on the phone. He knows we're coming."

"I'm Mr. Squires."

"You're the Squirts the Clown?" Squirrel blurted. "I'll be—I would've laid odds that you were the butler."

Squires' brow furrowed. "I beg your pardon," he huffed.

"Hey, it's a joke. You're a clown, aren't you?" Squirrel looked to Howie for support. "Get it? He's a clown. He should know about jokes, shouldn't he?"

"I'm sure he does," Howie replied, smiling through clinched teeth. "But he isn't working now as a clown."

"Your friend is correct." Squires' tone was measured and clipped. He directed his visitors to the two chairs in front of his desk. The massive dark-oak desk and brown-leather chair he seated himself in looked as if they cost as much as Howie's car.

"Now, what is it that you wish?" Squires made a show of looking at his watch. "And I need to remind you that I don't have much time. I'm a very busy man."

"I understand," Howie said. "As I told you on the phone, we've been asked to investigate the death of Donna Mae LaBelle."

"Yes, but I believe I made it quite clear that I didn't know the woman. So I don't see how I can possibly be of any help."

Squirrel ran his finger back and forth across the highly polished desk. "Say, Eddy, besides clowning, what other kind of work do you do?"

The veins in Squires' temples bulged as he glared at where his desk had been touched. "For your information, *sir*, I am the vice president of the First National Bank in downtown Minneapolis."

"You mean that big fancy one with the white pillars?" Squirrel let out a low whistle. "Man, Eddy, you sure know how to pick 'em."

Squires sat motionless for several moments, coldly staring at the little man who had had the nerve to touch his desk. "If you must call me by my given name," he finally said, "the name is Edward."

"My associate here is new," Howie said, interceding. He gave Squirrel a stern look. "He tends to get a little overzealous at times."

"Yeah, I'm still learning the ropes of detective work. I'm here to see how—ouch!" Squirrel gave Howie a puzzled look. "What did you kick me for?"

49

"Didn't you say you came along because you wanted to *quietly* observe?"

"I did?" Squirrel shot a glance toward Squires. "Yeah, I did. That's cool. I'll keep my trap shut. Go ahead and do your thing, boss." He nodded toward Squires. "Eddy looks like he's in a hurry."

Howie turned his attention to Squires. "You told me over the phone that you've never heard of Donna Mae LaBelle."

"That is correct."

"How about your partners?"

"What about them?"

"Was one of them seeing her?"

"I wouldn't know that." Squires folded his hands on the desk. "I don't get involved in their personal lives. Ours is strictly a business relationship."

"I see." Howie didn't believe the guy, but this wasn't the time to push the issue. "I'd like to talk to them," he said as Squirrel reached over and picked up a glass paperweight. "Could you give me their names and phone numbers?" he asked, with a sidewards glance at Squirrel.

"I suppose I could." Squires didn't take his eyes off Squirrel. "There is Arthur Wentworth. His clown name is High Pockets."

"High Pockets!" Squirrel exclaimed. "How did he get a goofy name like that? Bet you five-to—ouch!" He rubbed his leg and grinned sheepishly at Howie. "Sorry, boss. I forgot." He reached into his jacket pocket for an imaginary key, brought it to his lips, and ceremoniously turned the key as though locking his lips shut. His face lit with a smug grin as he dropped the key in his shirt pocket and then patted the pocket.

Howie wrote down Wentworth's telephone number. "What does he do for a living?"

"Arthur works at the Fireside Dining Club as a waiter." Squires paused. "Are you familiar with it?"

Howie nodded. The Fireside Dining Club was a pricey establishment in northeast Minneapolis. The Club (as regulars called it) boasted that every table had a view of a fireplace. The atmosphere was great, the food was even better, but the prices were outrageous. "And how about your other partner?"

Squirrel dropped the paperweight. It bounced off the arm of his chair and landed with a thud on the carpet. Squires' face flushed bright red. Squirrel picked up the paperweight, polished it on his sleeve, and placed it back on the desk. "Not even a scratch," he said.

"And the name of your other partner?" Howie quickly asked.

Squires shot daggers at Squirrel several moments before replying. "Jack Beamer."

"What's his line of work?"

"Real estate." Squires eyed Squirrel. "His clown name is *Smiley.*" He moved the paperweight out of Squirrel's reach. "It's crystal and very valuable," he told him.

"Is that so?" Squirrel's nose twitched. "I would've bet my last sawbuck it was glass."

"How about Oscar?" Howie asked. "Who's he?"

Squires put his elbows on the desk and clasped his hands together. For the first time since Howie and Squirrel had come in, a hint of a smile crossed his lips. "Jack will have to answer that question for you."

"Can I catch him at his office this afternoon?"

"Yes. He usually works until six or later." Squires abruptly stood up. "Now, if you'll excuse me, I must leave for a very important engagement." He came around the desk, walked to the door and opened it. "Gentlemen, if you please."

"Thank you for your time," Howie said as he and Squirrel left. They hadn't gotten more than a few feet when they heard the door lock behind them.

"So what do you think?" Squirrel asked as they walked toward the elevator.

"I think the guy's hiding something."

"I knew it! I just knew it!" Squirrel's nose began twitching. "I could sense all along that he wasn't on the level. And I bet you ten-to-one that he bought that paperweight in some dime store and just polished it up to make it look expensive."

Howie pushed the button for the elevator. Edward Squires, II, also came across as polished. Too polished for his own good, in fact. Whatever he was hiding, Howie was determined to ferret it out.

Chapter 14

As Adam drove to Les McGuire's place of business he wondered what Howie and Squirrel had found out that morning from Squires. He called the office around one o'clock, but got no answer. After seeing McGuire, he'd stop at Howie's on the way home.

He didn't mind following up on McGuire mainly because he felt he owed it to Bernadine since he hadn't had much to do with her in high school. His avoidance of her had more to do with him than her. In those years he'd steered clear of most people. The only close relationship he'd allowed himself to develop was with Mick and Howie, and that had started in junior high.

Throughout his high school days, other kids had pegged him as a moody loner who acted as though he didn't need anyone. And that was true to a certain extent. He now found it ironic that he was studying to be a minister since that profession would require him to be outgoing and social. His struggle, however, was whether the ministry was the right place for him. He still could be moody and needed time to be alone, but only because he wrestled with how to put his religious convictions into practice.

Because of his convictions, he and Howie had differing views on the ethics of detective work. While Howie felt it was okay to bend the rules to fit the situation or even to make up his own rules, Adam went through agonizing inner turmoil whenever the work asked him to compromise what he was being taught in seminary. The paradox, however, was that he found detective work appealing, and that he was good at it.

Somehow, he needed to bridge the gap between the two professions. Wasn't solving cases a way of helping people, and wasn't helping people part of what a minister was all about? One of his classmates once told him that perhaps he should consider becoming a social worker. Social work, however, didn't appeal to him. Helping out a former classmate by investigating what was going on with her brother was more to his liking. So was investigating possible murder cases.

After parking the car on the street across from Les' Used Car Lot, he sat there for a moment, watching a man in a short-sleeve Hawaii-print shirt show a car to a customer. The guy in the Hawaii shirt had to be Les, though he looked much heavier than what Adam remembered. He couldn't hear what Les was saying, but by the way he smiled and patted the hood of the car, he was obviously trying to convince the customer that the car was for him. The customer, however, shook his head and walked away.

The smile disappeared from Les' face and he headed back to the wooden-framed building that served as his office. The building, a weathered-yellowed structure with a flat roof, wasn't much larger than the size of a double garage. From where Adam sat, it looked as if it could use a fresh coat of paint. A little greenery around the place would also help.

"I suppose now is as good of a time as any," Adam said as he got out of his car and trotted across the street. More than a few of the cars on the lot looked like rejects from other used car lots. He paused at the office door, deciding whether he should knock, and then just walked in.

The odor of stale cigarettes and burnt coffee filled the small office. The furniture consisted of a couple of four-drawer metal filing cabinets, two wooden chairs for customers, and a vinyl-covered card table sitting in one corner. A coffee pot along with a stack of Styrofoam cups sat on the table.

Les McGuire sat behind a gray metal desk smoking a cigarette. The room had been partitioned, and Adam wondered if the door behind Les led to an inner office or storage room. Or maybe the guy kept a cot back there to take a nap whenever business got slow.

Les stood up, smiled, and extended his hand with a hearty, "Good morning. Les McGuire here. Great day to buy a car, isn't it? What do you say I help you find the car of your dreams? I've got some real gems out there." He stubbed out his cigarette in an ashtray already filled with cigarette butts. "I know just what you're looking for and I'll tell you what I'm going to do. Just because it's a beautiful day and I'm in a great mood, I'll give you a sales price. How's that for a deal?"

"Do you remember me?" Adam asked.

The smile froze on Les' face. "I don't think so," he said and then snapped his fingers. "Oh, wait a minute. Sure, I remember you. I usually don't forget a face, but I've been swamped with customers all week. Weren't you in here a couple of months ago looking for a car?"

Adam shook his head. Even though they'd been in high school together, there was no recognition on Les' part. The guy had put on weight and looked more like he was in his forties rather than his late twenties. Dark bags hung below his eyes and although he had thick bushy brown hair, sprinkles of gray dotted the sides. One side of his jaw had the purpling shading of a recent bruise. "We were in high school together," Adam said.

"We were?"

"Yeah. You were two years ahead of me. I'm Adam Trexler. Class of '59."

Les stared at Adam for several moments. "Sorry, but I can't place you." He took a cigarette pack out of his shirt pocket, plucked one out, lit it, and took a deep drag as he slid the pack back into his pocket. "So what are you here for if not for a car?" His tone turned as unfriendly as his eyes.

"Sales have been slow. I don't have any money to give to the North High Alumni Fund if that's what you're here for, and I'm not interested in going to any class reunions."

"Actually, I'm here on a business matter. I work for the MAC Detective Agency down on Third and Broadway." At his puzzled look, Adam explained. "We're located above Kass' Drugstore."

"Oh, yeah. Good old Kass. I remember him. A short, fat, bald-headed guy. Is he still there?" Adam nodded. Les took another drag off his cigarette. "So you're a detective? What brings you here to see me? One of my customers complain?"

"No, your sister, Bernadine, is concerned about you." Les rolled his eyes as soon as his sister's name was mentioned. "She thinks that you may be having some sort of trouble so she asked if we'd check to make sure you were doing okay."

"She did, huh?" Les picked some tobacco off his tongue before taking another puff. "She's going to drive me crazy some day. I swear, she's more like a mother hen than a sister." He pointed his finger at Adam. "You tell my sister I'm doing fine. Her problem is that she doesn't approve of my life style."

"Maybe she has a reason." Adam gestured toward Les' face. "How about that bruise on your cheek? Is that a result of your life style?"

"This?" Les raised a hand and stroked his cheek. "It's nothing."

"What happened?"

"I told you it's nothing. I wasn't watching where I was going."

Les' unconvincing tone and the fact that he wouldn't make eye contact supplied Adam with a different answer. Howie was right. You can always pick up more when dealing with someone in person. "You sure nothing's wrong?"

"Look, I'm doing fine," Les snapped. "And you can tell Bernadine to keep her nose out of my business." He looked out the window. "I've got to be going. There's a customer waiting for me."

"I can wait if—"

"Forget it. I've nothing more to say on the matter." Les stood up. "Stop in again when you're in the market for a good used car. I sell nothing but the best."

As Adam left, the door behind Les opened. "You can attend to your customer later," the man said. "If he comes in, brush him off."

Les' face still hurt from being slapped around by the guy, yet still he questioned him. "How am I supposed to do that?"

"Tell him you're busy."

"Since you're holding the gun, I guess you're the boss."

"I'm glad you see it from my perspective." The man paused. "You did very well with that detective. Let's hope that your customer out there doesn't make the mistake of coming in here. It could be most unfortunate for him if he did."

Les glanced out the window. The "customer" was Harold, a Broadway wino who regularly came around every few days. He would check out the cars and then leave without saying a word. "You don't have to worry about that guy."

"Good, because I was getting lonesome in the back room." He motioned for Les to sit down at his desk. Watching to make sure Les did as he was told, the man slid a wooden chair in front of the desk and sat down. "Right now, I'm your only customer, get it?" He lowered the gun. "Don't try anything funny. Believe me, I'll use it."

Les swallowed. He was scared, but he knew the man wouldn't kill him. After all, he had something that the man wanted.

"Now, let's see...where were we before the detective so rudely interrupted us?"

"You were asking about the key in a not so friendly way," Les said as he touched his bruised cheek.

"Yes and I was very disappointed that the key was missing when I checked the car."

When the '61 Chevy Impala first came in, Les had taken it out for a test run. The body was clean, but the engine sounded like it needed an overhaul. He figured that when he and a customer took it out for a test ride, he would turn up the radio nice and loud; that way it would cover up the knock in the engine. It was quite by accident that when checking the fuses he found the key taped underneath the dashboard.

"I think it's time that we make a deal," Les said. "I've got what you want, and whatever that key opens up, I want a share."

The man's lips curled into a sneer. He rose from his chair, walked around the desk and put the gun to Les' temple. "This is my deal."

Chapter 15

At Howie's request, his partners had stopped by the office. He liked having frequent meetings as a way of keeping everyone up-to-date on their current cases. Squirrel had also dropped in to offer his help. How the little guy knew about the late afternoon meeting was anybody's guess since Howie hadn't mentioned it earlier when he and Squirrel were trying to track down Hatchaway's totem pole.

Mick and Adam had taken their usual seats while Squirrel perched himself on the windowsill, his feet dangling a few inches above the floor. Adam had already reported about his cool reception from Les McGuire, and Howie had just finished telling about the visit with Squires that morning. "I'm going over to see Jack Beamer after we're done here," he announced. "The more information I have for Margo when I call him later tonight, the better to keep him off my back."

"It's going on five now," Adam said. "Is Beamer still going to be at work?"

Howie checked his notes. "Squires said that Beamer usually works at his office until six or later so I've got plenty of time."

Mick glanced at Squirrel, whose eyes continually darted back and forth between the three detectives. He gave the reformed street hustler a wink before turning his attention to Howie. "Are you taking your new partner with you when you go see Beamer?"

"I...ah..."

"Come on," Squirrel pleaded, his voice rising in pitch. "I'll be good."

Howie pinched the bridge of his nose and closed his eyes. Squirrel had peppered him with questions all afternoon about being a detective and if Howie thought that he had a chance of becoming one himself. He answered all of Squirrel's questions, but hedged about his odds of getting into the detective business. The wannabe detective had a lot to learn, but if enthusiasm were any indicator, then the chances were in his favor. The guy could prove to be a pain at times and his quirky habits annoying, but his exuberance grew on you. He glanced at Squirrel. "Are you sure you want to go?"

"Am I sure?" Squirrel cried, his eyes growing wide. "What kind of question is that? You bet I'm sure!" In his excitement, he almost slipped off the windowsill.

"What did you and Squirrel do after visiting with Squires?" Adam asked Howie.

"We spent most of the time checking around the area to see if we could dig up any clues about that missing totem pole."

"Any luck?"

"Nope. A lot of the people recalled seeing it in front of the store, but none of them had any idea who would've taken it and why."

"Somebody knows something," Squirrel said. "I'd lay you four-to-one that—" He took note of the stern look Howie gave him. "Okay. Scratch that betting stuff. I forgot. It was a mere slip of the tongue." He hopped off the windowsill and, putting his hands flat on the desk, leaned toward Howie. "Somebody must've seen something. I can feel it in my bones."

"Good. Hang on to that feeling," Howie said. "But for the time being get your mind on clowns."

"I can't figure out that Squires character," Mick said.

"What do you mean?" Howie asked.

"The way you described him, it's hard to imagine him as a clown. He sounds like a snob."

"You can say that again," Squirrel chimed in. "Man, his nose got all out of joint simply because I touched his precious old paperweight." His squeaky voice rose even further in pitch. "You'd think it was made of gold or something. The guy probably bought it at the dime store. I don't trust him." Having said his piece, he went and sat back down on the windowsill.

"Howie?"

"Yeah, Adam?"

"Do you think Squires' lying about not knowing Donna Mae?"

"It wouldn't surprise me if he was. The guy didn't even so much as blink an eye when he said he'd never heard of her."

"How about his body language? Nonverbal clues are just as important as the verbal ones. Did you get any clues from that?"

"None whatsoever. Either the guy was telling the truth or he was the smoothest liar I've come across. I'm curious what kind of story we'll get from his partners."

Adam turned to Mick. "If Squirrel's going with Howie, why don't you come with me to see Bernadette's brother?"

"Sure. I can do that."

"I thought you've already seen him," Howie said.

"I did," Adam replied, sounding a little defensive. "But like I told you, he wasn't very open to my visit. Since Mick knew him in school, he might be more open to talking to him."

"Sounds like a good plan to me." Howie turned his eye toward Mick. "Won't you be missing supper with Mary again?"

57

"We had lunch together today. She understands. Besides, after shopping all morning with her, I'm ready for a little detective work."

"Good luck, then." Howie slipped his notepad into his shirt pocket, stood up, and motioned to Squirrel. "Ready to go?"

Squirrel scrubbed his hands together and gave Howie a mock salute. "Okay, boss. Whatever you say. I'm ready for action."

On the way to Beamer's office, Squirrel carried on nonstop chatter. "Man, am I glad you asked me to come along. It's going to be cool to watch a bona fide detective like you in action, not like those phony TV detectives...except maybe Joe Friday on *Dragnet*. Do you ever watch that?"

"No," Howie said, not having much time or desire to watch TV.

"Friday always knows what he's doing." Squirrel's nose twitched. "Of course, he's no match for you and your hero, Bogie. And I agree with Kass."

"About what?"

"What he says about you."

"And what's that?" Howie asked as he slowed the car around the corner.

"Don't you know?"

"No, why don't you tell me."

"Be glad to." Squirrel gave Howie a toothy grin. "Kass is always saying that you're going to be famous some day."

"Oh, I don't know about that."

"Come on, boss. You will be. I'd give you odds on that...that is, if I was a betting man...of which I no longer am."

Howie smiled to himself. Squirrel had a habit of laying it on thick. When Howie had first gone into detective work, he'd wondered about his abilities. He'd been the class clown in high school and many of his former classmates thought he was kidding around when he told them his plans of opening up a detective agency. In that first year, he came close to giving it up. After a couple of years and several tough cases, however, he felt more confident.

"How much longer before we get there?" Squirrel asked.

"Not long."

"So tell me, boss. What kind of approach are you going to use with this guy?"

"I'm going to make it sound like Squires implied that Beamer could've been dating Donna Mae."

"But he wasn't, was he?"

"I don't know, but it'll be interesting in seeing Beamer's reaction."

"You mean what he says?"

"That but also how he reacts and the look in his eyes." Howie glanced at Squirrel. "But you let me do all the talking. Okay?"

Squirrel gave him a thumbs-up. "Sure enough, boss."

"And don't touch anything?"

"Hey, boss, whatever you say."

"Good. And quit calling me boss." For the rest of the drive, Howie listened as his protégé talked about opening up his own detective agency one day. Squirrel assured him that he would open it in another part of town so as not to compete. "You don't know how relieved I am to hear that," Howie told his future competitor.

Howie pulled out his notepad from his shirt pocket, checked the address he had for Beamer's office, and dropped the notepad on the seat besides him. "It should be in the next block," he said as he slowed the car.

Beamer's real estate office sat on the corner of Plymouth and Penn in north Minneapolis. A modest one-story, white-framed building with large glass windows in front, it looked as though it might have been a café at one time. Howie parked the car around the corner, and he and Squirrel walked up to the front door. He paused for a minute before opening the door. "Remember, Squirrel. I'll do the talking."

"Yes, sir!"

Howie opened the door and walked in with Squirrel tagging along. A small wooden desk with stacks of manila folders upon it occupied the middle of the room. The beige shag rug looked as though it never had been cleaned. Two high-back chairs sat before the desk. A three-by-four foot chalkboard was on the wall to the left. The chalkboard had a dozen or so addresses listed upon it. The third and the sixth addresses were crossed out and marked sold. A door behind the desk was partially opened and a muffled male voice could be heard coming from inside the back room.

"What should we do now?" Squirrel asked as the two of them stood looking around.

"We'll just have to go and knock on—" Before Howie could finish his sentence the door opened and out walked a man dressed in a brown-and-yellow checkered sport coat, light-tan slacks, white shirt, and a mustard-colored tie. He wasn't much taller than Howie. The man's rosy-red chubby cheeks looked as though "Auntie" had pinched them all too often. It was his smile, however, that was most striking, a big smile that stretched from ear-to-ear, revealing beautiful white teeth. "Hi there," Howie said. "Are you Mr. Beamer?"

"That's me. Call me Jack." He motioned to the chairs in front of his desk. "Why don't you two sit down and take a load off. I'll get you some coffee and then I'll find you the house of your dreams."

"We're not looking for any houses," Howie said as he and Squirrel sat down. "My name is Howie Cummins. I'm investigating the death of Donna Mae Labelle."

"Who?"

"Donna Mae LaBelle."

"Are you cops?" Beamer looked at Howie's sidekick, but Squirrel just shook his head while pointing to Howie.

Howie gave him his business card. "No, I'm a private detective." He gave a sideways glance at Squirrel, surprised at how quiet he had been thus far. "And this is my associate. We're wondering if you could tell us anything about Miss LaBelle."

"I would if I knew who you were talking about." Beamer scanned Howie's card and set it aside. "Why are you coming to me? Is this someone that I'm supposed to know?"

"We've talked with Edward Squires. He referred us to you."

"He did, huh?"

"Yes, Mr. Squires seems to think that you were dating Miss LaBelle."

"Edward said that?" Beamer shook his head. "He must be confused. That's simply not possible."

"And why's that?"

"For two reasons. First is like I told you. I never heard of her. And second, even if I did know her, I wouldn't have dated her."

"And why's that?"

"Because I'm a happily married man."

"How about your other partner, Arthur Wentworth?" Howie asked, not accepting "married" as a valid defense. "Was he seeing her?"

"I don't know. You'll have to ask him."

Squirrel leaned over to Howie and spoke softly but loud enough to be heard by Beamer. "Ask him about Oscar."

Beamer broke out in laughter, chuckling so hard that his jowls quivered. "Oh, I doubt she would've dated Oscar."

"And why's that?" Howie asked.

"Because Oscar's the type that women may think is cute, but they wouldn't go out with him." He continued to chuckle.

Squirrel looked at Howie triumphantly. "Told you he's a dummy!"

Beamer's smile disappeared. "I beg your pardon?"

Howie quickly spoke up. "My associate here thinks that Oscar might be one of those dummies that ventriloquists use."

"Ah...I see." Beamer turned to Squirrel. "I can assure you that Oscar is very much alive and is quite a unique individual."

"We'd like to talk to him," Howie said. "There's a few question I'd like to ask him if he doesn't mind."

"Oh, I'm sure he wouldn't mind." Beamer's eyes twinkled. "He's in the back room. Would you want me to ask him to come out?"

"We'd appreciate that."

Beamer got up, opened the door behind him, and disappeared into the next room.

Howie watched as Squirrel picked up a miniature figurine of a clown from Beamer's desk. "Put that back."

"Don't worry, boss. It's safe in my hands." Just then Beamer came out with Oscar. "What the—" Squirrel's mouth dropped open and the figurine slipped from his hands and shattered on the floor.

Chapter 16

Adam and Mick crossed the street to Les McGuire's used car lot. Even though Adam had been rebuked on his initial visit with Les, he felt it important to try again. Bernadine had seemed so worried about her brother, he wanted to help her. Helping people was one of the reasons he gave for deciding to study for the ministry. When he had first shared that reason with his partners, Mick had given him full support and had encouraged him. Howie, however, with a smirk he didn't try to hide, had quipped, "Yeah, I suppose you could help people that way, but detectives help in ways that preachers never could."

Adam caught hold of Mick's arm and pointed to the broken window next to the entrance door to McGuire's office. "Do you see that?"

"Wow!" his partner exclaimed as they stepped onto the curb. "Somebody did a pretty good job on it, didn't they?"

"It wasn't broken when I was here earlier. I wonder what happened."

"Some kid probably tossed a rock through it. It happens at our school every now and then. Kids today just don't have respect for property."

"But it wasn't broken from the outside," Adam said as they walked closer.

"How do you figure that?"

"Just look at the glass on the ground." Shards of windowpane could be seen scattered on the ground several feet in front of the broken window. "Something was tossed through the window all right, but from the inside."

"Hey, you're right." Mick slapped Adam on the shoulder. "Good work. Howie would be proud of you."

Adam glanced around. "Something isn't right here."

"Let's go in and find out," Mick said as he led the way. He opened the door and walked in with Adam right behind him. They both stopped just inside the entrance and stood open-mouthed at Les McGuire, sitting at his desk, holding a blood-stained handkerchief to his lip. In addition to the bruise Adam had seen earlier, Les now had a nasty gash on the left side of his forehead, and the beginnings of a pretty good black eye. His torn shirt looked as if it was missing a couple of buttons. Papers were scattered on the floor; the two chairs were tipped over; all four drawers of the file cabinet hung opened, empty of their contents. Everything on the desk had been swept onto the floor.

Adam noted that the door behind Les' desk stood ajar. He kept his eye on the door, his adrenalin surging, wondering if the instigator was still there. "Are you okay?"

"Yeah, yeah, I'm all right."

"What happened?" Mick asked. "This place looks like a tornado went through it."

"I had some trouble with kids."

Adam stared suspiciously at Les. "Kids?"

"Yeah. Teenagers. High school." Les took the handkerchief from his mouth, revealing a cut and badly swollen lip. "I caught them going through my stuff. They must've been looking for money. We got into one hell of a fight."

"How many were there?" Mick asked.

"How many? Uh, there were two." Les winced as he felt his lip. "When they found out that I wasn't going to back down, they split."

Mick moved closer. "Do you need a doctor?"

"I'm not seeing any damn doctor!" Les snapped, his tone belligerent, as though Adam and Mick had been the intruders.

"How about the cops?" Adam asked.

"What about them?"

"Did you notify them?"

"No, but I will." Les sneered. "What are you guys here for, anyway?"

"I came back to see how you were doing," Adam said. "I brought Mick Brunner with me. I think you guys know each other from high school."

"We were in biology together," Mick said. "Are you sure we can't help you in any way?"

"Not unless you're here to buy a car."

Adam didn't buy Les' story. "Look. Like I told you before, your sister's worried about you." He glanced around at the room. "And it looks like she has a right to be."

"I told you that I don't need your help." Les tossed the bloody handkerchief on the desk. "Just tell Bernadine to stay the hell out of my life!" He jabbed his finger at Adam. "And as far as that goes, I don't want you coming around here anymore. Do you hear me?"

"Hey, Les, we're just trying to help," Mick said.

"When I need your help, I'll call." Les got up from his desk, knelt down, and began picking up the papers on the floor. "Now get out so I can clean up this mess."

The door closed behind Adam and Mick as they left the office. Les moved to the window and pulled aside the curtain, watching until the two detectives got to their car. After his unwelcome visitors drove away, he went to his phone and dialed the number his assailant had left. Why the guy didn't tell him his name was anybody's guess. As he waited for an answer, he remembered how he had stood up to the guy when the jerk pulled out the gun. Les had used every ounce of energy to keep his voice under control so as not to reveal his terror.

"You kill me and you'll never get the key."

"I'll just have the pleasure of shooting you then," the man had threatened as he shoved the barrel of the gun against Les' temple.

With his stomach in knots and sweat running down his face, Les had held his ground. "Look, what do you say we partner up? We'll split the take. I'll take forty. You can have sixty." The man's only response was the cock of the gun. "Okay, okay. Seventy-thirty. That's better than nothing. I'm not worth losing seventy percent of whatever you're after, am I?"

That had been nearly an hour ago, and as Les now waited for the man to answer the telephone, he felt confident about having been at the top of his performance as a salesman. His ploy had worked. The man had put away the gun, and instead had pulled out a pair of brass knuckles. Les felt fortunate to have protected himself as well as he had. Once his attacker had tired of bouncing him off the walls, the man had torn the place apart. To Les' relief, however, the key was never found.

"This is your new partner," Les nervously said as the man finally answered. "I'm calling for a couple of reasons. The first is that two detectives were just here."

"Police detectives?"

"Naw." Les fumbled in his shirt pocket for his pack of cigarettes, his hands still shaking from his encounter with the guy. To his annoyance, his cigarettes were gone. The smokes probably had fallen out when he was being tossed about the office. "They were a couple of guys who opened up a detective agency here on the North Side."

"What are their names?"

"Mick Brunner and Adam...I forget his last name."

"Why did they come to see you?"

"Because of my stupid sister. She thinks I'm in some kind of trouble. She hired them to check up on me."

"What did you tell them about the office?"

"That I caught some teenagers going through my stuff here and we got into a scuffle."

"Did they believe you?"

"I think so."

"Are they coming back?"

"No. I told them to stay out of my life."

"And what was the second reason you called?"

"To tell you that I may be just a used car salesman to you, but I've got brains." Les spotted his pack of cigarettes across the room on the floor.

He could use one right now. "I don't ever want you pulling that stuff with me again." He touched his swollen lip. "Do you understand?"

After a long pause at the other end of the phone the man finally answered. "Yes, I understand. I understand perfectly."

"Okay, now that we're partners, how about telling me your name?" The only answer he got, however, was a click and the dial tone.

Chapter 17

"That's a monkey!" Squirrel screamed as he jumped up and scooted behind his chair. His nose twitched at twice its normal rate and his eyes shifted between the monkey and the door leading outside. "Don't you need some kind of permit to keep a beast like that in the city?"

"Oh, please!" Beamer said, rolling his eyes. "He's harmless."

The "beast" hugging Beamer's neck reminded Howie of one of those monkeys that teamed up with organ grinders. Years ago he had seen a movie that had an organ grinder as the main character. In the movie, the white-faced, long-tailed monkey wore a red fez and held out a tin cup for passers-by to toss their coins in. Oscar, minus the fez and cup, could have stepped right out of that movie.

"Are you sure that thing is harmless?" Squirrel asked.

"Quite," Beamer replied, amused by Squirrel's reaction. "Just act friendly and you'll be fine."

"Good monkey," Squirrel said as he dug into his pocket and pulled out a package of gum. "Does the nice monkey want a stick of gum? It's Juicy Fruit."

Oscar stared at Squirrel's offering for a moment, screeched something, and shifted his eyes toward Howie.

"Suit yourself." Squirrel put the gum back into his pocket.

Howie didn't like the way the "nice" monkey was looking him over with his beady eyes. Oscar's pointed yellow teeth looked as though they could inflict some serious damage. "Is this some kind of joke?" he asked Beamer.

"I can assure you that Oscar is no joke." Beamer's eyes twinkled with amusement. "He's a valued member of our clown act. Ever since we got him a couple of years ago, our bookings have doubled." He moved around the desk and sat on the edge of it. Oscar settled in his lap but continued staring at Howie. "Don't be alarmed. Oscar won't hurt you. Will you, my little monkey friend?" Beamer leaned toward Howie. "Would you like to hold him?"

"I don't think so," Howie said, drawing away.

Beamer turned to Squirrel.

"How about you?"

"No way!" Squirrel put his hands in front of him and backed away. "The only monkeys I like are the ones I see in the zoo…in cages."

"Take it easy," Howie said, trying to settle Squirrel down. He didn't want to antagonize Beamer. "Don't be so scared of him." He offered the monkey a winsome smile. "Oscar won't hurt you, will you, little guy?"

Oscar raised his eyebrows and bared his teeth at Howie. Beamer chuckled when Howie jerked back. "I think he likes you," Beamer said.

"Is that right? He sure has a funny way of showing it."

Beamer gently scratched the top of Oscar's head. "You don't have to be concerned about Oscar. Raising his eyebrows and baring his teeth is his way of showing his affection."

"Well, you better tell him to brush those fangs more often," Squirrel said in a tone hinting of sarcasm. He stepped back when Oscar began screeching, glaring at him with eyes nearly popping out. "What's he saying?"

"I don't know exactly." Beamer reached into his pocket and took out a peanut. As soon as Oscar took the peanut, he settled down, but kept his eye on Squirrel. "I don't think, though, he was very happy with what you said."

Squirrel wrinkled his nose. "You mean that monkey can understand what I say?"

"Not exactly, but he understands the tone of your voice and reacts to it."

"What does Oscar do in the act?" Howie asked.

"Oh, he's a very smart little guy." Beamer got up and set Oscar on the desk. He gave him another treat and told him to stay. "He does a number of tricks." Beamer gestured to Squirrel. "Have a seat and we'll give the two of you a little demonstration."

"Is it safe?" Squirrel asked.

"Oh, sure. Oscar loves to show off for an audience."

Squirrel pushed his chair back further from the desk and sat down, all the while keeping his eye on Oscar.

"Oscar. Dance." Beamer made a circular motion with his hand. The monkey, with his long tail curled behind him, twirled around like a ballerina doing a pirouette. When Oscar finished, Beamer reached into his pocket, took out a handful of peanuts, and held them in the palm of his hand. Oscar grabbed the peanuts, glaring at Squirrel. Whenever he looked at Howie, however, his eyebrows rose and he bared his teeth.

"Does he do anything else?" Squirrel asked.

"Let me get you two a cup of coffee and I'll show you." Without saying another word, Beamer walked over to the coffee maker, poured two cups of coffee, came back, and set them on the desk. "Now, how about some sugar in your coffee?"

Squirrel shook his head. "I'll take mine black."

"I'll take some sugar," Howie said.

"Splendid!" Beamer turned his attention toward Oscar who seemed to know what was coming. "Sugar, Oscar…get sugar."

The monkey hopped off the desk and scurried into the back room out of sight. Within a minute he came back, climbed onto the desk, and scampered over to the two cups of coffee. Howie and Squirrel watched in amazement as Oscar dropped a couple of sugar cubes in both cups of coffee.

"Hey!" Squirrel cried. "I said black."

Beamer shrugged. "Oscar thinks everybody should have sugar in their coffee." He handed the cups to Oscar's audience. "Please take a sip. Oscar gets upset when people don't appreciate his sugar trick."

Squirrel glanced at Howie, gulped, took a couple of sips, and made a face as though he had taken poison.

Howie peered into his cup at the dissolving sugar cubes. He gave a nod to Oscar, smiled, pretended to take a sip, and put the cup back on the desk. "That was good, Oscar." No sooner had Howie spoken the words than the monkey hopped from the desk into his lap, crawled up his chest, and put his hands around his neck. Time stood still as he and Oscar were eyeball to eyeball.

"I'm impressed! He really likes you," Beamer said as Oscar began checking his new friend's head for fleas. "He doesn't do that with just anybody."

Howie nodded. Squirrel was right. Oscar needed to start brushing his teeth. He also could use some breath mints as well.

Chapter 18

The birthday party was nearly over. He was glad, he'd grown weary of playing the clown for a bunch of eight-year-old brats. But he had to admit, clowning was a rather clever cover. After all, who would suspect a guy who spent his time making others laugh? The cops wouldn't. He still found it amusing that he and his partners had done a benefit show for a police officer who'd been shot answering a domestic. So many of the cops there that night thanked him for the laughs, some even had tears in their eyes. All of them told him to feel free to give them a call if he ever needed help. *Fools! If they only knew Johnny LaBelle and I had killed a cop in a shoot-out.*

"Mr. Clown, will you go over and scare Todd for me?" a blond-haired girl in a pretty, new party dress asked. "He took my piece of cake."

He shook his head and attempted to mime that he was a clown and clowns don't scare people, but the stupid kid didn't get it.

"Can't you talk?" she asked, wrinkling up her nose and looking at him as though he was a windup toy that had been broken.

Another girl joined her. "Clowns don't talk, Sally."

"Why's that?"

"I don't know. Maybe they don't have any tongues."

The blond girl's mouth dropped open. "Mr. Clown, don't you have a tongue?"

He opened his mouth, stuck out his tongue, and pointed to it.

"Yuck!" the other girl said. "You have an ugly tongue. Come on," she said to the blond. "Let's go play Pin the Tail on the Donkey."

Without so much as a good-bye, the two girls turned and walked away. As he watched them go, he was tempted to rip out their tongues and pin *them* on the donkey. When the blond girl turned and looked back at him, however, he smiled and waved. *Jab yourself with the pin, kid.*

"Would you care for some punch?" the mother of the birthday boy asked.

He nodded, took the plastic cup from her, and then watched her walk away. Not bad looking he thought, and wondered if she would like to make it with a clown. As he took a sip of the punch, his thoughts turned to Les McGuire. *So that dimwitted used car salesman thinks he has brains, does he?*

Once I get what I want from him and then put a bullet hole in his head, we'll see if any gray matter oozes out.

"Hey, you, Clown!" A chubby boy with red hair shouted. "Do some more tricks."

Two other equally obnoxious boys joined their chubby friend. "I hope he's not going to juggle balls again," said a curly-haired boy, rolling his eyes.

"Yeah, that's really dumb," said his friend.

He looked at the three boys and smiled. *It wouldn't be if I stuffed them down your throats.*

Just as he began juggling, though, the chubby boy and his two friends walked away. "That dumb clown can't do anything but juggle!" he heard one of them complain. His nostrils flared as he fought the urge to go after the three brats and introduce them to Mr. Angry Clown.

"I like juggling, Mr. Clown."

He turned to see a boy of six or seven wearing a party hat and looking at him with wide eyes and an innocent smile. He returned the kid's smile and began juggling.

Chapter 19

Squirrel had a pretty good hunch who on the North Side might know something about the missing totem pole. If he could get a lead on that pole, Howie and his partners would really be impressed. They might even ask him to team up with them. Three-to-one they wouldn't. But if they did, that would be cool.

He headed up Broadway looking for his old friend, Hoots. The North Side had more than its share of characters and Hoots would top the list. So nicknamed because he stayed up most of the night walking the streets, Hoots had been a fixture on Broadway as long as anybody could remember. If anything happened on the street during the night, Hoots would know about it. Nobody knew his real name or where he disappeared to during the day. Nobody could even ever remember seeing him during the daylight hours, causing those with fanciful imaginations to spread the rumor that he was a vampire of the night. Squirrel didn't put much stock in the rumor and had laid seven-to-three odds against it. He would have given better odds, but Hoots was so skinny and pale that he did look as though his blood had been sucked out of him.

If Hoots could be found anyplace, it would be at one of the local hamburger joints playing pinball machines—or as he called them, "the ding-a-lings." Squirrel located his man at the third place he checked.

At half past midnight, the Rainbow Café was nearly deserted. A bored waitress shared a cup of coffee with her lone customer at the one end of the counter. At the other end of the counter by the cigarette machine, Hoots worked the flippers on the pinball machine while slamming the sides of it with his palms. His body shifted back and forth as he tried to maneuver the steel ball. Red and white lights flashed and bells clanged every time the ball pinged off the bumpers.

"Come on! Come on, baby! I need that!" Hoots kept banging the side of the ding-a-ling until a red tilt sign flashed. "Damn!" he cried and slammed his fist on the glass top so hard that the coffee cup sitting on it jumped.

"Hey, Hoots!" the waitress yelled from the other end.

"What?"

She smirked. "If you break it, you're going to have to pay for it."

Squirrel leaned against the cigarette machine. He noted that Hoots hadn't chalked up any free games. "Not doing so good tonight, huh?"

"Hi, ya, Squirrel. What's cooking?"

"I've been looking for you."

"Well, you've found me." Hoots dug in his pocket, pulled out several nickels and tossed them on the glass. "Hell, all I needed was five thousand more points and I would've got myself a freebie." He picked up his coffee cup, took a gulp, swished it around like mouthwash, and swallowed it. "I could've done it easy if this damn thing hadn't tilted."

"You're losing your touch," Squirrel said.

"The hell I am. The ding-a-ling screwed me." Hoots put a nickel in the slot and the machine came to life. "So, where've you been?" he asked.

"Around."

Hoots looked toward the waitress for a moment. She was pouring coffee for her customer. He lowered his voice. "Hey, Squirrel, is it true what I hear on the street about you?"

"That depends. What are you hearing?"

"That you're working for the gumshoes."

"I'm not exactly working for them." Squirrel wondered what Howie and his partners would say at being called gumshoes.

"So what are you doing, then? Running errands for them?"

"No. They're using me as a...advisor."

"Advisor? What in hell does that mean?"

Squirrel puffed up what little chest he had. "Whenever they are dealing with a tough case, they call on me."

"Is that so? Man, I've lived to see everything." Hoots sniggered. "Now I can die a happy man. Squirrel has reformed and went to the other side. Next thing you know, you'll be teaching Sunday school."

"Very funny." Squirrel's nose twitched. "Hey, Hoots."

"What?"

"Did you hear anything about that totem pole that was stolen from Hatchaway's antique store up on Broadway?"

"Hear about it? Man, I saw it happen."

"You did?"

"Yep." Hoots finished his coffee and handed the cup to Squirrel to set on the counter. "You know nothing happens on the street without me knowing about it."

"Who took it?"

"Kids."

"What do you mean, kids?"

"A bunch of college kids."

Hoots shot his first ball.

Squirrel waited to ask more questions, knowing Hoots didn't like to be disturbed while playing the ding-a-ling. After dinging and ringing through six thousand points on his first ball, Hoots turned toward Squirrel. "I'm on my way." He grinned, revealing two gold-capped teeth. "You just watch. I'm going to make this sucker pay."

"How do you know they were college kids?"

"Easy. One of them had a University of Minnesota jacket on."

"What did they do? Just carry it off?"

"Naw. They dumped it in the back of a pickup, covered it with a tarp, and took off." Hoots smirked. "Strictly amateur stuff."

"Did you report it?" Squirrel asked, knowing that Howie would want to know.

Hoots gave Squirrel a look as if his friend had gone tilt. "Are you nuts? After the last time they picked me up for loitering, I've got nothing to do with those flatfeet."

Squirrel waited while Hoots played the second ball. "Anything else about those kids that night?" he asked after his friend racked up an additional four thousand points.

"Nope."

"Okay. Thanks for the info. I owe you."

"No problem." Hoots cocked his head. "Hey, Squirrel."

"Yeah?"

"How about a little bet? I'll give you two-to-one odds that I'll reach thirty thousand on this game."

"I don't think so. It's late and I've got to go." Squirrel started to walk away, stopped, thought about it, and then went back. "Make it three-to-one, and you've got yourself a sucker."

Chapter 20

So far the morning hadn't started well for Howie. He'd had a restless night and that only contributed to his already irritable disposition. For some reason he had no hot water for his shower and would have to talk to Kass about it. When he tried to fix breakfast his last two slices of bread burnt in the toaster. The smoke from the burnt toast was so bad that he had to open the kitchen window. He tried to fix himself a couple of eggs, but the yolks broke when he flipped the eggs. With no yolk to dip his burnt toast in, he set the eggs aside, threw away the toast, and rummaged up two stale cake donuts.

With a fresh brewed cup of coffee and his donuts Howie headed for his office. He shut the door to his living quarters hoping the burnt smell would soon clear out. No sooner had he sat down at his desk and opened his desk drawer for the bottle of bourbon than his office door opened and in walked Bernadine McGuire—the last person he felt like seeing. He closed his drawer with a sigh. If Saint Bernadine knew about the liquor, he'd be in for a lengthy sermon about the evils of alcohol and how, if he didn't change his ways, the flames of hell would be waiting to consume him.

His visitor stopped by his poster of Bogie, eyed it for a moment, and shook her head in disapproval. "Howard, it's beyond me why you have such an interest in that man. Don't you realize that all those Hollywood-type leading men are nothing but womanizers and boozers?"

"Have a chair," Howie said, swallowing the temptation to wisecrack that women and booze were the very reasons he got into detective work in the first place. He eyed his breakfast. "Can I get you a cup of coffee and a donut?"

"I don't drink coffee," Bernadine replied, adding, "It's not good for your digestive tract." She turned up her nose at the donut he was holding out to her. "No thank you." She sniffed the air and looked around the office. "Howard, what is that smell?"

Howie glanced at the desk drawer containing his bottle of bourbon. "What do you mean?" he asked, keeping his tone nonchalant.

She sniffed the air again. "It smells like you've burnt something."

"Oh, yeah. It's toast," Howie said, feeling relieved, but a little surprised that she didn't have a nose for sniffing out booze. "It's a little

73

burnt, but I can get you a piece," he offered in a tone as friendly as he could muster. "I'll just put some jelly on it and you won't even know the difference."

She looked at him as though he had suggested she should take up smoking. "I think not," she huffed.

"Suit yourself." Howie took a sip of coffee, wishing he had had the chance to spike it before the Saint came in. If he was on his way to hell, he might as well enjoy the ride. "So, what are you here for?"

"I want to know if you have come up with anything on my brother, Lester, yet." Her eyes narrowed, causing the lines in her face to appear even sterner. "Goodness knows, you've had sufficient time," she chided.

Howie leaned back, interlaced his fingers, and put his hands behind his head. He offered her a smug smile. "I want you to know, Bernadine, that I've given the case top priority."

"You have?" She sounded surprised.

Howie nodded. "Adam has already gone to see him."

"He has?"

"That's right."

"So what did he find out?"

"Your brother wouldn't admit to anything." Howie leaned forward, folding his hands on the desk. "He made it very clear that we should stay out of his life," he said, almost adding *that especially applies to you.*

"I don't care what he says," Bernadine snapped. "I know there's something wrong. He's just not himself." Although her eyes pleaded, her tone was demanding. "You're not giving up, are you?"

"No, no. In fact, Adam and Mick went to see him again yesterday. I was expecting to hear from them today."

"And you haven't?"

"Well, Bernadine," he said, stretching out the syllables of her name, "it's barely past nine o'clock in the morning. I'm sure they'll come by later on. When they do I'll give you a call and let you know what they found out."

She took a deep breath, appearing more relaxed than when she first came in. "Howard, I would appreciate that. Thank you." Her gaze turned inward for a moment. "If I have been hard on you, it is only because I'm so concerned about my brother."

"I understand. You're under a lot of stress." Several long seconds ticked off as he waited for her to get up. "Is there something else?" he asked when she didn't give any indication that she was going to leave.

"In high school I had a crush on you," she blurted out.

"You what?"

"I had a crush on you."

Howie glanced at his desk drawer. He could use a stiff shot—maybe two.

"I wanted to get to know you better but I was too shy." Her eyes softened. "I almost asked you to the Sadie Hawkins' Dance. You seemed to be such a free spirit and fun loving person. No wonder you were the class clown."

"Well, I was young and foolish in those days." He wanted to erase that image so that people would take him seriously as a detective. Most of his former classmates found it hard to believe that the one time class clown was now a private investigator.

"May I ask you a personal question? Have you been going to church?"

"Have I what?"

"Church. Have you been going?"

Howie wanted to tell her it was none of her business. He had enough of that religious crap from Adam. "Why do you want to know?"

"Because of the kind of work you're involved in. I'm sure detective work brings you into contact with some very unsavory characters. And I would think that you would want to keep spiritually rooted."

"You don't have to worry about that." Howie flashed a winsome smile, hoping to loosen her up. It had always worked with other women. "With Adam studying to become a minister, he's got enough religion for the two of us." His grin faded as Bernadine sat there with a stern look on her face as if he had just uttered blasphemy.

"You shouldn't kid around about such things." Her voice quivered with emotion. "Don't you realize, Howard, that your very soul is at risk?"

To his relief, the downstairs entrance door slammed shut. "Sounds like somebody's coming up."

"I hope it's one of your partners so I can find out about my brother."

Howie recognized the footsteps. He waited until the office door opened and Squirrel came jaunting in.

"I didn't know you were busy," Squirrel said. He twitched his nose at Howie's visitor. "I'll come back later."

"No, come on in," Howie quickly said. If Saint Bernadine wanted to save souls, she could try her luck with Squirrel. Odds weren't in her favor, however. Probably fifty-to-one. "I want you to meet someone," he said. "This is Bernadine McGuire. She graduated from high school with me, Mick, and Adam."

"Hi, ya, Bernadine." The little guy plopped down in the chair next to her. "The name is Squirrel."

"Squirrel?" Her eyebrows rose. "That's a very unusual name."

"You think so?" Squirrel's nose twitched several times. "Hmmm. You know, I never thought of it that way." He gave Howie a glance before turning his attention back to her. "So what were you guys talking about, the good old days at North High?"

Bernadine shook her head. "I was just telling Howard about how important it is to be spiritually grounded."

"I know just what you mean," Squirrel said.

Howie's mouth nearly dropped open.

Squirrel continued. "You can never get too much religion I always say. In my book, it's good insurance to get connected with that Big Guy in the Sky."

"You are so right." Bernadine's face lit up as though she was at a prayer meeting. "It sounds like you've had a personal experience. Have you?"

"You bet your bible I have." Squirrel's thin lips formed a smug smile. "And I'm proud to say that I've turned my life around."

Her eyes glowed with approval. "That is so thrilling to hear." She gave Howie a knowing look before turning her attention back to Squirrel. "Maybe you could be a positive influence on Howard."

"Hey, that's a great idea. I never thought of it that way before. It'd be a way to repay him for showing me the ropes on being a detective."

Howie sighed as he massaged his temples. *How's it possible to get a headache so early in the morning?*

For the next ten minutes he leaned back in his chair and stared at the ceiling as Squirrel shared his story of how he turned from a life on the street to seek the straight and narrow. Squirrel's description of his transformation sounded as though it was nothing short of a miracle how he came to his senses and turned away from a "pathway leading straight to the hot flames of the furnace down below". Bernadine sat on the edge of her seat, drinking in every word as Squirrel spun his tale.

"If the two of you want to continue this," Howie finally said, "why don't you go someplace else to do it? I have a few cases to work on." He directed his next words at Bernadine, not caring if she heard the sarcasm in his voice. "You haven't forgotten about your brother, Les, have you? And do you still want me to work on finding out what's going on with him, or have you changed your mind?"

"Of course I haven't. I just get so enthralled when I hear how God can transform lives." Bernadine sighed deeply as she clutched her hands in front of her chest. "Oh, Squirrel, thank you so very much for sharing such an inspirational story."

"Hey, that was only part of it."

"You mean there's more?"

"Oh, sure," Squirrel said.

"I so look forward to hearing the rest."

"No problem. We'll have to get together over a bottle of—a cup of java and I'll tell you the whole story."

"That would be absolutely delightful." Bernadine got up to leave. "Howard, wasn't that a wonderful testimonial?"

"Yeah. Terrific." Howie shot a glance at Squirrel. The former street hustler sat with his arms crossed and a look of contentment. "One could even say unbelievable."

"Oh, I so agree," she said. "What a witness. I simply must hear more."

Howie massaged his aching forehead. "Are you two sure you don't want to go and have that coffee now?"

"Can't do that, boss," Squirrel said.

"Why not?"

"Because I came up here on account of detective business."

"Perhaps another time," Bernadine said as she left.

Squirrel waited until his new admirer shut the door behind her. "She's not a bad chick, but could use some makeup and different clothes."

"I'm sure the two of you would make a perfect couple."

"Oh, no, boss." Squirrel waved off Howie's suggestion. "Don't get me wrong. I'm not about to get tied down with any dame. I'm free and easy and want to stay that way. So she's all yours for the taking. I promise I won't get in the way."

Howie needed to find some aspirins. He would take three or four and wash them down with something stronger than coffee. "Why are you here?"

"Like I told you…detective business." Squirrel flashed a toothy grin. He huffed on his fingernails and buffed them on the front of his shirt. "I've got the lowdown on that totem pole."

"You do?" Howie took out his notepad, feeling hopeful. Maybe the morning would have a bright spot after all. "Let's have it."

"My friend, Hoots…you know Hoots, don't you?"

"Yeah. Tall. Skinny. Looks like a scarecrow."

"That's Hoots all right."

"So what about him?"

"He saw the whole thing go down." Squirrel's nose began twitching. "It was college kids who took the totem pole."

"How did he know they were college kids?"

"A couple of them had University of Minnesota jackets on. I did some further checking with another one of my sources and I found out that a fraternity over there is having some kind of big party tonight. I figure the totem pole might be the guest of honor or something. You know how crazy college kids are."

"Good work." Howie flipped a page in his notepad. "I don't suppose your source happened to have the name of this fraternity house?"

Squirrel gave Howie a thumbs-up. "You think I'd come here without the whole scoop? When Squirrel does a job, he does it—"

"Just give me the name. Okay?"

"It's Della Phil or something like that."

"You mean Delta Phi?"

"Yeah, that's it." Squirrel watched as Howie wrote in his notepad. "What are we going to do, boss?"

Howie rolled his pen between his thumb and forefinger for several moments. "I'm going to call Mick and Adam, and we're going to pay Delta Phi a visit tonight."

"Why not go over there right now?"

77

"Because they'll probably keep the totem pole under wraps until the party. We don't want to tip our hand."

"Smart thinking." Squirrel stood up, placed his palms on the desk and leaned toward Howie.

"Hey, boss. Can I go along tonight, too? What do you say? I won't get in the way."

Howie closed his notepad and gave him a grin. "Sure, why not? After all, you got us the lead."

Chapter 21

Howie had Squirrel ride along with him as they headed toward the University of Minnesota campus. Mick and Adam followed in an old Ford pickup that Mick had borrowed from his uncle. Squirrel chattered nearly non-stop and although he was better at yakking than listening, nevertheless, Howie still enjoyed his company.

"What's the truck for?" Squirrel asked as they turned onto University Avenue.

Howie glanced at his passenger to determine if he was serious. "Just how big do you think my trunk is?"

"What?"

Howie looked over at Squirrel, but the guy hadn't made the connection. How he could be so streetwise while, at times, so lacking in common sense was a mystery. "A seven foot totem pole isn't going to fit in my trunk. That's why we need the truck."

"Oh, man, I get it now," Squirrel said as he slapped himself in the forehead. "I sure have a lot to learn about this detective business, don't I?"

At shortly after ten they arrived at the Delta Phi fraternity house and parked around the block so as not to draw attention. They got out of their vehicles and walked back toward the house. The moon rising above the trees and rooftops illuminated the cloudless night sky. A slight chill in the air could be felt. Delta Phi, a massive two-story brick structure with an open porch encased by white pillars at each of the porch's four corners, sat in the middle of the block. Only a light from an upstairs room could be seen coming from the house.

"Do you think the party's over?" Squirrel asked as they stood in front of the house.

"Why would it be over?" Mick asked

Squirrel shrugged. "I don't know." He glanced at the frat house. "Maybe they have a test tomorrow morning and they went to bed early."

Howie put his finger to his lips. "Shhh." Music could be heard coming from somewhere in back of the house. "Do you hear that?"

"That sounds like string instruments," Adam said.

Mick nodded. "Harps, I think."

"Harps?" Squirrel glanced back and forth between the three detectives. "What are they doing? Having some kind of religious service?"

"I wouldn't take any bets on that," Howie said. "The party must be in the backyard. Come on, let's go around the side." He led them around the right side of the house through a wooden gate that posted a *No Trespassing* sign. Enclosed by a wooden fence, the backyard extended some thirty yards deep.

"They've got a bonfire going," Mick whispered.

"What are they doing? Roasting hot dogs?" Squirrel asked.

Howie rolled his eyes at him.

"Hey, how should I know what they do at these things? I never went to college. I didn't even finish high school."

"You never finished high school?" Mick's mouth dropped open. "You're kidding."

"Nope."

"What happened?"

"I was caught in ninth grade for playing poker during lunch. They kicked me out for a few days, and I never went back."

"You should consider going back and getting your diploma."

"Why should I? I learned all I wanted to know from the streets."

"Guys, save the discussion for another time," Howie said, noting the concerned teacher coming out in Mick. "Just keep your eyes open for that totem pole."

"Will you look at that?" Squirrel exclaimed. "They're got sheets draped on them!"

"Keep it down," Howie whispered.

Squirrel lowered his voice a smidgen. "What's going on?"

"It's a toga party," Mick explained.

"How do you know that?" Squirrel tugged at Mick's sleeve.

"Because when I was in college we had a toga party in my junior year. It starts off quiet, but it gets wilder as the night goes on."

Squirrel pointed to the left of the bonfire, near a massive oak tree. "There's the totem pole!" Several young women danced around the pole while a blond, curly-haired young man sat in front of it playing what looked like a miniature harp.

"Okay," Howie said. "We've found it. Let's go get it." He walked into the open and headed directly for the totem pole, his partners and Squirrel coming behind him. Within moments a muscular young man intercepted them. The young man blinked his glazed eyes a couple of times as he swayed back and forth. The laurel wreath on his head slipped to one side, nearly falling off before he pushed it back on.

"Hey, where are your togas?" the young Greek god slurred. "Everybody's got to have a toga." He squinted as he scanned the four of them. "What frat house are you guys from?"

"Who's in charge here?" Howie asked.

"In charge?" The would-be enforcer blinked his eyes a couple of times as though trying to focus. "You're not with the University police, are you?"

"We're detectives on official business. I'll ask you one more time. Who's in charge?"

"My friend, Kurt."

"Where is he?"

"Over there at the keg. The guy with the dark hair." The man continued to sway. "Say, you guys got a search warrant?"

"We don't need one for stolen property."

"Stolen property?" The news had a sobering effect. "What are you talking about?"

"That totem pole over there."

"Hey, man. We just borrowed it for our party. We were going to return it."

"Sure you were." Howie pointed to Mick. "You and Squirrel stay here. Adam, you come with me. We are going to have a little talk with Kurt."

"What are you going to tell him?" Adam asked as he and Howie walked away.

"Exactly what I told that other clown."

"What if he gives you trouble?"

"He won't."

Two of the young women who had been dancing around the totem pole now moved smiling toward Howie and Adam.

"Hello, there," one of the women said to Adam. "Are you a new member of Delta Phi? I haven't seen you around before."

"He's cute," the other young lady said, brushing up against Adam and running her fingers through his hair.

"Look, girls," Howie said, noting how uncomfortable Adam appeared to be. "We're here on business. We're not part of this fraternity."

"That's too bad," she cooed at Adam. "We could talk to Kurt and ask him to make you honorary members."

"You stay here with these two," Howie said to Adam.

"What for?"

"Just keep them occupied while I talk with Kurt." Howie paused. "And don't' worry, they're not going to hurt you." Although Adam gave Howie a reluctant look, he did as he had been asked. As Howie walked away, he heard one of the women ask his partner if he was going steady with anyone.

"Is your name, Kurt?" Howie asked the dark-haired kid who had just filled a glass with beer.

"That's me." He grinned and offered Howie the drink.

"No thanks." Howie explained that they were detectives and that the totem pole was stolen property. Kurt's grin disappeared.

"I didn't know it was ripped off." Kurt pointed to the guy that Howie had left with Mick and Squirrel. "Pete said he borrowed it from a friend. He thought it'd be great for the party. He told me that the chicks would go wild over it."

"Well, they'll have to go wild over something else. We'll be taking the pole back to its owner."

"You're not going to report this to the University, are you?"

"Not if you cooperate." The fact that Howie promised that their party could go on without interference was all that was needed to make Kurt fully cooperative. Kurt had Pete and several other guys haul the totem pole back to Mick's pickup.

"We appreciate the help," Howie said, once the totem pole was secured in place.

"Hey, no problem," Pete said and then shook hands with Squirrel. "Thanks a lot for agreeing. The chicks will eat you up."

"What was that all about?" Howie asked Squirrel as Pete and his friends went back to their party.

Squirrel brought his hand up to his mouth, huffed on his fingernails a couple of times, and made a show of buffing them on the front of his jacket. "I'm going to be their mascot."

Chapter 22

Howie slid onto a stool at the soda fountain, having stopped to share the good news with Kass that the totem pole had been recovered. "Looks pretty slow in here this morning."

Kass nodded his agreement and went about filling the straw dispenser. "It was pretty busy when we opened up with the usual morning rush." He looked over his shoulder at the clock above the ice cream cooler. "For some reason at eleven, we always seem to go through a lull." He offered Howie a shrug. "Business will pick up later this morning. It always does." His eyebrows shot up and the expression on his face changed to one of sudden realization. "What are you doing here? You don't usually come in this early. Is something wrong?"

"No. In fact, everything's great. I just wanted to let you know that we got the totem pole back last night."

"You did? That's terrific!" A broad grin swept across Kass' face. He leaned over the counter and gave Howie a hearty slap on the back. "I knew you and Mick and Adam would do it. You boys are getting better with every case." He pointed to the wall behind him. "That's where I'm going to hang your pictures when all of you become famous. Then I can brag to everybody that you boys got your start above my drugstore." He stuck out his chest and beamed. "Then my drugstore becomes a famous historical landmark and I can retire."

"Thanks for the confidence, but don't hold your breath."

"What did Stuart W say when he got his totem pole back?"

"I didn't get a chance to talk to him. It was nearly midnight when we returned it last night so we just set it in front of his store and left a note taped to the front door." Adam had questioned whether they should leave the pole unguarded, but Squirrel promised that as the newly appointed mascot of Delta Phi, he would vouch for them not taking it again.

Kass took the top off of a second straw dispenser and began replenishing the glass container. "So when are you going to talk to Stuart W?" he asked. "If I know him, I'm sure that he'll want to show his appreciation."

"I tried to call him this morning, but the line was busy. I'm on my way over there now."

"That's good. He'll be so pleased that he got his good luck charm back, and just in time for his sale next month." Kass' eyes twinkled with excitement. "You boys did a great job, and so fast."

"We'll have to give Squirrel credit on this one." Howie shared how the little guy had learned from his friend, Hoots, that college kids had taken the totem pole. "I have to say that this has been one of the easier cases we've worked on."

"I'm glad to hear that. You boys need to have an easy one every now and then."

Howie nodded. He felt confident that having the totem pole returned would generate a lot of publicity for him and his partners. Between Kass and Hatchaway, the word would get around Broadway how the MAC Detective Agency solved the case so quickly. The agency wasn't having a problem with cash flow at the moment, but you never knew. Although they had several irons in the fire now, he didn't think finding out what was going on with Bernadine's brother would take much of their time either. Margo's hiring them to investigate the death of Donna Mae, however, was a different story.

"Can I fix you something to eat?" Kass asked.

"No. I've got to go. I've got a long day ahead of me." Howie hopped off the stool and stretched for a moment. "After we returned the totem pole, Mick suggested that we get a bite to eat to celebrate our success. I didn't get more than five hours sleep last night. I won't be coming in tonight to work. Is that okay?"

"No problem." Kass screwed the top back on the straw dispenser. "Are you working on that other case concerning the woman who died?"

"Yeah. I'm driving up to International Falls to visit her parents. Maybe I'll get some clues from them."

"Good luck, but don't work too hard," Kass admonished, adding in a fatherly tone, "International Falls is a long way, so drive carefully."

Howie left the drugstore, went to his car, and headed over to Hatchaway's. On the drive to the antique store, his thoughts turned to the Donna Mae case. She had been dating a clown, but which one? And even if she had dated Squires or one of his partners, it didn't mean that whoever dated her murdered her as Margo suggested. If she had been dating one of those guys, and they had nothing to do with her death, why then would they deny it unless...unless they were hiding something else? But what? Perhaps the guy was married and didn't want his wife to find out about his having a fling. Or maybe Donna Mae was going to dump him?

Howie put those thoughts aside as he parked in front of the antique shop. When he didn't see the totem pole in its usual spot, he feared that it had been taken again. His fears were alleviated, however, when he noticed it looking out the window from inside the store. No sooner had he walked into the place than Stuart W came bounding toward him as if he had regained twenty years of his life.

"Thank you so much for finding my totem pole." Hatchaway grabbed Howie's hand and shook it as vigorously as if pumping water in the backyard of an old farmhouse. "I was so delighted when I saw it this morning." Before Howie could say a word, he slapped a check in his hand. "Here's your fee. You've certainly earned it, and to show you my appreciation I want to give you a little bonus."

"That's not necessary. I'm happy to do it for a friend of Kass'."

"But I insist. You don't realize how much it means to have Charlie back. My anniversary sale is now a guaranteed success."

Howie slipped the check into his pocket. "I see you moved it inside."

"Oh, yes. A couple of my friends did that for me. I'm not about to take any chances now. Charlie's been so much part of me that I had difficulty getting a decent night's sleep knowing someone else had him." Taking Howie by the arm, Hatchaway led him toward the counter in the middle of the store. "I've got something for you." He reached underneath the counter and got a wrapped package, the size of a shirt box. "Sorry about the brown wrapping paper. I didn't have anything fancier." He set the package on the counter next to the teapot.

"This isn't necessary. You've already paid me."

"I know, but allow me to show my gratitude for doing such a fine job. You made an old man happy." Hatchaway gestured toward the package. "Go ahead and open it."

Howie tore off the paper. As soon as he opened the box, however, he caught his breath.

"That there is a genuine Colt revolver," Hatchway announced.

Unsure what to say, Howie offered a polite smile. He had sworn not to carry a gun in his work. JD, his police detective friend, had told him right from the beginning they had met, "Don't try to outshoot the bad guys, outsmart them."

"How do you like it?" Hatchaway asked.

"Well, I…it's very nice, but…I don't use a gun."

"This isn't for your use. It's a symbol."

"Symbol? I'm not sure what you mean."

Hatchaway picked up the revolver. "This is a Colt Frontier Six Shooter, also known as a Peacemaker. These were sold between 1873 and 1907. I figure this one here…" He turned the Colt over a couple of times. "This one dates back to the 1880's. You can mount it on your wall as a symbol of being a law enforcer."

"Thank you." It would be useless to explain that he was a private detective and not a police officer. "I'll find a spot for it in my office." He took the revolver from Hatchaway and examined it.

"See those notches filed on the handle?"

Howie nodded.

"More than likely the sheriff killed four outlaws with that gun."

"This thing isn't loaded, is it?"

"Oh, gracious no. I don't keep loaded guns. I may be a crazy old coot, but I'm not that crazy." Hatchaway reached into his pocket. "But these go with it. They're 44 caliber cartridges, same caliber as the famed Winchester 73 carbine. Did you ever see the movie *Winchester 73* starring Jimmy Stewart?"

"I'm afraid not."

"Oh, you should. It's a wonderful movie."

"Maybe I'll have to see it sometime." Howie slipped the cartridges into his pocket. "I need to be going now."

"Let me wrap that for you." Hatchaway took the Colt and rewrapped it in paper and placed it in a box. "There you go," he said. "You wouldn't want to walk out of here with a revolver in your hand. Somebody might think you just robbed the place. You wouldn't want anyone to think that, would you, now?"

"No, that wouldn't be good." Howie picked up the box.

"Now, you drop in anytime, you hear. The tea is always on."

"I will, and you hang on to that totem pole."

"Oh, you can be sure that I'm not going to let Charlie out of my sight." Hatchaway raised his teacup as though making a toast. "Here's to good times and good luck ahead."

Chapter 23

Two hours after Howie left Hatchaway's antique shop, Les McGuire walked into the place. Someone had once pointed Hatchaway out to him, but that had been a couple of years ago. He figured, though, that the elderly gentleman sitting in a rocking chair drinking a cup of tea had to be him.

Hatchaway stood and set his cup on the counter. "Hello there, would you like a cup of tea? I brewed it myself." He eyed Les. "Say, don't you manage that used car lot up on Broadway?"

Les nodded, not pleased that he had been recognized. "I don't manage it. I own it."

"You don't say. Well, I'm Stuart W Hatchaway," he said, extending his hand. "Pleased to have another businessman come into my store." The two of them shook hands. "Now, how can I help you? I hope you're not looking for antique cars because I don't have any in stock right now." He chuckled at his own joke. "But I do have some old license plates that date back to the 1930's that might interest you. They're on the back table. Would you like to look at them?"

"I don't think so." Les pointed to the front of the store. "I'm interested in that totem pole you have there."

"Isn't that unique? A lot of people come in to look at it. Some even have their picture taken with it."

"I'm not interested in having my picture taken with it. I want to buy it."

Hatchaway shook his head. "Sorry, son, but that's the one item in the store that isn't for sale."

"I'll pay you good money for it." His new partner had instructed him to offer twice what the totem pole was worth, and had given him the cash to complete the transaction. Les figured to get the totem pole cheaper and then pocket the rest. "Whatever you paid for it, I'll go thirty percent above it."

"That's a fair offer, but I told you that it's not for sale."

"Okay, Mr. Hatchaway, I can see that you drive a hard bargain. I understand and respect that. After all, I'm a businessman also. I'll tell you what I'll do. I'll pay you fifty percent over and above what you paid for it."

87

Stuart W's eyebrows knotted together. "It's not for sale at any price."

Les kept his smile, but inside fumed at the old man's stubbornness. "Are you sure you won't change your mind?"

"Absolutely."

"Here's my card in case you reconsider." Les set the card on the counter. "Give me a call. I'm sure I could even be persuaded to go as high as seventy-five percent."

Les left and hurried back to his office where he made a phone call he dreaded. It was answered on the first ring.

"Hi, this is Les."

"Did you get it?"

"I tried, but no deal," Les said, determined not to let the cold tone of his partner intimidate him. "I even offered the stubborn old fool one hundred and fifty percent over what he paid for it, but he turned me down. He said he wouldn't sell it at any price."

"That's most unfortunate."

"So what do we do now?"

A long pause elapsed before the reply came. "I believe you have a pickup truck among your used cars, don't you?"

"Yeah, so?"

"Have the pickup in the back alley of the antique store tomorrow night."

"What time?"

"Nine-fifteen."

"But he closes at nine."

"Just do as I tell you...and Les?"

"Yeah?"

"Don't forget to bring the money I gave you."

Chapter 24

Adam parked his car, got out and headed toward the entrance of the Fireside Dining Club, one of the more exclusive supper clubs in northeast Minneapolis. He wondered if he should have worn a tie, but he wasn't planning to dine there, only check on Arthur Wentworth. He waited for the doorman to open the door and then walked in, going directly to the maitre d' dressed in a tux standing behind a podium. The man finished taking a reservation over the telephone and gave Adam a warm smile.

"Good evening, sir. Your name?" he asked, his eyes fixed on a sheet of paper on the podium.

"I don't have a reservation."

The smile turned cool.

"Well, then, I'm afraid that you'll not be able to dine with us tonight. All of our tables have been spoken for. Perhaps if there's a cancellation…"

"I'm not here to eat."

The man's eyebrows rose. "Oh?"

"I'm here to speak with Arthur Wentworth. I believe he works here as a waiter."

"I'm sorry, but staff members aren't permitted to have visits during working hours."

"This isn't a social call." Adam hardened his tone, putting an edge to his voice. "I'm with the MAC Detective Agency and I'm working on a case." He handed him a business card.

The man's eyes widened a bit. Within moments, however, he regained his composure. He glanced around before lowering his voice. "Arthur isn't working tonight. He's off for the next several evenings."

"May I ask you a few questions about him?"

"I don't know Arthur that well." He moved from around the podium. "Is he in some kind of trouble?" he whispered.

"No. I just need to ask him some questions. Is there someone else here that I might speak to?"

"Well…there's Charles."

"Who's he?"

"Our chef."

"May I talk to him?"

He looked down his nose and sniffed his reply, "Later perhaps. I'm sure Charles wouldn't want to be bothered at this moment."

"Why don't you let him decide that?" Adam said, frustrated with the man's increasingly patronizing attitude.

"Another time would—"

"I'll bring the police with me when I come back." Although a bluff, Adam had to chance it. "How would you like that for your evening crowd?"

The muscles in the man's jaw tightened. He drew in a deep breath, letting it out in an audible sigh as though this whole scenario was beneath him. "Very well if you put it that way," he huffed. "I'll take you to Charles and let him decide what to do with you. Please follow me."

Adam followed him through the main dining area. The smells of filet mignon, baked salmon, and a variety of pasta dishes filled his senses. The chaos in the kitchen area surprised Adam: cooks shouting orders; pots boiling; eggbeaters twirling; waiters flying in and out. And in the center of all the chaos stood a tall lean man dressed in white and wearing a chef's hat.

"Charles?"

"Stephen, don't you see I'm busy? Table four sent their salmon back, table sixteen is insisting on a dish that's been off the menu for months."

"I'm sorry but this gentleman insisted on seeing you. He's a private investigator and wishes to ask some questions about Arthur Wentworth."

Charles eyed Adam for a moment. "If you can wait fifteen minutes, I'll have some time to spend with you."

"That's fine."

"Just stay out of our way."

The fifteen minutes stretched into twenty-five and then forty-five minutes. Adam continued to be amazed at the buzz of activities. Two cooks had a heated discussion about what seasonings should be added to the preparation of a ravioli dish. One word from Charles stopped the dispute. He scurried from station to station: stirring and tasting a soup, making sure the lettuce was crisp for the salad, giving a final approval on a plate presentation, inspecting the fish fillets. Finally, he made his way over to Adam.

"Five minutes. No more."

"Thanks. Tell me what you know about Arthur Wentworth."

"Not very much. Arthur is a quiet individual who keeps to himself. He shows up on time. He does his job and then leaves without socializing with the other staff."

"Do you know much about his personal life?"

"Only that he does clowning on the side. When he mentioned that to me one night I was really surprised. You know, him being so quiet and everything."

A young man carrying a large ceramic bowl rushed up to Charles. "Is this the consistency you want for the dressing?" Charles took the wooden

90

spoon from the man's hand. After stirring the dressing, he nodded and then praised his assistant, who went away looking as though the Pope had just blessed him.

"How long has Wentworth worked here?" Adam asked.

"About three months." A frown appeared on Charles' forehead. "I have to say that even though Arthur said he had experience working in an establishment such as ours, he seemed a little rough around the edges."

"Are you saying he lied?"

"You'll have to ask him that question."

"By any chance, do you know where he spends his days off?"

"Not usually, but this time I do since he had to ask my permission to take Saturday evening off. He'll be attending a clown convention."

"Do you know where?"

"I believe it's at a hotel in downtown St. Paul."

Chapter 25

Howie arrived in International Falls in the early evening. The drive from Minneapolis had taken nearly five hours. He checked into a local motel and called Donna Mae's parents, arranging a time to visit with them later that evening. Since the LaBelle's were still under the impression that their daughter's death was a suicide, until he had definite proof to the contrary, he would leave it at that. He went out to grab a bite to eat before driving out to the LaBelle's.

Donna Mae's parents lived in an older two-story wood-framed house with a screened-in front porch. The house and the yard appeared to have been well taken care of over the years. Howie rang the doorbell and waited. A slightly built man in his mid-fifties answered the door, squinting at him from the other side of the threshold. "Are you the detective who called?"

"Yes, I'm Howie Cummins. I appreciate the time you and your wife are giving me, Mr. LaBelle."

"Call me Cliff." He led Howie into the living room and had him sit in a recliner rocker. On the coffee table sat a plate of cookies. "I hope you like homemade oatmeal chocolate chip cookies...they're my wife's specialty. Excuse me." Cliff went to the doorway of the kitchen. "Sarah, he's here. Would you come join us and bring the coffee?" He turned to Howie. "You do drink coffee, don't you?"

"I'd love a cup, thank you."

Sarah brought in a silver tray with a sterling silver coffee pot, fine china porcelain cups, and light-blue cloth napkins. She poured coffee into the cups, served Howie and then her husband. As Howie watched the woman, she moved with such grace and quiet dignity that she could easily be the grandmother whom everybody would love to have. "Do you take it with sugar or cream?" she asked as she sat next to her husband on the couch.

"Black is fine." Howie sensed that Sarah was waiting for him to try her cookies. He picked one up and she smiled. "They look good," he announced as he took a bite. "Delicious." He followed it with a sip of coffee. "I appreciate you two seeing me. I know it must not be easy for you to have lost your daughter."

Cliff picked up a cookie, broke it in two, and dunked one of the halves in his coffee. "As a parent you never dream that you'll outlive your kids. It's a parent's worst nightmare."

"I remember Donna Mae playing with her dolls," Sarah said with a catch in her voice. "I still have two of them in the guest bedroom." She dabbed at the corner of her eye with her napkin. "She was such a wonderful daughter."

"I'm sure she was." For a change, Howie found himself wishing Adam were with him. His partner was more sensitive in these situations. "I hope you don't mind me asking some questions?"

Cliff shook his head and laid his hand on Sarah's. "We understand you're only doing your job."

"Thank you." Howie reached into his pocket and took out his notepad. "Did your daughter ever do or say anything that might indicate anything that she might be depressed enough to, ah…"

"Take her life," Cliff said without emotion.

Howie nodded.

Sarah spoke up. "Donna Mae was the type of person who would never let anything get her down."

"Did your daughter ever talk about the people she was dating?"

"Donna Mae didn't date a lot," Sarah said. "She had plans for her life and didn't want to be tied down."

"What kind of plans?"

"School, for one thing. Once she finished her schooling, she wanted to travel. Now, does that sound like a person who would end her life?"

"No," Howie replied, beginning to understand the inner strength of Donna Mae's parents.

"And I was praying for a grandchild some day, but…" She took a deep breath as her husband patted her hand. "I know she was dating a gentleman who owned a business in downtown Minneapolis."

"Margo?"

Cliff put his cup down. "Yes, that was his name. We never met him, but Donna Mae told us that he treated her right. As her parents, that was the most important thing." He paused. "Do you know him?"

"Ah, yes, I've met Margo."

Sarah placed her napkin in her lap and took another cookie. "Donna Mae told me that he had a wonderful, fun-loving personality and that he was a self-made man."

"I'd agree with her." Howie swallowed a smile. "Margo certainly has a very unique personality. He was broken up about what happened to Donna Mae."

"Is he the one who hired you?" Cliff asked.

Howie hoped his face didn't reveal his surprise. "Yeah, that's right. Like I told you on the phone, I was hired by someone to investigate what possibly could have caused Donna Mae to do what she did. Margo was that person. He really cared about your daughter."

"That was very nice of him. I hope we get the opportunity to meet him some day." Sarah glanced at Howie's cup. "Would you like some more coffee?" she asked. "And please have another cookie. I made them especially for you."

"Thank you." Howie held out his cup for more coffee and took another cookie. "Besides Margo, was she dating anyone else?"

Cliff tugged at his ear. "Not that we know of." He turned to his wife. "Did she ever mention anyone else to you?"

Sarah shook her head.

"You have to understand that Donna Mae was one of the most popular girls in her high school," Cliff said. "She had all the dates she wanted. And that continued for several years after high school. We thought for sure she'd meet the right man, settle down, and have a family."

"In this day and time, women have so much more opportunity," Sarah said. "My Donna Mae had a lot to live for."

"So it sounds like she had lots of friends..."

"Lots," Sarah said proudly.

"And I would guess very few, ah, people who didn't like her?"

"I could say that I can't think of a single person. She was a beautiful girl. The boys she graduated with from high school would see me on the street and ask when Donna Mae was coming up to visit again. They were just waiting to ask her out, hoping she would say yes."

"So even though she had lots of opportunities to date, she didn't take them?"

Sarah offered a sad smile. "That's correct."

Cliff gave a sideways glance at his wife. "You have to understand that after her brother died, she didn't date for a long time."

"Her brother?" Howie set his cup down, feeling he was out of his league with this kind of stuff. If only Adam was here. "I'm so sorry to hear that," he said, feeling that no words would be adequate. "You have my sympathy."

"Thank you," Cliff said.

Several long moments passed without a word. Howie knew he had to carry on. He wondered if something about the brother could provide a clue. He had gotten nowhere with his questions about Donna Mae, and he didn't have any other pertinent questions to ask. From what he had heard from her parents, Donna Mae led a pretty normal life. "I didn't know she had a brother."

"Oh, yes, she and Johnny were very close." Cliff looked away for a moment. "She was devastated when he was killed."

"What happened?"

Cliff looked at his wife. She nodded as if acknowledging that it was okay to share the story. "Johnny was always a good boy and he would've been able to get a decent paying job here at the paper mill if he had liked school more. He was smart enough, but he was just one of those kids that formal education didn't set well."

"He got good grades in junior high," Sarah said.

"That he did," her husband added. "But in high school everything went wrong. His grades were terrible and then we found out that he was skipping classes. His teachers told us that he was nothing but trouble at school. He was always getting into fights."

"I didn't understand that," Sarah said. "He never gave us any trouble and he always helped around the house. He even helped me with dishes." Her eyes revealed a sense of pride. "Not every teenage boy would do that. He was such a good son."

"I'm sure he was."

Cliff continued with the story. "Johnny quit school and moved down to the cities. He worked at odd jobs down there and after several years, got into some real bad company. After that, he always seemed to have money. And then one day we got a visit from the police here. The police chief and the pastor of our church sat in our living room and told us that our Johnny had been killed in a shoot-out with the police down in the cities."

Howie saw the pain in their eyes, but still needed to ask the question. "What were the circumstances of his death?"

"The police surrounded the house Johnny was holed up in and told him and his two partners to come out. They didn't." Cliff took a deep breath. "He and another man were killed."

Sarah spoke up. "A police officer was also killed, and another one wounded. That was just awful. We were told, though, that it wasn't Johnny's gun that had fired the bullet that killed the officer."

"Johnny and the two other men stole some very valuable merchandise," Cliff said. "I never found out what. I never wanted to."

Howie put away his notepad. "You said only two were killed. What happened to your son's other partner?"

"Somehow, he got away," Cliff said. "The police never found him, and they sure wanted to because they figured he was the one who had shot the officer. Jake Peterson, he's the police chief here, told us that even though it happened five years ago, the case is still open. The stolen property was never recovered."

"So the other guy got away with the loot?"

Cliff shook his head. "The police believed that the stolen property was still in Johnny's possession, but they never found it. They figured that he stashed it away. I heard that an insurance company had offered a big reward for the recovery of the stolen items, but to this day nobody has ever found any of it."

"What kind of person was Johnny? I mean, what kind of things did he like?"

"Johnny was very kind and considerate," Sarah said. "And he loved music."

"Especially Rock 'n' Roll music," Cliff added. "When he was living here, I always had to tell him to turn his record player down...and he always did."

95

"My son also liked to collect oddities," Sarah said.

"What do you mean?"

She smiled. "He liked being different. For a whole year he saved his money from working at the grocery store here...this was when he was in eighth grade. With his money he bought an authentic Japanese sword."

"He also bought a footstool made out of an elephant's foot," Cliff said.

Sarah scrunched her nose. "I didn't like the elephant's foot. Every time I looked at it, all I could think of was that poor animal."

Cliff brushed some cookie crumbs off the front of his shirt. "Like I said, after he moved to the cities he had lots of money to buy collectables. At one time he had a knight's suit of armor, a nickel slot machine that actually worked..." He went on to name half dozen or more unusual items that his son had collected over the years.

"What happened to all those things?" Howie glanced around the house. The LaBelle's appeared to have very conservative tastes.

"Donna Mae took them," Sarah said. "She initially thought it'd be one way to keep the memory of Johnny with her. She didn't have space for everything, however, and sold all but a few items."

"By any chance do you know who she sold it to?"

"No, I'm afraid not," she said apologetically. "I'm not being very helpful, am I?"

"Oh, no," Howie said, reassuring her. "Both of you have been very helpful." He glanced at his watch. "I need to be leaving now. Thank you for the coffee and cookies."

Sarah fixed him a bag of cookies for the trip back to Minneapolis. "It's a long trip and you'll get hungry," she explained.

When he got back to the motel, he took out his notepad and was reviewing his notes when the phone rang.

"Howie, this is Cliff LaBelle. After you left, my wife and I talked some more and we remembered there was one other item that Johnny acquired that he really liked. It was something our son was quite proud of."

"What was it?"

"A totem pole."

"A what?"

"A seven foot tall totem pole."

Chapter 26

Howie called his partners from the motel in International Falls to set up an early afternoon meeting with them at his office the following day. Without going into details, he informed them that he had something very interesting to share about the LaBelle case. The next morning, he left the motel shortly before seven and drove straight through to the Cities. Worn out from a restless night in a strange bed, he brewed himself a pot of extra-strong coffee. Now, as he sipped his third cup, he waited until his partners had fully absorbed what he had shared about Donna Mae's brother, Johnny.

"That's hard to believe," Mick said. "When did you say this all happened?"

"Five years ago."

"Wow."

"Her poor parents," Adam said. "Having their son killed in a shoot-out with the police and then losing their daughter. How're they doing?"

"As best as can be expected." Howie leaned forward. "But there's more to the story about her brother, Johnny. Get this. He collected all sorts of odd stuff including...a totem pole."

"What! Does this have any connection to the case we just finished?"

Howie shrugged. "I don't know."

"Maybe it's just a coincidence," Mick pointed out. "Do they know what happened to it after he was killed?"

"Yeah, Donna Mae got it."

Adam was quick to ask the next question. "Did Margo ever mention seeing a totem pole at her place?"

"No, and I wouldn't suspect that he would've seen it there."

"Why?"

"Because according to her parents, she got rid of it along with the other stuff."

"Who did she sell it to?"

"I don't know. Her parents didn't have that information."

"Could it be the same totem pole that we just recovered for Hatchaway?" Mick asked.

"That's my thought." Howie opened his notepad and glanced over his notes. "This whole case is getting screwier by the day. Here's what we're dealing with thus far. The cops are calling Donna Mae's death a suicide. As far as they're concerned, the case is closed. But then Margo comes along and hires us because he doesn't believe that she'd do that to herself and he suspects some guy she was dating killed her. We find out that the guy she was dating does clowning on the side, but there are three clowns and we don't know which one." He flipped a page in his notepad. "Then I find out that she not only had a brother, but he and one of his partners were killed in a shoot-out."

"And the police don't think that the other guy got away with the loot," Adam said. "Is that right?"

"That's right. But don't ask me how this all ties in...if it does."

"Do we assume that Margo's right when he says that Donna Mae didn't commit suicide?" Mick asked.

"I think so, but not because of Margo." Howie sipped his coffee. It tasted bitter without any bourbon, but it was keeping him awake. "Based on what her girlfriend told you about Donna Mae's plans for going to school and what I got from her parents, she had too much to live for. My guess is that she didn't pull the plug on herself."

"Who killed her then?" Adam asked.

"Probably the guy she was dating."

"And the guy she was dating is into clowning," Mick said.

Howie nodded. "And that leads us to the assumption that it had to be one of those three guys on the business card you got."

"So we assumed she was killed," Adam said. "But why should we assume that it was one of those three guys that we're currently investigating?"

"It has to be," Mick said.

"Not necessarily. Maybe the girlfriend misunderstood her." Adam turned and faced Mick. "Sure, she was dating a clown but that doesn't mean it was one of the guys from that group."

"Oh, come on. Use some common sense on this. Who else could it have been?"

"Quite a few other guys."

"How did you come to that conclusion?"

"I did some checking. There're a number of people who are into clowning as a hobby. There are even clown clubs out there."

"But she had this card indicating these particular three guys," Mick argued.

"That doesn't prove anything."

"Sure it does!"

"Hold on you two," Howie said. "Even though there could be any number of others, I'm going on the assumption that it is one of those three guys. That's all we have to go on for now." He looked to Adam for further argument, but his partner said nothing. "Squires and Beamer told me that they never heard of her. I can't say I believe either one of them. Mick, did you find out anything more on Squires' background?"

"A little. He's not married and lives alone. Other than clowning, he doesn't seem to have any other interests. Nobody I've talked to knows much about his background. And he's been at the bank for about three years."

"What kind of reputation does he have there?"

"Hard-nosed and impersonal." Mick paused. "I talked to a couple of employees. The word is that he's made some bad personal investments and might have to declare bankruptcy. If he does that, the bank wouldn't keep him on. And according to the people I talked to, nobody would shed a tear if he was let go." He crossed his arms and leaned back as though he had presented a solid case for the prosecution. "As far as I'm concerned, Squires should be our number one suspect."

"Just because he's having financial problems doesn't mean he killed Donna Mae," Adam said. "What would be his motive?"

"You've got a point," Howie said. They needed to discover a motive for why Donna Mae was murdered. "We haven't established a reason for anyone wanting to kill her."

"How about money?" Mick said. "Maybe Squires was embezzling from his bank and needed to cover it before he was caught. If he was hard up for cash, he could've killed her for that."

Howie finished off the remainder of his coffee. "Maybe...if she had any money. She lived modestly and her parents told me that she was planning to borrow money from them to go to school this fall. I checked with JD. According to the police report, there was nothing taken from her house."

"Maybe it was a crime of passion," Adam said. "Maybe she was going to break up with the guy and go back to Margo."

Mick shook his head. "No, that can't be it. According to her friend, she really liked the guy she was dating. Her friend said that Donna Mae could've even been in love with him."

"Then maybe she found out something about him and he killed her to keep her quiet," Adam said.

"You mean, if Squires, for example, was embezzling from the bank and she found out about it," Mick said. "That could be a motive for murder."

Adam's eyes narrowed. "I thought those were rumors."

"Rumors that could be based on truth."

Howie listened with interest to the give-and-take between his partners and although what Adam was saying was plausible, it just didn't sit right with him. He was about to suggest they sleep on it when he heard the downstairs entrance door slam shut. The footsteps on the stairs sounded heavy so it had to be a man. And the guy had to be in pretty good shape since he was taking the stairs two at a time.

"Come on in, JD," Howie hollered just as the door opened and in walked Jim Davidson. At nearly six feet, cold gray-blue eyes, square jaw, and the build of a linebacker, he looked every bit the part of the hard-nosed veteran police detective.

"You're getting pretty good at that, Howie." JD closed the door behind him. He greeted Mick and Adam, then walked over and leaned against the wall by the window.

"What brings you up here?" Howie asked.

"I understand that you guys located a missing totem pole."

"With Squirrel's help," Mick said.

"Is that so? Maybe there's hope for the little guy yet. Where did you find the pole?"

"At a frat house at the U of M," Howie said. "They were using the pole for one of their toga parties. You know college kids."

"Yeah, believe it or not, I was one for a year." A hint of a smile crossed JD's face. "Of course, I wasn't in any fraternity."

"You didn't come up to talk about your old college days, did you?" Howie said.

"What did Hatchaway say when you returned his totem pole?"

"He wasn't there," Adam said.

"We left it in front of his store," Mick added. "It was so late at night that we didn't want to wake him. We thought it'd be a nice surprise in the morning."

"I talked to him the next day," Howie said. "He was happy to get it back. I'm going to do a follow-up visit with him tomorrow."

"That's not going to be possible," JD said.

"Why's that?"

"Because he's dead."

Chapter 27

"Dead!" Did the excitement of getting the totem pole back prove too much for the old guy? One glance at his partners told Howie that they were just as stunned as he was hearing the news of Hatchaway's death. "What happened?" he asked. "Did he have a heart attack or something?"

JD appeared tired, as though he'd been up all night. "If only it was that simple. Then I could go home early tonight, crack a few beers, and watch the ballgame on TV."

"What are you trying to tell us?" Mick asked.

Adam spoke up. "I think he's saying that Hatchaway didn't die of natural causes." He eyed the police detective. "Am I right?"

"You've got it." JD squeezed the bridge of his nose. When he spoke, his tone was matter-of-fact. "We got the call mid-morning when one of his customers thought something wasn't right. Hatchaway's place usually opens at nine, but the doors were still locked at ten. When the officer arrived at the scene he could see through the windows someone lying on the floor by the cash register. The officer broke in and when he discovered that Hatchaway was dead, I was called in. It didn't look right to me so I had the lab boys do some preliminary testing of the teacup on the counter next to the body."

Mick's eyes widened. "Do you think he was poisoned?"

"No doubt about it. The lab boys found traces of potassium cyanide powder on the counter. The teacup had traces in it as well."

"Potassium cyanide?" Howie felt angry that someone would murder a harmless guy like Hatchaway who only wanted to share his passion about antiques with others. "That's some powerful stuff."

JD nodded. "It can kill you in a matter of minutes." He rubbed the cleft in his chin. "There's one thing that has the lab boys confused, though."

"What's that?" Mick asked.

"Hatchaway should've been able to taste that something wasn't right with his tea. He drank nearly the whole cup."

"He told me he had a terrible cold," Howie said. "Might that explain it?"

"If it affected his sense of taste, it could."

Howie curled his hand into a fist. Even though he only visited with Hatchaway a couple of times, he had grown fond of the guy. "Any idea of who did it?"

"None what-so-ever." JD's tone hardened. "Look, guys, I'm going to share something with you off the record. It stays off the record. You got that?" He waited until he got the nod from the three of them. "We know that the tea was loaded with this stuff, but we don't know how it got into his cup. Both the back and front doors were locked."

"Couldn't someone have locked them after they left?" Mick asked.

"Yeah, except both doors had been locked from the inside with dead bolts. There was no way that someone could have done that from the outside."

"How about an unlocked window?" Adam suggested. "There's got to be some windows in the back where he lives."

"There are two windows back there, but both were locked. The only possible entry we found was an open transom above a side door, a space so small that a baby would've had a hard time wriggling through."

"You don't think he could've taken his own life?" Howie didn't believe that Hatchaway would do such a thing, but needed to ask the question if only to bring it to the table.

JD folded his arms and leaned against the wall. "I considered that, but it's not very likely. The shoe repair guy next door to the place told me that the day before yesterday Hatchaway had come over with a pair of shoes to be repaired. All the time he was there, Hatchaway talked about his anniversary sale coming up and how great it was going to be." He shook his head. "In my book, there's no way that he would've taken his own life."

"Was anything stolen from the place?" Howie asked.

A hint of a smile crossed JD's face. "You've been in that store. With all the junk in there, it'd be hard to say if anything was missing. I can tell you that money was still in the cash register and he still had his wallet on him."

"How about enemies?" Mick asked. "Did he have any?"

"Not according to the people we talked to. The old guy was well liked around Broadway." JD paused. "Right now, we've no suspects, no motive, and no idea how the crime was committed. It's going to make for some late nights, but an interesting case."

"So, how are you going to handle it?" Howie asked.

"Same way we do on most cases like these. We'll keep dogging it until something turns up. It could be a day, a month...hell, even years." JD checked his watch. "Look, I've got to go. It's going to be a busy day. I just wanted to stop in to let you guys know about this since you found the totem pole for him. If you hear anything, give me a call."

"Sure, no problem," Howie said. "Where are you headed now?"

"I'm going down to talk to Kass. He doesn't know about it yet. I want to ask him a few questions."

Adam shot Howie a concerned look. "Kass is going to take it hard. I'm going with JD."

"Go ahead." Howie appreciated Adam's sensitivity. "And ask Kass to come up for a few minutes afterwards."

"Glad to have your assistance," JD said to Adam. "See you guys." He stopped and stood in front of the movie poster. "Bogie, make sure these hot-shots leave some of the bad guys for the police department." He gave a tip of his head and left with Adam.

As soon as the office door closed, Mick leaned forward and spoke in a whisper as though JD was on the other side of the door listening. "When you asked if anything was stolen, you were thinking about that totem pole, weren't you?"

"That's right. Apparently, it wasn't, though."

"How do you know that?"

"JD would've mentioned it since he knew that we recovered it for Hatchaway." JD had proven to be a good mentor, not to mention a valuable resource. Howie owed him big time, but also felt an obligation to Hatchaway. The totem pole may have been returned but the case wasn't closed, and wouldn't be closed until they found out whoever murdered Hatchaway. "I can't shake the feeling that the totem pole figures into this some way."

"How?"

"I'm not sure."

"But if he was killed because of the totem pole..." Mick watched Howie play with the pencil. "You don't think those college kids from the frat house had anything to do with his death, do you?"

"I'm pretty sure we can rule those guys out. I can't think of anyone from that night who would even come close to being a suspect." The image of Hatchaway's body lying amidst his beloved antiques flashed through his mind. "Maybe his death didn't have anything to do with the totem pole. For all I know, the guy had a stash of dough hidden in a potbelly stove."

"So what do you suggest we do?"

"Keep our eyes and ears open. This case isn't finished as far as I'm concerned. JD and his boys can handle it from the cops' angle. We'll handle from ours." The downstairs entrance door banged and the stairs began to creak. "Adam and Kass are coming up now," Howie said. He and Mick waited in silence.

"Sorry about your friend," Mick said as soon as Kass came in.

"Thank you." Kass walked over and, at the insistence of Adam, sat in the chair next to Mick. Adam sat on the windowsill.

"How're you doing?" Howie asked Kass.

"I still can't believe it. I just talked to Stuart W the other day and he sounded so happy. When Detective Davidson told me that he was dead, I was shocked. I...I just couldn't believe my ears. I still find it hard to believe." Kass looked to Adam. "Thank you again for being there."

"How much did Davidson tell you?" Howie felt more comfortable dealing with facts. Adam could deal with Kass' grief.

"Only that Stuart W was found this morning after the police was called. The detective asked me if he had any enemies. He made it sound like the poor man was...murdered." Sadness enveloped Kass' face. "What happened?" he asked, but quickly added, "No, I've no right to ask that. Your detective friend told you things in confidence. I don't want you to break that trust. I know Stuart W is dead and I surmise that someone caused his death. That's all I need or want to know for now."

"Thanks," Howie said, relieved that he didn't have to lie to Kass. He had been prepared to say that the police had no idea of the cause of death. The fewer people who knew about the details of the case, the better.

Mick reached over and placed a hand on Kass' shoulder. "I'm sure you'll miss him. He seemed to be such a nice guy."

"He was a wonderful man and a loyal friend."

Howie opened his notepad and picked up a pen. "When did you say was the last time you talked to him?"

"It was the next day after you boys returned his totem pole. We talked on the telephone for a half hour or so."

"And what time of day was that?"

"Early afternoon. He sounded so relieved to have his totem pole back. It was the happiest day of his life and he was looking forward to the anniversary sale." The grief lines on Kass' face softened. "He told me that he was very indebted to all of you boys. The two of us were to go out for a celebration dinner once the sale ended. The last thing he said to me was that his luck had changed for the better." He sighed as his whole body sunk further into the chair.

"Why don't you take the afternoon off?" Adam said.

"I agree," Mick added. "You certainly could use it."

"No, I'd rather go back to my drugstore." At the mention of his drugstore, Kass' body seemed to reenergize. "That'll be the best thing for me." He rose from his chair. "Thanks for coming down," he said to Adam. "Thanks to all of you." He offered an appreciative smile and left.

Adam walked over and sat down. "Any theories concerning Hatchaway's death?" he asked Howie.

"Like I was telling Mick, I've got a gut feeling that the totem pole might have something to do with all of this, but exactly what, I don't know. Here's what we do know. Donna Mae's brother had a totem pole and he was killed. Donna Mae got her brother's totem pole and she was killed. And now, Hatchaway."

"It has to be the same one, don't you think?" Adam asked.

"It sure seems like it."

"Do you think it has anything to do with the guy she was dating?" Mick asked.

"We're going to find out." Howie pointed to Adam. "You stay with Wentworth. Mick, you got Squires. That leaves Beamer for me." He closed his notepad and slipped it in his shirt pocket. "Now, is there anything else?"

"You should know about Squirrel," Adam said.

"What now?"

"I talked to him while I was waiting for Kass."

"Is he coming up?"

"No, he told me to tell you that he's going over to the University of Minnesota. He wants to check to see if those college kids had anything to do with Hatchaway's death."

"What? How did he even find out about it?"

"I don't know, but he's going back to that frat house. He said that it was his duty as their mascot."

Chapter 28

The Delta Phi fraternity house appeared quiet as Squirrel strolled up to the front door and knocked. He looked around but didn't see any signs of life at the other houses on the street. He knocked a second time, but again no answer. Unwilling to give up, he pounded on the door with a fist.

"Come on in," a deep male voice yelled.

Squirrel opened the door and peeked in, wondering what he was getting himself into. He quietly closed the door behind him, moved through a short hallway, and peered into the living room. The place didn't fit his idea of a frat house. No leftover beer or whisky bottles, no broken lamps, no holes in the wall, no lingering booze odors, and most surprising (and disappointing), no young women running around in their underwear.

"Hey, Eric, I'm out in the kitchen," the deep voice boomed.

Eric? Who's Eric? Squirrel sucked air through his teeth. He cautiously moved toward the sound of the voice.

"I'm fixing myself a sandwich," the person continued to shout. "If you're hungry, I'll fix you one and then we'll hit the books."

Squirrel hadn't stepped a foot into the kitchen when he stopped in his tracks. At the counter by the sink stood the biggest guy he had ever seen. The giant with the crew cut had Mick by a good six inches. And whereas Mick was well built, this guy looked more like one of those Japanese wrestlers Squirrel had seen on television…the ones with pigtails and diapers.

"Hey, you're not Eric," the sumo wrestler announced casually as though having strangers pop in the house was nothing unusual. He studied his visitor. "Say, weren't you here with those detectives the other night?"

"Yeah, I…ah…was," Squirrel replied, trying to figure out if that was in his favor. He would hate being tossed out by the guy. But, ten-to-one, he could outrun the big lug. He eyed the nearest exit.

"No, wait. Don't tell me. You're Beaver. Right?"

"The name is Squirrel," he replied, hunching up his shoulders.

"Oh, yeah. Now I remember." He cocked his head as though recalling the events of that night. "We adopted you as our mascot, didn't we?"

"That's right."

The giant walked over and extended his hand. "I'm Monk Peterson. Please to meet you, Squirrel."

Monk's hand enveloped Squirrel's, and for a moment, the newly adopted mascot thought his hand would be crushed. "You've got some pretty big mitts there," Squirrel said as Monk released his grip.

"It helps me handle the pigskin."

"Pigskin?"

"Yeah, football."

"You play for the team here?"

"I'm the starting center." Monk chewed off a hunk of his sandwich. "You want something to eat?"

Squirrel shook his head.

Monk leaned up against the counter and took another bite of his sandwich. Three more bites and it would be history. "Hey, man, I'm glad you showed up."

"Oh, yeah? How's that?"

"I need you guys to investigate a case for me."

Squirrel's eyebrows shot up. Adrenalin surged through his body. That Monk had taken him for a real detective started Squirrel's nose twitching.

"You don't have to first check with your partners, do you?"

"Oh, no." Squirrel huffed on his fingernails and buffed them on the front of his jacket. "They'll go along with whatever I say."

"Have a chair, then, and I'll tell you all about it."

"Sure thing." Squirrel sat down at the kitchen table. "Hey, Monk."

"Yeah?"

"I'll take that sandwich now. Working on a case always makes me hungry."

Chapter 29

"A clown convention?" Howie laid his pencil on the desk, leaned forward, and cocked his head at Adam. "Did I hear you right? You did say a *clown* convention?"

"That's right."

"I didn't know they had such things."

"They do and it's going to be this weekend. That's why Wentworth's not working at the restaurant Saturday night."

"Then that must mean Squires and Beamer will be there," Mick said.

"That's what I thought," Adam replied. "And if you ask me, those three are closer knit than they make out to be."

Howie rocked in his chair as he studied his two partners. By asking the right questions and using the process of deduction, Mick and Adam were thinking more like detectives every day. The two of them had come a long way since their first case, and he was pleased to have them working with him. Sometimes his biggest challenge, being the *boss*, was keeping one step ahead of them. "Where's this convention going to be held?"

"At the Hotel Fleming in St. Paul," Adam said. "Why?"

"Because I've got an idea." Howie got out the telephone book from the bottom drawer of his desk and turned to the Yellow Pages. He kept flipping until he found the listing he was looking for and ran his finger down that page. "Ah, here it is."

"Here's what?" Mick asked.

"Just hang on." Howie picked up the phone, dialed, and gave a knowing nod to his partners while waiting for someone to answer. "Hello. I'm calling about the clown convention this weekend. Is that right? Great." He gave his partners a winsome smile. "I wonder if you could give me the details." He jotted the information in his notepad. "So we don't need to make reservations?" Mick mouthed a question but Howie waved him off. "Is that so? And that's it?" He squinted at Mick and Adam, sizing them up for what he had in mind. "Oh, no, that's no problem. Thanks for the information."

"Thinking about going?" Adam asked.

Howie nodded.

"But we'd be spotted in ten seconds," Mick said.

"No, we won't." Howie closed his notepad and put the telephone book back in his drawer.

"What do you mean? Why won't we?" Adam asked.

"Because we're going to dress up as clowns."

A startled expression flashed across Mick's face. He opened his mouth, but no words came forth.

"You're kidding!" Adam said.

When Howie didn't reply, Mick spoke up. "I think he's serious." He nudged Adam. "He's got that look about him."

"Look guys, everybody going to that convention is going to be dressed as clowns. It's a perfect cover. We'll walk around and blend into the crowd."

Mick's face registered disbelief. "Are you sure that's going to work? Won't they spot us as frauds?"

"Not if we do a good job in our clown makeup." Howie leaned back in his chair and cupped his hands behind his head. "Nobody's going to recognize us. We'll be able to stand right next to Wentworth and his partners, and listen in to what they're talking about. Who knows what we might pick up?"

"I don't know about this," Adam said with a note of skepticism.

"Don't worry about it," Howie said. "Just trust me on this. All we have to do is to walk around and keep our eyes and ears open."

Howie's phone rang ten minutes after his partners left the office. "MAC Detective Agency. Howie Cummins speaking."

"I just got back from that frat house," Squirrel shouted. "I met Monk Peterson. He's the center on the football team. The guy's huge. Must weigh five hundred pounds. And you should see his hands. They're ten times the size of mine. I've never seen such a big guy. He's—"

"Slow down, will you? And you don't have to shout."

"Sorry, boss, I'm just so excited about this case I got for us."

"What case?"

"The one I picked up from Monk."

Howie closed his eyes and sighed. "Don't tell me that you said yes."

"What else could I do?"

"You could have said no."

"But I'm their mascot."

Howie held the phone away from his ear while he took a couple of deep breaths. He had a feeling he'd want a stiff shot of bourbon after this phone call. "Okay, what's the case about?"

"I don't want to tell you over the phone."

"What do you mean you don't want to?"

"I want to tell you in person."

"Listen, I—"

"I'll catch you tomorrow afternoon at the office. Got to go."

"Wait a—hello? Squirrel? Damn!" Howie hung up the phone and sat there for several moments muttering. He massaged his temples, opened his desk drawer, and took out his bottle of bourbon.

Chapter 30

Les McGuire reached for the phone on the second ring.

"What happened to you?" The man on the other end of the line made no attempt to disguise his anger. "I waited for nearly an hour. Are you trying to pull something?" A chilly tone crept into his voice when he spoke again. "Because if you are, you're going to wish you hadn't."

"Look, I couldn't help it," Les said. "The cops drove by. It wouldn't have looked right for me to be sitting there in the pickup so late at night. Didn't want to arouse their suspicion."

"Why didn't you drive away, wait for a few minutes, and come back?"

"I did, but they came back. I couldn't risk staying any longer," Les lied, not wanting to fuel the man's fury. He especially didn't want him to know that he had panicked when he saw the police car the first time. "So what are we going to do now?"

"I'll have to give it some thought."

"Are we still going to need my truck?"

"Of course we're going to need your truck," the man snapped. "Just be ready when I call."

Les didn't like the idea of playing chauffer, but whatever the reason the man wanted the totem pole, it involved money, and he wanted his cut. "When can I figure on you calling again? I can't be by the phone day and night. I've got a thriving business to run." A prolonged silence followed. Les felt a jolt of fear.

"I'll call you in the next couple of days," the man finally said. "Stay close to that phone."

The telephone clicked in Les' ear. He placed the phone back on the receiver and sat staring at it for several moments. Only when he reached for his pack of cigarettes, did he realized that his hands were shaking.

After he had hung up on McGuire, he walked over and sat in front of the lighted mirror and began applying the greasepaint. He applied the white base, used his powder sock to set the makeup, and gently brushed the excess away. Taking the grease pencil, he outlined his eyes in black and drew teardrops at the corners of each eye. He stared at his reflection, his mind going back to the day five years ago when Johnny LaBelle had called him after the heist.

"Don't worry, I've got it stashed in a safe place," Johnny had said.

"Where?"

"I'll just keep that to myself for now."

"Don't you trust me?"

Johnny laughed. "As much as you do me."

It had been a mistake to let Johnny take care of the haul. They should have split it three ways right afterwards. But no, Johnny and their other partner had argued in favor of stashing it for a few months until things cooled down. "What if something happens to you?" he asked Johnny.

"What's going to happen to me?" Johnny replied in his usual cocky manner. "You know something I don't know?" He laughed again and then got serious. "Look, the stuff is under lock and key, and I have the key."

"But if the cops nab you, they'll get the key."

"No they won't."

"How can you be so sure?"

"Because I hid the key in my sister's car."

"Is that so?"

"Don't get any funny notions. Even with the key, you still wouldn't know what it goes to."

"Quit playing games! If you want your sister to stay healthy, you better level with me."

Several long seconds elapsed before Johnny replied. "Hey, man. Don't get so worked up. I'll tell you what the key is for when I see you in a couple of days."

As he applied red rouge to his cheeks, he recalled that day of the shoot-out with the cops. Just after Johnny had been shot in the chest, he had knelt next to him and asked what the key fit.

"Pro...promise...take care...my sister? Give...give her...my share."

"Sure thing."

Johnny coughed up blood, but still managed to get the words out. "Tot...totem pole."

"What about it?"

"Wro...wrote...in...in..."

"You wrote a note what the key fits to and hid it in the totem pole?" he asked, but Johnny was already dead.

Now, as he sat staring into the mirror, his mouth twisted into a sneer. He had been lucky to escape that day. And after killing the cop, he skipped town, having barely slipped through the police dragnet. He had taken care of Johnny's sister, all right, but not in the way Johnny had thought. He had waited five long years to recover the loot and now that he almost had his hands on it, nobody—*nobody*—was going to get in his way.

Chapter 31

Squirrel sauntered casually into Howie's office as though nothing were amiss. The little guy froze in his tracks, however, as soon as he saw the three detectives. Within an instant, his initial surprised expression turned into one of amusement. "Why are you guys dressed up as clowns?" He put his hand to his mouth stifling a laugh. "You're not planning to run away and join the circus, are you?"

"Don't get wise," Mick muttered as he adjusted the blue suspenders holding up his yellow baggy pants. He pointed to Howie. "Ask him. It was his idea."

Dressed in a one-piece red, white, and green striped outfit, Howie was adding the final touch: his red sponge-ball nose. His size sixteen black-and-white clown shoes required concentration to walk without tripping and he wondered how he was going to navigate the stairs, let alone drive a car. A bushy orange wig and large red bow tie completed his attire.

Squirrel moved closer to inspect the three of them. "Where did you guys learn to put on that makeup?"

"The man at the clown shop gave us some pointers," Adam said, retying the rope holding up his pants. Dressed as a hobo, he carried a stick with a blue-and-white handkerchief bag tied at the end. He had no wig, but wore a black derby that looked like something he'd found in a trash can.

"Aren't you afraid someone will recognize you in those outfits?"

"Not a chance," Mick said. He adjusted his straw-colored wig and then tucked in his multi-colored polka dot blouse-like shirt. "My own mother wouldn't know me," he added as he stuck a beanie hat topped with a propeller on his head.

Squirrel chuckled. "And if she did, three-to-one she probably wouldn't admit it."

Howie pointed his forefinger at Squirrel. "I hope you didn't come up to hassle us."

"No way, boss."

"So why are you here?"

"To tell you about the case."

"What case?"

"The one I picked up at the frat house for us. You didn't forget about it, did you?"

Although curious as to what Squirrel had committed them to, they were running late and Howie was anxious to get to the hotel. "Make it fast. Spare us the details."

"Sure thing, boss." Squirrel began pacing back and forth in front of Howie's desk. "Monk Peterson, he's the football player I told you about. His parents were swindled when they bought lakeshore property up north." His energetic tone and the rapid twitching of his nose signaled that he was ready to take on the case himself. "The realtor misrepresented the property and Monk wants us to investigate the crook."

"Tell him to get in touch with a lawyer."

"But you're going to want this case," Squirrel said.

"And why's that?"

"Because Beamer was the realtor!"

Chapter 32

The Hotel Fleming, located in the center of downtown St. Paul, dated back to the turn of the century. The hotel, a historic landmark, was well known for its huge elegant ballroom with high fresco ceilings and crystal chandeliers. Howie parked in the hotel parking lot. He ignored the silly grin on the parking lot attendant as he handed him the keys.

"I look funny in this getup," Mick said as they walked toward the hotel's entrance.

"You're supposed to look funny," Howie said. His oversized shoes flapped on the cement as he walked. "You're a clown. Start acting like one and you'll blend right in."

Adam tapped Howie on the arm. "Just exactly how's a clown supposed to act?"

Howie shrugged. "How should I know? Just watch the other clowns and do as they do."

The three detectives entered the ballroom, amazed at the sight of hundreds of clowns in all shapes and sizes, and dressed in every colorful outfit imaginable. One walked by holding a pink parasol and hanging onto a leash that stretched out in front of him as though there was a dog at the end of it, except there was nothing leading him but an empty dog collar. Another whizzed by on a unicycle. Nearby, another pretended he was juggling as several others applauded his antics.

"I feel like I've died and gone to clown heaven," Mick whispered.

A clown wearing a long blond wig and a sequined emerald-green evening gown that flared out at the bottom sashayed up to Howie. "Hi, I'm Cuddles," she said, fluttering two-inch false lashes. "And may I ask your name?"

"Ah...Howie Smith," he replied, realizing with a start that Cuddles was actually a man.

"No, no, no, I mean your clown name."

"Oh...ah..." Howie glanced up at the chandeliers. "Ah...Crystal. And these are my two friends."

Cuddles curtsied. "And your names?"

Before Mick and Adam could reply, a voice came over the loud speakers asking everyone to be quiet and give their attention to the stage.

"That's Bon Bon," Cuddles said. "He's the Master of Ceremonies for this evening's entertainment."

"Welcome everybody to the Midwest Eighteenth Annual Clown Get-together," Bon Bon said. "Would everyone please gather closer to the stage?"

"Come on," Howie told his partners behind his hand. "Let's go and see if we can spot our guys."

"But how're we going to know them?" Mick asked. "If we think they won't recognize us, how do we expect to recognize them?"

Howie scratched his head. The wig made his scalp itched and he wondered how long he would be able to put up with it. "You can always tell a person by their eyes." Noticing several clowns wearing oversize sunglasses, he shrugged. "Well, just do the best you can."

"...and now if we could have a moment of silence..." Bon Bon announced, "...to remember those friends who are no longer with us and who have departed to that big circus in the sky."

"Let's move up toward the stage and then fan out." Howie and his partners took the opportunity to slip away quietly through the crowd.

Bon Bon spoke into the microphone again. "We begin our program this evening by having a contest for the best impromptu act." Many of those in attendance with bicycle horns honked their approval. "I shall randomly pick three from the crowd. Those three may then choose whomever they wish to do their act with."

"I think I see Beamer," Howie whispered, gesturing toward a clown wearing a full-length orange coat covered with smiley faces. He moved to within several feet of their suspect.

"You there, in the red, white, and green striped outfit," Bon Bon said. "You'll be our first contestant." He waited for a moment and then pleaded, "Would someone hit that clown over the head with a foam rubber mallet?"

A Keystone Cop tapped Howie on the shoulder with his nightstick. "I think Bon Bon's talking about you," he said as he pointed toward the stage.

Howie looked toward the Master of Ceremonies, glanced around, and then pointed to himself. "Me?"

"Yes, you," Bon Bon said. "You're our first contestant. Choose your partners and come on up."

Howie shook his head. "Oh, no, you mean...I can't...that is—"

The crowd roared and applauded. Somebody pushed Howie toward the stage.

"As you see, we won't take no for an answer." Bon Bon pulled an oversized alarm clock out of one of the pockets in his baggy pants. "Now choose your partners to do your skit. You have two minutes to talk it over with whomever you select."

"You guys are coming with me," Howie said, grabbing Mick by the arm.

"Are you crazy?" Mick said, trying to pull free. "What do we know about clowning? We'll make fools out of ourselves!"

Adam cast a worried look in the direction of the stage. "We're not going to do this, are we?" he asked Howie.

Others were beginning to stare. Howie knew if they didn't act fast, they'd blow their cover. "Come on. The more time we waste, the more people notice us. Let's do it and get it over with."

"You've got to be out of your mind!" Adam said. "What are we going to do?"

Sweat trickled down Howie's temples. He wondered if his makeup was coming with it. "Any ideas?" he asked Mick.

"Yeah. We could leave."

Bon Bon walked up to the microphone again and looked in Howie's direction. "Ready, yet?"

Howie held up two fingers to signal he needed some more time.

Mick whispered as he looked in Bon Bon's direction, "Oh, man, I hate the thought of going up on that stage."

"I don't think you have to worry about that," Adam said. "We're going to fall flat on our faces even before we get up there."

"That's it!" Howie said

"What are you talking about?" Mick asked.

"We're not going up on stage. Here's what we're going to do." Howie and his partners huddled. After he shared his idea, the three of them headed toward the stage. When they got to within ten feet of the stage, they stopped and scratched their heads. Each pointed in a different direction. Howie bopped Mick and Adam over the head with a rubber bat he had borrowed from one of the clown spectators and then used it to point to the stage. Mick and Adam scratched their heads again as if to indicate they weren't sure what he was trying to tell them. He smacked them over the head again and pointed to the stage area. This time Mick and Adam nodded.

Bon Bon and the audience roared with laughter as Howie and his partners ignored the side staircase to the stage and tried their best to climb onto it from the front. Although the stage was waist high, they made it appear as though they couldn't negotiate it. They tried to swing one leg up on the stage but promptly fell backward, which brought another round of laughter. The biggest laugh came when Howie instructed his partners to get down on their hands and knees, and then attempted to use them as a stairway. The human stairway collapsed, however, as soon as Howie began to climb.

"Oops!" Bon Bon declared as the audience clapped and horns honked their approval.

"Who are the new guys?" Squires asked Beamer and Wentworth as the three of them stood in the middle of the crowd watching what was going on. "I haven't seen them before."

"We've seen them before, all right," Beamer said.

"What are you talking about?" Wentworth asked.

"You fools, it's those detectives who've have been snooping around and asking questions."

"What!" Squires' tone reflected his indignity. "How dare they invade our privacy like this!" He turned to his partners. "What are we going to do about them?"

Beamer sneered. "For now, let's just enjoy their little charade."

The skit ended when Mick pointed out to Adam the side stairway leading to the stage. Adam took the bat from Howie and whacked him over the head. Mick grabbed the bat from Adam and took his turn with Howie. After walking dazedly around in a circle, their leader fell to the floor as though he had been knocked out. Mick and Adam stood over Howie's body and scratched their heads. They picked him up, and carrying him by his hands and feet, proceeded to struggle up the stairway unto the stage. Once they got up to where Bon Bon stood at the microphone they dropped him and wiped the not so imaginary sweat from their brows.

"Splendidly done," Bon Bon announced, applauding loudly.

As Mick and Adam took their bows, the whole room erupted into wild applause. Two clowns dressed as firemen ran up to the front of the stage carrying a hose and a fire hydrant. One hooked up the hose to the hydrant and pointed the hose's nozzle at Howie while the other turned the valve on the hydrant. When the water sprayed from the hose hitting Howie in the face, the audience erupted with even greater pandemonium.

Bon Bon nearly doubled over in laughter. He took to the microphone. "Now, that will be a hard act to follow." As it turned out, he was right. While the next two acts were funny, by the end of the night, Howie and his partners had won hands down.

Later that evening, Howie walked into his office to find Squirrel sitting in one of the leather chairs with his feet up on the desk.

"Where are your partners?" Squirrel asked as he took his feet down.

"I dropped them off." Howie wanted to get out of his costume, take a long hot shower, and relax by having a shot of bourbon.

"How was the convention?" Squirrel was ready to hear the full details of the evening.

"Terrific. Just terrific," Howie said sarcastically.

"Didn't you find out anything?"

"Not a thing. We spotted Beamer and his partners, but couldn't get close." Howie wasn't about to share the story of their impromptu skit. The fact that many in the crowd mobbed Howie and his partners and asked permission to use their routine took the three detectives by total surprise. After nearly an hour of other clowns talking with them, they decided it was time to leave. He and his partners made a pact to keep what happened to them a secret. They could only imagine what future clients would say if they ever found out about their undercover escapades. "What are you doing here anyway?" he asked.

Squirrel jumped up out of the chair, slapped his hands together, and vigorously rubbed them back and forth. His eyes danced with excitement. "Have I got some great news for you! I did some checking on the Beamer guy with a friend of mine who sells real estate on the side."

Howie walked over and sat down in his chair, tossing his fake nose, his wig, and hat on the desk. "So what did you find out?"

"He knows Beamer from a few years back. Told me that the guy's married."

"I already knew that."

"But did you know that he cheats on his wife?" Squirrel's eyes doubled in size. "My friend says the rumor is that he makes it with other women while wearing his clown getup."

"Look, we're not investigating the guy's marriage or his quirky sex life. We want to know the motive he may have had for murder."

"Selling real estate is like detective work. It's either feast or famine."

"What are you getting at?"

"For the past several years, it's been famine and Beamer desperately needs dough." Squirrel's eyes lit up. "And what better motive for murder than that?"

Chapter 33

Howie heard someone yell his name. He rolled over and looked at the alarm clock on the nightstand. A few minutes before seven. "Go away," he muttered, pulling the covers over his head. He had gotten to bed late last night. Squirrel's information that Beamer was in financial trouble proved interesting but wasn't as helpful as it first seemed. Money could be a motive for murder, but there wasn't any indication that Donna Mae had any. The fact that she was planning to borrow from her parents to pay for schooling was proof enough.

"Okay, maybe Beamer didn't kill her for her dough," Squirrel had argued. "But he could've thought she had money."

"Possible, but not likely," Howie had replied. "If Beamer did it, there had to have been some other motive."

"Like what?"

"I haven't figured that out yet."

Squirrel stayed to have coffee and a sandwich as his consulting fee. When he finally left, Howie discovered that getting the clown makeup off proved harder than anticipated. For a full fifteen minutes, he stood in the shower allowing cascading water, as hot as he could stand it, to massage his face. Before going to bed, he poured himself a nightcap, sat down at his desk, and relaxed by reading several articles in *Police Gazette.* He hit the sack well after midnight. Although exhausted, he tossed and turned for the next several hours before falling asleep. The morning intrusion, however, had come way too early.

"Howie, are you in there?" the man now yelled again.

"Just a minute!" Howie yelled back, pretty sure who the voice belonged to. He rolled out of bed, slipped on a pair of pants and a tee shirt, and stumbled barefoot into his office. He was still focusing his eyes when Margo loomed in front of him. "Do you know what time it is?" Howie snapped, wishing he would have locked his office door when he had gone to bed.

"I thought you detectives got an early start," Margo said with no hint of apologizing. At least he looked as though he had had a restful night's sleep. "I wanted to get to you before you started your day."

"My day's still asleep under the covers." Howie yawned. "Come on into the kitchen while I fix some coffee."

The two of them sat at the table drinking coffee and munching three-day-old glazed donuts dunked into the black liquid. "Now, just what is it that you wanted to talk about?" Howie asked as he poured himself a second cup.

"I want to know what the latest is on the case." Margo put his hand over his cup indicating he didn't want a warm-up. "I'm going nuts thinking that the guy who killed my Donna Mae is still out there some place free and easy."

"Look, these cases don't get solved overnight." Howie blinked his eyes a couple of times; he was just beginning to feel awake. "Did she ever talk about her brother?"

"Brother?" A look of puzzlement swept over Margo's face. "I didn't know she had one. How did you find out about him?"

"I went up north to talk with her parents." Howie hesitated, not wanting to disclose all of the information at this time. It wasn't that he didn't trust Margo; rather there was still too much speculation. He didn't want the big guy to jump to any false conclusions and go running off half-cocked. "Look, right now we don't have much to go on."

"Have you found out who she was dating?"

"Not yet." Howie sipped his coffee. "Look, I've got to be up front with you. Although I'm convinced she didn't commit suicide, that doesn't mean someone killed her."

"What the hell are you talking about?"

"It could be that she went out into the garage, started the car, and then got distracted...or she was tired and closed her eyes for a moment." Howie paused. "Those things happen. And maybe the car was old and the exhaust system was defective."

Margo slammed his fist on the table. "She did have an old car, but she traded it for a newer one." His lip curled in anger. "And she got screwed on the deal."

"That's too bad," Howie said. "I'll tell you what. I'll check with the car dealership to see if there had been any work done on the exhaust system. Maybe some mechanic screwed up. Did she get it around here?"

"Yeah, right up on Broadway."

"Where on Broadway?"

"Some dump of a used car lot called McGuire's."

Chapter 34

Howie and Mick walked into Les McGuire's office around five in the afternoon. Whether McGuire and Donna Mae's death were connected Howie wasn't sure but he wanted to cover all the bases.

"I told you guys I've got nothing to say to you," Les said as soon as the two detectives walked in. He angrily turned his attention to a stack of papers on his desk.

"We just want to ask a couple of questions," Howie said. He and Mick took seats in front of Les' desk. "It won't take long."

"If you don't get out of here, I'll call the cops."

"Go ahead. Here's their number." Howie took out his notepad, scribbled a telephone number on a sheet, ripped the sheet off, and tossed it on the desk. "You'll be talking to Detective Jim Davidson. He's with the Fifth Precinct here on the North Side." He turned to Mick. "JD would be happy to come over and listen to his complaints, wouldn't he?"

"Oh, yeah. He'd be here in no time flat."

Les stared at them sullenly. He made no move toward the phone.

"Tell you what," Howie said, reaching for the receiver. "I'll even call him for you."

"Okay, you win," Les snarled as he snatched the phone out of Howie's hand and slammed it back down on the hook. "Ask your questions and then get out of here so I can go back to work."

"My, my. You're a little testy this afternoon," Mick said. "Having a hard time pawning off those junks out there to customers?"

Les gritted his teeth. "Just ask your questions, okay?"

Howie opened to a blank page in his notepad and pretended to study it. "Did you take a trade-in from a woman by the name of Donna Mae LaBelle?"

"How should I know?" A huffy tone crept into Les' voice. "I do a terrific business here. Hundreds of customers come through here every month. You can't expect me to remember every one."

"Who are you kidding? You're lucky if you get ten customers here a month," Howie said. "She traded a light-blue '61 Chevy Impala for a green '64 four-door Buick." He closed his notepad and returned it to his pocket, looking expectantly at McGuire.

"Like I told you. I do a lot of business."

Mick reached for the phone. "I guess we'll have to make that phone call to Davidson after all."

"Wait a minute!" McGuire's huffy tone disappeared. "Hey, I remember her now. The woman drove a hard bargain. She made out like a bandit. I got robbed on that deal."

"I bet you did," Howie said. "There's a blue '61 Chevy Impala in the corner of your lot. We'd like to have the keys for it."

"What for?"

"To take it for a test drive."

"I know what you're thinking, but that isn't hers," Les said. "I sold her car two days after it came in."

"We'll take it out for a spin, anyway," Howie said. "Unless you've got a problem with that."

Les opened his mouth as though he was going to refuse. His eyes shifted between the two of them. Perspiration formed above his upper lip. He slid his fingers back and forth along the edge of his desk. Finally, he reached behind him, plucked a set of car keys from a pegboard filled with keys, and tossed them on the desk. "Go ahead. Take it for a spin. It runs like a top. And if you like it, I'll give you a good deal."

Without another word, Howie picked up the keys and he and Mick left. They got into the Impala, started it up, and drove off the lot. In the rearview mirror, he noted that Les had come out of his office and watched them drive away. They hadn't gone more than a couple of blocks when Howie pulled onto a side street and parked. "Let's give this the once-over while we've a chance."

"What are we looking for?"

"I'm not sure. Just anything out of the ordinary." Howie opened his door. "We'll start with the trunk." After checking the trunk, they proceeded to check the back and front interior. They found a dime and two pennies, a gum wrapper, and underneath the front driver's seat, a hairpin. The ashtrays were clean. They checked the glove compartment, but found nothing of interest.

"What are you doing?" Howie asked as Mick looked under the dashboard.

"My uncle Jake use to tape a five dollar bill under the dash in case of emergencies. Maybe—well, what do you know?"

"What?"

"Have a look." Mick pointed to a spot just to the right of the steering wheel column. "Do you see those markings?"

"Yeah. What's that from?"

"Looks like residue from Scotch tape. Something was taped under here and by the looks of it, it was there for a long time."

Howie bent over to examine what Mick had pointed to. The marking wasn't longer than a couple of inches. He sat up, settled back into the drivers' seat and stared out the window for several moments before turning to Mick. "What do you think was there?"

"I don't know. Emergency cash like Uncle Jake's?"

"Perhaps," Howie said. "But the question is did Donna Mae take it before she traded the car in or did McGuire find it?"

"If it was emergency cash, she would've taken it with her."

"I agree." Howie started the car and pulled away from the curb. "But that doesn't explain why McGuire wasn't too happy about us taking this car. Unless..."

"Unless what?"

"Unless it wasn't cash. And whatever it was, Donna Mae didn't know about it when she traded the car in. McGuire could have found whatever was taped under that dashboard."

"Should we confront him when we get back?"

"Let's keep it to ourselves for now. He'd just deny it, and we've no proof of anything. We don't even know what it was or if it had anything to do with Donna Mae's death."

McGuire hung the keys to the Impala back on the pegboard as he watched the two detectives leave. As soon as they were out of sight, he got on the telephone. He lit a cigarette while waiting for his partner to answer. "It's me, Les. Listen, a couple of detectives were nosing around here."

"What did they want?"

"They took the Impala out for a test drive." Les took a drag off his cigarette. "Do you think they know about the key?"

"I doubt it."

"What were they doing then?"

"Just fishing in the dark."

"Even if they don't know anything, they're beginning to get on my nerves," Les said. "What are we going to do?"

"Don't worry. If they get too close, I'll take care of them."

Mick went home after they left McGuire's. Howie decided to make a return visit to Beamer's. This time, he'd try a different approach. He'd try to get on his good side.

Beamer didn't seem all that surprised to see him again.

"What brings you here, Detective? Don't tell me that you're in the market for buying a house?"

"Not today. I stopped because I want to find out more about the finer points of clowning. It interests me."

"Is that so?" Beamer eyes twinkled with amusement. "And I can see why. You and your partners did a pretty good job the other night at the convention."

Howie face registered surprise. "How did you know we were there?" he asked, laughing a bit.

Beamer chuckled. "Those of us in clowning are a pretty close-knit group. We always know when someone new shows up." He paused. "Your makeup was passable, but I recognized you immediately." He paused again, longer this time as he studied him closely. "You were there on business I presume...perhaps checking on me or one of my partners."

"You've got me on that." Howie flashed his winsome grin. There wasn't any way he could lie his way out of this, but maybe he could use it to his advantage. "We thought we'd talk to a couple of people and find out a few things about the three of you."

"And did you?"

"Yep, and all we got were good reports. You guys have a pretty good reputation."

"I'm pleased to hear that from my fellow clowns. It's always nice to get that kind of affirmation from your peers." Beamer folded his hands on the desk. "Does that mean, then, that your investigation of us is over?"

"I would guess so." *Just as soon as I clear up a few minor details. Like which one of you is lying to me, and who had the motive for killing Donna Mae.* "If you don't mind, I'd like to ask a few questions about clowning."

"So you've been bitten by the clowning bug?"

"You might say that." Howie believed that people tended to make slip-ups when they're put at ease. "Are you willing to share a few secrets of the trade?"

"For you, of course. We probably should start with the makeup. You can—" The ringing of the phone interrupted the lesson. "I'm sorry. I should get that. It could be one of my customers." He picked up the telephone. "Beamer here. Service with a smile. Yes...yes...ah, I'm with someone right now...I see...okay. But what am I going to do about Oscar?" He glanced at Howie and raised an eyebrow. "Hmmm...that's a possibility. I'll see what I can do. I'll call you back if I can't." He hung up and rose from his chair. "I'm sorry but I need to leave."

"That's too bad."

"If you want to learn about clowning, we certainly can meet again."

"Good, I'd like that very much."

Beamer hesitated. "I'm really in a bind right now. Can you help me out?"

"I don't know. That depends on what you need."

"It's Oscar. I don't want to leave him alone and I can't bring him with me. Could you watch him?"

"What?" Howie tried to conceal his surprise. "Baby-sit a monkey?"

"I can assure you that he won't be any trouble."

"I, ah...don't know..."

"Please, Mr. Cummins. I would be in your debt."

Yes, you would. "The thing is that I have to get back to the office."

125

"That's no problem. You can take him there. I know where your office is. I'll pick him up when I'm done. It'll be only for a couple of hours. Besides, he likes you."

"I don't know, Beamer. Are you sure about that?"

"Oh, yes. If he didn't like you, he'd claw you or pull your hair. Just be careful, though, when he meets a stranger. If he starts chattering loud, sticks his chin out, and raises his eyebrows, those are signs that he doesn't like the person. He loves women, though." Beamer glanced at his watch. "How about it? Will you do it?"

Howie thought about it while Beamer held his breath. What a unique opportunity to get in with Beamer, and maybe his partners. Finally, he said, "Sure, why not?"

"Great! I knew I could count on you," Beamer said, a big grin on his face. "And just remember, baring his teeth is his way of smiling."

Chapter 35

Oscar proved to be better behaved than Howie expected. Only once on the drive back did he start chattering and jumping up and down on the back of the passenger's seat. His reaction was triggered when Howie pulled up to a stop sign and a heavyset guy in the car next to them rolled down his window and made a face at the monkey. If the passenger's window had been open, Oscar would've jumped out and attacked the big ape.

Howie took Oscar to the office, amused when his new friend bared his teeth at the movie poster. "Bogie," Howie said, "that only means he likes you." He led Oscar by the hand into the kitchen thinking that the little guy might be hungry. After searching the cupboards, he handed Oscar a two-day-old donut. "You stay here and be a good monkey." Oscar took a couple of nibbles and tossed the donut aside. "So you're fussy, huh? Just wait here and I'll bring you back a nice treat." Howie hurried down to the drugstore and found Kass working behind the soda fountain.

"Hi, my boy," Kass said, greeting him with his usual broad smile. "And what can I fix for you?"

"A banana split."

"Coming right up."

"And make that to go...with an extra banana and heavy on the whipped cream please...but skip the toppings."

Kass raised his eyebrows but said nothing. Within a few minutes Howie headed back to his office. When he walked in he found Oscar sitting on the desk. As soon as the monkey saw Howie, he twirled around and clapped his hands. "Is that for me or the banana split?" Howie asked. "Well, whatever...come on out to the kitchen. You can sit at the table and eat there." Oscar obediently followed and when his treat was set on the table, he jumped onto a chair.

"Enjoy yourself," Howie said as he placed a spoon next to the banana split. "I'm going to be in the office doing some work. If you need anything, just...ah, do whatever monkeys do."

Oscar looked at him and bared his teeth. He picked up the spoon, scratched his head with it, and tossed it onto the floor. Within moments, his hands were deep into the whipped cream.

Howie hadn't been at his desk very long when the downstairs entrance door slammed shut and footsteps could be heard coming up the stairs. *Now who's this? A new client?* He waited for his door to open and got up from his chair to greet his visitor when who should walk in but Bernadine McGuire.

"Have you found out anything about my brother yet?" were the first words out of Bernadine's mouth. No "hello" or "how are you" or "nice to see you again" Howie noted glumly.

"Why don't you sit down?" Howie hoped that if she made herself comfortable, some of the harsh lines in her face might soften. It was going to be bad enough to tell her that they hadn't found out very much. And he didn't dare share anything about her brother's involvement with Donna Mae's car. Something like that might send her over the edge, and no telling what she might do. "We're making progress," he offered.

"Good. So tell me." Bernadine leaned forward, a determined look in her eye. Before Howie could reply, terror replaced her determined look. She shrieked as Oscar jumped up on the desk, his mouth covered with whipped cream.

"Don't worry," Howie said, "he's—"

"Foaming at the mouth!" Bernadine screamed. She jumped up, nearly tipping her chair, and then positioned herself behind it.

"That's not foam, it's—"

Bernadine screamed again as Oscar leaped onto her chair. Before Howie could say a word, she ran to the office door, yanked it opened, and flew down the stairs. Oscar turned around to face Howie. The monkey sat on his haunches, raised his eyebrows, and scratched his head.

"I'm with you," Howie said. "I don't understand women either." He grinned at his new friend. "I hope you're enjoying your banana split." Oscar bared his teeth, chattered something affirmative, and scampered back to the kitchen.

When the downstairs door slammed again, Howie thought Bernadine had decided to come back. By the sounds of the footsteps and the voices, however, he realized it was Mick and Adam.

"What's with Bernadine?" Mick asked as he and Adam walked in. "She nearly ran us over coming out of here."

"Yeah," Adam said. "She shouted something about a rabid beast up here."

"Was she referring to you by any chance?" Mick asked, trying to keep a straight face, but failing.

"Yeah, right." Howie shot Mick a stern look. "Why don't you wait and see for yourself?" The sound of tiny feet could be heard coming down the hallway from the kitchen. Within moments Oscar appeared and made a flying leap onto the desk. Besides a mouth covered with whipped cream, his cheeks bulged with banana.

"Holy cow!" Mick slid his chair back in alarm.

"Is that thing friendly?" Adam asked, his hands gripping his chair as if he were ready to bolt.

"What's the matter, boys? You're not afraid of a little monkey, are you?"

Mick flinched when Oscar bared his teeth. "He doesn't bite, does he?"

"Don't worry. He's just smiling."

"Well, somebody needs to give him the name of a good dentist," Mick said.

"Where did he come from?" Adam asked.

"He belongs to Beamer. His name is Oscar and I'm taking care of him for a few hours. That's whipped cream on his mouth. He just got done eating a banana split."

"Are we in the monkey sitting business now?" Mick asked, still tense at the confrontation.

"Look, I went back to Beamer's with a few more questions," Howie explained. "While I was there, he got a phone call and said he needed to go. He asked if I could watch Oscar for him and I agreed. I thought it'd be a good way of getting in with them."

"Did he say what came up that was so urgent?" Mick asked.

"No, but I figure if I took care of his monkey, he'd be more open to me coming around. I told him I was interested in clowning. While he's giving me pointers, I hope to learn some other things. People are more apt to talk freely when they don't feel threatened."

Mick kept his eye on Oscar. "So, you're counting on him dropping some clues as to who may have dated Donna Mae?"

"That's right."

"But what if he's the one who dated her?" Adam pointed out. "He's not going to let that slip."

"We'll see about that. Remember what JD always says. 'The good guys win by outsmarting the bad guys'." Howie leaned back in his chair. "I don't plan on being outsmarted."

The phone rang. Before Howie could answer it, Oscar ran to it, lifted the receiver, and held it with two hands high above his head.

"Thank you, Oscar," Howie said. "I'll take that." He took out his handkerchief and wiped off the sticky receiver, then propped it on his shoulder and leaned back in his chair. "MAC Detective Agency. Howie Cummins speaking."

"Mr. Cummins. My name is Grant Larson. I'm a cousin of Stuart W Hatchaway's."

"Oh, yes...I'm terribly sorry for your loss Mr. Larson."

"Thank you. It was a shock to us all."

"I'm sure that it was. So, what can I do for you?"

"Actually, I'm calling because the family feels that since you made Stuart W so happy, finding his totem pole, well, we agreed you should have it as a token of appreciation."

"What?" He rocked forward in his chair, and dropped the handkerchief on the desk. "Did I hear you right? You want to give me the totem pole?"

"That's right."

First a monkey, now a totem pole. What next? Howie let out a puff of air. "That's very kind of you, but really—"

"Please, it'd mean so much to us. And I know Stuart W would want you to have it."

Howie drummed his fingers on the desk. If the totem pole had anything to do with Hatchaway's murder, it could provide a clue. "Well, if it means so much to the family, I'll be glad to take it."

"Wonderful! We're having a going-out-of-business sale starting at nine tomorrow morning. Why don't you come a half hour early and we'll get it for you. That way you'll beat the crowd."

Howie agreed and hung up the phone. It rang again. This time it was Jack Beamer.

"How's my little friend doing?" Beamer asked.

"He's making himself right at home."

"I'm glad to hear that." Oscar's owner paused. "Mr. Cummins, I need to ask a really big favor from you."

"And what's that?"

"Could you keep Oscar overnight? I know it would be an inconvenience," he said before Howie could interrupt, "but I can't get anyone else. My wife's quite sick and needs to go to the hospital."

Howie glanced at Oscar, who bared his teeth at him as though he sensed what was being asked. "Okay, but can you pick him up tomorrow?"

"I will. Thank you so much. I'll get him around noon. And Mr. Cummins? I owe you one."

Howie smiled to himself.

You sure do, buddy, and I'm going to collect.

Chapter 36

He stood in a shadowed entryway across the street from the antique shop and glanced at his watch. A half hour yet until the store opened. He had heard about the going-out-of-business sale, and had come for the totem pole. With Hatchaway out of the picture, there would be no one to oppose him.

A red convertible pulled up in front of the store. He was stunned to see the detectives get out and walk into the shop. He lit a cigarette and kept his eye on the front entrance.

What the hell is going on? He felt a flush of anger, then a surge of alarm. *Were they there to investigate Hatchaway's death? But no, they couldn't be. The plan...and the execution of it...had been foolproof.*

He stepped deeper into the shadows, his eyes on the store across the street.

Ten minutes passed, then fifteen. The store was due to open in fifteen minutes. Finally the door opened. He watched in disbelief as the three detectives carried out the totem pole and loaded it into the backseat of the convertible.

"Damn it!" He tossed a cigarette into the gutter and hurried to his car, cranking it just as Cummins pulled away. He wheeled after them, following at a discreet distance. They traveled down Broadway for several blocks and turned left onto Third Street where they parked on the side street next to Kass' Drugstore. He pulled over to the curb and put the car in neutral, watching as they removed their cargo from the backseat of the convertible, and carried it through the street entrance of Cummins' apartment building. He sat staring after them for long moments, struggling with his temper. "That's not the end of this," he muttered. "I'll be back. You can count on that." He slammed the car into gear and drove away.

"Come on, guys," Howie encouraged as he stood at the top of the first landing. "We're almost there."

"What do you mean *we?*" Sweat ran down Mick's brow. "How come we're carrying this thing?"

"Yeah, it's your totem pole," Adam said.

"Just hang on. I'll get the door for you." Howie took the next dozen steps two at a time, swung open the door, and waited for Mick and Adam. As his partners struggled up the remaining steps, he glanced into his office. Papers from his desk had been scattered all over the floor, his movie poster hung crooked, and the phone was off its receiver. Oscar, however, was nowhere to be seen.

"Don't drop it," Howie said as the two laborers approached the top of the stairs.

"We're going to drop it on your head," Mick said. "You don't know it, but this thing weighs a ton."

The scampering of feet behind Howie caught his attention. He turned to see Oscar leap onto the top of the back of his chair.

"You little scamp." He shook a disciplinary finger at Oscar. "You're in big trouble, little guy. No more banana splits for you."

Oscar raised his eyebrows, barred his teeth, and leaped from the chair onto the desk, knocking the telephone to the floor. He peeked over the side of the desk to see what had happened to the telephone, flashed his teeth again, and twirled around in what could only have been interpreted as a victory dance.

"What's going on in there?" Adam yelled from the stairway.

"It's just our little friend making a monkey out of himself," Howie growled. Within moments Oscar leaped off the desk, ran toward him, climbed up his trousers, and came to rest on his shoulder. He placed his hands atop Howie's head, steadying himself, and curled his long tail around the detective's neck. From his new perch, he chattered at a startled Mick and Adam as they stumbled into the office, and laid the totem pole on the floor.

"Don't worry," Howie said. "He likes you."

"That's comforting to know," Mick replied.

Adam gestured at the totem pole. "Where do you want that thing?"

"Stand it up in the corner by the couch." Tiny fingers dug into Howie's scalp. "Quit it," he scolded.

Mick chuckled. "What's he looking for...fleas?"

"Just put the pole in the corner wise guy."

They managed to stand the pole in the corner. After admiring it for a moment, they went over and collapsed into their chairs. "I'm bushed," Mick said. "That was hard work."

Oscar scooted down from Howie and approached the totem pole. He paused and then proceeded to climb it. Once he got to the top, he sat down, crossed his arms, and gave the world below a triumphant look.

"Sure is a mess in here," Adam said. "What happened?"

"Ask the guy on top of the totem pole." Howie picked up his phone, then knelt to retrieve some papers. "Aren't you guys going to help?"

His partners gave each other a knowing smile. "Yeah, about as much help as you gave us lugging that totem pole up the stairs," Mick said. For the next several minutes, he and Adam looked on as Howie picked up the papers. Oscar watched from the top of the totem pole, chattering encouragement to his benefactor.

A tapping at the door caught Howie's attention. "Come on in. It's open."

The door slowly opened and Bernadine McGuire peeked in. She scanned the area, and cautiously stepped in. The totem pole caught her attention. "Oh, my," she uttered and moved closer to look at it.

"Bernadine, I wouldn't—" Before Howie could finish, Oscar leaped from the pole onto her head.

The poor woman screamed and then fainted.

Chapter 37

While Mick and Adam revived Bernadine, Howie diverted Oscar's attention with food. He took the monkey into the kitchen, set him on a chair, and told him to stay put while he fixed him one of his specialty sandwiches. He cut the sandwich into four parts and set it in front of Oscar. "Here, this should keep you out of mischief for a while." He headed back to his office. To prevent any further disruptions, he closed the door behind him. "How's she doing?" he asked his partners.

"She's beginning to come around," Mick said as he fanned Bernadine's face with one of Howie's magazines.

Bernadine moaned. She opened her eyes, sat up, and tried to focus on the two people kneeling beside her.

"Hi, Bernadine," Adam said. "Are you okay?"

"Yes, I think—" Her eyes filled with dread. "Where did that beast go?" She grabbed Mick's arm with such force that he winced. "It's still not here, is it?" She scanned the room, her eyes settling on the totem pole, no doubt expecting to see "the beast" lurking on top.

"Don't worry," Adam said. "Howie's got Oscar locked up in the kitchen."

"Oscar?" Bernadine's eyes registered puzzlement. "Who's Oscar?"

"Oscar's a monkey," Howie said gently. "He belongs to someone with a clown act. Oscar's part of the act."

When her face still registered puzzlement, Mick explained, "Howie agreed to monkey-sit for a while."

Bernadine looked at the three of them as though they had lost their minds. She quickly stood up, brushed and straightened her skirt, and pointed toward the kitchen. "I'm not staying here! Not while that…that beast is still loose." Before anyone could reply, she turned and rushed out the door.

"Maybe it's not all that bad having Oscar around," Howie said, listening to the woman fly down the stairs.

"Come on," Adam said. "You're not serious, are you?"

Mick nudged Adam. "Of course, he is. Just look at that devilish gleam in his eye."

A crashing noise came from the kitchen. "Speaking of devils." Howie opened the door leading to the kitchen. "I've got to see what that little scamp is up to now." He hadn't gotten halfway down the hallway when he yelled to his partners, "Lock the office door before anybody else comes in!"

"What did you say?" Mick yelled.

"Hurry! Lock the door!"

"Watch out!" Adam cried. "Here he comes."

Adam and Mick jumped aside in amazement as the monkey dashed through the office and skidded to a stop in front of the door leading downstairs.

"What's he doing?" Mick asked as Howie came rushing back into the room.

"I don't know." They watched Oscar eye the door.

"He's curious about something," Adam said.

Oscar jumped up and grabbed the doorknob. He hung on with one hand while trying to unlock the door with the other. On his third try, he succeeded in unlocking it.

Mick let out a low whistle. "I wouldn't have believed it if I didn't see it for myself."

Done with his task, Oscar jumped to the floor, twirled around several times, and bared his teeth at them. Mick and Adam stepped back in alarm.

"He's just smiling," Howie reminded his partners.

Oscar made a flying leap onto the desk, sending the papers Howie had just collected scattering in every direction. Unperturbed at the mess he made, the little rascal held out his hand, palm up.

"I think he wants a treat," Adam said.

"How did he learn to unlock doors like that?" Mick asked.

"I don't know," Howie said ominously. "But I've a hunch it's not part of the clown act." He opened the top drawer of his desk and found a package of gum. After unwrapping a stick of gum, he showed it to Oscar. "Here's your treat, but you've got to work for it." He pointed to the door. "Oscar, go lock the door."

Oscar sat unmoving.

"Maybe he doesn't like gum," Mick said.

"Offer him something else," Adam suggested.

Howie pointed to the kitchen area. "Oscar, do you remember the sandwich?" He put his hand to his mouth and pretended he was eating a sandwich. "Sandwich, Oscar. If you want another, go lock the door." He pointed to the door.

Immediately, Oscar leaped off the desk and ran to the door. He jumped up and grabbed the doorknob as he had done before and on his second attempt, locked it. After dropping to the floor, he did a twirling victory dance.

"That's one smart monkey," Mick said. "What kind of sandwich are you going to fix him?"

"Same as the last. Liverwurst with pickles."

"Liverwurst with pickles?"

"Hey! That's all I had to work with. Anyway, I slapped some peanut butter on it. He likes it that way." Howie gave Mick a winsome smile. "How about you?"

"How about me what?"

"Can I fix you one too?"

"You've got to be kidding..."

Les McGuire picked up the phone, hoping it might be a potential customer. He hadn't sold a car for a couple of weeks now and his finances were hurting. "Hello, McGuire's Used Cars. I've got the best deals on the North Side."

"Be ready with your pickup tomorrow night."

Several seconds passed as Les debated a nasty comeback.

"Les, did you hear what I said?"

"Yeah, all right." He wished he hadn't picked up the phone. "Where are we going?"

"To pay a visit to the MAC Detective Agency."

"Why?"

"Because he's got the totem pole."

Les fumbled in his shirt pocket for his pack of cigarettes. "You mean he's got that thing up in his office?

"That's right."

Les took a moment to light his cigarette. After a long drag, he felt calmer. "You know he's not just going to hand it over to us."

"I know that."

"So how are we going to get it?"

"Leave that to me. We'll go around midnight. He'll be asleep by then."

"But what if he's not?"

There was a low chuckle on the other end of the line.

"Then that would be his mistake."

"You know, there's something strange about this totem pole," Howie said.

"What do you mean, strange?" Adam asked

Howie, staring at the pole, folded his arms. "Well, what have we got? Johnny LaBelle was killed in a shoot-out with the police. Whatever was stolen was never recovered. Donna Mae inherited this thing from him and, I'm convinced, sold it to Hatchaway."

"I see what you're getting it," Mick said. "Do you think Donna Mae discovered some secret about this pole before she sold it, and that's why she was killed?"

"That's a possibility," Howie said. "And what if Hatchaway was killed because the killer was after the totem pole?"

136

"But how could Hatchaway be killed if the killer couldn't get inside?" Adam asked.

"I haven't figured that one out yet."

"Uh oh," Adam said. "Here comes Oscar. And he looks a little under the weather."

Mick chuckled. "Who'd blame him after eating those sandwiches?" He watched as Oscar made his way up to the top of the totem pole. "I say we give the totem pole a thorough going over."

"I agree," Adam said.

A scratching sound caused them to turn their attention to Oscar. The monkey was picking at the right eye of the Thunderbird carving on top of the totem pole.

"What's so interesting up there?" Adam asked.

"There's only one way to find out." Howie slid one of his office chairs next to the totem pole and climbed upon it. He handed Oscar to Adam, who in turn set the monkey on the floor.

"Do you see anything?" Mick asked Howie.

"Not yet...wait a minute."

"What is it?" Adam asked.

"Looks like this eye is loose." Howie motioned to Mick. "Get me the letter opener on my desk." He waited until his partner came back, and then used the letter opener to pry the eye out. "Well, what do you know?" He tucked a finger into a hole behind the eye.

"What did you find?"

Howie jumped down from the chair. "Somebody hollowed out a space behind that eye. And look what I found." He showed them a slip of paper with printing on it, and a key.

"Wow!" Adam moved closer. "What's that key for?"

"Let me see it," Mick said. He took the key from Howie and examined it. "It looks like it could be for a safe-deposit box or locker. And hey, there's a number on it."

"What is it? Howie asked.

"It looks like 137." He handed the key back to Howie. "What's on that slip of paper?"

"One word: *DOG*."

"What's that suppose to mean?" Adam asked.

Howie shook his head. "I have no idea."

Chapter 38

"D-O-G?" Mick handed the slip of paper to Howie. "What in the world do you think that means?"

"Your guess is as good as mine." The key held more interest for Howie. A locksmith friend of his could possibly provide a clue. If need be, he would even consider showing the key to JD. As a cop, JD would be naturally curious, but, as a friend, wouldn't ask too many questions. Of course, if JD knew that the key had been found hidden in the totem pole it would be a different story. No doubt the seasoned detective would pull rank and confiscate the key as evidence in the Hatchaway murder. That, however, wasn't going to happen. Howie slipped the key in his pocket and showed the paper to Adam. "Do you have any ideas about what that refers to?"

Adam studied the printing. "It could be cryptic."

"What do you mean?"

"Just this." He handed the paper back to Howie. "If you read it backwards it would read *GOD*."

Concern flashed in Mick's eyes. "What are you trying to tell us?"

"Mick, I'm not trying to tell you anything." Adam looked as though he wished he hadn't brought it up.

"Does it have anything to do with Damien and the kind of stuff we dealt with in our first case?" Mick cast a worried look toward Howie.

"I don't think so," Adam replied in a reassuring tone, no doubt realizing that his observation had upset Mick.

"Don't worry about it," Howie said. "I have a gut feeling that Damien's out of the picture on this one." None of them could forget their first case and what Damien had done to Mick in that country cemetery south of the Cities. "I tell you what. Why don't we take a break this afternoon? We can discuss it tomorrow morning."

"That's fine with me," Adam said. "It'll give me a chance to go over to the library and catch up on some reading." He glanced at Oscar curled up in a ball on the couch, holding his tummy. "What are you going to do about the monkey? He's looks sick."

Howie checked the time. Half past ten. "Beamer said he'd be here by noon, but Oscar looks like he could use some tender loving care right now. I'm going to call Beamer and see if he's in. If he is, I'll run Oscar over there."

Adam tapped Mick on the arm. "What are you up to this afternoon?"

"I'm going with my wife to see the doctor."

Alarm spread across Adam and Howie's faces.

"Is she okay?" Adam asked.

"As okay as a woman can be who is going to have a baby," Mick replied, beaming.

"What?" Howie said. "Did I hear you right?"

Mick nodded as his grin widened.

"Congratulations!" Adam said. "That's great news!" He reached over and slapped his partner on the back. "When is she due?"

"We're not sure exactly. It'll be around Christmas. The doctor will probably give us a date this afternoon."

"So you're going to be a daddy, huh?" Howie frowned, wondering whether Mick would continue to work with them in the detective agency.

"That's right, and don't worry. I'll keep on working with you."

"Was I that obvious?"

"Like an open book."

"I'll have to work on that." Howie smiled, got up and came around his desk. He shook hands with Mick. "Congratulations. And tell Mary that as well."

"I will. So, you know what we're doing this afternoon, how about you?"

"After I get Oscar home, I'm going to relax and do some reading. Maybe I'll take in a movie to clear my mind."

"Are you working tonight at the drugstore?" Adam asked

"Yeah, I'm scheduled for a full evening."

"Why don't you talk to Kass to see if he has any ideas about what the slip of paper means?" Mick asked. "Maybe it was something Stuart W did and Kass might know about it."

"I just may do that." Howie often sought Kass' opinions on certain cases, knowing that his friend wouldn't press him for the full details.

Adam walked with Mick to the door. He opened the door, paused, and turned to look back at Howie. "What time you want to see us tomorrow?"

"Why don't we make it around nine?" Howie hadn't slept well for the past several nights. "If I can, I'm going to try to sleep in tomorrow."

After his partners left, Howie called Beamer's office. The realtor answered on the first ring.

"I'll be there in an hour," Beamer said as soon as he heard that it was Howie.

"Don't bother. I'll bring him back now. He doesn't seem to be feeling too well." After hanging up, Howie lifted Oscar, carried him down to his car, and drove to Beamer's office. His sick passenger lay quietly on the seat during the entire time. He dropped Oscar off, telling Beamer he would be in touch with him, and headed back to his office. After a quick bite for lunch, he picked up one of his *Police Gazette* magazines and headed for the couch, intending to read a couple of articles. Midway through the first, however, he couldn't keep his eyes open. He laid the magazine aside and let them close.

It was after four when Howie woke up. For the first time in days, he felt rested. He took a shower, changed clothes, and fixed himself a sandwich and a cup of coffee for supper. That done, he called his locksmith friend about the key and was told that the key could fit any number of things. That was disappointing, but not unexpected. He also called JD and asked if he had ever heard of the expression DOG and what it could mean.

"Sure, I've heard of it."

"Really?" Howie took out his notepad and pen. "So what does it refer to?"

"Will you keep this to yourself?"

"Of course. You know I will." The clock ticked away the seconds as Howie waited for a reply. He was just about to say something when JD spoke up.

"It refers to a four-legged creature that barks."

Howie tossed his pen on the desk and closed his notepad. "Thanks, wise guy," he said as JD chuckled at the other end of the line.

"What's this about, anyway?" JD asked.

"A case we're working on. That's all I can tell you."

"That's not telling me much."

"So, seriously, you don't have any idea what it refers to?"

"Not a clue."

For the next fifteen minutes, Howie reviewed his notes on the Hatchaway case, and then headed for his evening's work. When he walked into the drugstore, Kass was busy straightening up the magazine rack by the front entrance.

"Hello there, my friend." Kass gestured to the magazines and shrugged. "The customers never put them back right."

"Let me give you a hand with those." The magazines in order, the two headed for the soda fountain. Howie sat on a stool at the end while Kass stepped behind the counter.

"Do you want something to eat before you start? I'll be happy to fix it for you."

"No, thanks. I already ate. I'll just have coffee."

"Are you boys working on any new cases?" Kass asked as he poured Howie his drink.

"No, but I've a question for you on one of them."

Kass grinned. "You may have a question, but I can't guarantee you that I'll have an answer."

Howie sipped his coffee and set it aside. "Don't feel so bad. I don't have any answers either."

Kass studied him for a moment and then came around the counter. He took the stool next to Howie and placed his hand on his shoulder. "My boy, you're too quick to come down on yourself."

"Maybe, but I'm supposed to be a detective. It frustrates me when Mick and Adam ask me questions and I don't have answers."

"Do they have a problem with that?"

"No, they're supportive, but..."

"Tell me something. Haven't you solved all your cases in the past?"

Howie nodded. "Not as fast as I'd like, though. And luck played a big part in a couple of them."

"Let me ask you a question." Kass folded his hands on the counter. "Do you think your hero, Bogart, solved all his cases with a snap of his fingers?"

"No, but—"

"And don't you think he got frustrated at times?"

"Okay, Kass, I get your point."

"Good. Now if you still want me to, I'm open to listening to what's frustrating you." He leaned toward Howie. "And you know whatever you tell me stays between you and me."

"I know." Howie checked to make sure no customers were within hearing range. Even though there were none, he still lowered his voice. "We're working on a case now and there's a note connected with it that I can't figure out."

"What does the note say?"

"D-O-G."

Kass scratched his chin. "Could they be initials that stand for something?"

"I considered that, but I can't come up with anything."

"Maybe you should call your friend, Detective Davidson."

"I did, but he didn't have a clue." JD had been curious, but hadn't pressed him for details. Howie appreciated that they had the kind of relationship that respected each other's boundaries. It wasn't that he didn't trust Davidson as much as it was his desire to solve the cases on his own with as little help as possible.

"And how long has Detective Davidson been on the force?" Kass asked.

"Eighteen-plus years..." Howie gave his mentor a half smile. "Okay, you've made your point." He glanced at the clock. "I think it's time for me to get to work...Kass?"

"Yes?"

"Thanks."

Chapter 39

Les McGuire slipped into the phone booth, leaving the door cracked open for fresh air. After dialing, he scanned the various numbers scratched on the metal framing while waiting for his party to answer.

"Hey, it's me," Les said when his partner answered.

"Where are you?"

"Just where you told me to be. I'm in the phone booth across from the drugstore."

"Has Cummins left yet?"

"Yeah, ten minutes ago he went back up to his apartment."

"Good. Now, if he's the kind of hardworking detective I think he is, he'll be at his desk for an hour or so."

"How're we going to do this?"

"The same way we did Hatchaway."

Les fumbled for the pack of cigarettes in his shirt pocket. "But you're just going to use sleeping powder this time, aren't you?"

"Why do you ask?"

"Hell, you know why." He glanced outside. Although he saw no one, he lowered his voice anyway. "I didn't know you were going to kill the guy."

"I didn't... *we* did."

It was best not to argue with him. Les took a drag off his cigarette. "How do you know that Cummins will be drinking anything?"

"I don't for sure."

"So what if he isn't?"

"Then we go to Plan B. You remember Plan B, don't you, Les?"

Les let his cigarette drop on the floor and ground it out with the sole of his shoe. He recalled how he'd been worked over when he'd refused to give up the key he found in Donna Mae's car. If Plan A was dangerous, Plan B was deadly. "You're... you're not going to kill him, are you?"

"Why?"

"Because that would really get the cops on our trail. I don't—"

"Just have your pickup ready. Park down the street and keep the engine running. I'll be making the call from that telephone booth so make damn sure you take care of the light in it. And remember, when I give you the signal, come get me...and Les? Don't make me wait."

Howie had just taken a sip of coffee and was in the middle of reviewing case notes when the phone rang. He glanced at the clock, wondering who could be calling at such a late hour. Margo came to mind. "MAC Detective Agency. Howie Cummins speaking." He expected to hear Margo's gruff voice demanding the latest on what they had found out about who killed Donna Mae.

"Are...are you the guy investigating the death of the LaBelle woman?"

"Yeah, I'm handling it." The caller's voice was muffled as if he held something over the phone. "Who is this?"

"It...it doesn't matter."

Whoever he was, he sounded jittery. Howie didn't press for a name. If he did, the guy could get spooked and hang up. Glancing at his watch he jotted down the time. This could be the possible break in the case he had been looking for. "What do you want?"

"There's something you should know about her death."

A surge of adrenalin shot through Howie. His hand tightened on the phone. "Why don't you come up to my office and we'll talk about it?"

"I...I can't do that."

"Why? What are you afraid of?"

"I...I just can't do it. It...it wouldn't be safe."

"Okay, that's okay." Howie heard traffic noise in the background. "We'll talk over the phone."

"Do...do you have a phone in your kitchen?"

"Yeah. Why?"

"Go...go and pick it up and...and looked out the window. I'm in the phone booth across the street."

"Hang on. I'll be right with you." Howie hurried into the kitchen, grabbed the phone on the counter, and moved to the window. A shadow of a person stood in the darkened telephone booth across the street, his back turned to Howie.

"Okay I'm here," Howie said. "So tell me now what you know about Donna Mae."

"I knew her quite well. She was a nice woman, but uncooperative."

Although the caller's voice was muffled, the fear had been replaced by a confident calm, even smugness.

"What do you mean uncooperative?"

"It's too bad she cut her life short. You think the dame could have been depressed?"

Howie talked fast, hoping the guy would slip up and reveal something that would identify him. "What would she be depressed about?"

"About her brother."

What did this guy know about Donna Mae's brother? Howie cocked his head toward his office, thinking he heard a noise. Then the guy in the phone booth moved. Howie's attention snapped back to his caller.

"Are you still there?" the man asked.

"Yeah. Tell me what you know about her brother."

"Johnny was very protective of his sister. If he hadn't been killed, she might still be alive today."

"What makes you say that?"

"The woman thought I was quite charming."

"You were dating her, then?"

A muffled chuckle came across the line. "Don't jerk me around, Cummins. I know what you're trying to do."

"And what's that?"

"You'd like to connect me with her death."

"Is there a connection?"

"What do you think?"

"Why don't you come up and discuss it face to face?"

"I don't think so."

"Wait a—" The harsh sound of the dial tone buzzed in Howie's ear. He watched as the man struck a match and lit a cigarette. Within moments, a Ford pickup pulled up to the curb in front of the booth. The caller, head down and face hidden, exited the telephone booth and slipped into the passenger's side. Howie tried to get a license number as the truck sped away, but couldn't make it out. His first instincts was to dash down to his car and follow his unidentified caller, but the caller and his accomplice would be long gone before he could even get his car started. Instead, he headed back to his desk and sat down. He took out his notepad, flipped it open, and wrote down the essence of the conversation. After rereading what he had written, he opened his desk drawer, took out his bottle of bourbon, and topped off his coffee. For the next ten minutes, he reviewed his notes on Beamer as well as on Squires and Wentworth.

The caller had to be one of those three, but which one? And what about the getaway driver? Who was he?

The words in his notepad began to blur and he blinked his eyes trying to focus on what he had written. He attempted to get up, but fell back into his chair, and then the room began to spin.

"What's the matter, kid?" Bogie said as he stepped out of the poster. He walked toward Howie and took a seat in the chair.

"Is that really you?" Howie blinked and rubbed his eyes.

"Who else would it be?" Bogie gave him a crooked smile. He reached in his pocket, pulled out a pack of cigarettes, shook one out, lit it, and then offered one to Howie.

"No, I...ah...don't smoke."

Bogie shrugged and put the pack back. He took a drag and blew out a near perfect smoke ring that floated past Howie. "Well, what do you know, kid? I always wanted to do that in the movies, but never could get the hang of it." He settled back and crossed his legs. "You look a little edgy tonight. Working on a tough case?"

"Yeah. I've got a murder case on my hands and I think I just talked to the man who did it."

"You mean that wise guy who called you from the phone booth?"

Howie nodded. He could barely keep his eyes open.

"You should've pulled out your rod and plugged him from the kitchen window. It would've been a tough shot, but you might've gotten lucky."

"I...I don't carry a gun."

"You don't, huh? Well, just watch your back, then."

"I will."

"This is a tough business, but you're doing a good job."

"Thanks."

"You're looking a little sleepy, kid. Why don't you catch some shuteye? We'll talk later. See you around."

"Yeah, I...ah...sorry, Bogie, but I just got to..."

Chapter 40

Les lit a cigarette and stared at the totem pole standing in the corner in the room behind his office. Even though they had driven the side streets, the trip from Cummins' place had been nerve racking. He had been sure that the cops would stop them. And if they had been pulled over, how would he have explained the totem pole in the back of his pickup? He had pleaded that it was too risky, but his words were just brushed aside. Les didn't want the thing to be taken to his office, but his new partner had insisted. The look in the man's eyes warned Les not to argue.

They had arrived at the used car lot shortly after midnight, parked the pickup in back of Les' office building, and lugged the totem pole through the back door into the storage room. Les immediately had gone back out and moved his truck behind the building so it couldn't be seen from the street.

Now, as Les took a drag off his cigarette, he considered the turn his life had taken. He hadn't always been honest in his business dealings, but he had never been mixed up in anything like this. Although the cool night air helped, his shirt was still damp from perspiration. There were no windows in the storage room to open for ventilation, but that was okay. He didn't have to worry then about anyone seeing a light. He had turned the lights off in his main office, locked the door, and even pulled the shades.

"Do you think anybody saw us bring it here?" Les asked.

No reply came as he continued examining the totem pole acting as though Les was non-existent.

Les watched with interest as his partner slowly slid his hand up and down the pole, stopping every so often and rapping the wood with his knuckles. From the very beginning, Les had asked him what was so important about the totem pole, but received no answer.

"I hope you'll find whatever you're looking for soon," Les said. "I wouldn't want the police to come snooping around."

"Don't worry. Nobody saw us." He walked over to a chair where Oscar sat and gave him some peanuts.

"Did you have to bring that monkey in?" Les touched the side of his face where Oscar had clawed him. "We should've left him in the truck."

"Be careful what you say. You don't want to hurt his feelings again. He'll think he's not wanted." He gave Oscar a handful of peanuts. "Our little friend here has been more important to this operation than you."

"What are you—?"

"Shut up! All you did was drive the truck. If it wasn't for him, we wouldn't have gotten the totem pole." He walked over to the totem pole and began to examine it.

Les reluctantly conceded the point, relieved that they hadn't needed to go to Plan B. One murder was enough. "Okay, but now that we got it...what are you looking for?"

"I'm not sure. Johnny was pretty tricky in these matters."

"Who's Johnny?"

"My guess would be that he hollowed out a section. It would be just like him to do something like that." He stepped back and studied the totem pole. "Let's lay it on its side."

Les helped lay the totem pole down as Oscar watched from the chair. Not trusting the monkey, he kept a watchful eye on the animal. "I'll help you look," he said. "It might go faster." For the next fifteen minutes they examined the pole. "Hey, look at this! One eye of the bird carving is loose!" Les exclaimed. His partner shoved him aside and took out a pocketknife to pry out the eye, exposing a hollow compartment.

"Nothing's in there," Les said.

"I can see that," he snapped, the tone reflecting the cold anger in his eyes.

Les needed a cigarette. "What...what were you looking for?"

"The answer to what the key you have fits."

"Maybe old man Hatchaway found it."

"I don't think so."

"Who then?"

"That meddling detective, Cummins." The man turned to Oscar. "Is that true?" Oscar jumped down from the chair, scampered over, and peered at the spot where the piece of wood had been pried up. "Is that true?" he repeated. Oscar raised his eyebrows and barred his teeth.

"What are we going to do now?" Les asked.

"I don't know, but Mr. Cummins is beginning to get on my nerves."

Chapter 41

Howie raised his head off the desk and groaned. Tiny men wearing hard hats jackhammered inside his brain. His arms and neck hurt. It hurt even to raise his eyelids. He needed something wet (preferably bourbon) for his dry mouth and lips. His office door opened and a blurred shape came in. "Is that you, Bogie?" he asked.

"What are you talking about?"

"Just a minute." Howie tried to swallow, but couldn't. He reached for his coffee cup and managed to wrap both hands around it. He lifted the cup to his lips, paused, and stared into the cup. Only when he blinked his eyes a couple of times did things begin to come into focus. Soggy coffee grounds didn't appeal to him even though they smelled of bourbon. He set the cup aside.

Bogie walked toward him.

"Are you okay, Howie?"

"My head feels like it's going to explode."

"Ten-to-one you've been on the sauce, haven't you?"

"I just had a little bourbon with my coffee. Then I got that phone call...or did I have coffee after the call?"

"What phone call?"

Howie rubbed his eyes. His detective hero appeared shorter and needed a haircut. "Bogie, you don't look like yourself."

"Howie, I'm not Bogie!"

"What?" Howie rubbed his eyes again and blinked until he could clearly focus on the person standing in front of his desk. "Squirrel?"

"That's right, boss."

"What are you doing here? What happened to..." His gaze drifted to the movie poster on the wall. Bogart had resumed the role of protecting Mary Astor. "I guess I must've been dreaming or something."

"You sure must have been." Squirrel's nose began twitching.

Howie raked a hand through his hair. "What time is it anyway?"

"It's nearly nine on a Wednesday morning." Squirrel picked up Howie's coffee cup and sniffed the contents. He dipped his finger into the wet grounds, and touched his finger to his tongue. "Hey, boss, I don't know for sure, but I bet you were slipped a Mickey Finn."

"A what?"

"A Mickey Finn! Somebody doped your coffee."

"But how..." Howie tried to recall what happened last night. "I remembered drinking coffee and going over my notes. Then the room began to spin."

"What happened then?"

"And then..." He glanced around the room. "I...hey, wait a minute. It's gone."

"What's gone?"

"The totem pole."

Squirrel glanced around. "Are you sure you didn't dream it was here?"

"No, Mick and Adam carried it in here. We set it up in the corner by the couch."

"Well, it's not there now. Who would've taken it?"

"Give me a second to think this through." Howie massaged his temples. The men in the hard hats were hopefully done for the day. "It had to have been the man in the phone booth."

"What man?"

"But how did he slip me that Mickey Finn?"

"What phone booth?"

"The one across the street from the drugstore. I was in the kitchen talking on the phone to this guy."

"A different guy?"

"No. I don't know. Be quiet. He was telling me about..." Howie glanced at his coffee cup and then to the empty corner where the totem pole once stood. "Oh, man, this whole thing was a set up." He reached for the phone.

"Who are you calling?"

"Mick and Adam."

Howie's partners arrived at his office within fifteen minutes after receiving his phone call. Mick positioned himself by the window, sitting on the sill. Adam sat in the chair next to Squirrel.

"Who do you think doped your coffee?" Mick asked after Howie finished sharing the events of last night.

"Don't ask me." Howie sipped his coffee, spiked with bourbon to make sure the men with the jackhammers didn't come back. "Someone slipped in while I was on the phone in the kitchen."

Adam gnawed at his lip. "So while the guy kept you busy on the phone, his partner came in and doctored your coffee."

"Yeah, that's about it." Thinking back on it, Howie chastised himself for not having checked out the noise he heard while he was on the phone. It was an amateur mistake, and though he chided himself for making it, he wouldn't share that part of the story with his partners.

"The boss sure was out of it," Squirrel said. "He thought I was Bogie when I came in."

Howie shrugged, giving his partners a *don't even ask* look. "Whoever took the totem pole must have known that Johnny LaBelle had hidden the key and the note in it."

Squirrel's eyebrows rose. "What key? What note?"

Howie hesitated, thinking that Squirrel had provided valuable assistance in their last case and had proven that he could keep things to himself.

"Come on," Squirrel pleaded as though reading Howie's thoughts. "I've helped you guys out before. You can trust me."

Howie opened his desk drawer, took out the two items, and handed them to Squirrel.

"So what's this key for?" Squirrel sucked air through his teeth as he examined it.

"We were hoping that you might know."

"You've got me. If I was a betting man…" He shot a look at Adam. "Which I'm not, I'd say it was to some kind of storage locker."

"That's what we think, but which one and where?" Howie took the key back from Squirrel. "There's got to be thousands of them around."

"How about those letters *D-O-G*?" Squirrel handed the slip of paper back to Howie. "What do they stand for?"

"That's what we're also trying to figure out."

Mick spoke up. "I was hoping that you might have some idea."

"Hmmm." Squirrel began tapping his front teeth with the end of his fingernail. "Maybe it refers to the dog catcher."

Howie stared at Squirrel, then opened his desk drawer, slipped in the key and note, and closed it. "What should our next move be?" he asked his partners.

"I think we should go after Wentworth," Adam said.

"Why him?"

"Because he doesn't seem to be who he's pretending to be. Even the chef at the restaurant where he works implied that. I say we see him tonight."

"I'll go along with that," Mick said. "It'll give us a chance to size him up."

"Wentworth is one of those clowns, isn't he?" Squirrel inched to the edge of his chair, his eyes glued on Howie.

Howie directed his words to Mick and Adam. "Okay, we'll confront him tonight at the restaurant." Squirrel leaned forward hopefully, but Howie waved him off. "Sorry, you can't come with us on this one."

"Aw, come on! Why not?"

"Because I said so, and I'm the boss."

If Wentworth were the killer, things could turn dangerous. And although that wouldn't scare Squirrel away, Howie didn't want any chances of the little guy getting in the way.

Chapter 42

Howie and his partners arrived at the Fireside Dining Club a little before seven. They had called earlier for a reservation, making sure Wentworth would be their waiter. Within moments of being seated, their suspect appeared.

"Would you gentlemen care for a before-dinner drink?" Wentworth asked while handing them menus. Dressed in black slacks, white long-sleeve shirt, gray vest, and a black bow tie, he looked quite debonair. "We have a fine selection of wines."

"I think we'll pass," Howie said.

"Very well, sirs. I shall be back in a few minutes to take your orders."

"He seems to know his job," Mick said after Wentworth left to attend to an older couple several tables away.

"We'll see about that," Adam said.

Mick glanced around uneasily. "This sure is a fancy place. I should've worn a tie."

"Don't worry," Howie said. "We won't be here long."

"And at these prices, we won't be coming back." Mick set his menu aside. "It costs a small fortune to eat here." He smirked. "But this is on our expense account, isn't it? After all, I got that baby coming the last of December."

"Just a minute." Howie took out his wallet and checked his cash—three tens and a one. "Twelve bucks. That's our limit."

Adam opened a menu and studied it. "That looks like it'll just about cover our soup and maybe a small dinner salad for each of us."

"Here he comes," Howie said. "Let me do the ordering."

"Have you gentlemen decided yet?"

"Yes, we'll each have some soup."

"May I suggest our specialty? It's wild rice and is quite good."

"Ah...." Howie glanced around the table and got nods from Mick and Adam. "Sure, that will be fine."

"A cup or bowl?"

Howie checked the prices on the menu. "A bowl."

"And besides soup, what else would you like?" He pointed to the right-hand side of the menu. "Our special tonight is our filet mignon—a bargain at that price and we serve the choicest, most tender steak in town."

"We'll just have the soup tonight."

Wentworth raised a suspicious eyebrow. "Very well, sir. I'll bring it right out." He gathered the menus and walked away. At the door to the kitchen, he stopped to talk to another waiter. Both of them looked in the direction of Howie and his partners.

"Okay, here's the plan," Howie said after their soup was served. "When he comes with the check, I'll identify who we are and tell him that we need to talk to him about Donna Mae."

"What if he balks?" Mick asked.

"Then I'll tell him we'll just have to tell his boss that we need to talk to one of his employees about a murder in which he may be a suspect."

Adam nodded. "That should do it."

After they finished their soup, Wentworth came back. "Gentlemen, would you care for dessert this evening? We have an excellent chocolate mousse tonight."

"We'll skip dessert," Howie said. "We'd like the check and then we'd like to talk to you…alone."

"I don't understand." Wentworth's face registered a hint of apprehension. "Was there something wrong with the soup?"

"The soup was fine, but we want to have a little chat with you about Donna Mae LaBelle."

If Wentworth recognized the name, he did a good job hiding it. "I don't know what you're talking about."

"We're talking about the murder of Donna Mae LaBelle."

Wentworth glanced around as though to make sure no one had overheard the word "murder." He lowered his voice. "Who are you guys?"

"I'm Howie Cummins. These are my partners, Mick Brunner and Adam Trexler. We run the MAC Detective Agency over on the North Side. We're investigating Donna Mae's death, and we're here to talk to you." Howie handed him a business card.

Wentworth looked at the card and handed it back. "I have nothing to say."

"Is that right." Howie put an edge to his voice. "Then we'll just have a little talk with your boss."

A look of concern flashed through Wentworth's eyes. He took a quick look around. "Okay. Ah, I would suggest the men's room. I can give you ten minutes."

On the way to the restroom Wentworth spoke to another waiter. "Cover for me, will you? I'm going on a short break."

"Mick," Howie whispered. "Stand guard outside while we're in there with him. Okay? Don't let anybody come in."

"But what if they ask about what's going on?"

"Make up something. Tell them that one of the sinks sprung a leak or the toilets are being repaired. Just give us ten minutes with this guy alone."

Howie let Wentworth and Adam go in first. "Remember," he told Mick. "Ten minutes."

When Howie walked in, Wentworth and Adam were near the far sink, standing quietly as a middle-aged, balding man washed his hands in the first sink. Howie shot him a glance and he left without drying his hands. A quick check of the stalls showed they were alone.

"What is it that you want?" Wentworth asked, his tone revealing a defiant cockiness.

"What was your involvement with Donna Mae LaBelle?" Howie stationed himself between Wentworth and the exit door. "We believe she was killed by someone in that little clown group you belong to."

"And since you're a member of that group, you're a suspect," Adam said.

"Our number one suspect right now," Howie added.

Wentworth's chuckle wasn't the reaction Howie expected. "Do you think something's funny?" he asked.

"I'm afraid the joke's on you guys."

Howie and Adam exchanged glances. "You better start explaining yourself," Howie said.

Wentworth leaned against the washbasin and folded his arms. A smug smile crossed his face.

"I'm an undercover agent for the Mutual Fidelity Insurance Company out of Minneapolis. Donna Mae's name came up in an investigation we're handling."

Although taken by surprise by the revelation, Howie kept his tone even. "Have you got some ID?"

"Sure, no problem." Wentworth reached into his back pocket and pulled out his wallet. He opened it and handed Howie a card.

"Claims investigator? What are you investigating?"

"The theft of some rare coins by Johnny LaBelle and two other men five years ago. Johnny and one of his partners were killed afterwards in a shoot-out with the police. The third man got away. The coins are still missing. And although I have no proof, I believe that either Squires or Beamer was that man who got away."

"How much is this collection worth anyway?" Adam asked.

"Close to a half-million."

Adam let out a low whistle as he and Howie glanced at each other.

"And if I can't recover them, my company is out that money because they were insured with us. I've been on the trail for quite some time now." Wentworth glanced at the door. "Look, I've got to get back to work. I don't want to blow my cover here."

"Sure, but a couple more questions," Howie said. "What do you know about Donna Mae?"

"Not much. I know of her, but I've never met her. I wish I could have. She could've provided me with some answers."

"Do you know if Squires or Beamer were dating her?"

"If they were, they kept it to themselves." He eyed the door again. "My time's up. I really have to get back."

"Okay." Howie slipped Wentworth's card into his pocket. "We'll be in touch," he said, still shocked by the revelation.

Chapter 43

Jack Beamer waited for his partners to get comfortable before getting to the business at hand. He poured coffee for himself and Wentworth, and tea for Squires. Wentworth, with dark circles under his eyes, looked as though he could use a cup of strong coffee. Squires also looked tired, but seemed more bored than anything. Although skilled at clowning, Squires often gave the impression that he had lowered himself to associate with a "realtor" and a "waiter." With Beamer's work in real estate, he took pride in having a knack of reading people. Squires wasn't what he seemed to be—underneath his snobbish personality lay a dark side. Wentworth wasn't who he seemed to be either, but then again, Beamer had to admit that neither was he.

"I'm glad you two could come," Beamer said. "I hope you aren't being harassed too much by those detectives."

"I wish they'd leave me alone." Squires set his cup of tea aside after only taking a sip. He crossed his legs and folded his hands on his lap. His frown accentuated the hard lines in his face. "It doesn't look good at the bank when some detective comes around and starts asking questions about me."

"It sounds like you only had one coming around," Wentworth complained. "All three came to see me at the restaurant last night."

"They'll get tired of playing their games and go away," Beamer said. "After all, we've nothing to hide, do we now?"

"Why did you want to meet with us?" Squires glanced at his watch. "I have a board meeting to attend later this morning."

"I've taught Oscar a new trick."

"You did?" Wentworth's eyes lit up with curiosity. "That's great."

"You called a meeting for that?" Squires huffed.

Beamer noted Squires' scowl. Although the man had used Oscar upon many occasions, he never seemed happy in sharing the spotlight with a monkey. Oscar, however, had a fondness for Squires.

"Let's see this trick," Wentworth said.

"Coming right up." Beamer stood and opened the door to the back room. "Oscar, come in here. I've got a treat for you." Within moments the monkey ran in chattering and hopped on the desk. Beamer reached into his coat pocket and pulled out a couple of pistachio nuts. Oscar grabbed his treat and sat chewing while looking wide-eyed at Squires and Wentworth.

"This is the new trick?" Squires asked, his mouth twisting into a sneer. "Watching Oscar eat pistachio nuts?"

"No, no. Just wait." Beamer turned to the monkey. "Do you want another treat?" Oscar bared his teeth, twirled a couple of times, and sat on his hunches with his hands out and his tail curled behind him. Beamer laughed. "You're going to have to work for it." He opened the top right-hand drawer of his desk. "Oscar! Stick 'em up!" The furry performer scampered over to the open drawer, reached in with both hands, and lifted out a silver pistol. Squires and Wentworth's eyes grew large. Hooting and chattering, Oscar gamboled over to the edge of the desk and aimed the pistol at the two startled men.

"What the—?" Sweat popped out on Squires' forehead and he squeezed back into his chair. "Tell him to point that thing someplace else!"

"Come on, Jack, this isn't funny," Wentworth said, concerned but not as bothered as Squires. "That's not loaded, is it?"

Before anyone uttered another word, Oscar pulled the trigger using the forefingers of both hands. A red flag popped out with the word "BANG!" printed in bold black letters on it.

Beamer doubled up with laughter. It took several minutes before he could speak. "You should've seen the looks on your faces when he pulled that trigger. It was priceless. I should've had a camera."

Wentworth took a deep breath, cocked his head, and offered a nervous half smile. "You had me going there for a minute. That gun looked real." He turned to Squires. "What did you think?"

"Not funny," he said, mopping his forehead with a handkerchief.

"Come on, loosen up," Wentworth said. "You've got to admit it's a great prop. Can't you see this routine in our act?"

"I can," Beamer said. "And the audience will love it when Oscar pulls the trigger." He took the pistol from Oscar and gave him a handful of nuts.

Squires reached out his hand to Beamer. "May I see that thing?"

"Sure." Beamer pushed in the flag. "There you go. It's all set." He handed it to Squires.

"Hmmm, very interesting." Squires examined the pistol. "It's quite light, but certainly does look real." He pointed it at Beamer and pulled the trigger. The red flag popped out again. "Someone's certainly going to be surprised by this."

Beamer nodded. "They sure will be."

"I can think of lots of ways we could use it," Wentworth said.

Squires handed their new prop back to Beamer. "Now that you have mentioned it, so can I."

Chapter 44

Mick and Adam dropped by Howie's office around mid-morning, their faces reflecting the overcast, drizzly day outside. With Wentworth's revelation last night, they had lost their number one suspect. They needed now to rethink the connection between Donna Mae's murder, Hatchaway's death, and the clues found in the totem pole. Howie hoped that they would be able to connect some of the dots and begin to get a picture of how and if these things were related.

"Man, I'm still stunned at finding out that Wentworth's an investigator," Mick confessed as he settled in his chair and stretched out his legs. He cracked his knuckles, a sure indication that even with a new baby coming he wasn't his usual upbeat self.

Adam plopped in the chair next to Mick. "You're not the only one. I was sure we had the right man." He drew in a deep breath and let it out slowly. "Sorry I led you guys down a blind alley."

"Don't worry about it." Howie didn't want his partners to think that last night was a bust. Although Adam and Mick were discouraged, they needed to understand that these things happened when tracking down leads. Sometimes you hit pay dirt. Other times, you go home empty-handed. "Think of it this way, guys." Howie opened his notepad and drew a line through Wentworth's name. "Last night we eliminated a suspect. We now have it narrowed down to either Squires or Beamer...so that means we've made some progress."

Mick nodded. "I guess that's a good way of looking at it."

"That's a detective's way of looking at it," Howie said.

"Do you have someone in mind as a prime suspect now?" Adam asked Howie.

"I sure do." Although Wentworth could have been their man, Howie had never ruled out the realtor. "I'll go with Jack Beamer."

"I'm not so sure I agree." Mick sat forward in his chair, his eyes flashing. "Squires is a phony. In my book, he's hiding something. I'd go with him."

"So where do we go from here?" Howie asked. He drummed his fingers on the desk as the wall clock marked time.

Adam finally spoke up, directing his question at Howie. "Do you have any idea how you could've been drugged?"

"I'm still working on that."

"There's got to be a way to figure it out," Adam said. "We just can't keep coming up with dead-ends."

"Don't get so discouraged," Mick said. "Howie's right. We just have to keep plugging away at it."

Adam gnawed at his lip. "Yeah, I guess you're right. I just know that all these cases have to be related in some way."

Mick reached over and gave his partner a reassuring pat on the arm. "Sooner or later, a lead will turn up. Remember what JD told us."

"And what was that?"

"That the bad guys eventually always slip up."

Howie hoped that his partners were moving beyond feeling discouraged. Mick had the kind of personality that wouldn't allow things to get him down, and if they did, it wouldn't last long. Adam, though, tended to internalize his struggles and for long periods of time. The fact that he was now willing to move on and not dwell on the past was a good sign. He had struggled whether he should stick with his schooling to become a minister, but as far as Howie was concerned, there was no question as to what his partner should do. After all, Howie needed a good detective more than God needed another preacher. He picked up a pencil, rolled it between his fingers for several moments, and pointed it at Adam. "Okay. What's on your mind?"

"What? What do you mean?"

"Look, I can read you like a book. You've got something more to say, so let's hear it."

Adam shifted uneasily in his chair. "It's just that I'm still trying to figure out how that poison got into Hatchaway's cup with all the doors locked. And how did someone slip into your office and dope your coffee without you hearing him coming up the stairs?" Adam leaned forward, his eyes intense. "If we figure out the answer to either one of those questions, we'll have the answer to both. The pattern is similar so they have got to be connected."

"That sounds logical," Mick said. "Have you got any theories?"

"Right now..." Adam sunk back into his chair. "No."

The downstairs entrance door slammed shut. Howie cocked his ear and listened to the stairs creak. "Sounds like Squirrel."

Within moments the aspiring detective came bouncing in. After stopping at Howie's poster, Squirrel tilted it a bit to one side and then to the other. Once he apparently seemed satisfied that it was straight (not that it was ever crooked in the first place) he took his usual spot on the windowsill. "So what did you guys find out about that Wentworth character? Is he the one we're after?"

"No and we eliminated him as a suspect." Howie chose not to disclose Wentworth's undercover identity. Squirrel wasn't officially part of the agency and there was certain information that needed to be kept confidential. "How about with you?" he asked, wanting to get the little guy's inquisitive mind on something else.

"How about me what?"

"Anymore from your friend, Monk, at the frat house?"

"Oh, him. Not a thing." Squirrel sniffed the air. "He was supposed to call me." His nose twitched and he sniffed the air again. "That smells like fresh coffee brewing. I sure could use a cup." He smirked. "Unless you've got something else."

"I'll get you some coffee." Howie shot Squirrel a "keep-your-mouth-shut" look. If Mick and Adam hadn't been there, he would have been open to sharing a glass of bourbon with him. Instead, he got up, went into the kitchen, and came back with a cup of coffee for the reformed street hustler.

Squirrel took a sip. "How about some sugar to sweeten it up?"

Howie rolled his eyes. "Just a minute. I'll get some for you."

"Why don't you have your little friend get it?"

"Who are you talking about?"

"That monkey."

"Oscar, you mean?"

"Yeah. Doesn't he know tricks like putting sugar into coffee and unlocking doors?"

"That's right, but he's not—" Howie glanced at his office door, looked toward the kitchen, and then at his coffee cup sitting on his desk. "Oh, man." He slapped himself on the forehead. "Why didn't I think of that? It's so simple."

"What's so simple?" Mick asked.

"How my coffee was doped."

Adam gave Howie a stunned look. "You mean Oscar?"

"Yeah! If the little scamp can put sugar in coffee, why not poison? And he's small enough to squeeze through transom windows."

"You're talking about Hatchaway's place, aren't you?" Adam asked.

Howie nodded.

"I think you're on to something," Mick said. "And Oscar wouldn't make a sound coming up the stairs, would he?"

"That's right," Howie said.

Squirrel's eyebrows knotted as he gave the three of them a quizzical look. "Did I say something helpful?"

That evening Howie worked at the soda fountain. Margo came in shortly after eight. The big guy lumbered over and settled on the end stool. He waved Howie over. "Fix me one of those banana splits," he said in a tone more appropriate for his bar.

"What are you here for?" Howie asked, serving Margo his treat. "You didn't come in just for this."

Margo shoved a spoonful of ice cream and banana into his mouth. "I haven't had one of these for a long time. It reminds me of when I was a kid," he mumbled. After swallowing another spoonful, he pointed the spoon at Howie, and scowled. "I called your office, but nobody answered. I figured you might be working here tonight."

"Well, you found me. So, what do you want?" Howie asked, already knowing the answer, but irritated at the interruption.

"Hell, you know what I want. What's the latest on the case?"

"Margo, can't you see I'm working? Can't this wait until tomorrow?"

"Damn it! If I wanted to wait, would I be here?"

"This isn't exactly the place for us to discuss it."

"Let's go up to your office, then."

"I can't do that right now." Howie glanced around. A teenage kid sat at the far stool sipping a soda and reading a comic book. Several other customers milled about the aisles and Kass was busy straightening the magazine rack up front. "Listen, I'll call you tomorrow."

"The hell with that." His thick lips twisted into a sneer. "I'm not moving until I get some answers."

Howie let out an exasperated sigh. "Okay, let me tell you this. We made a connection with a totem pole and Donna Mae."

"Totem pole? Where in hell did she get something like that?"

"It was a gift from her family." It was close enough to the truth. "We figure the totem pole was important enough to somebody else and that person may have had something to do with her death."

Margo pushed his ice cream aside. "Did that thing give any clue as to why someone killed her?"

Howie nodded.

"So what did you find?"

"A key."

"Anything else?"

"Yeah, a slip of paper with some kind of notation on it." The kid at the other end of the counter glanced up from his comic book and stole a look at them. Howie lowered his voice. "We're not sure what the key is for and we haven't figured out the notation. It's going to take some time."

"Let me see the key."

"I don't have it with me."

The veins in Margo's temples began to throb. "Then tell me what was on the damn piece of paper!"

"I think we'll keep that to ourselves for now." Howie could picture Margo sharing the information with all the customers down at his bar. The guy would probably give out free beers to anyone who volunteered to help figure what the hell DOG meant.

Margo's nostrils flared as he glared at Howie. He got up, threw a couple of bucks on the counter, and stormed out.

Chapter 45

Adam set his coffee cup down on Howie's desk. He slumped back in his chair and brushed a shock of hair off his forehead. "So Margo stopped by last night while you were working?"

"That's right."

"And he wanted to know the latest on the case?"

"Yeah and he was pretty demanding. In fact, he was swearing under his breath as he left. The guy wouldn't wait until morning."

"Well, I don't blame him."

"What do you mean?"

"Howie, his girlfriend is dead and he believes someone killed her. He just wants answers. I'd be the same way if I were him." Adam paused, and then asked the question anyway. "What did you tell him?"

"I told him about the totem pole and that we think there might be a connection between it and Donna Mae's death."

"What was his reaction to that?"

"He wanted to know about everything we found out so far, and I do mean everything." Howie leaned forward to emphasize his next words. "And he was very curious about that key and the slip of paper."

"Curious like how?"

"He demanded to see them."

"Did you show him?"

"Oh, no. I told him some other time. I think the guy's tired of being a bartender and wants to play detective."

"That's not good."

"You don't have to tell me that," Howie said. "Margo needs to understand that he hired *us* to investigate the case and that if he'd just leave us alone, we'll get the job done. We don't need him gumming up the works."

"Did you explain that to him?"

"Naw. He left in a huff after I wouldn't tell him what was on that slip of paper."

"That's too bad."

The dark circles around Adam's eyes, caused Howie to wonder if his partner had been losing sleep over his misjudgment about Wentworth.

"Yeah, well, I'm not going worry about it. Margo's a hot head, but he'll cool down."

Adam sat quietly for several moments chewing on his lip. "Can I ask you something?"

"Go ahead."

"Now that Wentworth is out of the picture, what makes you so sure about Beamer? Why not Squires?"

"I suppose it could be Squires, but I'm going with Beamer because he's Oscar's trainer." Howie flipped to the page in his notepad where he had written down Beamer's telephone number. "And I'm going to call him now and ask if I can borrow Oscar for a couple of hours this afternoon."

"Why?"

"To get Oscar to do his tricks again...just to make sure he can do them." He picked up the phone, but didn't dial. "Why don't you get hold of Mick and we'll all meet back here around...let's say, around four-fifteen or so."

"Okay, I'll call him when I get home."

After Adam left, Howie dialed Beamer's number, confident that they were on the right track in solving how Hatchaway was poisoned. And once they had that piece of the puzzle, then they would be that much closer to the murderer.

Chapter 46

It had been easier than Howie expected to borrow Oscar. He'd explained to Beamer he wanted to impress a girl. Beamer bought it, no questions asked. Howie picked up Oscar shortly before three and was back at his office within a half hour. Setting coffee cups on the desk and sugar cubes in a bowl on the kitchen table, he put Oscar through the trick a couple of times. Each time the monkey did as asked. Oscar repeated the performance for Mick and Adam when they showed up a few minutes after four. The little trickster took off running into the kitchen. In less than a minute, he came back with two fistfuls of sugar cubes and dumped them into the coffee cups. After performing his task, he slapped his hands on top of his head, twirled in a little dance, and sat down on his haunches, his long tail curled behind him. He looked at Howie and held out his hands, palms up.

"Way to go, Oscar." Howie reached into his pocket and gave the performer a handful of peanuts. "So what do you think?" he asked his partners.

"That certainly supports our theory," Mick said. "But if we're right, Oscar here is an unwitting accessory to Hatchaway's murder."

At the mention of Hatchaway, Oscar raised his eyebrows and began to screech loudly as though confessing his guilt. Adam picked up a peanut that Oscar had dropped and gave it to him.

"I think it's time to call Davidson," Adam said.

"No," Howie said, irked by the suggestion. "We can handle this ourselves."

Adam stiffened. "Howie, you said that you would let JD know if we got any leads on Hatchaway's death."

"Look, if we solve this on our own, it would be good publicity for us. JD has enough on his hands."

"You're just avoiding the issue. We owe it to JD to call him. You *promised* you'd call if we got any leads."

"So what?" Howie kept his voice calm. "We've handled murder cases."

"But don't forget that JD helped," Adam snapped. "And he has more experience."

"We need experience too!" Howie's neck muscles tightened. "And running to the cops all the time isn't going to provide us that."

"We don't run to the cops all the time!"

"That's because I don't let you!"

"Hold on you guys," Mick said. "You both have good points." He locked eyes with Howie. "But I have to agree with Adam. You need to get in touch with JD. After all, you did promise him."

Howie started for a drink to ease the headache he felt coming on, then caught himself. Oscar sat quietly, his inquisitive eyes shifting back and forth amongst the three of them.

"Okay, you win," Howie said. "I'll call him the first chance I get."

Adam picked up the receiver, and held it out to Howie. "Call him now."

"What's the matter?" Howie said, glaring at his partner. "Don't you trust me?"

"Come on, it's not that." Adam softened his tone. "Both Mick and I know why you don't like going to the police."

"We trust you, Howie," Mick said. "But in this case, JD has a right to know. If we expect to get inside information from him, we have to keep our part of the bargain. It can't work just one way."

Howie snatched the phone away from Adam. His partners were right, of course, but nevertheless, he hoped their friend wouldn't be at his desk.

The police detective answered on the second ring.

"JD, this is Howie." He glanced at his two partners. "I think we have a lead on how Hatchaway's tea got poisoned."

"Let's hear it."

"It, ah...was Oscar."

"Oscar who?"

Howie shifted uneasily in his chair. "Oscar's a monkey."

"A what?"

"A monkey." He waited for a reaction, drumming his fingers on the desk, and feeling ridiculous.

"Listen, kid, I hope this isn't some kind of joke because I'm not in the mood. The chief has been chewing my butt all day."

"Wait a minute. Give me a chance to explain." Howie already regretted making the call.

"Oscar's part of a clown act and—" Oscar leaped into Howie's lap, causing him to drop the phone.

"What the hell's going on?" JD asked.

"Nothing. I, ah, just dropped the phone." Howie took some peanuts out of his pocket and coaxed Oscar to the other side of the desk. "The monkey belongs to a guy by the name of Jack Beamer. He uses him in a clown act. One of the tricks Beamer taught Oscar is to put sugar cubes in a cup of coffee."

JD laughed. "So what? I've got a blond secretary who does the same thing and I bet you she's a hell of a lot better looking."

"Be serious, now."

"Listen. If I went to the chief and told him that our prime suspect is some monkey who's been trained by a clown to put sugar into a coffee cup, do you know what he'd do to me? He'd assign me to the school patrol." JD paused, and then added, "Look. You're going to have to get me something better than that to go on. Call me when you have something more concrete...like a *human* witness."

Howie smiled and hung up the phone.

"What did he say?" Mick asked.

"He wasn't too impressed. It looks like we're on our own until we can come up with something solid." Howie tried not to show his delight at the outcome of the conversation. "He wants witnesses."

"That's impossible," Adam said, rolling his eyes in exasperation.

"So what do we do now?" Mick asked.

"Put the screws on Beamer," Howie said, his confidence rising. "When I return Oscar I'm going to confront him to see how he reacts." When Oscar stuck out his hand, he gave the monkey a couple more peanuts. "And Mick, why don't you come with me?"

Adam's face went blank. "And just exactly what do you want me to do?"

Howie suppressed a triumphant smirk. "Why don't you track down Wentworth?"

"For what purpose?"

"Find out as much about Beamer as you can," Howie replied, ignoring the coolness in Adam's tone. "I want to know everything he knows about the guy."

"And if he asks me why all the questions?"

"Tell him we have to keep it to ourselves for now. He's an investigator, he should understand." Howie slipped his notepad into his shirt pocket. "And tell him...we'll keep him informed."

"I'll get on it right away." Adam headed toward the door and paused just as he opened it. "I'll give the restaurant a call and find out what time Wentworth works tonight. That way I can be waiting for him when he comes in."

"Good luck," Mick said as Adam left.

Howie motioned to Mick. "Okay, let's take Oscar home." He stood and held out his hands. "Let's go, Oscar." The monkey chattered a reply, raised his eyebrows, and leaped into his arms.

"Now I know what to get you for Christmas," Mick quipped as they headed for the door.

Chapter 47

On the way to Beamer's office, Oscar sat in the backseat eating peanuts. Whenever they stopped at a stoplight and a car pulled up next to them, Oscar jumped up and down and made faces at the people in the other vehicle.

They arrived at Beamer's in twenty minutes, parked the car, and walked up to the door. The realtor was sitting at his desk talking on the telephone, but nevertheless waved them in. As soon as Howie set Oscar down, the monkey ran into the storage room behind Beamer. Howie and Mick took seats and waited while Beamer talked on the phone. From the gist of the conversation, it sounded as though Beamer was attempting to close a deal on a piece of property. He didn't have much luck. After he hung up, he turned his attention to his two visitors.

"Oscar has taken quite a liking to you," Beamer said to Howie. "I hope he behaved himself." He closed a manila folder and slid it aside. "Did you teach him any new tricks?"

"No, but he showed us some old ones. Like putting sugar into coffee."

"And locking and unlocking doors," Mick added.

"He's a clever little fellow, isn't he?" Beamer said, seemingly unaware of the trap the two detectives were laying for him.

Howie chose his next words carefully, anxious to watch Beamer's reaction. "It's too bad that he's an accessory to a murder."

Beamer's smile flickered as his eyes darted between the two detectives. "What in the world are you talking about?"

"I'm talking about Stuart W Hatchaway. We have reason to believe that Oscar was given a command to slip into Hatchaway's store and put something into his cup of tea."

"Only it wasn't sugar," Mick said. "It was poison."

"You two are serious, aren't you?" Beamer swallowed hard. Beads of sweat popped out on his forehead. "Are you thinking that I had something to do with that man's death?" He mopped his brow with a handkerchief. "You've no right to come in here and accuse me of something like that." He picked up the phone. "I'm going to call my lawyer."

"Go ahead," Howie said. "And I'll call a friend of mine down at the Fifth Precinct. Detective Jim Davidson. He would love to have a little talk with you after I tell him what you trained your monkey to do." He saw a hint of surprise in Mick's eyes and hoped his partner wouldn't give away his bluff. "So why don't you dial your lawyer. Go ahead. I'll wait."

Beamer wet his lips, his eyes shifting between Howie and Mick. "Look, I don't want to cause any trouble." He put the phone down. "Are you positive Oscar's involved in this?"

Howie nodded. "We have a witness."

"Who?"

"Can't tell you that, but I can tell you they're ready to testify."

"Whatever happened to that poor man, I didn't do it." Beamer's face grew desperate. "Sure, I trained Oscar to do those tricks, but I swear to you, that's all I did."

Howie had Beamer right where he wanted him. He kept the edge in his voice. "If you didn't do it, who did?"

"I don't know."

Howie picked up the phone. "I guess I might as well call my friend, then."

"Wait a minute." Beamer breathed a sigh of relief when Howie hung up the phone. "If you're looking for suspects, it could've been either one of my partners. They've borrowed Oscar a number a times." He lowered his voice as though sharing a secret. "There has always been something about Arthur Wentworth that was suspicious to me. That man has never seemed to be the person he said he was."

"Is that so?" Beamer was protecting his own skin. Howie decided to let him play it out. "And what kind of person does Wentworth seem to be?"

"He's mysterious-like." Beamer appeared more at ease now that he had shifted suspicion on one of his partners. "He works as a waiter at a restaurant in northeast Minneapolis, but that's all I know about him. He never talks about other things in his life and he's very secretive about his past."

"How about your other partner, Arthur Squires?" Mick asked.

"If I tell you this, you'll keep it in confidence?"

"Of course," Howie said.

"You probably already know that he's vice president of a bank in Minneapolis, but did you know that he's having financial troubles?"

Howie took out his notepad to convince Beamer he was giving them a key piece of information. "What kind of troubles?"

"I've no proof about what I'm going to tell you, but I've heard that he's made some bad investment decisions."

"Is that so? How did you hear about that?"

"I attend a monthly luncheon meeting of Minneapolis businessmen. A couple of months ago I overheard some of them talking at the next table about this banker who was having financial problems. When they mentioned Squires' name, my ears perked up."

"Are you implying that he's desperate for cash?" Howie asked.

"Oh, yes. He never talks about it, but I can tell."

Mick leaned forward. "Desperate enough to murder?"

"I...I don't know. I suppose if one is desperate enough...maybe."

Howie and Mick asked several more questions about Squires' background. Beamer cooperated, but offered no further information that might prove useful. That was okay. Howie didn't mind if Beamer got the impression that the suspicion they had concerning him had now been shifted to his partners. "Your cooperation has been useful," Howie said as he and Mick got up to leave.

"I wish I could've been more helpful." Beamer's smile reappeared and his professional demeanor returned. "If I can be of any further assistance, you know where to find me."

"That's good because we may need to talk to you again," Howie said. "In the meantime, keep our visit to yourself."

As soon as Howie and Mick were outside and walking to their car, Mick asked, "So what do you think?"

Howie glanced back at Beamer's place. "I think the guy was lying through his teeth."

Chapter 48

Adam headed home to call Wentworth's place of work. If Howie expected Wentworth to share information, Adam would make sure the flow of information went both ways. Howie didn't always honor the agreement with JD to exchange information, but Adam wouldn't do that to Wentworth. Howie might be right that detective work often needed to push ethics into the shadows in order to hunt down the criminals, but Adam was determined to do what he could to keep it in the light. He sat down at the desk, looked up the number in the phone book, and gave it a call.

"Fireside Dining Club," a man's voice answered on the second ring. "How may I help you?"

"You have an Arthur Wentworth working there as a waiter. Could you tell me what time he comes in tonight?"

Several seconds passed before the man replied. "I'm afraid that Mr. Wentworth is no longer in our employ."

Adam's jaw dropped. "What do you mean? I was just there last night and he was working."

"Indeed," the voice said dryly. "He quit after he finished his shift."

Adam hung up the phone and sat unmoving, chewing on his lip. The only way to find out what was going on would be to go to the insurance company where Wentworth worked as an investigator. For whatever reason the guy quit, he must have come up with something and no longer needed his cover as a waiter. Whatever that *something* might be, Adam wanted to know.

He was out the door and down to his car within minutes. Luck was with him as he arrived at Wentworth's place of work twenty minutes before closing. He parked his car and hurried into the front lobby. An attractive young woman with a pixie haircut and eyes to match looked up from the reception desk and offered a practiced smile.

"Hello. May I help you?" she asked.

"Yes. I'm here to see Arthur Wentworth." Adam made it sound as if he had an appointment: a lie that made him uneasy, but would have made Howie proud.

She frowned. "A Mr. Who?"

"Wentworth. Arthur Wentworth."

"Just a minute. That name doesn't sound familiar." From her desk drawer, she took out a booklet, and began paging through it. "This is our company directory, but I don't see Mr. Wentworth's name here. Are you sure you have the right insurance company? There's another one two blocks away."

Adam reached into his pocket and pulled out the business card Wentworth had given Howie. "He must work here. Here's his card." He handed the card to her.

"Let me ring that department." She eyed Adam while she waited. "Hello, Mr. Campbell. This is Cindy. We have a gentleman here who says he has an appointment with a Mr. Arthur Wentworth." As she spoke, she kept glancing at Adam. "But Mr. Campbell, he showed me Mr. Wentworth's business card. Yes...yes...oh, I didn't know. What should...okay. I'll tell him that. Thank you."

"Is there a problem?"

"Mr. Campbell will be right down. He'll explain everything." She offered an apologetic smile. "This is my first week here and I'm still learning the ropes."

Within a few minutes a tall dark-haired man in a professionally tailored business suit stepped off the elevator and walked up to Adam. "You're the gentleman who had an appointment with Arthur Wentworth?"

Adam nodded.

"I'm Bill Campbell. Wentworth used to work for me."

"Used to?" Adam hid his surprise. "When did he quit?"

"May I ask the nature of the business you have with Mr. Wentworth?"

"My name is Adam Trexler. I work with the MAC Detective Agency." Adam kept his tone low-key in spite of his growing excitement. "We're investigating a case and he was one of the persons we were questioning. He led us to believe that he worked as an investigator for your company."

"He did up until a year ago."

A year ago! Adam fought chewing on his lip. "What happened? Did he quit?"

Campbell paused. "Come with me for a moment." He led Adam away from the receptionist to an area where they could have some privacy. "What I'm going to tell you is off the record," he said, his voice a whisper. "Do you understand?"

"Of course."

"We had to let Mr. Wentworth go because we suspected that he was padding his expense account."

"Did you confront him with it?" Adam asked, his stomach muscles tightening.

"Oh, yes, but he denied it. We considered taking him to court, but our lawyers informed us that we didn't have a strong enough case."

"How long did he work for you?"

"Two years, and that was long enough." Campbell waited, smiling at a woman who walked past them, then continued. "Believe me, I should know because he was under my supervision. I continually had to be checking up on him."

"I see," Adam said, his mind racing, overloaded with all the startling information. "Anything else you can tell me about him?"

"Like what?"

"Do you know anything about his private life? What he did in his spare time? Who he socialized with?"

Campbell shook his head. "I can't answer any of those questions. The man kept pretty quiet about what he did outside of work. I don't know what kind of case you're investigating, but if he's involved in any way, I hope you nail him. He caused me a lot of grief."

Adam made it back to Howie's office a few minutes after six, feeling vindicated about his initial suspicions about Wentworth. When he walked in, he found Howie sitting at his desk paging through a magazine.

"You're not going to believe this." Adam plopped into a chair. "Wentworth pulled the wool over our eyes."

"What are you talking about?"

"You know he told us that he worked as an investigator for an insurance company?"

"Yeah, so?

"Well, he hasn't worked there for nearly a year. And get this. He was let go because they suspected him of cheating on his expense account. They didn't prosecute him because they couldn't prove it."

"Why that no good—" Howie slammed his palm on his desk. He grabbed his phone and dialed a number.

"Who are you calling?" Adam asked, wondering if he should've followed through on something himself.

"Beamer. I want to find out if he has any idea where Wentworth is."

"Do you think he'll tell you? I mean, can you trust him?"

"No way do I trust him, but I think he'll be more than happy to give us any information when we're going after one of his partners."

"We're going after Wentworth tonight?"

"You bet we are if we know where we can find him. Just hang on." Howie raised a hand and spoke into the phone. "Beamer? This is Howie Cummins. Listen, I need to know where I can find Wentworth tonight. It's important." He took out his notepad and picked up a pen. "Okay. What time will he be there? Gotcha." He hung up the phone. "Bingo. Wentworth is out at the Excelsior Amusement Park. He's scheduled to work from six until closing. We'll catch him as he leaves."

"Are you going to call Mick?"

"Yeah, and Squirrel. That amusement park is a big place. We could use an extra pair of eyes."

Chapter 49

"We've got half an hour before the place closes."

Howie pulled into the nearly empty gravel parking lot of Excelsior Amusement Park, parking in a spot in the far corner where the lighting was poor. After shutting off the ignition and headlights, he glanced at the multi-colored lights of the Ferris wheel. Music from the old-fashioned carousel could be heard in the distance. Turbulent dark clouds rumbling in the west charged the hot and sticky night with a sense of foreboding.

"Man, listen to the crazy people on the rollercoaster," Squirrel said from the backseat where he and Adam sat.

"You'd scream too," Mick said. "That thing heads out toward the water. You feel like you're going to end up in Lake Minnetonka."

Squirrel scrunched his nose. "You wouldn't catch me on that thing."

Mick rolled down his window. "Smell those foot-long hot dogs! I sure could go for one...and with mustard and relish and lots of onions."

Squirrel tapped Howie on the shoulder. "Do I have time to win one of those big panda bears?"

"I don't think so."

"Come on, boss. I want to win it for this dame I know. It'd just take me a minute to knock down a stack of milk bottles."

"I said no."

"Then how about the ring toss at the pop bottles? That would just take a second."

"Some other time, Squirrel," Howie said, a note of irritation in his voice. "Right now, we need to check our plan so there's no misunderstanding. Mick, you and Adam cover the north gate. Stay near the bushes so the people coming out won't spot you."

Mick glanced at Adam and Squirrel in the backseat. "You hear that, Adam? Me and you."

"Sounds good."

"What about me?" Squirrel asked, his voice hardly containing his excitement.

"You come with me," Howie said. "We'll stake out the west gate."

"What do we do if we see Wentworth?" Mick asked.

173

"Rush in and jump the bum!" Squirrel piped up.

"Wait a minute," Howie cautioned. "We're not going to take him in the park and we aren't going to get physical if we can help it. We'll wait until he walks out to his car."

"Why don't we just go in and take him down?" Squirrel sounded disappointed. "Then there won't be any chance of him slipping away."

"He's not going to get away from the four of us," Howie said. "And we're not taking him in the park because we don't want to cause a scene."

"Howie's right," Adam said. "That wouldn't look so good if four guys jumped a clown."

"And we're not sure how other people would react," Mick added. "I'd hate to have to fight off people coming to the defense of a clown."

"Okay, okay, I get you." Squirrel's nose twitched several times. "Man, you really have got to think of all the angles being a detective, don't you?" He vigorously rubbed his hands together. "So we wait until he gets to his car and *then* we pounce on him."

"I don't want him roughed up if we can help it," Howie said. "But we're not going to let him go anyplace until he answers some questions."

"Which car is his?" Squirrel asked.

Adam pointed at a car on the other side of the lot. "It's that tan Plymouth over there. We checked it out the other night when we went to his workplace."

"Come on, let's go," Howie urged before Squirrel could ask any more questions. "The park should be closing in twenty minutes. Give us a hand signal if you see Wentworth," he said to Mick and Adam.

Wentworth stood in the dingy shadows near the employee's shack having a cigarette. It was the only place where he could go and have some privacy. The park's manager told him that it wouldn't be wise to smoke while working. "You're a clown," he had said. "It'd set a bad example for the kids."

Thunder rumbled in the distance as Wentworth flipped his cigarette into the darkness. He had recognized the detectives immediately when their car pulled in. They hadn't seen him. He waited until he was sure they weren't looking in his direction before slipping back into the park's main area. He wasn't sure how he'd handle it, but he wasn't about to let them take him. Not now. Not when he was this close.

"I think all the people are nearly out of the park," Squirrel said. "But I didn't see any clown come out."

"Let's just wait." Howie looked across the way where Mick and Adam had staked out the north gate, but they indicated that they hadn't seen Wentworth, either. For another twenty minutes he and Squirrel waited in silence next to the bushes as park employees came through. Another fifteen minutes went by and a short squat man smoking a cigar came out to lock the gate.

"Are you the last one out?" Howie asked as he and Squirrel walked up to the man.

The man looked at them with apprehension. "Yeah. Why do you ask?"

"I'm a private detective. My name's Howie Cummins and this is my… ah…associate." He handed the guy his card. "We're investigating a case."

"Glad to meet you. The name's Jerry Houser, but they call me Curly. I'm the park's manager." He puffed on his cigar. "So, what do you want to see me about?"

"This has nothing to do with you. We're here to see Arthur Wentworth. We were told that he was working here tonight. We need to talk to him."

"Wentworth…Wentworth." Curly scratched his head. "I'm not sure who that is. Is he a regular employee here?"

"He's a clown and he's in big trouble," Squirrel blurted out. He stepped back when Howie shot him a stern glare.

"Wentworth is supposed to be working here as a clown," Howie explained. "And if he didn't show up, he's going to be in trouble with his boss."

"Oh, I know who you're talking about." The man shoved the cigar to the corner of his mouth. "Wentworth, huh? I never knew his name before. His clown name is Highpockets, isn't it?"

"That's right."

"That's the only name I know him by." Curly worked his cigar to the other side of his mouth. "The guy's pretty good with the kids. He's been here a number of times." He picked pieces of cigar off his tongue. "Doesn't he use a monkey sometimes?"

Howie nodded. Curly sounded like he could stand and talk all night. "Could Wentworth still be inside?"

"Naw, that's not possible."

"Are you sure?"

"Sure, I'm sure. I'm always the last one out." He took the cigar out of his mouth, flicked off the ashes, and stuck it back in. "Look, I'll tell you what I'll do. I'll take a quick walk around the park once to make sure."

"How about letting us go with—ouch!" Squirrel gave Howie an accusatory look. "You stepped on my foot."

Howie kept his attention on Curly. "Don't bother. We probably missed him when he left."

"Are you sure? It won't be any trouble."

"No, we're fine. Thanks anyway. We'll catch Wentworth tomorrow at his office." Howie signaled Mick and Adam. Within moments they joined him and Squirrel as they walked toward their car. He glanced back at Curly who, by now, had locked the gate and was heading toward a white pickup truck.

"We're not leaving, are we?" Squirrel asked. "Wentworth's in here. I can feel it in my bones. I'd give you four—no, make that five-to-one odds that he's still here. We can't be giving up now when—"

"Just hold it," Howie growled. "We aren't going anywhere."

"Then why did you give that guy the impression that we were leaving?"

"Because I didn't think he'd let us in on our own, and I didn't want him following us around in there."

"So what's your plan of action?" Adam asked.

"For now, we're going to act like we're getting ready to go." Howie noted that Curly had started his truck. "As soon as that manager leaves we're heading back."

"But the gate's locked," Mick said.

"We can break the lock," Squirrel suggested. "It's easy to do." He gave them a sheepish grin. "Or, so I've been told."

Howie shook his head. "That's not a good idea, Squirrel."

"Why?"

"Because a broken lock would be reported and the park manager would tell the police that we were the last ones seen here. We'll just climb the fence."

"Wow! That's an even better idea! Now we're getting down to the nitty-gritty business of detective work, aren't we?"

"Just stay close to me and keep quiet, would you?" Howie warned his over-eager helper.

Wentworth swore silently as he watched Howie and his partners hanging around their car and talking, biding their time until Curly left. Although there were four of them, he wasn't afraid. Let them come after him. He knew the park inside out. In the past couple of years, he had performed at least a dozen times and had come to know all the places a person could hide and not be noticed. If those detectives wanted to play games, he would be ready. He took one last look at them and headed for the Ferris wheel.

Chapter 50

"Squirrel, you come with me," Howie said, scanning the area.

"Sure thing, boss."

Howie pointed to the left. The eight-foot chain link fence seemed manageable. "We'll climb the fence by that telephone pole over there."

"What about us?" Mick asked.

"You and Adam go over the fence on the other end. When you get inside, make sure you check everything. Wentworth could be hiding anywhere."

"What if he slips by us and takes off?" Adam asked.

Howie studied Wentworth's car. He could leave someone to guard it, but he needed his partners in the park and felt uneasy giving the assignment to Squirrel. The little guy was brave, but physically, he was hardly a match for his own shadow let alone for Wentworth. "I tell you what. He's not going anywhere with four flat tires, is he?"

Squirrel's eyes widened. "Wow! Good thinking, boss."

"You guys go ahead," Howie said. "We'll take care of the tires."

"Why don't we just shoot them out?" Squirrel said as he and Howie headed toward the car.

Howie stopped and stared at his friend. "What did you say?"

"Just shoot the tires out." Squirrel's eyes danced with excitement. "They do that in the movies, don't they?"

Howie nearly laughed out loud until he realized that the guy was serious. "Squirrel, this isn't a movie set and we're not in a movie."

"I know, but can't we do it just this one time?"

"No."

"Why not?"

"Because, you know, I don't carry a gun."

"Maybe you should start." The little guy's nose twitched. "You never know when you may need one...like times like this."

"Come on. We're wasting time." When he and Squirrel got to Wentworth's car, Howie looked back just as Adam and Mick jumped down on the other side of the fence. They gave him a thumbs-up and headed in the direction of the Ferris wheel.

"Do you think Wentworth's the killer?" Squirrel asked.

Howie squatted and unscrewed the valve cap of the car's right-front tire. "I thought Beamer was, but now I don't know."

"My bet's on Wentworth." Squirrel's nose twitched again. "Why else would he lie unless he was covering his tracks? Don't you think?"

"I'm not sure what I think." Howie used the tip of his car key to depress the valve pin. The escaping air hissed into the night.

"I've got it, boss." Squirrel's eyes doubled in size. "Maybe Wentworth and Beamer are in it together."

"And maybe all three of them are in it together," Howie said. "I don't have the answers right now, but I plan to get some before we leave tonight."

"Anything I can do to help?"

"Yeah. Get started on one of the other tires."

"I didn't realize how spooky this place can be at night," Mick whispered as he and Adam made their way through the amusement park.

"Too bad we don't have any flashlights." Adam tried to distinguish shadowy shapes in the distance.

"Hey, look," Mick said. "Dodgem cars." They stopped at the mesh fence separating them from the ride. "I once rode these things six straight times. Man, I loved crashing into the other cars."

"And I thought you were just such a nice guy," Adam quipped, keeping his voice low. "Does your wife—" He broke off and glanced around, a frown on his face.

"What's the matter?"

"Did you hear something?"

"No. Did you?"

Adam cocked his head. A dog howled in the near distance and from beyond that came the rumbling of thunder. "I don't know. I'm not sure." He looked in the direction of the lake, but could barely make out the faint outlines of the speedboats people rented during park hours. "I guess it was nothing more than the waves hitting the dock."

The two detectives made their way past the Dodgem cars to an adjoining enclosed pavilion. A lone light bulb dimly lit the space inside. They peeked into the windows and tried the door.

"That's locked up nice and tight," Adam said.

"Where do you think we should try next?"

"I'd suggest the Ferris wheel."

Adam jumped at the sound of the new voice. He whirled around, staring at a man who had stepped out from behind the corner of the building and was pointing a revolver at them. His white clown face hung ghostlike in the darkness.

Adam's heart pounded in his chest. "Wentworth! How did you—?"

"Doesn't matter how." Wentworth moved closer. Light from inside the pavilion reflected off his baggy trousers, blousy shirt top, and bushy wig, giving him a surreal quality. "What does matter is that you do as I say." He motioned with the gun. "Start moving."

Adam didn't budge. "You're not going to get away with this."

"Yeah, give it up before you do something foolish," Mick said.

"I'm not planning to do anything foolish. Now get moving." Wentworth herded them at gunpoint, taking them to the Ferris wheel. He opened the gate and ordered them inside to the boarding platform. "Get in that seat and hurry up about it." Grudgingly, their eyes on the gun, they did as he had directed. "Put that safety bar down. I wouldn't want you to fall out." While keeping the gun on them, he moved to the operator's stand, took a set of keys from his pocket, and inserted a key into the control panel. Instantly, the Ferris wheel's lights lit up. "Have a nice ride," he called, and with a sneer, he pulled a lever.

Mick gasped as the ride began to rotate backwards.

"What's the matter?" Adam asked.

"I'm scared of heights." The Ferris wheel continued to move. Within seconds, they were halfway to the top. "This is not good!" Mick cried, gripping the safety bar.

"Just don't look down." Adam tried not to panic, and saw Wentworth looking up at them. "Fix on something off in the distance."

Mick turned his head slowly as if he were afraid to move. "You mean like that storm headed our way?"

Just as their car reached the pinnacle, the Ferris wheel jerked to a halt. The abrupt stop caused their car to violently swing back and forth.

"Quick rocking it!" Panic filled Mick's voice.

"I'm not doing it. Just sit still! It'll settle down by itself." A flash of lightning in the distance caught Adam's attention. One thousand one…one thousand two…at one thousand five, the clap of thunder reached them. The storm was a ways off, but moving rapidly in their direction. The wind picked up, shoving at their car.

"You're rocking it again!" Mick clung to the safety bar with both hands, his knuckles white.

"It's not me. The wind's picking up." Another flash of lightning lit the sky. One thousand one…one thousand two…At one thousand four the thundered boomed.

"What are we going to do?" Mick asked, his voice quivering.

"Don't worry. Just hang tight. Howie and Squirrel will get us down." No sooner had Adam uttered the words than the lights on the Ferris wheel went out.

Howie had just finished letting the air out of the fourth tire when Squirrel tapped him on the shoulder. "Hey, look! Somebody's cranked up the Ferris wheel."

"Damn! That's got to be Wentworth! Come on, let's go." Howie took off running.

"Wait for me!" Squirrel yelled as the first drops of rain pelted them.

Howie paused when he got to the chain link fence, figuring Squirrel needed help climbing the fence. But the little guy took a flying leap at the fence and was on top before Howie could get started.

"You need some help?" Squirrel asked, straddling the fence while he extended a hand to Howie.

"Just get out of my way." By the time Howie got to the top, Squirrel was on the ground on the other side waiting for him.

"Jump!" Squirrel yelled. "It's not that far."

Howie swung his leg over, ripping his pants leg in the process. Another couple of seconds and he was standing next to Squirrel. "I'll head straight to the Ferris wheel. You circle around. If you see Wentworth, yell out. Don't try to take him on yourself."

"Okay, boss." Squirrel took off, disappearing into the shadows.

Howie squinted at the Ferris wheel. Lightning flashed and he recognized the figures of his partners in a car at the very top. He moved cautiously toward the ride in case Wentworth had decided to use them as bait. Lightning flashed again and the wind picked up, bringing with it a torrential downpour.

Chapter 51

Squirrel worked his way around to the pavilion next to the Dodgem cars. The driving rain plastered his thick brown hair against his forehead. His soaked clothes became a second layer of skin. Every so often he glanced up at Mick and Adam stuck atop of the Ferris wheel.

Cold and shivering, he peeked through a window into the pavilion, wondering if Wentworth could be hiding inside. Lightning flashed and he got his answer. Less than ten feet away in the driving rain stood a smirking clown. Squirrel's first instinct was to rush him and take him down, but in the flickering storm light, he caught a glimpse of the revolver pointed at him.

"Don't do anything stupid," Wentworth said as he moved closer.

Squirrel's nose twitched. "Don't worry. I won't."

"Good, then you're smarter than you look." Greasy streaks of red and black paint ran down Wentworth's face. Lightning illuminated his grotesque appearance. He gestured with the gun. "Turn around and get going. I'll be right behind you."

"Where are we going?"

"The Tilt-a-Whirl."

"Why there?"

"You're going for a little ride."

"What!" Squirrel stopped and turned around. "How about the Caterpillar? It's got a cover that'll protect me from the rain." He sneezed. "Hear that? I'm going to catch pneumonia out here. Don't you—"

"Shut up! Get moving." Wentworth poked him with the gun and followed him to the Tilt-a-Whirl. After forcing his reluctant rider to climb into one of the cars, he made his way to the controls.

"Ohh, I'm going to get sick," Squirrel moaned. "I don't like things that spin around." He attempted to lift the safety bar. "I'm getting out."

"Stay where you are!" Wentworth shouted. "And don't think I won't use this gun." He kept the revolver pointed at Squirrel as he inserted a key into a slot on the control box. The ride began to move when he pulled a lever.

"Get me out of here!" Squirrel cried as the ride picked up speed. "Help!" he yelled as his car went into its first dip and spun around, slinging him against the side of the car.

Howie peered through the rain at the lights of the Tilt-a-Whirl, and immediately took off in that direction. When he got there, the ride was spinning around at full speed. As the cars whipped past he spotted Squirrel squashed against the corner of his car, pinned by centrifugal force. It didn't take Howie long to locate the control panel, but when he pushed the *Stop* button, nothing happened.

"Hang on!" Howie shouted as Squirrel whizzed by. The speed indicator had been turned to maximum and the lever broken off. The key in the control box had been snapped off in the panel. "I can't turn it off!" he yelled as Squirrel came around again.

"Get me out..." Squirrel's yell faded as he flew past.

Rain lashed at Howie. Lightning flashed. Out of the corner of his eye he caught a movement near the pavilion. With the next bolt of lightning he caught sight of a white-faced clown. "Wentworth!" he hollered. The person turned, looked in his direction, but kept on moving. "Hang in there, Squirrel!" Howie shouted as he took off after Wentworth.

Pleased that Howie had decided to come after him, Wentworth dodged around the corner of a building. He wanted to see how the meddling detective did one-on-one. He moved swiftly, but not so fast as to lose his pursuer. Whenever the lightning flashed, he made sure he stayed in clear view. Ditching the detective would've been easy, but Wentworth didn't want to ditch him. He wanted to make him regret that he had ever taken on the case. He paused and looked back. Cummins had stopped, obviously trying to determine which direction to go. "Did you lose something?" Wentworth yelled and waved his hands. Once he got Cummins' attention, he took off for the Fun House.

Wentworth's taunting angered Howie. He took out after him again, catching sight of him as he entered the Fun House. Mick and Adam were still stuck atop the Ferris wheel and Squirrel by now had turned green on the Tilt-a-Whirl. There wasn't anything he could do about them at the moment, but he could nab Wentworth and that's what they had come to do.

The entrance door to the Fun House had been left open. Howie entered into the maze passageway. During park hours, customers had to find their way through a lit mirror maze before coming to the stage platform inside the main area. Now, in complete darkness, it seemed to take forever to find his way through the maze. He had been in the Fun House several times over the years and was familiar with the arrangement. After the passageway, there would be boards that slid back and forth, and a section of floor that vibrated just before coming to the wooden stairway leading to the main floor. Tonight, however, there were no moving or vibrating boards, and the exit signs provided the only source of interior lighting. Every now and then, flashes of lightning lit up the area through the windows near the ceiling and in addition to the sound of rolling thunder, rain pounded the wooden roof.

Howie cautiously made his way down the staircase onto the main floor, giving his eyes time to adjust to the darkness. A gigantic barrel set on its side stood to his right. The Barrel of Fun invited customers to walk through while it revolved. He moved to the motionless barrel, thinking that Wentworth could be hiding inside, but he found it empty.

As Howie eased away from the Barrel of Fun to the other side of the room, a distorted shadow appeared before him. He froze, hands clammy, perspiration forming on his temples. Then he realized it was his own reflection in one of the curved full-length mirrors.

Taking a deep breath, he headed toward the wooden stairs leading up to the top of the slides where customers sat on gunnysacks to slide down one of the two slides leading back to the main area.

Howie climbed the stairs slowly, wincing halfway up when a wooden step creaked. He was nearly at the top when a flash of lightning showed him Wentworth crouched in a corner pointing a gun at him.

"This rain isn't letting up," Mick said.

"But the wind's dying down." Adam wiped the water off his face. He scanned the area. "Hey, look."

"What?"

"There's another ride going!"

"You're kidding! Where?"

"On the other side of the pavilion." Adam shielded his eyes from the driving rain. "I think it's the Tilt-a-Whirl."

Mick continued to hang on to the safety bar. "Do you think Wentworth got to Howie and Squirrel?"

"I don't know." Adam leaned and looked over the side of the car.

"Stop it!" Mick cried. "It's going to tip."

"Sorry."

"What were you doing?"

"If Wentworth stuck Howie and Squirrel on that ride, then that means there's no one to help us. We're on our own up here."

"So?"

"I'm not willing to wait."

"What are you going to do?"

"Climb down."

A flash of lightning illuminated the terror in Mick's eyes. "Are you nuts? In the middle of a rainstorm?"

Adam attempted to stand, but the safety bar wouldn't budge. "Mick. Push on the bar so I can squeeze out."

"Like hell I will!"

"But—"

"Just stay put, will you?"

Adam heard the fear in Mick's voice. "Okay. Take it easy."

"Thanks." Mick breathed a sigh of relief. "Just hang tight. Somebody's got to come sooner or later."

Howie lunged at Wentworth, knocking the gun from his hand. Wentworth threw him against the wall. Before Howie could recover, Wentworth was on him, his hands around Howie's throat. Howie gasped for air as he tried to pry Wentworth's hands free. The man was stronger than he appeared. Howie kneed him in the groin, breaking his grip, and slammed a fist into his stomach. Wentworth doubled over, choking. In the moment Howie attempted to catch his breath, however, Wentworth came back after him.

They struggled together, and tumbling over the edge of the slide, plunged down it. Howie hit the wall at the bottom hard, momentarily knocking the wind out of him. It took a second to regain his senses before realizing that Wentworth had gone.

A movement caught Howie's attention. Off to his right, Wentworth was running up the stairs to the stage. Howie took off after him, ran up the stairs, across the stage, and entered the maze. He swore under his breath when it took him longer to get through the maze than he wanted. By the time he found his way out, Wentworth was nowhere in sight.

Howie paused to catch his breath. The rain had stopped and the sky was beginning to clear. Down at the lake, a speedboat started up. Howie ran full speed for the dock but he was too late. The speedboat was gone and he didn't have to guess who had taken it.

When Curly, the amusement park manager, arrived, he told Howie that he had been called at home by his boss saying that he had better get over to the park. "The boss said he had gotten a number of calls from people," he explained as he chewed his cigar. "And they told him that there were some strange things going on. I came down to find out what the hell was going on."

Luckily, Curly had master keys to all the rides. Once he got Howie's partners down from the Ferris wheel, he used a pair of needle-nosed pliers to pull the broken piece of key from the Tilt-a-Wheel's control panel. Once he got that out, he used his key to shut the ride down.

Although shaky on their feet, Mick and Adam appeared okay. Squirrel, on the other hand, had to be helped off the ride. "Make the world stop spinning," he kept repeating, grabbing hold of Mick and Adam to steady himself. The little guy wobbled over and collapsed onto a bench, putting his head between his knees.

"You took a risk knocking that gun out of his hand," Adam said after Howie filled them in on his chase and the subsequent struggle with Wentworth.

"Yeah," Mick added. "You could've been killed."

"Yeah, right," Howie said with a crooked smile. Holding up the revolver he had retrieved at the Fun House, he pulled the trigger, and out popped a red flag with BANG printed in bold black letters on it.

Chapter 52

Wentworth swore under his breath, angry that his cover had been blown. He would deal with that, however. He still had time to finish what he had planned to do. He had come too far to quit now. Perhaps those detectives weren't as inept as he had thought, but he had outfoxed them at the amusement park. Using the Ferris wheel and Tilt-a-Whirl to neutralize three of them had been a stroke of genius. And he could've easily taken Cummins in that fight at the Fun House if he had wanted to stick around. Next time, he would finish the job.

He had hot-wired one of the speedboats to get away. He wasn't sure if they had anybody at his car in the parking lot to nab him, but he wasn't willing to take that chance. Besides, the lake provided a perfect escape route. It had been easy to get to a boat landing across the way. Now that he had docked, he needed a way of getting home. With all the houses along the lake, obtaining a car would be easy.

No one was home at the first house he tried, but his luck quickly changed. Just as he got to the next house, a car pulled into the driveway. A middle-aged man dressed in jeans, tee shirt, and wearing a Twins baseball cap got out, carrying a six-pack of beer.

"What the—" The man stopped suddenly, as if hitting an invisible barrier.

Wentworth gestured to the man's light-colored Chevy and then pointed to himself. He stepped closer, repeating the gestures, pleased by the nervousness in his victim's eyes.

"Can't you talk?" The man in the baseball cap asked, glancing at his car as if trying to understand. "And why are you dressed in that clown outfit?"

Without saying a word, Wentworth pointed in the direction of the lake and took a few steps closer.

"Did you...escape from the circus or something?" The man chuckled at his own comment, but his eyes reflected growing unease.

No more than five feet separated them. Wentworth pointed to something beyond the man, his eyes widening. The man turned to look. Wentworth rushed him and in one swift motion delivered a blow to his stomach. When the man doubled over, Wentworth grabbed the six-pack and swung it as a weapon into the man's temple, sending him crumbling to the ground. While the man lay dazed, he searched his pockets and found his car keys. He headed for the car, stopped, ran back, grabbed the six-pack, and left.

The drive to his apartment took less than a half hour. He parked on the side street in the shadows between streetlights and hurried to his building. Figuring he had a good hour's start on the detectives, he cleaned up, changed clothes, and packed a suitcase, planning to disappear for a while. He left, knowing that he wouldn't be back. Once he got to the car, he threw the suitcase in the backseat, climbed in, turned the ignition, and pulled away from the curb. He hadn't gone more than a couple of blocks when he noticed headlights in his rearview mirror. Was that car following him? He'd soon find out. When he turned left at the next corner, the car behind him turned left as well.

Chapter 53

Nearly five in the afternoon and Mick and Adam sat in Howie's office drinking coffee. Mick, still chilled from the previous night's rainstorm, nestled his cup in both hands. "How's Squirrel doing?" he asked.

"As of ten this morning, he was still out of it," Howie said. He had invited Squirrel to meet with them that afternoon, but he declined, claiming that the world hadn't stopped spinning.

Adam set his cup on the desk. Other than looking tired, he didn't show any ill effects from their ordeal at the amusement park. "I talked to Squirrel just before I came to see if he felt up to coming. I even offered to drive over and pick him up."

"And he still didn't want to come?" Mick asked.

"He didn't want to get into anything that moved. Poor guy, I can't help but feel sorry for him."

Howie took a sip of coffee, pre-spiked before his partners showed up. Although sympathetic toward Squirrel's condition, he chuckled about how green the little guy looked when he finally was rescued from the Tilt-a-Whirl. "Don't worry about him. He'll be okay in a couple of days. Let's focus on Wentworth."

"Okay. So where do we stand on him?" Adam asked. "Did you check with the insurance company?"

"Yeah, but they wouldn't give out any information on him. The guy I talked to informed me that all their personnel files are confidential."

"That's too bad," Adam said.

"Not all is lost, though," Howie said. "Beamer gave me Wentworth's address."

"What did you do? Lean on him?" Mick asked.

"Not in the least. He seemed quite happy to give out the information." Howie opened his notepad. "Wentworth has an apartment over on Como Avenue."

"Where on Como?" Adam asked.

"Not too far away from your seminary."

"We should check it out," Mick said.

"I already did. I tried to get the apartment manager to let me in. Told him I was a good friend. I even told him Wentworth had called asking me to bring his heart medicine. He didn't buy it." Howie got up. "Do you guys want any more coffee?"

Adam took another cup, but Mick declined, sneezing into his handkerchief. "I'm going home, have my wife make me some hot chicken soup, and then hit the sack."

"What are we going to do about Wentworth?" Adam asked.

"I've got to work at the drugstore tonight," Howie said. "But I'm determined to search his apartment tomorrow."

"Do you think he'll be there?"

"I doubt it. He's too smart to go back, but we might get lucky. We'll meet here around four and then go. Are you going to feel up to it?" Howie asked Mick.

"Yeah. All I need is some hot soup and a good night's sleep."

Howie didn't much feel like working at the drugstore but had promised Kass he would put in a couple of hours. Progress on the cases had been discouragingly slow. If they could get into Wentworth's apartment, he hoped for a break. Since starting the detective agency, he had experienced ups and downs. Downs came whenever he felt he should be doing more or when he had missed clues that he should have picked up on. Nobody told him that he wasn't doing a good job; it was his own high expectations. It was something he needed to prove to himself and make good on a promise that he had made to his dying father.

All of these things went through his mind as he wiped the counter. He was glad that business at the soda fountain was slow. He didn't feel like making small talk with customers or answering questions about the detective business. Most of the regulars who came into the drugstore knew about his work and were naturally curious about a detective's lifestyle. So many, however, expected his life to be similar to that portrayed on TV detective shows or mystery books that featured hard-boiled private eyes. They didn't want to think of a detective working behind a soda fountain serving banana splits and malts. And as far as women, they expected him to be involved with a beautiful dame with every case. If they only knew that his social life had taken a nosedive since he opened the agency. He had been too consumed with his work to have time for any gorgeous blonds or brunettes, either. Besides, he didn't know any.

"My boy, you haven't seemed yourself all evening," Kass said, having come over from minding the cash register up front. "You must have your mind on your cases, huh?"

"Yeah, I guess so."

"You sound discouraged."

"A little. I just wish I could come up with some leads on the cases I'm working on. It's not always easy."

"I'm sure it isn't." Kass picked up the straw dispenser and began to fill it. "But think of the cases you and the boys have solved. Weren't there times you got discouraged in those cases?"

Howie nodded.

"You're just too tough on yourself. Even Bogie gets discouraged at times." Kass set the dispenser aside, got a towel, and began wiping the counter. "Cases, like life itself, take many twists and turns along the way. You can't control everything that happens in life."

Howie respected the homespun wisdom. "So what you're saying is that I should just be patient?"

"Yes. Follow the leads as they turn up. Breaks will come. They always have in the past, and knowing you and Mick and Adam, they'll come with these cases too."

"I hope you're right."

Kass offered a warm smile. "You boys are good detectives and you'll find your leads." He shook his finger at him as though emphasizing his point. "And don't forget, you got Detective Davidson from the police department who's always ready to help out."

"Yeah, I know." *Why does everybody think I need help from the police?* Howie suppressed his irritation. "Thanks for the encouragement. You're a good friend."

Kass' round face broke into a wide grin and a twinkle appeared in his eyes. "I try, but remember I have an ulterior motive."

"And what's that?" Howie asked, grinning.

"When you and the boys become famous, I can brag to all my friends about knowing the three of you." Kass gestured to the wall behind him. "Your pictures will go up there so that everybody knows that my boys, the famous detectives, got started above my drugstore." His chest swelled with pride. "I might even create a special ice cream dish and call it the MAC-Sundae."

A few minutes after four the next afternoon Mick and Adam met Howie at the entrance to his apartment building. "Who's driving?" Mick asked, coughing through the congestion in his chest.

"I'll drive." Howie handed a slip of paper with Wentworth's address on it to Adam. "Do you recognize the street?"

"I sure do." Adam gave the paper back to Howie. "It's not far from the State Fair Grounds. It shouldn't take us more than a half hour to get there."

"With Howie driving," Mick said. "We'll be there in twenty minutes."

It actually took eighteen-and-a-half. Howie parked across from Wentworth's apartment building, an older two-story brick structure. They walked to the entryway and let themselves in.

"Do you think we should buzz him?" Mick asked.

Howie shook his head. "No. If he's home, he wouldn't answer and we don't want to advertise we're here."

"So, how are we going to get in?" Adam asked.

"I'm working on that." Howie spotted a boy, age seven or eight, in the hallway. He rapped on the glass and motioned for the kid to come to the door. The youngster cautiously walked up and stood some five feet away from the glass partition. Howie rapped on the glass again and pointed to the door. "Let us in, kid. We forgot our keys." The boy stared at them with suspicious blue eyes. Howie pointed to Adam. "Don't be scared. This guy's a minister."

"Not yet," Adam whispered. "Don't lie to him."

Howie smiled at the kid who continued to stare at them. "Open the door and I'll give you a quarter."

The blue eyes widened. The boy rushed to the door and opened it. "Where's my quarter?" he demanded as Howie and his partners came in.

Howie nudged Mick. "Have you got two bits? I don't have any change." Mick reached into his pocket and pulled out three quarters, a dime, and a couple of nickels. Howie gave the boy the money and then took another quarter from Mick and held it in front of the kid. "If you keep it a secret that you let us in, you can have this, too. Can you do that?"

The boy nodded, his eyes on the quarter.

"Now remember, kid, if you tell anyone that means you've broken your promise and God will get you." He looked at Adam. "Isn't that right?"

Adam's eyes narrowed, but he didn't say anything.

"I won't tell, Mister. Honest. Cross my heart and hope to die." The kid grabbed the money and ran down the hallway.

"You need to have a talk with Pearson," Adam said to Howie.

"Who's that?"

"Professor of ethics at the seminary."

"Well, Pearson is going to have to wait. Let's go."

They moved up the stairway and cautiously opened the door to the second floor, checking the hallway for any sign of their suspect.

"It's quiet up here," Mick said. "Everybody must still be at work."

"That's good. Nobody will bother us, then." Howie checked the apartment numbers. "It's the next one so stay alert."

"Do you think we should knock?" Adam asked. "I mean, just to see if he's home. He wouldn't know it was us."

"Mick, go ahead and knock," Howie said. "But disguise your voice. Tell him that you're the maintenance man come to fix the sink or toilet."

"But what if he doesn't have a problem?"

"People who live in apartments always have trouble with those things."

Mick cleared his voice and was just about to knock when Howie grabbed his arm.

"Wait a minute," Howie whispered. He tore a small piece of paper from his pocket notepad, wadded it, and popped it into his mouth. After chewing it for several seconds he stuck it over the peephole. "Okay, go ahead now."

"Maintenance! Here to fix your sink," Mick announced as he knocked on the door.

Howie put his ear to the door. "Once more," he whispered. After Mick knocked and announced his presence for the second time, Howie put his finger to his lips. A good half minute went by. "I don't think he's home."

"So what are we going to do?" Adam glanced down the hallway. "Should we get the manager to open the door?"

"I've tried that. No dice. He wouldn't do it without calling the cops first." Howie dug in his pocket and pulled out a small black leather case. He unzipped the case and took out a lock pick, brushing off the recriminating look Adam gave him. "This won't take long."

"You're breaking in. That's not right."

"I'm investigating a murder case and Wentworth's now the number one suspect. If we can get evidence this way to convict him, what's wrong with that?" Adam needed to leave his clerical collar with that ethics professor. Howie inserted the pick in the lock. In less than thirty seconds, they heard it click. "Bingo!" he said. "We're in."

They spread into the apartment with Adam coming in last, only after some hesitation. Howie shut the door, making sure it was locked. "Okay, let's check the rooms, one by one," he said. "We'll start here in the living room."

"Isn't he going to know that someone's been here if we go through his stuff?" Adam asked.

"Not unless you're planning to leave a note of apology," Howie snapped. "Let's get busy. I don't want to stay here any longer than we have to."

While Mick upturned the cushions on the couch and chairs, Adam went through the books on the two middle shelves of the bookcase. Ceramic figures of clowns filled the top and bottom shelves. Howie fanned through the pages of the magazines on the coffee table: several sports magazines, an outdoor fishing magazine, and the latest issue of *Popular Mechanics*. The center drawer of the coffee table contained decks of cards, a cribbage board, pencils, a half filled pack of gum, and other odds and ends. Nothing incriminating.

"Look behind the picture above the couch," Howie said.

Adam checked and shook his head. "Nothing."

"Okay, let's do the bedroom next."

The queen-sized bed appeared as if it hadn't been slept in. Mick looked under the mattress and the bed itself. Howie looked through the drawers in the nightstand while Adam checked the dresser.

"I don't feel right going through all his personal items." Adam closed the top drawer and opened the second drawer.

"Just remember we're investigating a murder suspect," Howie replied. "Forget the stuff they teach you at seminary for the moment."

"I know how he feels," Mick said. "I always tell my students that they should respect the property of others."

"Well, if it'll ease your minds, think of Donna Mae being asphyxiated in her car." Howie put an edge to his voice. "And then picture old man Hatchaway lying dead on the floor of his antique shop."

"Is that what you do?" Adam asked as he knelt down to examine the bottom drawer.

"Yeah, it keeps me focused."

Howie had no qualms breaking into Wentworth's place or going through his stuff. It didn't matter if it was ethical in the eyes of Adam's professor or Mick's students. Detectives had to do things that others might consider crossing the line. His police detective friend, JD, offered some advice when Howie was first starting out. "If you're bothered by the blurred distinction between right and wrong in this business, then you better get the hell out of it and open up a grocery store or something." It was advice that Howie never forgot, and hoped that his partners, especially Adam, would take to heart.

"What do you want me to check next?" Mick asked.

Howie glanced around. "Look in the closet—"

"Hey, guys," Adam said. "I've found something."

Chapter 54

"I found this hidden under some sweaters." Adam handed a brown letter-size envelope to Howie as Mick came over to join them.

Howie opened the unsealed envelope and took out two newspaper clippings on the coin theft Wentworth had claimed to be investigating. One dated January 12, 1963; the second, February 13 of the same year. The headline on the first clipping proclaimed *Heist Nets More Than Pocket Change.* The story described how three men robbed a coin collector at his home in south Minneapolis. The article characterized it as "a daring daylight robbery with the three men getting away with a rare coin collection worth an undisclosed amount".

Mick let out a low whistle. "Didn't Wentworth say those coins were worth a half million?"

"That's right," Adam said. "Enough to kill for."

"And look at this." Howie showed the second newspaper article.

Robber Killed in Shoot-out with Police

Based on a tip, the police tracked down Johnny LaBelle,
identified as one of three men who robbed Charles Atwood
of a rare coin collection in January. LaBelle and two other
men were staying at the Sleep Easy Motel in south Minneapolis,
and when ordered to surrender, LaBelle and his partners fired
at the police, killing one officer and wounding another. The police
returned fire, killing LaBelle and one of his partners. The third
suspect managed to escape. The rare coins were not in LaBelle's
possession and the police have no clues as to where they are or
who the third suspect might have been.

"You know what I think?" Adam asked Howie.

"What?"

"That Wentworth decided to track down those coins for himself."

Mick nudged Adam. "You mean instead of turning them in to the insurance company he was working for?"

Adam nodded. "Wentworth knew that Donna Mae was Johnny LaBelle's sister. My bet is that he dated her to probe her for information."

"But why kill her?" Mick asked.

"Possibly to cover his tracks. Maybe she found out what he planned and was going to tell the cops."

"That means he has the coins," Adam said.

Howie slipped the articles back into the envelope. "I don't think so. If he had, he wouldn't have stuck around. My guess is that he's still looking for them. I bet he got some kind of clue from Donna Mae and then killed her to keep her quiet."

"I wonder if it had anything to do with her car," Mick injected. "Whatever was taped underneath the dashboard could've been a clue where LaBelle hid the coins."

"How do we know that LaBelle even had the coins?" Adam pointed out. "The third partner may have them."

Howie scratched his chin. "That could be the case, but I have a feeling that those coins are still out there some place. After all, Wentworth was still looking for them after all these years."

"Wait a minute," Adam said, his eyes flashing with excitement. "I just thought of something. Do you think Wentworth could be the third robber?"

"How long had he worked at that insurance company?" Howie asked.

"A couple of years at least."

"That means he could've used his job as a cover while he looked for the coins."

"That's pretty slick," Mick said. "Getting paid for looking for something you had stolen in the first place."

"Where do we go from here?" Adam asked.

Howie slid the envelope back underneath the sweaters and closed the drawer. "Tomorrow we go back to that insurance company where Wentworth worked."

"But you said that they couldn't release any information," Adam said.

"Let's see what they say when we threaten to go to the newspapers. I'm sure the papers would love printing a story about a local insurance company who employed a robber and a murderer."

"Isn't that like blackmail?" Adam asked.

"You're not in ethics class now!" Howie snapped. "You're a detective working on a murder case."

"Don't you think I know that?"

"It's not real obvious. Let's get back to the office." Howie glanced around, making sure they were leaving everything the way they had found it.

Howie and his partners hadn't been back at the office for more than twenty minutes when the downstairs entrance door slammed and the creaking stairs announced that someone was on his way up.

"That's JD," Howie announced.

"I don't see how you can tell just by the footsteps," Mick said, shaking his head.

"He can't always be right," Adam said, a note of defiance in his voice.

Howie smirked at Adam. "Just wait and see." He leaned back in his chair, stretched his arms, laced his fingers, and used the cradle formed by his hands to nestle his head.

"I bet a buck it isn't."

"Mick, you've been hanging around Squirrel too much," Howie said.

The door opened and JD walked in.

The police detective closed the door, stood for a moment, and eyed the three young men. "What are you guys looking at me like that for?"

Howie glanced at Mick. "I was just telling Mick that he's been hanging around Squirrel too much."

"Whatever you say." JD walked over and leaned against the file cabinet. "We found Wentworth."

"Really?" Howie felt a twinge of jealousy that the cops beat them to Wentworth.

"Where did you get him?" Mick asked.

"We fished a stolen car out of a lake north of the cities. Wentworth was in it."

"What!" Howie's mind was spinning. "What happened?"

"We're not exactly sure. We're still investigating."

"How badly was he injured?" Adam asked.

"Bad enough. He's got a bullet hole in his right temple."

Chapter 55

By the stunned expressions on his partners' faces, Howie saw that he wasn't the only one shocked by the news of Wentworth's murder. Jack Beamer's name immediately popped into his mind. Circumstantial evidence could connect Beamer to at least two of the three murders. Howie was anxious to find out how much JD knew. He also wanted to stay one step ahead of the cops. "Do you have any idea who killed him and why?" he asked the detective.

JD shook his head. "We've had two murders. Hatchaway's and now Wentworth's. He hesitated as though wanting to gauge their reaction to his next statement. "And possibly a third. Donna Mae LaBelle."

"So you now think she was killed?" Mick asked in a voice reflecting a mixture of surprise and excitement.

"She's still listed as a suicide. Let's just say we're taking a second look." JD turned his attention to Howie. "You've been working on that case. You want to fill me in?"

Howie picked up a pencil, rolling it between his thumb and forefinger, and wondered what information JD could offer in exchange. "Maybe. That depends."

JD, expressing no hint of what he was feeling, watched Howie roll the pencil back and forth. A hint of a smirk formed on Howie's lips. The clock marked time as Mick and Adam shifted uncomfortably in their chairs.

"Sure, we will," Adam finally spoke up, casting a disgusted glance at his boss.

Howie tossed the pencil on the desk, angry with Adam for interfering with his planned bargaining. "We'll share what we have, but it has to go two ways. After all, we both want to catch the murderer, don't we?"

"I'll give you that," JD said, keeping his tone conversational. "You guys probably know more about how these deaths are connected than we do. So what have you found out?"

Even though JD was his friend, Howie wasn't about to give the police any kind of advantage. If the case was going to be solved, he wanted to solve it without the cops getting too much credit. "We're in the process of putting all the pieces together. I can tell you this. It was Donna Mae's boyfriend who hired us to investigate her death."

"So the boyfriend didn't believe her death was a suicide?"

"Not in the least."

"What's this guy's name?"

"Margo."

"How about a last name?"

"I only know him by Margo. He runs a bar called The Watering Hole."

"Isn't that on upper Hennepin?"

"That's right. You've heard of it?"

"Yeah. I've got a buddy who works vice. He's made a couple of arrests down there over the years." JD rubbed behind his ear for a moment. "Did this Margo have any suspects?"

"He thought it was some guy she was dating."

"And who might that be?"

"No idea."

JD's eyes narrowed.

Howie remained tight-lipped.

"But we've narrowed it down to a couple of suspects," Adam chipped in. "And both work on the side as clowns."

Howie shot a stern look toward Adam; he would talk with him later. In playing poker with JD, you don't broadcast your hand. "Okay, JD. Here's what we've got. It's not much, though. Mick found out that Donna Mae was dating some guy who was into clowning."

"How did you get the lead?"

"From a business card that she gave to a girlfriend. Wentworth was one of three guys involved in this clown act. "

"This girlfriend who coughed up the information. What's her name?"

"Beatrice Johnson," Mick said. "She lives here on the North Side."

"Have you got the address?"

"I don't have it anymore." Mick turned to Howie. "You must have it in your notes."

"I'll get it before I leave." JD walked over to the window, looked down at the street for a second, and leaned against the wall with his arms folded. "So what was the name of Wentworth's little group?" he asked Howie.

"Three Clowns and Oscar."

JD's eyes indicated instant recognition. "And isn't Oscar the monkey you told me about?"

"That's right."

"And the other two guys?" When Howie didn't reply, JD's tone hardened. "Look. I'm going to find out anyway. You can save me a few phone calls."

Howie shot an unforgiving look at Adam. "Jack Beamer. He's a realtor."

"And the other?"

"Edward Squires. He's vice president of a bank downtown."

"We thought Wentworth was our man," Adam said.

"Why's that?"

Adam answered without looking at Howie. "For one thing, he lied to us about working as an investigator for an insurance company."

"Tell him what we found in his apartment," Mick said.

JD eyed Howie. "You checked out his apartment?"

By the look JD gave him, Howie knew that the detective didn't want to know how they got into Wentworth's place.

"What did you find?" JD asked.

"Some newspaper clippings about a robbery that took place five years ago in south Minneapolis. Three guys robbed a man of a rare coin collection. One of three was identified."

"And his name?"

"Johnny LaBelle."

JD's eyes turned hard. "I remember that guy."

"Labelle and another man were killed in a shoot-out with the police," Howie said. "The third guy got away."

"I know." A cold anger crept into JD's voice. "A cop got killed in the shoot-out. One of my buddies got hit in the leg and chest. The creep who shot him got away."

"You want payback, don't you?"

JD shot Howie an icy look. "You damn right I do! I promised my friend that the case wouldn't be closed until the shooter was caught, even if it takes the rest of my career."

"Hey, cool it," Howie said. "I'd feel the same way. Anytime we can rid the streets of a bad guy is a good day."

"JD, you were never able to track down that third guy?" Mick asked.

"No. All the leads dried up like spit on a hot sidewalk. We don't even know his identity."

"That's too bad," Adam said.

JD unfolded his arms. "Tell me about this monkey again and how you think he fits into the death of Hatchaway."

"The monkey belongs to Jack Beamer," Howie said. "Beamer taught him to put sugar into coffee cups. He also was taught to lock and unlock doors."

"That's some smart monkey," JD noted. "I know some lieutenants who'd have a hard time doing that." He paused, amused by his own quip. "So you're claiming that this monkey put the poison into Hatchaway's tea?"

Howie nodded.

"Let me see if I got this straight," JD said. "This monkey gets into the store through the open transom above the side door and slips the poison into Hatchway's tea. Is that right?"

"That's what we figure," Adam said.

"Okay. So here's the big question. Why was Hatchaway killed?"

"The totem pole," Mick said.

Howie noticed the flicker in JD's eyes and realized for the first time since he had come, the detective wasn't tracking the connection. "The killer wanted the pole because it originally belonged to Johnny LaBelle."

"How did you find that out?"

"I visited his parents in International Falls. Labelle collected all kinds of odds and ends, including this totem pole. They told me that after their son's death, all his stuff went to his sister, Donna Mae. Somewhere along the line, Hatchaway got it. I'm not sure how."

"What's so special about this pole?"

When Howie hesitated, Adam spoke up. "Tell him what we found in it."

Howie sat quietly, seething about his partner's big mouth.

"Come on, Howie," JD said. "Fess up."

"First you promise that what I tell you stays in this room. I don't want it part of any written report."

"What if I can't do that?"

"Then no dice. I don't want our case being jeopardized by loose tongues. You know what I mean." Howie felt the stares of his partners. Adam especially wouldn't agree with what he was doing. He was counting on two things, however. The first was that JD was bluffing. The second, and more crucial, was his and JD's friendship. JD could be trusted to keep confidentiality. That couldn't be said of others who worked at his precinct. And JD would be the first to admit that the department had more leaks than a sieve.

The clock ticked off endless seconds before the detective responded. "Okay, you win this hand. Let's have it."

Howie pulled open his desk drawer, took out the slip of paper and the key. He handed them to the detective.

"We discovered those things in a secret compartment in the totem pole a couple of days ago," Adam said. "They were in a hollowed-out area behind one of the eyes of the Thunderbird carving."

"Clever." JD looked at the printing. "DOG? Is this what you called me about the other day?"

Howie nodded.

JD turned the paper over, rubbing it gently between his fingers, and then held it up to the light. After examining the paper, he studied the key. "This was it? Nothing else?"

"That's all we found." Howie leaned back in his chair. "I don't suppose you have any idea what those letters could stand for?"

200

"I'll have to give it some thought." JD paused. "Let me take these for a couple of days."

"I don't think so," Howie said.

Adam spoke up. "Why not?"

"Because I said so." Howie wasn't about to let JD take the items back to the station where everyone could stick their noses into the case. He leaned forward and reached out his hand, well aware of the scowl on Adam's face. "JD, I'll take those back."

"I could take them in as evidence."

"You could." Howie kept his hand outstretched. "But I'm counting on it that you're not going to do that."

JD pursed his lips, looked at the items in his hand, and gave them back. "Don't play that friendship card too often."

Howie put the key and slip of paper in the drawer and closed it.

"Tell me something." JD sat down on the windowsill. His tone turned conversational again. "If this monkey belongs to Beamer, he must be your number one suspect."

"He was, but then we figured it could be Wentworth," Adam said. "But now that he's been murdered..."

"Wentworth was a momentary diversion," Howie said. "But we always thought Beamer was our man."

"There's no proof, however, of his involvement," Adam said.

"But he trained the monkey?"

Howie nodded and Mick spoke up. "But Oscar was used by all three of them. Any one of them could've used the monkey that night."

"It looks like you guys could be on to something, but like I told you the first time, I'd be hard pressed to make a case that would stand up in court."

"Why's that?" Adam asked.

"For one thing, we have no fingerprints of monkeys on file. And secondly, I'd look pretty stupid bringing a monkey in for questioning. He might be an entertaining witness on the stand, but he wouldn't impress the judge. Although a couple of my peers would meet their equal if they tried to match wits with him."

Howie was anxious for JD to leave so he and his partners could discuss their next steps. The three of them could move faster on the case than the police. The sooner they could get to Beamer, the better. He noticed the detective checking his watch. "I suppose you need to leave."

"Yeah. There's another case I'm working on that I have to follow up on before I call it quits for the day. Do we agree that we'll keep in touch on this whenever something new comes up?"

"Will do," Howie said. *New* wouldn't apply to their ongoing investigation of Beamer. Even then, however, Howie would have to think about it. He wasn't intentionally deceiving his friend as much as helping him. Once the case was solved, he would explain to JD that he didn't want to bother him because JD had so many other cases going on. It might strain their friendship, but wouldn't break it. His partners, especially Adam, might present more of a problem in terms of what they thought he was promising JD. He would deal with that later.

Chapter 56

Les McGuire's partner parked on the side street around the corner from the used car lot and walked to Les' office, scanning the lot to make sure there were no customers. After approaching the building, he peered in the window. Les was alone, working at his desk. Perfect. Once again he checked the lot, and then stepped into the office, quietly locking the door behind him.

"I've got the slip of paper from the totem pole," he announced.

"That's great!" Les' eyes filled with greedy anticipation. "How in hell did you manage that? Where is it?"

"I've got it right here," he said, patting the pocket of his sport coat.

"Let's see it."

He reached into his inside pocket, took out a white envelope and laid it on the desk. When Les reached for it, he grabbed his wrist, twisting it. A thin smile crossed his face as he reached out his other hand, palm up. "You get to see it when you show me the key."

"Okay, okay, if that's the way you want it. Just let go of my hand," Les said, whining in pain.

He released his grip, pleased at the white imprints left on Les' wrist.

Les pulled open the bottom right-hand desk drawer and used it as a footrest. He bent over, untied his right shoe, took it off, and turned it upside down over his desk. A key clanked out, bouncing a couple of times across the desk. "I had the damn thing all along. You should see the blister I got from that," he said, slipping his shoe back on.

Satisfied, he slid the envelope toward Les and took out a handkerchief from his pocket to pick up the key. Just as he had thought, it was a key to a locker. *But what locker? And where?*

Les torn open the envelope and took the slip of paper out. He unfolded it, looked on one side and then the other. "Hey, what the hell is this? Is this some kind of joke? This paper's blank."

"Just like your head." He grabbed Les by the collar and slammed his head onto the desk again and again.

After wrapping up his business with Les, he drove to Cummins' apartment building and parked down the street. Just as he was getting out of his car, a man dressed in slacks and a navy blazer emerged from the building. *Damn! A cop!* He could spot cops just by the way they walked. He got back into his car and slammed the door. His next move would be rash but necessary. All he needed was the information on that slip of paper – when he got that, he would be home free. Once he found the coins and sold them to his contact, he could live comfortably for the rest of his life.

Perhaps in California. Maybe even Hawaii. Yeah, Hawaii would be nice. Sunshine and beautiful women. I deserve that. Johnny would be proud of me.

Promising to return, he started the car and drove away.

Chapter 57

After JD left, Howie and his partners brainstormed for another hour, but came up with few ideas. They agreed, though, that they needed to keep Beamer and Squires under surveillance—especially Beamer—now that Wentworth had been murdered. Just before Mick and Adam left, Howie reminded them that they needed to stay one step ahead of the police. He didn't need to spell out what he meant.

It was nearly nine o'clock and Howie had just finished going over his notes when the entrance door slammed downstairs. He leaned back in his chair and waited, too tired to guess who it might be. Soon his office door opened and the one person he least expected to see walked in. He was not thrilled.

"Hi, Bernadine."

She sniffed a reply. Her puffy, red eyes signaled that this wasn't a social call.

"What's wrong?" he asked.

"Lester has been severely beaten," she said, her voice breaking. "I just came from the hospital."

Howie rushed to offer her a seat. He watched her slump into the chair. "Tell me what happened."

"I don't know, exactly. The hospital called me at home. I got there as soon as I could, but there was nothing I could do. He looked so…" She worked a tissue in her hands between her fingers. "The doctors say that he may not regain consciousness for several days."

"Any idea who did it?"

Bernadine dabbed away her tears. "No, but it was by the grace of God that a customer just happened to stop by to see Lester about a car. He found my brother slumped over his desk in a…pool of blood!"

"I'm so sorry."

She leaned forward, her eyes pleading. "Will you pray with me?"

"Pray? Ah, you mean, like…to God?"

Without saying another word, Bernadine closed her eyes and bowed her head.

205

Howie stared at the top of her head. The ticking of the clock filled the awkward silence. A good minute passed. "Bernadine?" He waited until she looked up at him. "Look, ah, praying isn't exactly in my department. Adam's in charge of those things. He knows exactly what to say." He couldn't tell if the look on her face was one of disappointment or sadness at the thought that this non-praying detective would no doubt end up in hell.

"Oh, that would be wonderful. Be sure to thank him for me, then."

"I will. No problem." Howie took a deep breath, anxious to get on more comfortable grounds. "If you're up to it, I'd like to ask a few questions. Is that okay?"

She nodded.

"Did your brother ever mention anyone contacting him recently about a certain car?"

"I'm not sure what you mean. People are always calling him about cars." Bernadine used her tissue to gently blow her nose.

Howie realized he was just raising more questions for Bernadine. He wasn't about to tell her that Les may have found something tied in with what they discovered in the totem pole. He wouldn't mention Beamer's name, but a clearer explanation was needed. "What I mean is, did your brother happen to mention someone interested in something he may have found in a particular car? There's a possibility that he may have discovered an item in a car that recently had been traded in."

"Like what?"

"I'm not sure, but I think that whoever did this to him was after whatever he found."

"I don't understand," she said, her eyes revealing suspicion.

He chose his words carefully. If he even hinted that there was a possibility of this being connected to a murder case, she would go screaming to the police. "I can't go into details. It involves another case we're working on and I have to maintain client confidentiality. So he never mentioned finding anything?"

"Not at all."

"I tell you what. Let me do some more checking and I'll get back to you."

"Thank you. And don't forget to tell Adam to pray for my dear brother."

"Don't worry, I won't."

After Bernadine left, Howie checked the time. He would pay Beamer a visit tomorrow morning. He was the number one suspect. There had to be some connection between him and Bernadine's brother. If that turned out to be true, Les was lucky he hadn't been killed.

Chapter 58

Howie gulped down the rest of his special morning brew, making a mental note to restock his supply of bourbon. He checked the clock. A few minutes before eight. Grabbing the phone, he dialed Bernadine McGuire's number.

"Bernadine, this is Howie Cummins. How's your brother?"

"Howard, it's a miracle!" Bernadine sounded as though she could cry with joy. "I checked with the hospital just before you called and the nurse told me that Lester opened his eyes. Isn't that wonderful?"

"Ah...great. When can I talk to him?"

"I don't know. The nurse says he's still very groggy."

"Listen to me, Bernadine, it's important that I speak with him."

"I'll be seeing the doctor this afternoon. I can ask him then...Howie?"

"Yeah?"

"Please thank Adam for me."

"Thank Adam? What for?"

"His prayers for my brother's recovery."

"Ah...sure." He had forgotten to call his partner last night. That was okay. Adam could make the prayers retroactive. After getting Bernadine's reassurance that she'd call him as soon as she talked to the doctor, he hung up and headed out to his car. Determined to keep one step ahead of the cops, he droved to Beamer's office.

Howie walked into Beamer's place to find Edward Squires having coffee with him. Both had somber expressions. No doubt they already knew about Wentworth. Beamer offered him a chair and a cup of coffee. He sat down next to Squires, and wondered if their grief-stricken looks were for his benefit. He looked around for Oscar, but the monkey was nowhere to be seen.

"When did you guys find out about Wentworth?"

Beamer spoke up. "A Detective Davidson visited me last night."

"He came to see me as well," Squires said.

That JD had already made contact with them troubled Howie. JD hadn't been all that forthcoming about the case last night, but Howie couldn't fault him for not placing all his cards on the table.

207

"I don't know who could've done such a terrible thing," Squires said. "It's shocking. Arthur loved clowning. He especially loved to be around children."

"Yeah, Art could always make the kids laugh," Beamer added. "We'll miss him."

"I'm sure you will," Howie said, unconcerned if they picked up the hint of sarcasm in his voice. "So, what happens now?"

"We were just talking about whether we should go on with the act," Beamer replied. "We could get someone to take his place, but it just wouldn't be the same."

"Does that mean you're disbanding?" Howie wondered if they were both involved in the three murders, a possibility he hadn't considered until now.

"Oh, I wouldn't go so far as to say that," Squires replied, casting a sideways glance at Beamer. "We simply don't know at this point."

"It's just too soon to make such a decision," Beamer said.

"I agree," Squires said. "After all, we're still in a state of shock and disbelief. Arthur was such a decent fellow. I just can't understand."

"Perhaps you didn't know him as well as you thought."

Beamer gave Howie a puzzled look. "What do you mean?"

"Well, did you know who his friends were, or who he dated, or where he hung out when he wasn't with you guys?" Howie's question drew a blank look from Beamer. Squires, however, looked offended.

"What Arthur did in his private life was his own business," Squires said in a tone approaching arrogance. "We didn't ask about his social life and he didn't ask about ours."

"That's the way we all liked it," Beamer said.

Squires curled his lip in a sneer. "Personally, I don't have much respect for those who pry into the lives of others."

Howie was done playing Mr. Nice Guy. He'd hit them with some body punches and see how they reacted. "We all do what we have to do, don't we? Did you know that Wentworth wasn't really a waiter, but only used that job as a cover?"

"What are you talking about?" Beamer asked.

"If Arthur wasn't a waiter, what was he?" Squires asked, his eyes narrowing.

"An investigator for an insurance company."

Both men appeared stunned by the news. Maybe one was stunned and the other just acting. Or were both acting?

Squires shifted uncomfortably in his chair. "What was he investigating?"

"The disappearance of some valuable merchandise," Howie replied, noting that moisture had formed on Squires' upper lip.

"What kind of merchandise?" Beamer asked.

"I don't know," Howie lied. Good thing Adam wasn't there or he'd have to later explain that, at times, one had to lie to bait a trap.

Neither man, however, fell for it. Maybe he had said enough for the time being. Now, he would wait and watch. He'd meet with Mick and Adam later and discuss the best way of tailing these two phonies. As JD had told him once, "Outsmart the bad guys. Be patient, they always slip up. And when they do, nab 'em." Howie was determined to do just that, and do it before the cops got to them.

He set his coffee cup back on Beamer's desk, and stood up. "Unless either of you can give me any further information on Wentworth, I'll be going."

When he got back to his office he found Margo waiting for him. The owner of The Watering Hole was standing in front of the movie poster of Bogart. Howie wondered if his current practice of leaving his door unlocked so that clients and potential clients could wait in his office should be reconsidered.

"I always liked Bogart," Margo said as he pointed at the poster. "I bet I've seen this movie ten times. It never gets old." He gave Howie a crooked smile. "Just think. All that killing for that statue and all for shit."

Howie moved passed his visitor and sat down at his desk and picked up a pencil. He had things to work on. "What are you doing here? You didn't come here to discuss Bogie."

Margo walked over and dropped into a chair, his massive frame barely fitting into the contours of it. "Have you found out who killed my Donna Mae?"

"Our prime suspect was found dead."

"Who the hell was that?"

"A guy by the name of Arthur Wentworth."

"Who killed him?"

"I don't know."

Margo slammed his fist on the armrest of his chair. "Damn it! Now we'll never know for sure if it was him." His eyes locked onto Howie. "You said there were three in that clown group. Is one of the other two a suspect?"

Howie shrugged, having given as much information as he had planned. He didn't want Margo getting in their way by playing amateur detective. "You're just going to have to trust me on this. Let me do what you're paying me for."

"Damn it! I want to be kept informed!" Margo demanded.

"And you will be!" Howie shot back.

"I want this guy bad," Margo snarled, his eyes narrowing. "How about that stuff you found in that totem pole?"

"What about it?" Howie snapped.

"Could it be a clue as to who killed her?"

"Maybe. I don't know."

"Why in hell can't you tell me what was on that slip of paper?"

Howie's jaw muscles tightened. "Margo, it'd be better if you didn't know."

"Why the hell not?"

"For your own safety."

"Damn it! I can take care of myself. There isn't a guy out there I can't handle."

"Nobody said you couldn't. Just let us handle this, okay? No more questions."

Margo sat staring at Howie for several long seconds. "Sure, I...understand," he finally said, his tone softening. "But if you change your mind, I'd like to help." His lip curled as he leaned forward. "If I ever meet up with the guy who killed her...I'd take him apart a piece at a time."

"Look, I've got a lot to do today..."

The clock ticked off the seconds as the two men sat, staring at each other.

"Okay, I get your point," Margo finally said. He stood and glanced at the poster. "Bogart was my kind of man. He didn't take any shit from anybody...and neither do you."

After Margo left, Howie walked into the kitchen and poured himself a shot of bourbon. He slammed it down and then poured himself a second.

Chapter 59

Jack Beamer came out of the bathroom at the motel room wearing nothing but a towel and his clown makeup, and gave Angela the once-over. A buxom redhead, he'd met her at a local bar a couple of months ago. Although a bit past her prime, he still looked forward to an evening of the fun she could provide.

She slid her arms around his neck and rubbed cat-like against him. "Hey, baby, when are you going to leave your wife?" she asked in a low smoker's voice.

"Soon, baby, soon," he said, covering her neck in sloppy kisses. "She's out east visiting her sick mother. When she gets back, I'll ask her for a divorce." It was a lie that had served him well over the past couple of years. Women would wise up after three or four months but by then, he was tired of them anyway. Besides, there were other fish in the sea. Another evening or two of frolicking with Angela, he'd be looking again. After all, it was a very big ocean.

"Are you ready for me?" Beamer asked, tugging her toward the bed.

"What's your hurry? I thought you were going to bring me a nice present tonight?"

"I will, baby, I will. I'll hit it big soon. I've got a hot deal going on. It should be completed in a week or two." Beamer unwrapped the towel and tossed it aside. "Come on, I've been waiting all day for this."

"Wait, you're not going to wear that makeup again, are you?"

"Why not?"

"Because it's greasy and hard to get out of my hair," she whined.

"Don't worry about it." Beamer slipped into bed. "I'll give you some dough to get your hair done nice and pretty. And I'll get you a necklace to go with the pearl earrings I got you last week. How's that?"

"Oh, baby, you know how to treat a lady. But just one thing..." Angela glanced over at the nightstand. "Does that monkey have to watch?"

Jack just laughed, and tossed Oscar a peanut.

211

Chapter 60

For the past ten minutes Adam had paced in Howie's office as his startled partners looked on. The storm clouds that had come with him hovered overhead as he ranted, "Whoever it was meant business. If he thinks he can get away with this, he's crazy. So help me, if I ever get my hands on him..."

Howie had seldom seen his partner so angry. He was intrigued by Adam's darker side. Perhaps there was hope that his partner would shed the "turn-the-other-cheek" philosophy he was getting at the seminary. "Why don't you sit down and I'll get you a cup of coffee?"

"I don't want any coffee!"

"Hey, take it easy."

"Take it easy? How can I when some guy threatens my mother?" Adam dropped into a chair, his face in his hands. Within moments he jumped up, stormed over to the window, and scanned the street below.

Howie took out his notepad and opened it. "Let's go over this once more. What time did you get the call last night?"

Adam continued to look out the window.

"Adam? What time?"

Several seconds past before a reply came. "Around ten," Adam said.

"And you thought it was one of us?"

Adam turned and faced his partners. The dark circles under his eyes gave evidence of a sleepless night. "That's right."

Howie sipped his morning brew of coffee and bourbon, reflecting that Adam looked like he needed one. "Tell me exactly what he said again."

"I've already told you once," Adam snapped.

Howie exchanged glances with Mick. "I know you have." He intentionally kept his tone calm. "I just want to make sure I didn't miss anything."

Adam raked his hand through his hair and huffed in anger, "Whoever it was, the guy knew that we had found a note in the totem pole and he wanted it."

"And he didn't mention the key?" Mick asked.

"No. No mention of the key."

"That can only mean one thing," Howie said. "He already has a key and doesn't know about the one we found."

Mick scratched his head. "But why didn't he ask Adam to just tell him what was written on the note over the phone?"

"Simple," Howie said. "He doesn't trust us. He'll know by the handwriting on the paper that he has the original." He turned to Adam and prompted, "And you told him no way and he said..."

"He asked if I knew what happened to a certain used car salesman recently."

"Did he mention McGuire specifically?"

Adam gnawed at his lip. "No, and I told him his threats weren't going to scare us."

Mick spoke up. "And that's when he mentioned your mother?"

Anger flashed in Adam's eyes as he nodded.

Howie looked over what he had written. "What were his exact words?"

"He said, 'Who says I'll go after you or one of your partners?' I asked him what he meant and he said, 'Your mother works at that hamburger joint down the block from you, doesn't she? I was there the other night. She's a lovely lady.'" Adam walked over and fell into his chair. "Before I got a chance to say anything else, he said that he'd call tonight at the same time and that he'd better get a different answer this time. Then he hung up."

"Any background noises?" Howie asked.

"Not that I remember."

"And it didn't sound like either Beamer or Squires?"

"Whoever it was muffled his voice with a handkerchief or something over the phone." Adam got up and walked over to the window again.

Mick gave Howie a questioning look. "What are we going to do?"

"We'll wait for the phone call and follow his instructions. We'll leave it wherever he wants us to."

"Isn't that giving in?" Adam asked.

"We can't take a chance on something happening to your mother," Mick said.

"We're not giving in," Howie said. "We'll arrange for the pick up, but we'll be watching. And as far as your mother is concerned, we'll keep an eye on her after the pick up."

"Why afterwards?" Mick asked.

"Because here's my plan."

Chapter 61

It had been nearly twenty-four hours since Adam had told his partners about the threatening phone call he had received. Now, at two minutes past ten the next evening, he received the second call. Fifteen minutes later he was sitting in Howie's office. "He wants the slip of paper we found in the totem pole sealed in a white envelope and the envelope left on a bench at North Commons Park tomorrow morning at ten."

"Why the park?"

"I don't know. Maybe because it's public and accessible."

Howie leaned forward, placed his elbows on the desk, and clasped his hands together. "Tell you what. We'll make that into our advantage. Where does he want it left?"

"On a picnic table next to the tennis courts. He wants me to come alone, leave it, and then go. I'm to make the drop exactly at ten, no sooner, no later."

Howie picked up the phone. "We'll meet here at eight tomorrow. Mick and I'll be at the park at nine. You're going to have to drive yourself. Don't worry," he said as he began dialing. "We'll nab this guy."

"Who do you think it is?"

"It's got to be Squires or Beamer. My guess is Beamer."

"Why him?"

"It's just a gut level feeling, but if I was a betting man, I'd—hello, Mick. It's Howie. Listen. Adam got the call. Here's what we're going to do..."

Howie and Mick arrived at North Commons Park shortly before nine the next morning. "I'll park by the picnic area," Howie said. "That's far enough away so that nobody should notice the car. We'll head down to the baseball diamond across from those tennis courts. We should have a pretty good view from there."

"Are you sure he won't spot us?" Mick asked.

"Not a chance if we're under the bleachers. They'll provide enough cover." Howie pulled over and parked the car next to a station wagon. "Get the mitts and the ball from the backseat, will you?"

The idea of bringing baseball gloves and a ball was Mick's contribution to the plan. "It'll look like we're just two guys playing a little catch," he had said. To complete their deception, both wore jeans, cutoff sweatshirts, and baseball caps. Howie added sunglasses to his disguise.

They drifted across the athletic field tossing the baseball back and forth. After ten minutes they glanced around to make sure no one was observing them, and then ducked beneath the bleachers.

"How far would you say that picnic table is from here?" Howie asked.

Mick eyed the distance. From where they stood, the contour of the land gradually sloped upwards. "I'd say...ah, about fifty yards, but I can only see the top part of the table. There's too much of a slope."

"Don't worry," Howie said. "Unless the guy's crawling on his stomach, we'll be able to spot him from here."

"How long before Adam arrives?" Mick asked.

Howie checked his watch. "Another twenty minutes." He scanned the area. The tennis courts were empty, two female players having left a few minutes ago. A half dozen teenagers played basketball next to the tennis courts. An older man walked a golden retriever. On a bench next to the playground sat a young couple with their arms around each other. Watching the young lovers reminded Howie that he hadn't dated for quite some time. After they wrapped this case up, he'd have to work on his social life. For the next twenty minutes they waited quietly.

"See anyone suspicious?" Mick whispered.

"No. How about you?"

"Me either. Do you think—hey, here comes Adam."

They watched as Adam walked up to the picnic table. He looked around, took the envelope out of his pocket, and dropped it on the bench. Rather than leaving as he had been instructed, he lingered, his gaze roving around the park.

Mick nudged Howie. "What's he doing?"

"I don't know, but he better stick to the plan."

"I bet he's hanging around with the hopes of catching the guy."

"He better not be." Much to Howie's relief, Adam lingered less than a minute and left.

Howie and Mick continued to wait in silence. The basketball game ended and the players left. The two lovebirds on the park bench got up and walked away hand-in-hand, stopping every so often to kiss. Twenty minutes passed. Except for some kids using the playground, this section of the park looked just about deserted. Thirty minutes passed. Thirty-five...forty minutes went by.

"Maybe he's not going to show," Mick said.

215

"Let's wait another ten minutes." Howie wondered if the guy had spotted them and been scared off. The next several minutes went agonizingly slow. "Come on," he said, having a sinking feeling that something had gone wrong. "Let's see what's going on."

They quickly moved up the grassy incline. "It's gone!" Mick exclaimed as the picnic table came into full view.

Howie rushed to the table and checked the area, thinking that the envelope might have blown off. There was no sign of it anywhere. "Let's go this way," he said, starting off in the opposite direction from which they had come.

"Do you think he could've sneaked up to the bench and taken it without us seeing him?" Mick asked.

"Not unless he was two feet tall." He and his partner continued to scan the area as they moved. Within a short time, they came upon three young girls, ages nine or ten.

"Did you see anyone around here?" Howie asked the girl with brunette hair tied in a ponytail.

Her ponytail swished back and forth as she shook her head.

"Are you sure? This is important." Howie glanced around for other witnesses. He gestured toward the table where the envelope had been left. "We're looking for a man who walked up to that picnic table. You didn't see anyone go up there?"

The girl giggled and nudged her friend, a black-haired girl who immediately began sniggering. "No, but Alice said she saw a monkey running from that direction."

"A what!" Howie said.

"A monkey, but she's fibbing."

"I'm not fibbing. I did so see a monkey."

"Do you know where this monkey went?" Howie asked.

Alice continued to snicker as she pointed toward a small parking area near the horseshoe pits. "He ran to a car parked over there. A man opened the door and the monkey jumped in and the car drove away."

"Don't believe her, mister," said the girl with the ponytail. "She's making it up."

"No, I'm not," Alice said, sticking her tongue out at her friend.

"She's telling the truth," Mick said, sounding like a teacher defending one of his students.

The brunette looked at him with defiant eyes. "How do you know that? Are you the police?"

"No, we're private detectives."

"Really!" she exclaimed, her eyes enlarging to twice their size. "What did that monkey do?"

"He stole some bananas," Howie said. He nudged Mick. "Come on, let's go."

"Are you okay?" Mick asked Howie as they headed back to the car.

"I should've thought of this," Howie said, frowning.

"Don't be so hard on yourself."

Howie's head pounded from a lack of sleep, and from anger about not having anticipated this in advance. It had been a stupid mistake.

"But doesn't this prove it's Beamer?" Mick said.

"Maybe, maybe not. Remember, Oscar was used by all three of them."

When they got to the car, Howie paused before getting in. "We're tailing Beamer and Squires starting tonight." Without waiting for Mick to respond, he got in the car and slammed the door. After his partner got in, he threw the car in gear and peeled away.

Chapter 62

Three aspirins hadn't helped the headache that came from bungling the stakeout. Howie would pour himself a healthy dose of his own headache remedy as soon as Mick and Adam were out the door. He slammed shut the top drawer of his desk, chiding himself for not realizing that leaving the envelope in such an open area should've been a tip-off.

"So the plan didn't work out the way you had hoped," Mick said. "Who would've guessed that he'd send Oscar to grab it?"

Adam took up Mick's argument. "Howie, it wasn't a total bust. At least we know now that it's either Beamer or Squires."

"Yeah, but we would've known which one for sure if I would've thought of the obvious." Howie crumbled the paper he had been doodling on and tossed it at the wastepaper basket. He missed. "Whichever one it was, he knew that we were going to be there."

"But how would he know that somebody would be watching?" Adam asked.

"Because he's not stupid!" Howie snapped. He stared at the crumbled paper lying next to the wastebasket. Adam didn't deserve his ire, but he wasn't in the mood to apologize. He did, however, soften his tone. "I should've realized that he would've cased the area beforehand."

"You can't think of everything," Mick said.

Howie shot a stern look toward his partners. "Listen good, both of you. One of the first things you have to learn in this kind of work is to think like the bad guys in order to outsmart them. I didn't do that today. I blew it."

Mick and Adam looked at each other, but didn't respond. The clock ticked away the seconds while the truth of their boss' words hung over the room like a dark cloud.

"Well, it's a good thing we left a blank envelope," Adam finally said.

Mick agreed. "Yeah, but he's not going to be very happy about it."

"I tell you what," Howie said. "The two of you tail Beamer starting tonight and I'll follow Squires. That way, Adam, we'll make sure that neither one gets close to your mother."

After his partners left, Howie opened his desk drawer and took out the bourbon. He poured himself a shot and slammed it down.

A few minutes past seven that evening Mick and Adam watched as Beamer left his office with Oscar perched on his shoulder. The realtor drove to a motel near the airport. The two detectives parked across the street as Beamer got out of his car.

"What's he going to do with Oscar?" Mick asked.

"Your guess is as good as mine. I'm wondering what he's got in that duffle bag he's carrying."

Beamer walked up to a door on ground level and knocked. Within moments the door opened and he slipped in.

"Did you see who let him in?" Adam asked.

"Couldn't tell from this angle."

Adam rolled his window down and breathed in the cool night air. "Do you think he's meeting a woman?"

"It wouldn't surprise me. Squirrel said the guy cheats on his wife."

"But why bring Oscar? Isn't that sort of weird?"

Mick shrugged. "If you ask me, this whole case has been weird."

The two detectives sat for quite some time, their eyes focused on the door to the motel room. Every few minutes from the nearby airport, the roar of jets taking off and landing shattered the stillness.

"I don't like doing this," Adam said.

"What do you mean? What don't you like?"

"Spying on people."

"It's part of being a detective, isn't it?"

Adam waited for the deafening roar of a jet to subside. "That may be, but I still don't have to like it."

Mick turned toward his partner. "You know about these things more than I do, but doesn't God, in a sense, spy on us?"

Adam frowned.

"Just bear with me," Mick said. "Isn't God supposed to be with us all the time and can see everything we do? Isn't that what they teach you in seminary?"

"It's not the same thing."

"Why not?"

"Because God is God, and we are just us."

"So are you saying that it's okay for God to spy on people, but not us?"

"Hey, drop it, okay? You're sounding like Howie."

"Anything you say." Mick refocused his attention on the motel.

Several minutes passed before Adam spoke. "I'm sorry I snapped, but you know how I've struggled with this whole thing of becoming a minister."

"You like detective work, don't you?"

"Sure, but I'm not happy about some of the things we do."

"Like this?"

"Yeah, like this."

"Can't you see that what we're doing is for a good reason?" Mick shifted so he faced Adam. "We're sitting in this car across from a motel right now because we're trying to gather enough evidence to get a possible killer off the street."

"So the end justifies the means?" Adam asked defiantly.

"In this case it does."

"Even spying on a person's private life?"

"Even that."

"What if he's innocent?"

"What if he's not?"

"I feel like I'm talking to Howie."

Mick offered a sheepish grin. "I had this discussion with him earlier."

"What!"

"Don't get angry now. He figured that you'd feel uncomfortable doing this."

"And he knew it would come up, didn't he?"

Mick turned his attention back to the stakeout. For the next fifteen minutes, the two of them watched the motel without saying a word.

"What do you say we check that room out?" Mick said. "If it's just some woman he's seeing, then we won't have to sit here all night while they have their fun."

"That's fine with me. Have you got any suggestions?"

"Do you think the manager would give us a key?" Before Adam could reply, Mick answered his own question. "No, scratch that. Dumb idea."

"So what are we going to do? The sooner..." Adam rolled his eyes heavenward and waited while another jet passed overhead. "The sooner I get out of here, the better."

"How about if we bang on their door and yell fire?"

"Are you kidding?"

"Do I look like I'm kidding?"

"No...but do you think Beamer would fall for that?"

"Sure he would. Why wouldn't he? Besides, what have we got to lose? If he's the one, then he already knows that we're trying to nab him."

"But if he's innocent, we're invading his private life."

"You can't have it both ways."

Adam stared at the motel. "Okay. Let's do it and be done with it."

They got out of the car, walked across the street, and went up to the door, checking around them for potential witnesses. Seeing none, Mick nudged Adam. "Ready?"

Adam nodded.

"Fire!" Mick yelled as he pounded on the door. "Get out! The place is on fire!"

From inside a woman screamed. Within seconds the door flew open. Beamer, in clown paint, had only a bath towel wrapped around his waist. The frightened woman rushed past him and out the door wrapped in a sheet. In her panic, she tripped over it and fell, shrieking as it unwound from around her. The only calm one in the room was Oscar. The monkey was sitting atop the headboard, munching a banana, and watching the scene unfold.

Chapter 63

While Mick and Adam stood in the doorway of the motel getting an eyeful of Beamer's latest fling, Howie and Squirrel were off tailing Squires.

Squirrel had showed up at Howie's office just as the detective was leaving. When he heard what Howie was planning, he begged to come along. "It'll be my chance to get some more experience," he pleaded.

They parked down the street from Squires' office and waited for over an hour before their suspect came out, got into his car, and drove off. Howie started his car and followed him at a safe distance.

"Well, what do you know," Howie said after tailing Squires for nearly fifteen minutes. "Mr. Downtown Banker is headed toward the North Side. Now, what's a respectable gentleman like him doing slumming in our neck of the woods?"

"Don't be too shocked," Squirrel said. "When I was doing bookie work..." He gave Howie a sheepish sideward glance. "Which I've given up now that I've reformed. Anyway, you'd be surprised at the high-class people who sought me out. Why, I remember this one dame in her mink fur coat and fancy diamond jewelry—"

"Tell me later," Howie said. He slowed the car as Squires pulled into the parking lot of Billy's, a local bar that had the reputation of hiring former pro-wrestlers as bartenders.

"He sure knows how to pick them, doesn't he?" Squirrel said. "The cops are called to that dive more times than any other on the North Side."

"I'll let you out," Howie said. "You go in and keep an eye on him. I'm going to park around the block."

Squirrel's eyes lit up as though he had just rolled lucky number seven. "You mean I get to be a detective?"

"Just until I get there. Go in through the back. You can walk through and scan the place."

"And if I see him?"

"Don't do anything. Just find a spot where you can watch him. Have you got that?"

"Sure, no problem." Squirrel already had his hand on the door handle.

"Just do me one favor," Howie said.

"Name it."

"Don't draw any attention to yourself."

"Hey, boss, you can trust me."

Howie let his "trusted" detective out and parked around the block. On his way back to Billy's, he walked by boarded-up storefronts while occasionally sidestepping broken wine bottles.

He paused at the front entrance. Coming in this way was a risk, but he was counting on Squires having sought a more private spot in the back to conduct whatever business he had there. But why was he there? It certainly wasn't for the watered-down drinks or the ambience. The man could afford the high-class places in downtown Minneapolis where a glass of water cost more than most drinks at Billy's. *If he's looking for women,* Howie thought, *that would be another story.* Beamer had already shown his kinky interactions with the opposite sex. Maybe Squires was cut from the same fabric.

When Howie opened the door, a noisy, smoky atmosphere slapped him in the face. The only source of light came from pinkish bulbs randomly placed in the ceiling. It took several moments for his eyes to adjust. To his right sat a row of booths, perhaps five or six. He was trying to spot Squires when someone touched his arm.

"I saved a stool for you at the bar," Squirrel said.

Howie went with Squirrel and sat down.

Within moments a woman took a stool next to Howie. "Hi, cutie."

She looked to be in her mid-to-late forties, wearing white pedal pushers and a low cut, form-fitting sweater. Gold bracelets jangled with each movement of her hand.

"Why don't you and your friend buy me a drink?" she asked.

"Sure," Squirrel said. "What would you—ouch!" He rubbed his arm as he questioned Howie, "What did you do that for?"

"Move on, lady," Howie said. "We're going to be talking business."

She gave him a sultry smile. "Well, when you get done with business, honey, I'll be over at the jukebox. The name is Elaine." She brushed up against Howie as she got off her stool, her perfume overwhelming him. "Don't take too long, now," she said as she left.

"Where's Squires?" Howie asked Squirrel.

"In that booth by the rear entrance right across from the jukebox. His back is turned to us."

"Who's the bald-headed fellow with him?"

"I don't know, but before you came in, I went back and dropped a quarter in the machine to play some music. Up close, the guy looks like as sleazy a character as they come." Squirrel waved at Elaine who had positioned herself at the jukebox and was swaying to the rhythms of a song. "That dame's hot for us."

"That dame is old enough to be your mother." Howie averted his eyes when Elaine waved at him. "I thought you reformed."

"I did. I gave up gambling, not women."

223

A bartender, the size of a barn made his way over. "What'll you have?" he asked Howie.

"Give me a beer."

"Coming right up." The bartender turned to Squirrel. "How about you? Another one?"

"Naw, I'm still nursing this one."

Howie took a swig of beer the bartender served him and turned to Squirrel. "When you came in, were Squires and that guy already together?"

"No. Baldy was sitting at the bar. He saw Squires, walked over, and sat down with him."

Howie and Squirrel sat at the bar for another fifteen minutes, during which Squirrel ordered another beer but Howie declined.

"What are we going to do?" Squirrel asked.

"We just have to wait and see." Howie hoped that the booth behind Squires would open up, but the three guys occupying it ordered another round of drinks. Just as he was about to suggest to Squirrel that he should stand by the jukebox so he could overhear whatever Squires and the other guy were talking about, their suspect got up. Squires shook hands with his companion and left by the back door.

Squirrel hopped off his stool, but Howie didn't move. "We're not going to let Squires get away, are we?"

"We'll pick up the tail tomorrow again. I think we should have a little visit with his friend. I'm curious to see what this guy's connection is with Squires."

Howie slid into the booth in front of Baldy. Squirrel slid in on the other side to pin him in.

"What in hell do you think you're doing?" The man's rough voice matched his pockmarked face. He wore a dark sport coat and a light-colored shirt with a wide, open collar. A thick gold chain hung around his squatty neck. He looked to be in his early fifties. "Buzz off," he snarled. "Go find your own booth."

"We like this one." Howie kept his tone hard and threatening. Squirrel stared wide-eyed at him, no doubt surprised at hearing him come across like this. "We want to know what you and Squires talked about."

"Who's Squires?"

"The guy you were just talking to," Squirrel said. Although he was also trying to sound tough, his squeaky voice didn't help. "And don't deny it because me and my partner...we've been watching you."

"Maybe it's none of your damn business."

"We're making it our business." Howie gave Squirrel the cut-off signal.

"My friend here is a private detective," Squirrel said. "And he's got lots of cop friends and they don't mess around. They eat guys like you for lunch."

Howie rolled his eyes, wanting to put a cork in Squirrel's mouth.

"Hi, Sammy," a female voice said to Baldy. It was Elaine. "I've already met your friends, although I don't know their names." She eyed each of them. "You gentlemen ready for some company?"

"Beat it!" Howie snapped, his temper breaking.

Her smile froze on her face.

"Scram, I said!"

"Suit yourself." Elaine directed her attention to Sammy. "You should teach your friends some manners." She scowled at Howie. Turning on one very high heel, she walked away.

"Okay, Sammy," Howie said with a smile. "Tell us about Squires."

Sammy took out a pack of cigarettes from his shirt pocket and plucked one out. He lit it with a silver lighter, and then offered the pack around. Having no takers, he laid the pack on the table, and took a sip of his beer. "Even if you're a detective, I don't have to talk to you. I know my rights. You don't scare me."

Howie opened his coat, revealing the gun he had tucked in his belt. Squirrel's mouth dropped opened. Sammy said nothing, but a flicker of apprehension passed over his expression.

"Now, I'd suggest we have a nice conversation," Howie said. "Otherwise, we're going to take you some place where we can have a little more privacy."

"Like I said...you don't scare me." Although Sammy still tried to sound tough, his eyes betrayed a growing uneasiness. "I'm not going anyplace and you can't force me without making a scene. This is a public place and there are lots of witnesses. You wouldn't do anything so stupid."

"Who said I was smart?" Howie grinned, and leaned over and plucked the cigarette out of Sammy's mouth. He held it over Sammy's glass of beer for a moment, then let it drop into the brew. "Now I'm going to ask you once more. What were you and Squires talking about? And don't give me any runaround because I get impatient mighty fast." He noted the startled look on Squirrel's face. *Just keep your mouth shut and let me play this through.* He pulled out the gun and pointed it beneath the table at Sammy.

"What are you doing?" Sammy cried.

"Unless you're stupid, I think you can guess where this is aimed. If you still want to have a good time with your girlfriend over there, I'd suggest you start talking fast. This is a small caliber weapon and it doesn't make much noise. Place like this, it could go off and nobody would notice over the blare of the jukebox."

Beads of perspiration formed on Sammy's bald pate. "You're bluffing."

"Maybe I am." There was a click as Howie cocked the gun.

"Okay, okay. What do you want to know?"

"I've told you already. I don't like to repeat myself."

Sammy used a napkin to wipe his forehead. "Squires contacted me a couple of weeks ago."

"What for?"

"Man, I can't tell you that."

"What for?" Howie repeated.

"He...he needed some cash." Sammy gulped. He picked up his glass to take a swallow of beer, saw the cigarette butt floating on top, and set it back down. "I'm in the business of lending money to people on a short term basis."

"You're a loan shark?" Squirrel blurted out.

"Hey, watch it. I've got my pride." Sammy seemed to have forgotten the gun in order to defend his honor. "Loan shark's a nasty term. I'm a businessman."

"How much did he want to borrow?" Howie asked.

"Hey, give me a break. If word got out that I ratted on a client, I'd lose my customer base."

"I feel real sorry for you." Howie leaned over the table. "But if you don't tell me, you're going to lose something more important than your customer base."

Sammy wiped perspiration off his forehead and ran his tongue over his bottom lip. "Just a minute—don't get jumpy." He reached over and plucked the cigarette out of his drink, tossed the butt in the ashtray, and took a couple of gulps of beer. "Look, if I tell you this, you've got to keep it to yourself. Is that a deal?"

Howie smiled inwardly. JD was right about outsmarting the bad guys. "It's a deal," he said. "How much?"

"Two grand."

"How soon would he have to pay it back?"

"A couple of weeks."

"What would be the pay back?" Squirrel asked.

"Three grand."

"What! That's a fifty percent profit!" Squirrel shot a look toward Howie. "Can you imagine that? Making that kind of dough in just two weeks!"

"Hey, man," Sammy said, sounding offended. "I have to charge a high interest because it's high risk. I don't always get my money back."

"Did you give him the money tonight?" Howie asked.

"Are you kidding? We just finalized our agreement. I don't carry that much when I meet a guy for the first time. You never know what you're going to run in to...you know what I mean?"

"When does he get the money?"

"This Saturday."

On his drive back to his office, Edward Squires realized that he had forgotten to make it clear to Sammy that he didn't want to be called at the bank. He turned the car around, hoping the shark would still be there. When he walked in the front entrance and headed toward the back booth, he stopped in his tracks. That Cummins detective and his goofy partner were sitting in the booth with Sammy. "Those detectives are getting too damn nosey," he muttered. He quickly turned around and hurried back to his car. Slamming the door shut, he sat for a minute, trying to calm down. Something had to be done about them.

Howie and Squirrel spent another ten minutes with Sammy, pumping him for more information. He didn't know much more about Squires than the business they were conducting. Howie tucked the gun back into his waistband.

"Come on, let's go," he said to Squirrel. He glanced at Sammy. "We'll keep in touch."

Squirrel spoke up as soon as they had left the bar, his voice shaking with excitement. "Why didn't you tell me you carry a rod now? When you flashed that piece, you scared ten years out of my young life." He gave Howie a questioning look. "You wouldn't have shot him, would you?"

"If I had to."

Squirrel's mouth fell open. "Right there in the bar, you would've done it! Not even Bogie would've tried that. Wow! This is what being a detective is all about, isn't it? Life and death situations...living on the edge...having danger sit on your shoulder...being approached by beautiful women in seedy bars..."

"Squirrel."

"Rubbing out the bad guys...risking everything—"

"Squirrel!" Howie said again, but the little guy was on a roll. Howie reached inside his coat, pulled out the gun, and pointed it at him.

"Wha...what are you doing?" Squirrel stepped back. "Don't play around. That's not funny. Put...put that thing away, it might go off."

Howie pointed the gun at a tree and pulled the trigger.

227

Chapter 64

Howie couldn't help but be amused at the expression on Squirrel's face when he had pulled the trigger and a flag with the word *Bang* printed on it popped out. The reformed street hustler's eyes doubled in size and his hand flew to his chest as though his heart had just stopped.

"Man, I thought that gun was real!" Squirrel cried. "Where did you get that?"

"Wentworth dropped it."

"Where?"

"In the Fun House at Excelsior."

"How come you didn't show it to me then?"

"Are you kidding? After your ride on the Tilt-a-Whirl, you were too dizzy to see anything." Howie reset the flag and stuck the gun back in his waistband. An older gentleman on the other side of the street waved his cane at them and laughed. The old guy would sure have a story to tell when he got home.

After dropping Squirrel off at his apartment, Howie worked a couple hours at the drugstore. The time flew by as he lost count of the malts and sundaes he served. When he finished work, he dragged himself upstairs to his office. He poured himself a half glass of bourbon and sat down at his desk to go over some case notes. In less than ten minutes, his eyes were closing. He decided he'd had enough, even though it was barely after ten. He finished his drink, flipped off the lights and headed for the bedroom, hoping for a decent night's sleep. The next day he'd get up early, have a good breakfast, and resume working on the case. Though Beamer wasn't out of the picture yet, he'd given top priority to following Squires, their number one suspect.

He got up, had breakfast, and headed downstairs to talk with Kass. As soon as he stepped outside he found himself in a different world—one that had been transformed into a carnival. A gigantic Ferris wheel stood in place of the drugstore and Broadway had become the Midway. Crowds of men, women, and children milled about. He walked up to a man selling tickets to the Ferris wheel and discovered it was Kass.

"What happened to your drugstore?" he asked.

"Why, Howie, don't you remember? I traded it for a Ferris wheel."

After a brief conversation with Kass, he meandered through the crowds, stopping to watch people try their luck at winning a panda bear by throwing baseballs at milk bottles. Suddenly, he found himself chained to the back wall of a large canvas tent. Off to his right, a sign in bold black letters read: Shoot the Detective and Win a Stuffed Monkey. Directly in front of him not more than twenty feet away were clowns…hundreds of them…and all were lined up to try their luck. Those in the front lay their quarters down and picked up guns similar to the one Squires had dropped at the Fun House.

He struggled to break free, but couldn't. Off in the distance a calliope came to life, groaning out an eerie tune. The first clown stepped up. He looked familiar. Squires! Next to him stood Beamer. Beamer was the first to take aim. He pulled the trigger and Howie felt something whiz by his head. He turned and saw a bullet hole in the canvas. Beads of perspiration broke out on his forehead. The sounds of the calliope pounded in his head.

"My turn," Squires shouted as other clowns laughed and cheered. He took aim and fired. That bullet grazed Howie's arm.

Beamer smirked, pointed his gun at Howie, and yelled, "On the count of three. One…two…"

Howie awoke in a sweat. He turned on the nightstand lamp and checked the clock to make sure he was awake and that he was in his bedroom. Only a few minutes past eleven. Getting up, he found his way to the kitchen and poured himself a shot of bourbon. After downing a second, he headed back to bed. The phone rang just as he was about to switch off the light. He sat on the edge of the bed for a moment before stumbling out to his office to pick up the phone. "Howie Cummins here," he mumbled.

"This is Margo. I've got to talk to you."

Music and boisterous voices could be heard in the background. "Go ahead," Howie said. "I'm listening."

"I want—"

"Hey, bartender, bring us another round of drinks!" a man yelled.

"Just hang the hell on!" Margo shouted and then lowered his voice. "Listen, I can't talk right now. It's a zoo here. I'll call you when I get done with work. We close at one."

"No, no! I plan to be asleep by then."

"I'll stop by tomorrow morning then."

"You do that, but not too early." Howie hung up. Whatever Margo called about sounded urgent, but so was a good night's sleep.

Chapter 65

Howie had just finished his first morning cup of coffee and was sitting at his desk with his second cup when Margo dragged into his office. Sunken eyes, rimmed with dark circles, made the owner of The Watering Hole look like the lead in a zombie movie.

"You look beat," Howie said as his visitor slumped into a chair.

"Hell of a night." Margo stretched his long, muscular arms in front of him, and rubbed bloodshot eyes with the heels of his hands. "A couple of the regulars got carried away. It took forever to clean up after closing. Hell, I didn't get home until damn near two. Tossed and turned until four. Got up at six."

"What do you say we get down to business then? The sooner you tell me why you wanted to talk, the sooner you can go home and get some shut-eye." Howie took out his notepad and opened it to the page where he had notes concerning Donna Mae.

Margo leaned forward, his eyes now emitting the tense energy of a gathering storm. For a moment, he looked as though he might pound his fist on the desk. "I've just got to know who killed my Donna Mae!"

"I figured that's why you called." Howie took a sip of coffee, sorry for Margo. All the guy wanted was to find out who killed the love of his life. He couldn't blame him for that. "I tell you what. Let me fill you in as much as I'm able. You understand that I can't give you all the details."

"Why the hell not? I'm paying you, damn it! I've got a right to know!"

Howie didn't like being pushed. Although he could sympathize with him, he didn't want the guy botching up the case. He leveled a gaze at Margo and considered telling him to take a hike. But with a stack of unpaid bills in his desk, Howie couldn't afford to lose him as a client.

"Okay, I'll tell you what we know, but Margo, you've got to promise that you'll stay out of the way."

Margo's eyes narrowed sullenly, but he nodded.

"Good. Now, here are the basics. We think Donna Mae was killed because she found out the man she was dating had teamed up with her brother, Johnny, and another guy in a big heist five years ago."

"What did they hit? A bank?"

"No, they robbed a man of his rare coin collection."

"No shit. How much was it worth?"

"Plenty."

"Did they get away with it?"

"Not exactly. Donna Mae's brother and another member of the trio were killed in a shoot-out with the police. The coins were never recovered and the third member of the gang was never captured."

"So he made off with the loot?"

"I don't think so. It appears that Johnny stashed the coins someplace before he was killed. Neither the police nor anybody else knows where he hid them."

"So you think this jerk turned up and started dating Donna Mae because he thought she might know something about the coins?"

Howie picked up his letter opener, held it in both hands, turning it over and over before setting it aside. "That's the way it appears. The coins were never recovered."

"Any clues?"

"Just what we discovered in the totem pole."

"What does the key you found fit?"

"We're not sure. Maybe a safe deposit box."

"Have you tracked it down?"

"Not yet."

"Hell, it must be here in the Cities, don't you think?"

"Maybe. I don't know."

"How about that piece of paper? Doesn't that tell you?"

"It's coded. We haven't figured it out yet."

"I can help! Tell me what the damn thing says."

Howie drummed his fingers on the desk. If sharing the note with Margo kept the guy occupied for a few days, maybe it would be worth it. He opened his drawer, took out the paper, and handed it to him.

"DOG?" Margo scowled. "What the hell is that suppose to mean?"

"That's what we are trying to figure out." Howie took back the slip of paper.

"Hell, it could mean anything," Margo said. He settled back in the chair. "So whoever's after that information and the key is the guy who killed Donna Mae. Is that right?"

"I think you can make that assumption."

"And you thought you had the guy, but he was killed."

"That's right."

"How about the cops? Have they got any suspects?"

Howie had had enough. "Look, I've told you as much as I can," he said, irritated. "I promised my cop friend not to say anything since the case is still under investigation."

Margo knotted his eyebrows. He folded his arms against his massive chest. "All you guys stick together, don't you?"

The muscles in Howie's jaw tightened. "What do you mean by that crack?"

Margo's eyes darkened. "Nothing. I'm going home and get some sack time. It's going to be another tough night." He stood up and jabbed his finger at Howie. "Keep me the hell informed. You got that?"

Howie watched him leave. He opened his desk drawer and poured himself a drink, noticing but not concerned that his hand trembled as he raised the glass to his lips.

Chapter 66

Still smoldering from his morning meeting with Margo, Howie met with Mick and Adam in his office that afternoon. They had just finished reporting what happened at the motel with Beamer the night before.

"So he and his lady friend were all ready to…"

Mick nodded. "Oh, yes."

"And Oscar was all set to watch?"

"Yeah, just like he was at the movies but with a banana instead of a bag of popcorn." Mick grinned. "That little monkey has a kinky side to him."

Howie eyed Adam speculatively. "I think you should counsel Oscar on the wages of sin." Although Howie and Mick laughed, Adam didn't crack a smile.

"Why do you think Squires wants to borrow money from a loan shark?" Adam asked.

"Yeah," Mick said. "Why didn't he just give himself a loan? That would be easy for him, being in the banking business."

"Maybe he's already given himself a loan," Howie said. "A very special loan."

Adam frowned. "Are you insinuating he embezzled from the bank?"

"Could be." Howie set his notepad aside. "A person of Squires' standing must be doing something illegal if he's dealing with a loan shark. It wouldn't surprise me to find out that he's dipped into the cash drawer."

"But what would be his motive for killing Donna Mae?" Mick asked.

"I've been thinking about that." Howie rocked in his chair for a moment. "We might be dealing with two different issues here. Squires may be, as JD likes to say, one of those outstanding community citizens who crossed to the other side."

Mick leaned forward. "So you don't think he killed the Labelle woman?"

"I'm switching my bets back to Beamer on that one," Howie said. "But I wouldn't be surprised if the two of them are in this for the money."

"What do you suggest we do?" Adam asked.

"You and Mick continue to track Beamer. I'll deal with Squires. I'm also going to talk with Beamer's wife."

"Sounds good," Mick said. "Do you think she suspects that her husband is playing around?"

"I'm counting on it, because then she'll be more open to talking to someone with a sympathetic ear." Howie fielded a stern look from Adam. "Is there a problem?"

Adam's jaw muscles tightened. "You're taking advantage of her."

"How so?"

"By letting her think you care about what's going on with her marriage, when all the time you're just there to pump her for information."

"So?"

"Isn't that a little dishonest?"

Howie chose his words carefully. "What I care about is finding Donna Mae's killer. And if that means I've got to soft-talk a woman whose marriage is falling apart in order to get to her husband, who I think is the killer, I will."

"I wouldn't do it."

"I'm not asking you to, am I? Just remember. What they teach in seminary doesn't always work in the real world."

"How would *you* know what they teach?"

"I know one thing for sure. Killers aren't caught by preaching the golden rule. They're caught by those who aren't afraid to get down and dirty."

"Are you implying I can't do detective work?"

Mick held up his hands. "Whoa, wait a minute, guys. Let's all just calm down."

Adam shot up out of his seat, crossed to the window, and stood staring down at the street.

Howie regretted the sharp tone he had taken with Adam. The guy had enough of a struggle dealing with issues involved in becoming a minister. Working as a detective just increased the intensity of his internal struggles. "Look," he said, softening his tone. "I didn't mean to come down on you so hard."

"Come on, Adam," Mick said. "We're all tired and edgy with this case. Howie didn't mean it the way it sounded."

Several long seconds passed before Adam turned and faced his partners. "I guess I didn't help by getting on my high horse, either. Seeing Beamer's wife is probably the right thing to do. I just don't think I could do it." He headed for the door.

"Where are you going?" Howie asked.

"Nowhere. Anywhere. I've got to get out of here for a while." Adam paused at the door and glanced back at Howie. "I may not agree with you, but I understand you've got to do what you've got to do."

"Why don't you go and talk to Kass," Mick suggested softly.

Adam chewed on his lip. "I just may do that." He left, closing the door quietly behind him.

Howie picked up the phone and called Beamer at his office. As soon as Beamer answered, he hung up. "He's still at work," he told Mick.

"So what are you going to do now?"

"I'm going to pay his wife a visit and hope she's home." He copied Beamer's address from the phone book, and then he and Mick headed downstairs.

"Good luck," Mick said as they stepped outside into a cloudless, warm day.

"Thanks. You want to come along?"

"I would, but I promised Mary I'd help get ready for later. We have got another couple coming over tonight. We're going to share the news about Mary's pregnancy."

Howie looked toward the drugstore. "Do you think Adam went in to see Kass?"

"Stay here and I'll check." Mick walked to the corner and peeked in the window of the drugstore. Within moments, he turned toward Howie, and gave him thumbs-up.

Chapter 67

Kass stopped filling napkin holders, watching as Adam settled on a stool at the soda fountain. "You look troubled, my boy. Anything wrong?"

"Oh, it's been one of those days."

"Sorry to hear that."

"Yeah. Me too. But that's the way it goes sometimes."

"Anything you want to talk about?"

"I don't think so."

Adam sat silently, gnawing at his lip and watching his friend. After a couple of minutes, he glanced around to make sure there were no customers within hearing range. "Howie and I got into it," he quietly said.

Kass glanced over at him as he refilled napkin holders.

"It had to do with detective work," Adam continued. "We don't always agree on how it should be done."

Kass closed the holder he was filling and set it aside. "I've never been a detective, but I'd think wanting to be a minister and doing detective work could present conflicts."

"You've got that right." Adam ran his tongue over his bottom lip. "Kass, could I have a glass of water, please?"

"Of course." Kass scooped ice into a glass, filled it with water, and set it in front of Adam. He waited until his friend finished quenching his thirst. "Conflict isn't always bad, you know, especially when a person struggles to find their purpose in life."

Adam set the glass down. "You know me pretty well, don't you?"

"I should," Kass said, his eyes twinkling. "You've been coming in here since grade school." He paused. "I've told you about some of my relatives who died in the concentration camps during World War II, haven't I?"

"Yeah."

"Have I ever told you about my Uncle Hershel?"

"I don't think so," Adam replied, wondering what lesson of life this story would hold.

"Uncle Hershel was interned in one of those camps. He barely survived." Kass waved at an elderly woman who was leaving. "That's Mrs.

Clingwood. If I don't wave, she'll think I'm mad at her and I'll never hear the end of it." He scratched the top of his bald head. "Where was I now?"

"You were telling me about your uncle."

"Oh, yes." He cleared his throat. "As a prisoner, Uncle Hershel found himself doing things he never thought he would do."

"What kind of things?"

A flicker of sadness passed through Kass' eyes. "Things that went against his sense of right and wrong."

Adam stared at his glass, slowly sliding his finger around its rim. "So what you're saying is that there may be times when you have to decide whether or not to do something that goes against your values?"

Kass nodded.

"Doesn't seem right."

"That depends."

"On what?"

"It may be justified if it's for a greater purpose." Kass took his time to refill Adam's glass, allowing the younger man to reflect upon his words. "That must be true in detective work, Adam. You may not always feel right doing certain things, but they're done in order to solve the case, and right a wrong."

"Okay, but where do you draw the line?"

"Ah, that's a tough question. Each of us has to struggle to find the answer for ourselves."

"I was afraid you'd say that. I guess I...I was looking for a pat answer."

"There are none. Life is seldom black and white. There are only shades of gray." Kass poured himself a glass of water and took a sip.

"Why does it have to be so complicated, Kass?"

Kass shrugged. "Because God made us a complicated world. It's no Garden of Eden out there and He didn't leave us a blueprint for living in it."

"So where does that leave us?"

"To do the best we can."

Adam stared at the ice cubes melting in his glass. Finally, he moved his glass aside and got up to leave.

"By the way, whatever happened to your uncle?"

A gentle smile lit Kass' face and he winked at Adam. "After being liberated, Uncle Herschel became a private investigator. He devoted his life to tracking down those who ran such camps."

Chapter 68

On his way to see Beamer's wife, Howie reflected on what had happened between him and Adam. There was no question that his partner would make a good minister. Adam really felt for people and always tried to do what was right. Whether he could ever make it as a full-time detective was another question.

Then again, if the roles were reversed, Howie would never make it as a minister. The reason was simple. In detective work the boundary lines between right and wrong were often blurred. Howie had understood that right from the beginning. He didn't have any qualms about it. Adam tried to live by the maxim that you should do unto others as you would have them do unto you. In this business, you did unto others before they got the chance to stick it unto you.

A late model, dark-blue Buick sat in the driveway at Beamer's rambler. Howie pulled up, watching a petite, plain woman with long brunette hair carry groceries through the side door of the house. He parked in front, got out, and walked up to the woman who had just lifted out another bag of groceries. As he approached, she eyed him with a certain amount of apprehension.

"Mrs. Beamer?"

"Yes?"

"I'm Howie Cummins from the MAC Detective Agency. I'd like to ask you some questions."

She scowled slightly.

"About what?"

"The murder of Arthur Wentworth."

Apprehension transformed into alarm.

"Why do you want to talk to me?" she asked defensively. "He was my husband's partner."

"Wentworth's name came up as part of a case I've been hired to investigate and I just want to talk to everyone who may have known him. This is just a routine investigation. Actually, you're the sixth person I've talked to today."

She shifted her bag of groceries from one arm to the other, resting it on her hip.

"I'd like to get your perspective on Mr. Wentworth," Howie said gently, ready to work his winsome charms on her. "You may think you don't have much to offer, but every little piece of information is important. May I have a few minutes of your time? I promise it won't take long."

She hesitated but finally nodded her okay.

"Good. Why don't you let me help you with your groceries?" Without waiting for her reply, he picked up a couple bags and followed her into the house.

"Just set them on the table," she said as they walked into the kitchen. "Let me put away a few cold things and then we can talk." After she put the milk and other items into the refrigerator, she turned to him. "Would you like a cup of coffee?"

"Thanks, but you don't have to bother."

"Oh, it's not any bother at all."

"Are you sure? In that case then, I'd love a cup." To share a cup of coffee was perfect. People opened up more in a relaxed atmosphere. Besides, Beamer's poor wife sounded like she craved company. Knowing what he now knew about her husband, Howie figured she probably spent many evenings alone. He sat at the table, watching her pour the coffee. The lady wore little makeup. Her thin eyebrows matched the color of her pale-brown eyes. She was one of those unfortunate women for whom a trip to the beauty salon would be a waste of time.

"Here you go," she said with a warm smile, setting his coffee on the table. After pouring herself a cup, she sat down across from him. "I hope you don't mind sitting in the kitchen?" Her tone sounded apologetic.

"By no means. This is very homey." Howie took a sip of watery coffee. "This really hits the spot. Best coffee I've had in a long time."

"Thank you." Flattered, she gave him a mousy smile and seemed to relax a bit more.

"I bet you and your husband spend a lot of time in here having coffee and talking," he said, hoping she would take the bait. She did.

"Not as much as I'd like," she said regretfully, and with a hint of anger. "He's so busy with his work. I tell him that he should relax more, but he says his work provides a roof over our heads."

"He's lucky to have such an understanding wife."

"Thank you." She sipped her coffee. "Now, you wanted to know about Mr. Wentworth, didn't you?"

"Yes."

"Well, I'm afraid I can't tell you too much. I only met him a couple of times."

"So, you weren't involved with their clowning activities?"

"I'm afraid not. Jack didn't want me around. He said that, for him, it was a diversion from all the pressures of life. I guess men have to be with men at times." She gazed at her cup for several moments and offered a weak smile. "Every now and then I get together with some of the girls I graduated from high school with. We go bowling— I guess it's the same thing."

"And it sounds like fun." Howie cleared his throat. "So your husband doesn't talk much about his clowning?"

"No, why do you ask?"

"I just thought if he did, he might've mentioned some things about Wentworth. I figured that maybe you picked up on some things that he may have forgotten to tell me."

"Jack doesn't talk much about his outside activities when he gets home. He likes to sit in front of the television and watch the ball game. He says it's his only way of relaxing." She lowered her eyes as if confessing something about herself.

"Mrs. Beamer, I—"

"Call me Doris. Mrs. Beamer sounds so...so old." She glanced at the back of her hands. "Lord knows I feel ancient as it is."

"Okay...Doris. And please call me Howie. Your husband has certainly impressed me with his vast knowledge of the real estate business. How long has he been in that line of work?"

"Only since we've been married."

"And how long has that been?"

"Four years next month."

He gave her his best smile.

"Happy anniversary in advance."

"Thank you."

"What did he do before he got into real estate?"

"I'm embarrassed to say I don't know. When we first started dating, he told me that he was between jobs." She glanced at his cup. "May I warm that up for you?"

"Sure, why not? You make a great cup."

She got up and refilled their cups before continuing. "You have to understand my husband. He doesn't like to talk about his past. He's a very private person."

"Does he keep a lot from you?" Howie asked, the underlying implication of his question made clear by his tone.

For a long time Doris Beamer didn't say anything. Only the hum of the refrigerator's motor interfered with the silence.

"It started a couple of years ago," she said, slowly rotating her wedding ring. "Jack began staying away more and more nights, claiming he had nightly business meetings. At first, I believed him because I know there are odd hours in his line of work. But then I began to notice little things. Like the scent of perfume on his shirts. One night he said he'd be working late at his office. I decided to check. I drove by. The office windows were dark. I knew then."

"That had to be hard."

Her voice grew angry. "Maybe if I could've convinced him to have children...but he didn't want any. At least if I had a baby, I'd have someone to keep me company in the evenings. I wouldn't care then what he did." She blinked back tears and shivered as if cold.

240

After a long period of silence, Howie cleared his throat. "Listen, Doris, I need to go."

She reached out and caught hold of his arm, stopping him.

"Do you know the crazy part of all of this?"

Howie shook his head. More tears came, but they now flowed from eyes filled with a seething anger.

"I still love him, but one day he may find out I no longer need him."

Jack Beamer looked forward to spending several hours with Cindy. Since those detectives interrupted his fun the other evening, he was ready for some real action. He had called his wife and explained that he had a meeting tonight with a potential buyer. Doris sounded different over the phone. In the past, she had always folded without question. This time, however, she asked some rather pointed questions. *What time can I expect you home? Is there a number I can reach you in case I had to? What client are you with?* When he tried to sidestep her questions, she had gotten angry with him and hung up. He had never heard her get angry before. That concerned him. Their anniversary was next month. He would take her out to a movie and dinner, and buy her some roses. That should settle her down and keep her happy.

Chapter 69

After Howie left Doris Beamer, he decided to have a talk with Angela Drake. According to Mick, the Drake woman worked at the same bank as Edward Squires. Miss Drake, a bank teller, had dated Squires at one time. Howie went back to his office and called her at the bank. Once he explained who he was and why he wanted to talk with her, she agreed to meet at a local restaurant after work.

The restaurant, on France Ave in Edina, wasn't crowded at this time of day. Howie walked in and found her waiting for him. A slender woman with long dark hair, she wore a white long-sleeve turtleneck sweater and a pleated black skirt. He slid into the booth across from her.

"Hi, Miss Drake, I'm Howie Cummins. Glad you could make it," he said with as much charm as he could, entertaining thoughts that his social life might have a chance of being recharged. Angela Drake was the exact opposite of Doris Beamer. A gorgeous brunette with a beautiful complexion and smile, and body to match, she was a female work of art that would fit anyone's idea of what a private eye would have adorning his right arm.

"I don't have a lot of time," she said.

"Why's that?" he asked, his eyes on her full lips.

"I'm meeting my fiancé in a half hour. We're going shopping and then out to supper. We're getting married next year and we have to start planning."

Damn. Jolted back to reality.

"Congratulations," Howie said, trying to sound sincere. "Since you're short on time, I'll get right to it. What can you tell me about Edward Squires?"

"Not much. Like I told you over the phone, we only went out twice."

"Why wasn't there a third date?"

"He was too much of a stuffed-shirt for me."

The waitress came by, and Howie ordered coffee while Angela ordered a glass of lemonade. After they were served, he resumed his questioning. "What did you talk about on those dates?"

"Mostly me," she replied, blushing at her answer. "He did talk a little about clowning, though. That he was involved in that kind of thing surprised me."

"Did he ever talk about where he came from? What kind of job he had before coming to the bank? Anything like that?"

"He never talked about his past, if that's what you mean. It's not that I didn't ask." She lowered her eyes for a moment. "But every time I asked questions about him, he'd brush them aside and change the subject, mostly turning the conversation back on me. It was flattering, but sometimes a girl gets tired of talking about herself."

Howie pushed his coffee aside and leaned forward on the table. "How about his dealings at the bank? Did you hear anything about those?"

"What do you mean?"

"You know what I'm talking about. There are always rumors floating around the workplace. Any about him?"

"Mr. Cummins, how would I know?" she said defensively. "I'm just a lowly teller. Edward was the vice president. You know, I was really surprised when he asked me out." She took a sip of lemonade, leaving a rich, red imprint of her lipstick on the glass.

"Come on, Miss Drake," he said, turning on the charm. "Give it some thought. Bank tellers and secretaries know more about what's going on at work than anybody else."

"Well..." She smiled, and Howie noticed she had dimples. "I did overhear a couple of managers talking over coffee break that he might be having some financial difficulty. Nothing came of it. I mean I didn't hear anything more so I guess it must've been just a rumor."

"Where did the two of you go on dates?"

"Both times we had dinner at very exclusive restaurants. If he was having financial problems, he didn't let it show."

"Did he ever try and get fresh with you?"

Her eyes widened in surprise. "Not in the least. He was always a perfect gentleman, but..."

"But what?"

She waited for a waitress to pass. "There was this one time when the waiter brought the wrong soup. Edward got quite upset. The waiter apologized, but when he came back with the soup we had originally ordered, it was lukewarm. I thought it was sort of funny, but Edward became furious. He raised such a fuss that the manager gave us our meals on the house. He was still fuming about it when he brought me home."

"So he's got a temper?"

"Oh, yes."

"Were you ever frightened of it?"

"Not for myself." She glanced around and lowered her voice. "But I think he could get violent if he really lost it. I felt so bad for that waiter. I mean, after all, what's the big deal about lukewarm soup?"

"Anything else you can tell me about him?"

"Not that I can think of. Why are you investigating him?"

"I just needed to check on him through an independent source. He could be a witness in an upcoming court trial." He gave her a cautioning smile. "Let me give you some friendly advice, Miss Drake. Don't mention to Squires or to any of your friends that you met with a detective about him."

"Oh, I won't."

"Good. Because if you did, you could be in a lot of trouble when this case comes up to trial. And I would think you'd want to keep your name out of this if at all possible."

Her mouth dropped open. "I don't want to cause any trouble. I promise I won't tell anyone."

Angela left. Howie stayed for a second cup of coffee. Although Beamer was still his primary suspect, Squires was rapidly closing the gap.

Chapter 70

Adam sat quietly as Howie finished briefing him and Mick on his visits earlier with Doris Beamer and Angela Drake. Although he disagreed with Howie's methods, he had to admit they got results.

"Doris Beamer is a volcano ready to erupt at any moment," Howie said. "And apparently our banker friend can throw quite a tantrum when he wants to."

"So Angela Drake thinks Squires' temper could become violent?" Mick asked.

Howie nodded.

"Violent enough to commit murder?"

"I didn't ask her that, but we can't rule it out as a possibility."

"Did that change your mind on Beamer?" Adam asked.

"No, it just convinces me that Squires was involved in some way."

"Well, I think he's the killer," Mick said.

"What have you got for us to do?" Adam asked Howie, refusing to judge either Beamer or Squires until they got more conclusive evidence.

"You and Mick go up to the hospital and see if McGuire's up to talking. If he is, try and find out what happened to him."

"What if he doesn't want to talk?"

"Oh, I think he might be more than willing to talk considering he got his face bashed in. Don't be afraid to press him. I'd go myself, but I'm due to work at the drugstore in an hour, and tomorrow morning Squirrel and I are going to pay a visit to Jack Beamer."

"Sounds good to me," Mick said. "Anything else?"

"That's it for now."

Mick nudged Adam with an elbow. "Let's go, partner. The sooner we go, the sooner we're done."

For most of the ride to the hospital Adam remained quiet. He didn't like what they were doing.

"Howie never misses an angle, does he?" he said as he pulled into the hospital parking lot. "McGuire just had his brains knocked out, and he wants us to pump him for information."

"You've got to remember we're working on a murder case here."

Adam parked the car, switched off the ignition, and sat for a moment, his hands gripping the steering wheel. The conversation with Kass had helped, but nagging questions kept coming up. "Mick, don't you ever struggle with some of the things we do?"

"I don't know if I'd say I struggle with them. Some times I feel a little crummy about some things, but it passes."

"How do you work through it?"

Mick sat thoughtfully for a moment. "I guess I just remind myself of the why we're doing the things in the first place. After we solve a case, I look back on certain things that we did that may have bothered me at the time and I discover that they weren't as big of a deal as I thought when I consider the whole picture." He paused to give Adam a meaningful look. "Howie's got a point when he says that right and wrong isn't always black and white."

"But shouldn't there be situations where you draw the line?"

"Of course there are."

"Then what do you do after you've drawn the line and you're asked to cross it?"

"I guess you have to be honest with yourself."

Adam gnawed at his lip, trying to understand how Mick could be so matter-of-fact about an issue that kept him up at night. "And what does that mean when it comes to detective work?"

"Either you decide to compromise your standards or..."

"Or what?"

"Walk away."

"You mean from being a detective?" Adam had struggled with whether he should walk away from the ministry, but that was because he felt he couldn't live up to the standards. Though detective work challenged him in terms of where to draw the line, he loved the excitement. He felt as much drawn to being a detective as he did to becoming a minister...maybe even more so.

"Give it some time," Mick said. "Don't walk away from it now. You're too good of a detective. Besides, you keep Howie and me in check. You may just find out as time goes by that you'll need to reevaluate where you have drawn the line."

"Why, because the work will have hardened me?"

"No, because you'll realize you've drawn the line too quickly."

Adam listened to the faint wailing of a siren in the distance. It got louder as it came in their direction...an ambulance on its way to the hospital. "I'll think about it. Thanks."

"Sure." Mick opened his car door partway. "What do you say we go up and pay McGuire that visit?"

The two detectives stopped at the receptionist desk in the lobby. "Take the elevator to the fourth floor and turn to the right when you get off," the receptionist instructed. "Mr. McGuire's room is about halfway down from the nurses' station."

246

"What if there's a nurse in his room?" Adam asked as they rode in the elevator. "Do you think she'll let us talk to him if he's still in rough shape?"

"We'll tell her we're relatives."

"Really? Just where do you draw the line, Mick?" Adam asked as the elevator doors opened.

"My lines are drawn with a pencil. Sometimes I have to use an eraser."

There was no nurse in Les' room, but his sister, Bernadine, sat in a chair by his bed. She rose to meet them as they walked in.

Les McGuire had bandages wrapped around his forehead. His left eye was swollen shut and the right side of his jaw had several stitches. It would leave a nasty scar. As bad as he looked, at least he had no IV's or tubes coming out of his body.

"He's improving," she whispered. "He's even spoken to me."

"What did he say?" Mick asked.

"He called me by name."

"Anything else?"

Bernadine smiled at her brother. He appeared to be resting comfortably. "He mumbled something about his car business. I couldn't understand everything but I got the impression that he wants me to take it over for him for now."

"You would do that?" Adam asked.

She nodded. "Even though we haven't always seen things the same way, we stick together when times are tough. I've been praying for him."

"Do you think we could speak to him for a minute?" Mick asked.

"Is it really necessary?" She grew silent for a moment. "I mean, he's doing better, but I'm not sure if he'd be up to it."

"Maybe she's right," Adam said, shrugging uncomfortably.

Mick placed a hand on Bernadine's shoulder. "Look, I know this is hard, but you do want to find out who did this to him, don't you?"

"Yes, but..."

"And whoever did it is still out there someplace. As long as he's free, your brother isn't safe."

Bernadine nodded. "You're right. Go ahead, but don't press him too much. He's still very weak."

"We understand," Mick said. "Why don't you go home for a while and get some rest?"

"Oh, I don't know if I should." She gave a worried look at her brother.

"Look," Mick said. "If there are any changes the hospital will call. For Les' sake, you need to take care of yourself as well. You can come back this evening."

She took in a deep breath. "I guess you're right." She picked up her purse and gave one last look at her brother.

As soon as Bernadine left, Mick and Adam moved over to the side of the bed. "Les, this is Mick Brunner. Adam Trexler's with me. We want to know who did this to you."

Les' one eye opened slowly. He turned his head ever so slightly and his lips moved.

"What's he saying?" Adam asked.

"I don't know." Mick bent over and put his ear close to Les' mouth. A moment later he straightened up.

"What did he say?"

"I'm not sure."

After his visitors had left, Les McGuire opened his eye and scanned the room. He had fooled Brunner and his partner by pretending he was out of it. It had bought him a little time. His head pounded, his mouth was dry, his whole body hurt, but he had to get out of there. There were a few unfinished things he had to do. Somehow he would find the strength to crawl out of bed, get on his feet and go do them. He was determined to get those coins. Once he sold them, he could make a new life for himself. Perhaps, he would open up a new car dealership in Florida. *Yeah. Miami would be nice. No more selling old junky cars. No more cold Minnesota winters.* Even more importantly, however, was moving someplace where his partner would never find him again.

With great difficulty, he slowly moved back the covers, struggled to sit up, and finally managed to sit on the edge of the bed.

Chapter 71

"Do you think he's here?" Squirrel asked as Howie parked in front of Beamer's office. "It's barely nine. Maybe he doesn't come in this early or maybe he takes Tuesday mornings off."

"He's here, all right."

Squirrel's eyes nearly doubled in size as he stared at Howie with awe. "Wow! That's terrific! That's some of that detective intuition, isn't it?"

"Not quite."

"How did you figure then?"

"His car's parked in the lot next to the building." Howie opened the car door. "Come on. Let's see what he has to say, but remember let me do the talking."

"Okay, boss. Whatever you say." Squirrel scooted out of the car and waited for Howie to join him on the sidewalk. "Are you going to tell him that you've talked to his wife?"

"I don't think so." Howie recalled the cold anger in her eyes, and wondered what kind of reception Beamer had gotten when he had come home last night.

"Does Mick still think Squires is the killer?"

Howie nodded.

"How about you?"

"He's certainly a suspect, but in my book, Beamer's the guilty one." Howie glanced at the real estate office to make sure Beamer wasn't peering out the windows.

Squirrel's eyes danced with excitement. "How are you going to get him to crack?"

"You're sure full of questions today."

"Hey, boss, I've got to learn, don't I? So how are you going to get him to break?" Squirrel persisted as the two of them started up the sidewalk.

"If I can catch him in a lie, I'll confront him."

"If that doesn't work, I know how to get him to talk."

Howie stopped and eyed Squirrel suspiciously. "How?"

Squirrel buffed his fingernails and offered a smug smile. "I have my ways."

"You do, huh? And what have you got in mind?" Howie couldn't imagine Squirrel strong-arming Oscar the monkey into confessing.

The little guy reached into his pocket. "Using these."

"Squirrel!" Howie exclaimed. "Where did you get those brass knuckles?"

"One of my connections got them for me."

"Put them away, will you?" Howie waited until Squirrel slipped his tools of persuasion back into his pocket. "You've been watching too many gangster movies. Come on. We're wasting time out here." He started toward the entrance.

Squirrel hurried to catch up. "Okay, but they're yours to use."

"I don't think so." Howie laughed to himself. Adam would be shocked to know that he had standards as well. He would never think of resorting to brass knuckles, but then again, if the situation called for them...

They walked into Beamer's office and found it empty. An opened manila file folder containing papers lay on the desk. A nearly full cup of coffee sat to the right of the folder. Howie felt the cup.

"What are you doing?"

"Think about it, Squirrel," Howie said, keeping his voice to a whisper. "What do you think I'm doing?"

Squirrel's nose twitched. "Oh, I get it. If it's still hot, it means it was just poured."

"Good! Now you're beginning to think like a detective."

"I am?" Squirrel threw out his chest as though he had just graduated from detective school. "Was it hot?"

"Not even warm."

"So where is he?"

"Probably in the back room."

"Maybe he's teaching the monkey a new trick," Squirrel said. "Do you think so?"

Howie shrugged and rapped on the desk with his knuckles. "Hey! Anybody here?"

Squirrel tiptoed over to the door and pressed his ear to the door. "Not a sound."

"Something's not right here," Howie said. "Let's see what's going on in there." He opened the door and stepped inside. "Oh, man!"

"What's wrong?" Squirrel cried, peering into the room over Howie's shoulder.

"It's Beamer!" The real estate agent lay face down on the floor in a pool of his own blood. A wooden chair had toppled over beside him. Howie rushed over to him, dropped to one knee, and felt for a pulse.

Squirrel leaned against the door frame, his face drained of color. "How...how is he?"

"Not good."

"What do you mean, not good?"

Howie stood up. "Not good as in good and dead."

250

Chapter 72

It had been a little over ten minutes since Howie had put the call into Jim Davidson. While waiting for Davidson, he went through Beamer's file cabinet and desk. He also checked the place for Oscar, but the monkey was not to be found.

Squirrel had designated himself as the lookout, taking a position next to the window and peeking out every so often while Howie checked the area. "The cops just pulled up!" he cried.

Howie closed the desk drawer. Although he had found several receipts from a motel near the airport, he didn't find anything that connected Beamer to Donna Mae LaBelle. "How much time do I have?"

"They're out of their car and are casing the area," Squirrel said, his nose now twitching. "They're looking in this direction!"

"Hang tight. This will only take a minute." Howie used his handkerchief to wipe clean the handles on the desk drawers, file cabinet, and anything else he might have touched. He checked the desk to make sure he had put everything back in place.

"Man, hurry up! Here they come!"

Howie moved to the front of the desk and casually took a seat, gesturing his nervous friend over. "Just take it easy and relax," he said as Squirrel plopped down in the other chair next to him.

Squirrel rubbed his palms on his pants legs, folded his arms in front of him, crossed his legs, and began jiggling his foot.

Within moments the door opened and JD, along with two uniform police officers, walked in. "Malloy, you go out and put up the tape," Davidson said to the taller of the two officers. "Be sure to tape off the parking lot."

"The whole lot, Detective?"

"Yeah, the whole lot. That's the victim's car out there and we don't want anyone messing with it." Davidson turned his attention to the other officer. "You stand outside the door and watch for the coroner." After the second officer left, JD offered Howie a half-smirk. "So you've got another body for me, huh? You're sure drumming up the business."

"Just want to keep the North Side's finest working."

"You guys didn't touch anything, did you?"

"Of course not."

"Like hell you didn't. I just hope you were smart enough to wipe your prints off." JD gestured to Squirrel. "What's he doing here?"

"Hey, give me a break, Detective. I'm on your side."

"He's with me," Howie said. "I'll vouch for him."

A smug grin swept over Squirrel's face. He raised his hand and waved it back and forth.

"What do you want?" Davidson asked with a note of irritation in his tone.

"I was just wondering. How did you figure that the car in the parking lot belonged to Beamer?"

"You tell him," Davidson said, giving Howie a look as though asking if he really wanted to vouch for this character.

"They ran a check on the license plate."

"We're done with detective school now," JD said. "Where's the body?"

"In the back room," Howie said. "It's pretty bloody."

"You guys mind if I go outside?" Squirrel asked. "I need some fresh air."

"Go ahead." Howie led JD to where Beamer's body lay.

Davidson scanned the room for several minutes before squatting to examine the body. "Shot in the temple just like Wentworth."

"How do you suppose this went down?"

JD stood up. "I figure somebody came in, took Beamer back here, and shot him."

"Do you think it was a robbery?"

"Naw. The desk doesn't look like it's been touched and his wallet is still in his back pocket." JD squatted again, examined the body for a minute and stood.

"Got any suspects in mind?" Howie asked.

"Sure."

"Who?"

"The monkey," Davidson quipped without missing a beat. He glanced around, puzzled. "By the way, where is that monkey?"

"I don't know. He's not here."

"There you go," JD said, still keeping his poker face. "The monkey did it and took off for the jungle. Case closed. Now I can go on my vacation."

"Come on, get serious. Who's your suspect?"

JD stared at Howie for a moment. "This isn't official, but my bet's on his partner, Squires. Trouble is I ran a check on him."

"And?"

"The guy's clean. Not even a speeding ticket. Of course, he could've changed identities. In any case, I'm going to have to take him in for questioning." JD gave Howie a hard look. "You don't by chance have any idea where I can find him?"

"None whatsoever. If it was Squires, he probably skipped town by now."

"He might've, but that would only prove his guilt," JD said. "If he's as smart as I think he is, he's going to play it cool and stick around. He knows we don't have anything on him. After I'm done here, I'm going up to his office and put the squeeze on him."

Howie was anxious to start following up on his own leads. "You need me for anything?"

"Yeah, you and Squirrel are going to have to give a statement."

"Do we have to go down to the station?"

JD offered a hint of a grin. "If it was anyone else but me, you would. But since I'm such a nice guy, I'll take your statements here."

After Squirrel came back in, Howie shared with JD the information that his partners had followed Beamer to a motel where he had a rendezvous with a woman. He also mentioned his visit with Beamer's wife, but only because he figured JD would find out anyway as part of his investigation. He didn't mention, however, her seething anger. "So after interviewing his wife, I decided it was time to pay Beamer another visit."

"He brought me along as his backup," Squirrel said with a proud grin.

"Anything else you want to tell me?" JD asked Howie.

"Like what?"

"Don't give me those innocent baby blues. Like how this ties in with the case you and your partners have been working on."

"Look, I've told you everything." Howie wasn't about to reveal that Beamer had been his number one suspect all along. But now that he was dead, he would turn his attention to Squires. He hoped he could nab the guy before the police did. JD might get angry with him for not being totally open, but he'd get over it.

JD asked a few other, mainly routine, questions for his report, and dismissed them. "Be sure to keep in touch if you find out anything else."

"Will do."

"One more thing."

"Yeah?"

"No more bodies, okay? I've got a week's vacation coming up and I want to be able to take it."

Howie gave JD a half-smile before he and Squirrel headed for the door. He would drop Squirrel off, go back to his office and call Adam and Mick to inform them of Beamer's death. In order to get a head start on the cops in finding Squires, he would ask his partners to come up to his office for a meeting. The sooner they got on this, the better.

On the way back to the North Side, Howie kept going over in his mind the financial problems Squires had and how that tied in with Beamer.

Did Beamer find out that Squires was after the coins? Had he tried to horn in on him because he needed the money? And what about Wentworth? Why had he been murdered?

"Hey, I just thought of something!" Squirrel blurted out.

"And what's that?"

"What happened to the monkey?"

"I don't know. Davidson asked me that same question."

"Do you think he witnessed Beamer's murder?"

"That could be."

"If that's the case, then the killer took him." Squirrel paused. "My theory is that we're going to find that monkey dead because of him being a witness."

"I wouldn't worry about that. It's not like Oscar is going to name the killer."

"You can let me off at the next corner," Squirrel said.

Howie pulled over to let him out. "How come you're getting off here?"

"I'm going to go talk to one of my contacts."

"Who's that?"

"Louie 'the lip' Lotterman. He used to do circus work whenever one was in town. You never know. Louie might've heard of someone trying to sell a monkey. If that's so, and I find out who, it'd break this case wide open."

Howie stifled a chuckle. "Good luck with Louie. Call me if you find out anything."

After dropping Squirrel off, he drove to his apartment. He fixed himself a sandwich, poured himself a cup of coffee, and sat down at his desk to call Mick and Adam. He had just taken a bite of his sandwich when he heard unfamiliar footsteps coming up the stairs. *Bogie, if this is a new client, let it be a nice, simple easy case.*

The door flew open and his "new client" walked in, holding a gun on him.

Chapter 73

Squires' hand was shaking, but he kept the gun pointed at Howie. "I need your help."

Howie stared at him, his eyes narrowed. "That's a funny way of showing it."

"The police think I killed my partners."

"Did you?"

"No! I swear to you I'm innocent."

Howie kept his voice calm. He had a gut feeling that if Squires pulled the trigger, it wouldn't be a red flag popping out of the barrel. "Guns make me nervous. Especially when they're pointed at me. Why don't you put that thing away and then we can talk?"

Beads of perspiration formed on Squires' forehead. "Oh, no. I'm not taking any chances of being turned over to the police."

"Okay, have it your way." By keeping his own nerves under control, Howie hoped Squires would relax a bit. "Let's talk. You said partners. That means you knew about Beamer's death. How did you find that out?"

"I stopped by his office this morning. I...I found him in the back room. It was horrible."

"Why didn't you call the cops?"

"I don't know. I...I just panicked."

"What happened to the monkey?"

"I took him with me. I didn't want to leave him there."

For a guy who said he had panicked, it seemed odd he'd still had the presence of mind to take Oscar. "Tell me about Beamer," Howie said.

"I don't know what he was involved in, but he asked me to check on a key for him."

"Why you?"

"Because of me being a banker. He wanted to know if the key was the kind that would fit a safety-deposit box, like one you'd find at a bank."

"And was it?"

"No. I checked with the locksmith who handles that for our bank. He said it wasn't that type and he had no idea what it would fit." Squires sounded calmer, but the hand holding the gun still shook.

"Why don't you sit down? You can still hang on to the gun. I'm not dumb enough to make a play for it." Howie watched as Squires moved to one of the chairs, pulled it further away from the desk, and sat down. The gun, however, was still aimed at him. "You say you need my help. What do you mean by that?"

"Do you believe me when I tell you that I didn't kill my partners?"

Howie hoped he sounded more convincing than he felt. "If you were the killer, you wouldn't be here asking for my help...would you?"

A hint of relief flickered in Squires' eyes.

"But if you want my help, you're going to have to be honest with me. Can you do that?"

"Of course."

"Okay. Let's start with Sam, the loan shark. Why are you dealing with him?"

"That's a personal matter," Squires said defensively.

"Look, if you want me to trust you, you're going to have to come clean."

Squires hesitated as his gaze turned inward. "My parents were divorced when I was less than a year old," he began softly. "I was raised by foster parents. It's not something that I'm proud of. Don't get me wrong. They were good to me, but I always had this sense of abandonment. My therapist told me that my temper is misdirected anger. I've been working on that all my life."

Howie wasn't moved by his story. If the guy wanted to spill his guts about his childhood, then he could talk to Adam. His partner was a good listener and more sympathetic to stuff like that. "That doesn't explain you hooking up with Sam."

"I'm coming to that." Squires swallowed hard. "For the past three years, I've spent a lot of money looking for my birth parents. I hired a private investigator who specializes in such things. Several months ago he located my mother."

"What about your father?"

"He died five years ago, and didn't leave anything to my mother. She's living in poverty. I needed money to resettle her. I couldn't stand to see her living in the slums. Going to Sam was the only way I could get my hands on some quick money. I knew what he was, but I didn't care."

"How were you going to pay the money back?"

"I don't know. I didn't think that far ahead. I just wanted a better life for my mother before she..." Sadness flickered in his eyes. "I want her remaining years to be happy."

"You can prove all of this?"

"Certainly." Squires' eyes sought understanding. "I'm not a liar and I'm not a killer. You have to believe me."

"Do you think that whoever killed your partners is going to come after you?"

"Yes."

256

"But you don't know why?"

Squires shook his head. "Will you help me?" he pleaded.

"I've got to talk it over with my partners first."

"You do that, then." Squires rose from the chair, lowered the gun down to his side, and moved toward the door.

"How am I going to get in touch with you?" Howie asked.

"I'll contact you. I've got to check on a couple of things myself."

"What things?"

"I'll tell you when we talk next. Maybe by then, you'll believe me. I'll have the proof."

As soon as Squires left, Howie poured himself a shot of bourbon, one for his nerves, and a second for the hell of it before calling his partners.

Chapter 74

Howie had just finished jotting down notes on Squires' visit when Adam and Mick rushed into his office.

"I can't believe the guy would come here," Mick said as he sank into a chair. "Man, you're lucky he didn't shoot you."

"Take it easy, Mick." Adam took the chair next to his partner. "It sounds to me like Squires came here to prove his innocence."

Mick cracked his knuckles. "But if the guy's innocent, why did he have a gun? And how do we know it wasn't the same gun that killed Beamer and Wentworth?"

Adam looked to Howie.

"Hey, listen, I went back and forth on all of this myself."

"And what did you decide?"

"That the guy didn't have anything to do with the murders of his partners."

"How can you say that?" Mick asked, incredulous.

"Look. You guys didn't see Squires. I did. And he didn't have the look of a killer. He was scared to death, shaking like a leaf."

"So, what does that prove?"

"Beamer had been shot point-blank. JD told me that whoever did it had to have been a cold-blooded murderer. Squires didn't have that look in his eyes."

Mick shifted uneasily in his seat. "I don't know about this."

"It's time to call JD," Adam said.

"We can handle this ourselves!" Howie snapped.

"This is an ongoing police investigation," Adam shot back.

"Damn it, this is our investigation too!"

"Howie, we can't leave JD out of this. We owe it to him. If we don't bring him in on this, he's going to be crucified by his chief."

Howie realized Adam was right. If it had been anyone else other than JD, he wouldn't have any qualms about hanging the guy out to dangle in the wind. He picked up the phone and dialed. It rang several times before anyone answered.

"Fifth Precinct. Rogers speaking."

Howie hesitated, surprised, and glanced back and forth between his partners. "Ah, isn't this Detective Jim Davidson's phone?"

"It is, but he's not at his desk at the moment. Can I take a message?"

"Tell him to call Howie Cummins. He's got my number."

"Cummins? Are you with that detective agency down on lower Broadway?"

"Ah...yeah. Why?"

"JD's talked about you. He said that you and your partners do a hell of a job with only a few years of experience."

"He said that?" Howie winked at his partners.

"He sure did, and he doesn't give out compliments that often. He—wait a minute, he's coming back now—hey, JD. Phone for you. And you owe me a beer for serving as your personal secretary."

Howie heard the phone change hands.

"Davidson here."

"Hey, JD. It's Howie."

"I hope you didn't call to tell me that you've found another body."

"No, but you're going to be interested in who I had a visit from."

"What happened? Monkey show up?"

"No, wise guy, it was Squires." Howie could picture JD suddenly straightening in his chair.

"When?"

"About an hour ago. The guy just walked into my office. He knew about Beamer's murder and was afraid that he'd be considered a suspect."

"So what did he want from you?"

"He says he's innocent and needs my help."

"Is that so? Doesn't he know that we'll want to question him?" Davidson's voice remained even, giving no indication that he was surprised at what he had just been told.

"Sure, but he's convinced you guys will think he's the killer and throw him in the slammer. And if he's locked up, he can't prove his innocence. I think I can get him to talk to you if you promise that you're not going to arrest him on the spot."

"Be reasonable! How in hell can I promise that?"

"Sorry. That's the deal."

"Damn it! Whose side are you on, anyway?"

"I'm on the side of solving my case," Howie said, determined not to be intimidated. "And right now, I'm betting that Squires is innocent and that he may be able to provide the clues I need."

Several seconds passed. When Davidson finally spoke, Howie could hear the restrained anger in his voice. "Okay, Cummins, I'll play your game...for now. But he's got to agree to share everything he knows."

"Don't worry, he will."

"I'm not worried. It's you who should be worrying because if you're wrong on this, you're aiding and abetting a killer. If that turns out to be the case, you can kiss your detective agency good-bye because the only clients you'll have will be the low-life scum."

The reality of Davidson's words hit hard. "Okay," Howie said. "I'll be in touch with you as soon as I hear from Squires."

Edward Squires made a quick trip to the office he and his partners had shared. He wanted to go through the folders in the bottom drawer of the file cabinet. A couple of weeks ago he had run across a receipt Beamer had placed in their accounts payable. At the time, he didn't think much of it. Now that Beamer had been murdered, he hoped that it would provide a clue as to who killed him.

Howie sat at his desk staring at his half empty coffee cup. His partners had left with the understanding that he would call them as soon as he had heard from Squires. As far as his conversation with JD, he had only shared with them that Davidson agreed to meet with Squires. He didn't tell them about JD's chilling prediction of what would happen to their detective agency if it turned out that Squires was the killer.

The ringing of the phone jarred him. Although too soon for Squires to call, he still hoped it would be him. "MAC Detective Agency. Howie Cummins speaking."

"It's me, Margo." His tone was coated with anger.

Howie squeezed his eyes shut. Margo was the last person he wanted to talk to right now. "What do you want?" he asked curtly, hoping that the guy would get the message that he was too busy to talk.

"You got any news for me?"

"No."

"How about that Squires guy?"

"What about him?"

"Damn it. Did he knock off Beamer?"

"How did you know about Beamer?"

"It was on the news. So did Squires ice him?"

"No."

"How can you be so damn sure?"

"Because he was just up to my office," Howie blurted out, suddenly realizing, but then not caring, that he had given out that information.

"What the hell was he doing up there?"

"Look, all I can tell you is that I'm pretty sure Squires didn't do it, and that we're at a dead end right now."

The clock ticked off several long seconds before Margo spoke. "You're going to keep working on it, aren't you?"

"Sure."

"Call me if you come up with anything."

After Howie hung up, he took a couple of aspirins, washing them down with lukewarm coffee. Margo's constant calling was getting on his nerves.

No, that wasn't exactly true. Everything about the case was getting on his nerves. For the first time in nearly a year, he wondered if the detective business was for him.

Chapter 75

It had been nearly forty-eight hours since Squires had shown up at Howie's office. Howie wondered if JD had been right about the guy's guilt. Once he finished working at the soda fountain, he would head upstairs and call Squires at home. To find him in might be a long shot, but one he needed to take in order to feel that he was doing something. As he wiped the counter, he wondered if Squires would ever contact him. His partners, especially Mick, felt that he'd set him up, and they had told him so the very next day.

"What do you mean, set me up?" Howie had asked, more irritated at himself than his partners.

Mick took the lead. "Adam and I think that his showing up at your place was a ploy. He used you to buy himself some time."

"You don't really believe that, do you?"

"Can you explain why he hasn't contacted you?" Adam asked.

It was a question Howie had no answer for. JD had even called him yesterday and asked if he had heard from Squires. When he said he hadn't, his friend was silent for a moment and then encouraged him to hang in there. By the tone of his voice, however, Howie could tell that the detective didn't believe Squires would ever call. But maybe the killer had gotten to him or he was laying low. More than likely, though, as his partners had suggested, Squires planned that whole scene at his office. Maybe he figured that once he got the gullible detective on his side, he'd have more time to put as much distance between himself and the cops. Howie mulled over these things as he wiped the counter.

"If you're not careful, you're going to rub a hole right through that."

"Oh, hi, Kass. I didn't hear you come up."

"That doesn't surprise me. You looked like you were deep in thought."

"Yeah, I was thinking about some things."

"Whatever they are, they seem to be pretty heavy on your mind." Kass took the towel from Howie and braced his arms against the countertop. "You've seemed preoccupied all evening."

"It's this case I'm working on. At times, it seems pretty cut and dry...and then the next moment, I'm not sure if I'm even on the right track.

To tell you the truth, lately I've been wondering if opening up the agency was a mistake."

"Don't talk nonsense. You're a good detective, and so are Mick and Adam." Kass waved to a customer leaving the store and then turned his attention back to Howie. "You just have the blessing and curse of youth right now."

"I'm not sure I understand."

Kass set the towel aside. "Youth is a blessing because you have so much to look forward to and experience. It's also a curse because when you're young, you don't want to wait. Eagerness leaves no room for patience." He paused. "Have you ever worked a jigsaw puzzle?"

"Sure, when I was a kid."

Kass' eyes twinkled. "Our childhood years are filled with such good memories. I remember working on puzzles with my grandfather. When I first poured out all those pieces onto the table, that big pile discouraged me. I never thought we would be able to piece it together. But then my grandfather started sorting the pieces, forming a part of the picture here and a part there. The important thing was not to become impatient, my grandfather would tell me."

"He was a wise man," Howie said.

"And when we got stuck on that puzzle, he told me that we should walk away from it for a time." Kass' gaze turned inward. "Ah, my grandfather...bless his memory. He said that there are valuable life lessons learned from putting jigsaw puzzles together."

Howie offered Kass a knowing smile. "And I would suppose your grandfather would say that those lessons could be applied to my line of work as well."

Kass nodded.

"So what you're saying is that in solving the case I might have to get away from it for a while. And when I come back to it, the clue I've been looking for hits me right smack in the face. Is that right?" Howie asked, feeling better now, and re-energized about the case.

"Yes, exactly," Kass said, his face beaming with pride. "You and my grandfather would've gotten along just fine."

The cowbell over the front entrance door clanged and in walked Jim Davidson. The detective scanned the store, spotted Howie, came over and sat down.

"I'm honored to have you in my place, Detective Davidson," Kass said. "Can I get you something to eat, maybe a sundae or banana split?"

"No thanks. I'm just here to touch base with this guy." JD turned to Howie. "You weren't home so I figured I'd check here."

"Do we need to go upstairs?"

"We can talk here. It won't take long." He gave a sideways glance toward Kass.

"You detectives talk," Kass said. "I think I hear the magazine rack calling me to straighten it up." He set a glass of water in front of Davidson and walked away.

JD eyed the water for a moment. "I don't suppose they serve anything here that I could use that for as a chaser?"

"I'm afraid not."

"That's the breaks," JD said with a shrug. He waited until Kass was out of hearing range. "We did some further checking on Squires..."

"And?"

"He's coming up pretty clean. Still a suspect, but there's no hard evidence. Has he contacted you?"

"Not yet. The last thing he told me was that he had to check out something."

"What was that?"

"He didn't tell me, but it was something that might give him a clue as to who killed his partners."

"Is that so? Well, if he's guilty, that's a clever cover-up, giving the impression that he's trying to solve the murder."

Howie frowned at the implication that he had been duped. "You've met him. Do you think he did it?"

"What little circumstantial evidence we have points to him. If you're asking about whether I think he could have pulled the trigger, my answer is yes." JD took a sip of water and, grimacing, set the glass aside. "Too much of that stuff can kill you." His tone turned serious. "Just watch yourself."

"Don't worry. I will."

"And call me as soon as you hear from Squires."

"Are you still willing to talk to him without bringing him in for questioning?"

"Yeah. You've got my word on that." JD slid off the stool. "See you around."

Howie worked for another hour before heading for home. Halfway up the stairs to his apartment, he heard the phone ringing in his office. He took the rest of the stairs two at a time, barged through the door, and rushed to his desk. When he picked up the phone, he heard a click at the other end. He hung up and went back to close his office door. Just as he closed it, the phone rang again. This time he caught it by the second ring.

"MAC Detective Agency. Cummins speaking."

"This is Edward Squires. I've got to talk to you. I just discovered something important."

"Go ahead, I'm listening."

"I can't talk now. I'm in a gas station and there's someone waiting to use this phone."

"Come up to my office, then."

"No, I'm afraid the police might be watching your place by now."

That possibility hadn't entered Howie's mind, and he wondered if JD would do that. But why not? If he were in JD's shoes, he'd be doing it. Although he trusted JD wouldn't do that to him, nevertheless, the possibility that he could angered him. "Okay, so where do you want to meet?"

"There's a coffee shop on the corner of Lyndale and Lake Street. Can we meet there tomorrow morning around seven?"

"Sure, I know the place, but why tomorrow if this is so important? Why not now?"

"Because there's one more thing I've got to check on." He lowered his voice to a whisper. "I think I now know who killed my partners."

Chapter 76

Howie had a restless night. He was up before the alarm went off, anxious to hear who Squires thought murdered Wentworth and Beamer. He hoped this would be the piece of the puzzle needed to solve the case. After washing and getting dressed, he considered calling JD. Then he changed his mind. He'd talk to the detective after meeting with Squires. That way, he could tell Squires about JD's willingness to talk to him without hauling him in to the station. Besides, this was his case. He wanted to solve it without the help of the cops. JD would understand…maybe.

The coffee shop Squires had arranged to meet at was nearly full. Howie arrived a few minutes before seven. Squires was nowhere in sight. He spotted a back booth opening up, went and sat down as the dirty dishes were being cleared from it. From his vantage, he had a direct sight to the entrance door. A young, attractive red-headed waitress stopped and he ordered coffee. His interest in her, however, waned as soon as he spotted the diamond on her finger.

Customers came and went but no sign of Squires. It was nearly seven-thirty when, after his third cup of coffee, he decided to order breakfast.

Why hadn't Squires shown up yet? Was he just being cautious in case I brought the cops with me? Maybe he'd had second thoughts. Or maybe Adam and Mick were right that he was stringing me along.

At ten minutes after eight he paid the bill and walked out of the coffee shop, having made the decision to drop by Squires' apartment.

Twenty minutes later he arrived at Squires' apartment building, parked his car in the lot, and sat for a couple of minutes. Squires' car was nowhere in sight, but that didn't mean anything. The guy was too smart to leave his car parked in plain sight as an advertisement to the cops to come and get him. Although the entrance into the apartment building required a key, he persuaded an older lady to let him in, explaining that he had come to surprise his sister whom he hadn't seen in three years.

"Thank you very much," Howie said after she had opened the door for him. "You don't know how much this means to me."

"I know most of the people in this building," the woman said. "What is your sister's name again?"

266

"Ah, you know, it's been so long since I've talked to her that I've forgotten her current married name. She's on her fourth marriage." Leaving the woman, Howie took the stairs up to the second floor.

Squires' apartment was at the far end of the hall. He knocked on the door, standing to one side so he couldn't be seen through the peephole. No answer. He knocked again but there was still no response. He tried the door, surprised to find it unlocked. Glancing down the hallway, he slipped inside, quietly closing the door behind him. A short entryway led into a stylishly furnished living room. If Squires had financial problems, his furnishings didn't reflect it. Howie was about to check the bedroom when a crashing sound like a glass shattering on the floor came from the kitchen area.

"Squires? It's Howie Cummins."

Without warning a small furry brown blur burst into the living room from the kitchen, flew past Howie, and disappeared into another room. It took him a moment to realize that the brown blur was Oscar. Moments later, the monkey inched his way back into the living room. With huge eyes and raised eyebrows, he peered at Howie. As soon as Oscar recognized his old friend, he scampered over and leaped into his arms.

"We're going to have to teach you to knock before you burst into a room," Howie said. "You could give someone a heart attack." He set Oscar on a chair and listened for any other sounds coming from the kitchen. "Squires? It's me, Howie Cummins. I'm alone. No cops."

With his hands clutching his long tail, Oscar screeched away.

"Shhh." Howie put his finger to his lips and moved across the living room toward the kitchen. As soon as he entered the kitchen, he stopped in his tracks.

Squires' body lay sprawled on the floor in a pool of blood. Howie rushed over, dropped to one knee beside the body, and checked for a pulse. Seeing no phone, he retreated back into the living room. The phone sat on an end table next to a high-back cushioned chair. He plopped down in the chair and dialed Jim Davidson's number.

"JD. It's me, Howie."

"What's the matter? You sound sort of shaky."

"I'm at Squires' apartment," Howie said as he glanced toward the kitchen area. "You're going to have to delay your vacation. Squires' dead. Shot in the head."

"Damn! I'll be there as soon as I finish up booking a robbery suspect. Don't disturb anything."

Howie hung up the phone and considered what he should do next. He wanted to know what, if anything, Squires had found out about who had killed his partners. "Sorry, JD, but I've got to do what I've got to do," he muttered and began searching the apartment. Going through each room, he opened drawers, searched closets, looked behind pictures frames, and even checked the bathroom medicine cabinet, making sure he wiped off his fingerprints on everything he had touched. He found nothing.

Davidson and two other officers arrived within twenty minutes. JD posted the officers outside the apartment door, asking one of them to go find the manager and tell him to stay put. "I'm going to want to talk to him after I'm done here," he said. Once the officers left, he turned to Howie. "All right. Show me the body. I want to see it before the lab boys get here." JD's attention was suddenly pulled to a noise coming from the bedroom. "What's that?" he asked, slipping his right hand inside his coat jacket.

"That's the monkey. I locked him in the bedroom so he wouldn't give you any trouble."

JD withdrew his hand from inside his coat. "What's the matter? Doesn't he like detectives?"

"He likes me, but I'm not too sure how he would react to you." JD muttered something under his breath that Howie didn't quite make out. "Come on," Howie said. "The body's in the kitchen." They walked into the kitchen. He stepped aside while JD eyed the area.

"You didn't touch anything, did you?"

"Of course not. I always do what you tell me."

"Yeah. Sure. I hope you were smart enough not to leave any fingerprints." The police detective squatted beside the body.

"How long do you think he's been dead?" Howie asked.

"I don't know." JD continued to examine the body. "I'd guess at the max...six hours, could be as little as two." He stood up. "How did you happen to be here, anyway?"

"Ah...just on a hunch. I got tired of waiting for him to contact me," Howie replied. "Can I go now, or am I a suspect?"

"Get out of here, but I'll want to talk to you later."

"Do you mind if I take Oscar?"

"Who?"

"Can I take the monkey?"

"Go ahead, be my guest. Hell, you'd be doing me a favor. It'll save me from taking him down to the station and booking him."

A half hour later, Howie, with Oscar in his arms, entered his office to find Bernadine waiting for him. As soon as she saw the monkey, she stiffened, her eyes filling with apprehension.

"Don't worry," Howie said. "I'll put him in the kitchen." He took Oscar into the kitchen, got a box of cereal from the cupboard, and poured him a bowlful. "Go ahead and make yourself comfortable...and stay out of trouble."

He walked back into his office. "So, Bernadine, what can I do for you?" he asked as he sat down at his desk.

"My brother's gone."

"Gone? What do you mean?"

"He left the hospital?"

"When?"

"It must have been just after Mick and Adam were up there on Monday afternoon. When I got up there that evening, Lester was gone. A nurse told me that he checked himself out against the doctor's advice." Bernadine paused, her eyebrows knitting together in a frown. "I don't know where he is. I tried to contact you a couple of times, but you were gone. I've spent the last couple of days checking with all his friends. Nobody has heard from him."

Startled by Bernadine's announcement, Howie wondered if Les could've killed Beamer. If he left the hospital on Monday and Beamer was found dead Tuesday morning…Sure the guy was in tough shape, but that wouldn't prevent him from pulling a trigger. And if he killed Beamer, could he have tracked down Squires?

"And you've checked his apartment?" Howie asked.

"Yes, he's not there, and he's not at his office. He shouldn't be walking around."

"What do you want me to do?"

"Find him!"

"I'll do what I can," Howie said. "Why don't you go home and get some rest," he told her. "You look exhausted."

"But I need to find my brother."

"Look, he may try to contact you at home."

His words struck a cord with her. She nodded and got up to leave. "Call me if you find out anything."

"Sure." After Bernadine left, Howie leaned back in his chair and stared at his movie poster. *Bogie, what in hell is going on with this case?*

Chapter 77

After Bernadine left, Howie made his way into the kitchen. Oscar had eaten most of the cereal and now sat atop the back of the chair looking out the window.

"If you see anybody out there who looks like a murderer, let me know, okay?"

Oscar turned and looked blankly at Howie. His only response to the detective's inquiry was to scratch the top of his head.

"Yeah, I know just how you feel. I haven't a clue, either." Howie made a pot of extra strong coffee, poured a cup, and grabbed a couple of cookies. When Oscar eyed the cookies, Howie gave the rest of the bag to him, and headed back to his desk. He hadn't slept well for the past two nights and wondered if he looked as exhausted as Bernadine.

Within moments, the furry beast scampered in from the kitchen and leaped onto Mick's chair, his bulging cheeks ready to burst.

Howie wagged his finger at him. "You little pig. How many cookies have you got stuffed in your mouth?"

The monkey's eyebrows rose. Besides a mouthful of cookies, the little scamp held cookies in both hands.

"You better give me those before you get a stomachache," Howie said, reaching out his hand.

Oscar's eyes doubled in size. He stuffed another cookie into his mouth, uttered some muffled- sounding rebuke, jumped from the chair, and dashed to the other side of the room.

"Suit yourself. Don't blame me if you get sick." Howie leaned back in his chair and watched Oscar climb to the top of the totem pole. Once atop his perch, he sat down, bared his teeth at Howie, and made a show of consuming his remaining cookie.

Howie chuckled at the audacity of his little friend and then settled his gaze on the movie poster. He stared at it for a good minute. "Bogie, did you ever get tired of chasing bad guys? Well, my trouble is I don't know who I'm chasing now. I was sure Beamer or one of his partners killed the LaBelle woman. Then one by one they were murdered." He leaned forward and took a sip of coffee. Opening the desk drawer, he brought out his bottle of bourbon, and took a swig before adding some to his cup. As he continued his conversation with Bogie, he took note of Oscar watching him with a curious expression.

"All I know is that all of this has something to do with those stolen coins. Sure, there were clues—a key and a note with 'DOG' written on it." He took the key out of his desk drawer and held it up. "But, what am I suppose to make out of this? It could be a key to a post office box or a gym locker or who knows what. And what does 'DOG' mean? I know…I know. Give it some time. I'll get a break. I suppose—"

The office door opened and Squirrel sauntered in. He scanned the room, noted Oscar on top of the totem pole, and offered Howie a questioning look. "Don't tell me, you're talking to monkeys now? Boss, are you sure you're okay? You look beat," he said as he walked over and settled in a chair.

"It goes with the territory." Howie slipped the key back in the drawer. "How are you doing?"

"Just got back from meeting a friend at the bus depot downtown. Man, I hate going down there. Those bus fumes make me puke."

Howie suddenly felt as though he had just emerged from a thick fog. "What did you say?"

"I said those fumes made me want to—"

"No, no, before that."

"I was telling you I was at the bus depot."

"That's it!" Howie cried as he snapped his fingers.

"That's what?"

"The missing piece of the puzzle."

"Puzzle? What puzzle?"

"Kass was right. Just give it time."

"Give what time?"

Howie picked up the phone and dialed. He gave a thumbs-up to Squirrel who sat staring wide-eyed at him.

"Adam, this is Howie. Call Mick and the two of you get over here as soon as you can. I think I have the answer to what the key and note we found in the totem pole is all about."

Chapter 78

Les McGuire checked into a motel as soon as he had left the hospital. Bernadine would be worried about him, but he didn't care. He needed to rest and make plans for the future without his sister sticking her nose into his affairs. His head and jaw still ached like hell, and his one eye was badly swollen, but in time, all that would heal.

Later tonight or maybe tomorrow or the next day he would go and get the loot for himself. There was no rush now that Beamer was dead. Les had found out all about him that day he had tailed him to the real estate office. Beamer hadn't been as smart as he thought. He deserved what he got.

As Les lay on the bed, he closed his eyes and reflected on how things had turned out. It was pretty smart to have had that duplicate key made. Also, he was damn lucky to have done it a couple of days before Beamer came into his office and beat the hell out of him. And talk about luck, it was just plain dumb luck that the old guy who made the duplicate key recognized the original.

"I haven't seen one of these for a few years," the old timer had said.

"So you know where that key comes from?" Les asked, hardly able to contain his excitement.

"Why sure. At one time, I had a locker down there myself." He held the key in front of Les' face. "See there that number?"

Les nodded.

"That's the locker number."

As Les now turned on his side, attempting to get comfortable on the lumpy motel bed, he relived the moment he walked out of that locksmith's shop feeling like he had the whole world by its tail. For the first time in his life, lady luck had smiled upon him. Soon he would be rolling in dough. All he needed now was some rest.

Chapter 79

Adam arrived at Howie's office within ten minutes. Mick rushed in five minutes later and took a place by the window. Oscar had greeted each of them from atop of the totem pole.

"Okay, everybody's here. Start talking," Adam said. Howie had told him and Squirrel that he would wait until Mick arrived before sharing his news.

Howie held up the slip of paper and the key they had found in the totem pole. "I'm pretty sure I know what these are all about."

"I gave him the answer," Squirrel said, a smug smile filling his face.

"I asked him how he was doing and..." Howie nodded at Squirrel. "Go ahead. Tell them what you said."

The little guy scooted to the edge of his seat. "I told him I met a friend at the bus depot."

"And as soon as he mentioned the bus depot, it clicked."

"I'm not sure I understand," Mick said.

"Think about it." Howie wanted his partners to make the connection as part of their ongoing learning experience. "What kind of buses are there?"

"Big smelly ones," Squirrel offered.

"But what's the place called?"

"The bus depot." Squirrel's nose twitched. "But I still don't get it."

"Mick, think of the buses," Howie said. "What kind are they?"

"They're—" Mick eyes' widened. "I see what you're getting at!"

"So do I!" Adam said, his voice revealing a growing excitement.

"What? Come on, guys, tell me." Squirrel's eyes darted between the three of them.

"Squirrel. What's the name of the buses?" Howie asked.

"They're, ah, Greyhound."

"That's right." Howie held up the note. "And the way I figure it, 'DOG' refers to the Greyhound Bus Depot."

"Oh, man!" Squirrel slapped his forehead. "Greyhound...Dog. I get it now. And that number on the key has to be a locker number. Right?"

"That's my guess," Howie said.

"So, what are we going to do?" Adam asked cautiously.

"We've got the key," Mick said. "Why don't we go down and open the locker?"

"And when we do," Howie said. "I'm hoping we'll find the coins."

"Coins?" Squirrel's mouth dropped open. "What coins?"

"So what are we waiting around here for?" Mick asked. "Let's go get them."

"We'll go, but only to check to see if they're still there," Howie said.

"What are you saying?" Adam asked. "That we're going to do this on our own? Without the police?"

"That's right. And if the coins are still there, we'll lay a trap."

"Come on, guys...what coins?"

"Laying a trap is a good idea," Mick said. "So does that mean we're going to stake the place out?"

"Exactly."

"And when do we start?"

"Right away. That's why I wanted you guys here. If we're lucky, and the coins are still there, that means the killer hasn't gotten to the locker yet."

Squirrel raised his hand.

"What is it?"

"What coins?"

"Coins that were stolen in a robbery five years ago from a private collection. They're rare and worth plenty." Howie turned to his partners. "One more thing. Bernadine was in this afternoon to see me. Les took off from the hospital after you guys visited him on Monday."

"And you found Beamer dead on Tuesday morning," Adam said.

"Oh, my gosh," Mick said. "If Les killed Beamer, do you think he could have killed Squires?"

"What!" Squirrel cried. "Another one bit the dust! It sure doesn't pay to be a clown now-a-days." He looked up at Oscar. "Poor guy...you're an orphan now."

Oscar raised his eyebrows but remained quiet.

"I don't know if Les is the killer," Howie said. "But whoever this killer is, just watch yourself." He paused. "So are we clear on everything now? Any questions?"

"Not me," Mick said.

"Me, either, boss."

Howie noted the continuing silence of Adam. "How about you? Any questions?"

"Don't you think we should call JD?"

"I just knew you'd ask that." Howie's tone turned hard. "We're going to catch this guy on our own without any police help."

"But we're dealing with somebody who's murdered at least four people. Maybe five with the LaBelle woman."

"So? You don't think we can handle it?"

Adam shifted in his chair. "It's not that."

274

"Damn it! What is it then?"

"You know how I feel. We should be cooperating with the police."

"We'll cooperate after we nail this guy. We'll hand him over to JD on a silver platter."

"But—"

"But nothing!" Howie snapped, his neck muscles tightening. "If you don't like the way I'm handling this, you don't have to take part."

"Howie, Adam's just trying—"

"Stay out of this Mick," Howie said, not taking his eyes off Adam. "You want off the case?" he asked.

Adam glared at Howie. Squirrel stared at them both with his mouth wide open. The clock marked the passing of awkward silence. Adam finally spoke. "I came this far with you guys. I'll finish it."

"Okay, that's settled," Howie said, still angry with Adam. "Let's get going. I'm anxious to check to see if the coins are there."

"And if they are?" Mick asked.

"Then we'll work in shifts. Mick, you and Adam take the first shift. You'll watch it until eleven tonight. Squirrel and I will take over after that." Howie got up and headed for the door.

275

Chapter 80

Howie and Squirrel entered the Greyhound Bus Depot shortly before eleven to relieve Mick and Adam who had been there since four that afternoon. Earlier, all of them had gone to check the locker area. Upon locating and opening locker 137, they had found a battered brown briefcase containing the stolen rare coins.

"Hot diggity dog! Now we're in business!" Squirrel exclaimed at their good fortune.

After quieting Squirrel, Howie replaced the briefcase's contents with a bag of washers he had bought at a local hardware store.

"What are you going to with the coins?" Mick asked.

"Keep them for a while."

Adam frowned. "Aren't you turning them over to the police?"

Howie brushed aside his annoyance. "Yeah, eventually, but I want to do it at the same time we nab the killer." He shoved the briefcase back into the locker, closed it, and turned to Mick and Adam. "We'll do this in shifts. You first. Squirrel and I will spell you later. Keep your eyes open. Follow whoever comes for that briefcase. If you can take him down, do it."

His partners exchanged nervous glances.

"Don't worry," Mick spoke up. "You can count on us. He won't get away."

"Good. We'll see you later. Come on Squirrel, let's go." They had then gone back to the office to wait. Squirrel napped on the couch. Howie, too tense to sleep, paged through one of his *Police Gazette* magazines. Shortly after ten, they headed back to the bus depot.

"Do you think the murderer showed up?" Squirrel asked as he and Howie scanned the main floor of the depot looking for Mick and Adam.

"We'll soon find out," Howie said, figuring that his partners would have contacted him if that had been the case.

The depot, built in the late 1930's was roughly the size of a couple of basketball courts placed side to side. Although late at night, the place was fairly crowded. Over the loudspeaker a man with a nasal whine announced that the bus to Rapid City, South Dakota was now boarding at Gate Three.

"There they are," Squirrel said, pointing to his right across the way.

Mick and Adam had stationed themselves by the vending machines. From their vantage point, they had a direct line of sight to the alcove of lockers.

Howie and Squirrel made their way over to them. "No luck, huh?" Howie asked.

Mick shook his head. "We thought we had something about an hour ago but it was just some guy trying all the lockers."

"We figured that he was hoping to find one open," Adam said.

"I know that scam," Squirrel piped up. "He finds an unlocked one, takes whatever stuff's in it, and pawns it." When Howie gave him the eye, he offered a sheepish grin. "Hey, I only know about that because one of my friends got caught doing it. I'd never think of doing it myself."

Mick yawned as he stretched his arms. "I'm ready to go home and get some sleep."

"Yeah, I could use some shut-eye myself," Adam said.

"Take off then," Howie said. "We'll see you tomorrow afternoon around four." After they left, he turned to Squirrel. "Are you staying for the duration?"

"Man, are you kidding? I wouldn't miss this for anything."

"Good. Now get away from me and act like you don't know me."

Squirrel bought a cup of coffee, picked up a discarded newspaper, and found a place to sit. Howie stood nearby next to the vending machines. Squirrel opened the newspaper, held it in front of his face, but turned his head slightly and spoke out of the corner of his mouth. "Did you know I used to hang around here a lot?"

Howie kept his eye on the locker area. An older lady carrying a shopping bag opened the locker opposite the one he was watching, put her bag in it, and closed it. "So, what kind of trouble were you getting into down here?"

"You've got to know this was before I turned over a new leaf."

"Don't be looking at me," Howie said. "Act like you're reading the paper."

"Okay, boss." Squirrel set his coffee cup on the floor and went back to paging through the paper. "I'd come down here and hustle bets. There were plenty of easy marks. People waiting for their bus to leave and were tired of playing the pinball machines. With a pair of dice, I could make fifty bucks on a good evening."

"I'm glad you reformed. Now, let's just keep our eyes open and cut the chatter."

"Who are we looking for?"

"Whoever approaches that locker."

By two in the morning, the station had quieted. Howie leaned against the vending machine, half dozing. He came fully awake as a familiar figure walked up to locker 137 and inserted a key into it. Stunned, he pushed off from the vending machine.

"Let's go!" he hissed as he ran past Squirrel.

277

Doris Beamer had just opened the locker by the time Howie and Squirrel reached her. "Need some help?" Howie asked.

Doris opened her mouth but no words came out. Her eyes doubled in size. "Wha... what are you doing here?"

Howie glanced pointedly at the briefcase sitting in the locker. "I was just about to ask you that very same question."

"I'm...just picking up some stuff," she said nervously.

"Is that right? And what would that be? Something that belonged to your late husband?" Howie's tone turned sharp. "You don't exactly seem to be the grieving widow." He nudged Squirrel. "Does she?"

"Not at all."

"Why did you kill your husband?" Howie asked. "Was it out of jealousy or just plain old-fashioned greed?"

"I don't know what you're talking about," she huffed, offended by the accusation.

"Oh, I think you do." Howie pointed to the locker. "Just like you know what's in that briefcase. You put on quite the little act for me the other day, didn't you?" When she didn't reply, he continued, "You discovered your husband was Johnny Labelle's partner. That's what you meant, isn't it, when you told me that even though you loved him, he'd find out one day that you didn't *need* him. You learned about the locker, somehow you got a key, and then, I'm betting you got rid of your cheating husband."

"I didn't kill him!" she snapped.

"Who did then?"

Her eyes took on a defiant look.

"You hired someone to do it...is that it? And then there's Squires and Wentworth...how about them? Did you get someone to kill them as well?" When she still remained silent, Howie turned to Squirrel. "Get the briefcase."

"Sure thing." As Squirrel reached in and got the briefcase, Howie grabbed Doris by the arm.

"Where are we going?" she fumed.

"To see a detective friend of mine."

"She's not going anywhere!" a voice snarled from behind them.

Chapter 81

Howie whirled around, his grip tightening on Doris' arm.

"Margo! What are you doing here?"

"Let her go!" Margo snarled, his eyes raging with fury.

"But she's—"

"*I said let her go!*"

To Howie's astonishment, as soon as he released his grip on Doris, she hurried to Margo's side, taking hold of his arm.

"Babe, I was so scared," she cried.

"I told you I'd watch out for you, didn't I?" Margo assured her, not taking his eyes off the two startled detectives.

Howie's brain spun like it was riding the Tilt-a-Whirl. He locked eyes with Margo to steady his thoughts. "So the two of you are in on this together, huh? Then *you* must have killed Squires and Wentworth..." His eyes shifted to Doris. Her thin lips had formed a tight, smug smile. "And then the two of you killed your husband. Is that it?"

"You can't prove shit," Margo said, his lips curling in a sneer.

Margo was too powerful for them to take on, but maybe he could be bluffed. Howie looked to the main area of the depot. "We'll just let the police decide that. They're here to talk to you."

Margo didn't flinch.

"You can't fool me, Cummins," Margo said. "There aren't any cops here. I can smell them a mile away."

Howie slipped his hand into his coat pocket. "Consider this, then. I have a gun."

"Oh, my god!" Doris gasped. She clung tighter to Margo's arm.

Margo grated a laugh. "Don't worry. He doesn't carry a rod." He gave her a sideward glance. "You get out of here now. I can handle it from here."

"But I don't—"

"*Go!*"

Howie took a step toward Doris as she hesitated. Margo moved between them, blocking his way. "You take another step and I'll break you in two." He gave Doris a gentle push. "Get going now!" She left in a hurry, casting anxious glances over her shoulder until she was out of sight. He pointed at Squirrel. "Get the briefcase."

"You're not going to get away with this," Howie said, furious.

"Shut up!" Margo shot a smoldering look at Squirrel. "What the hell are you waiting for? Get the damn briefcase!"

Squirrel gulped. "Boss, ah, what should I do?"

"Do what he says," Howie said grimly.

"Heave it over here!" Margo ordered.

Squirrel tossed the briefcase. With Margo distracted, Howie charged him, slamming into his chest with a thud, momentarily knocking the breath out of him and causing him to drop the briefcase.

"Why you—" Margo picked up Howie and hurled him crashing against the lockers. The explosion of body and metal echoed off the marble floor into the main area of the depot. Pain flared, and Howie slid to the floor, only half conscious.

As Margo bent to pick up the briefcase, Squirrel leaped onto his back, wrapping his arms around the man's massive neck.

"Help!" Squirrel yelled. "Call the cops, somebody!"

Howie began to crawl, inching his way toward the briefcase. Snorting like a bull, Margo twirled in a circle, shaking Squirrel off. The little guy careened off the floor into a row of plastic chairs and sent them clattering in every direction.

Margo reached for the briefcase, but Howie snagged it first and, using the last of his strength, flung it into the midst of gathering onlookers.

"I've called the cops!" a man yelled from the growing crowd.

"Damn you, Cummins!" Margo glared at Howie. "You'll pay for this!" He took off running, knocking to the floor whoever got in his way.

Howie clenched his teeth and slowly picked himself off the floor. He clutched his arm, holding it tight to his body.

"You okay?" Squirrel asked.

"Shoulder hurts like hell," he replied, wondering if he was going to pass out.

Squirrel retrieved the briefcase and came back to where Howie had slumped in a chair. "That guy doesn't know how lucky he was."

"What are you talking about?" Howie asked.

"I was only getting started." Squirrel hunched up his shoulders as he sneered, "The next time we meet, he's in for big trouble."

Chapter 82

It had been a week since Howie and Squirrel tangled with Margo at the bus depot. Witnesses had recounted to the police that Margo had tossed the two of them around like they were rag dolls.

One of the witnesses, a spry old man in his 80's, told the police officer, "That brute plowed through people like they were matchsticks. No one tried to stop him. Now, if I would've been younger..."

His arm now in a sling, Howie had suffered a severe shoulder separation when slammed against the locker. Squirrel, bruised and sore, complained more of dizziness than anything else. "Man, that guy spun me around so much I thought I was back on the Tilt-a-Whirl. He came on like a freight train in bib overalls."

Howie had turned the stolen coins over to the police. When he had tossed the briefcase into the midst of the gathering crowd, a woman had enough presence of mind to slip it into her shopping bag. "How much of a reward do I get?" she had asked the police.

The next day JD had stormed into Howie's office. He'd never seen his friend so angry. "What the hell were you thinking?" he yelled, slamming his fist on Howie's desk. "Damn it to hell! We're supposed to be working together."

"Come on, JD, be reasonable!" Howie shot back. "I didn't have time to call you. So why don't you sit down and we can talk this out."

"Listen to me and listen good! I'm only going to say this once!" JD braced his hands on the desk and leaned so close Howie could smell his Old Spice aftershave. Although not yelling anymore, his tone had turned icy. "You call me even if you hear so much of a rumor where Margo's *grandmother* might be. You hear that?"

Howie nodded, gritting his teeth, deciding not to further antagonize his friend with a smartass retort.

JD straightened. "Good, because this guy's suspected of killing three already. Let's not make it a fourth." Without giving Howie a chance to reply, he stormed out, slamming the door behind him. A couple days later, he called to check on Howie. He sounded like his old self, ending the phone call with a reminder that Howie could contact him day or night.

The police had staked out Margo's bar but he never showed up. One of the part-time bartenders posted a sign, *Closed Until Further Notice*, in the window. The cops had also staked out Margo house in south Minneapolis. No luck there either. Doris Beamer hadn't been seen since and was presumed to be with Margo.

Howie was mulling over Margo and Doris' whereabouts when his office door opened and his partners walked in.

"How's the shoulder?" Mick asked as he and Adam sat down.

"It's okay."

"Good thing it's the left arm," Adam said. "He can still write."

"And eat," Mick added with a smirk.

"If you guys came to cheer me up, you're not doing a very good job," Howie said, forcing a smile. The slightest movement sent stabbing pains through his shoulder. The medication helped, but only so far as keeping the throbbing at a tolerable level. The pain was a constant reminder of how he botched the case. He should never have allowed Margo to get away.

Adam glanced at Mick and took the lead. "Actually, we came to tell you that we've made a decision."

"All on your own? And what would that be?"

"Tell him, Mick."

Mick cleared his throat. "Now don't get angry until you hear us out." He paused as though waiting for their boss to comment. "We decided that one of us should take turns staying with you."

"What!" Howie winced. "You can't be serious! No way am I going to have a baby-sitter."

"Not a baby-sitter, a bodyguard," Adam said. "Margo's a dangerous character. And your arm's still in a sling."

"I don't care. What would people say?"

"They're not going to say anything," Adam argued.

"That's right!" Howie snapped. "And do you know why? Because they're not going to get a chance. Listen, I appreciate what you guys are trying to do. But I'll be okay. I'll keep the office door locked." It was a lie. No way would he lock the door. The wags on Broadway would have a field day with how the brave detective remained behind lock doors. "If anything comes up, I'll call you. Adam, you're only five minutes away. And Mick, you could make it here in less than ten minutes if you had to."

"But what if we're not home when you call?" Mick asked.

"Then I'll call Kass downstairs, or I'll call the cops, or I'll call Superman." He rubbed his throbbing shoulder. The next time he took his pain pills, he would take a double dose. "Besides, JD told me that he could have a squad car over here within three minutes if I need one." He didn't mention he'd refused JD's offer of having a police officer stay with him for a couple of days.

His partners exchanged glances. "I told you that he wouldn't go for it," Mick said.

Adam shrugged. "We had to try."
"Don't sweat it, guys, I'll be okay."
"Sure you will," Mick said. "After all, you can call on Superman."

Chapter 83

Howie had just finished pouring himself an evening cup of coffee in the kitchen when he heard his office door open. "Make yourself comfortable, Mick," he yelled. "I'll be right out." He glanced at the clock: a few minutes after eight. Mick had told Howie that he didn't think he could make it before eight-thirty.

"The wife and I are going out for dinner to talk about names for the baby due in December," he had explained.

Mick's early arrival probably meant that the naming process had gone smoothly.

"You want a cup of coffee?" Howie yelled, wondering what name they had decided on. Hearing no reply, he headed back toward his office. "Hey, are you hard of—" All thoughts of Mick fled when he saw who was standing in his office.

"Hello, Cummins." Margo's eyes shifted to the cup in Howie's hand. "Go ahead. I already had some earlier."

Howie set his cup on the desk and took his chair. He was no match for Margo, but if it came to that, he wouldn't go down easy. Still, with his arm in a sling and his shoulder hurting like hell, his best option was to stall and play it cool until Mick showed up.

Margo pushed a chair closer and settled in. "Finish your coffee. I'm in no hurry."

Howie glanced at the clock. Five after eight. "You really surprised me, showing up at the depot," he said casually.

"Hell, I could tell that by the look on your face."

"So why did you kill Squires and his partners?"

Margo's crooked smile turned into a sneer.

"You tell me, since you're so damn smart."

Howie took his time in forming an answer. "It wasn't just because one of them was dating Donna Mae, was it? It had to have been because you somehow found out about the coins."

"Do you want the full story?"

"Sure. And start with Donna Mae."

"Hell, I liked that dame. Always wondered how she would've been in bed. Too bad she got snuffed before I got to know her better."

"You mean, before you could learn more about her brother."

"Yeah, you can say that." Margo's sneer turned cold. "Then she started dating somebody else. When she was killed, I figured the guy who did her was after the loot."

"But you didn't know who he was. Is that right?"

"That's why I hired you. Pretty damn smart, aren't I?"

Anger simmered within Howie. He bit his lip to keep it from surfacing. "Why did you kill Wentworth?"

"Shit, I had no choice. He was getting too damn close to finding the coins."

"But he wasn't Johnny LaBelle's partner, was he?"

"I didn't know that until I tracked him down."

"So who was Johnny's partner?"

"You're the detective. You tell me."

"It had to have been Jack Beamer." The minute hand on the clock looked like it had barely moved since last time Howie looked. "What I can't figure out was how you got his wife to come in on the deal with you."

Margo calmly scratched his chin. "Man, that was the luck of the draw. Met her a year ago. She came into the bar a couple of times, lonely as hell. We struck up a relationship, had some romps in the sack, and that was the end of it."

"Until you found out that it was her husband you were after."

"Like I said, luck of the draw. Didn't take much to persuade her to help. She turned out to be one greedy broad."

"Where is she now?"

The look in Margo's eyes sent a shiver down Howie's spine.

"Let's just say I ditched her."

"You only used her to get to her husband. Isn't that right?" Howie asked, seething at how he had been duped by Margo.

"The dumb shit thought I was a client wanting to buy one of his crummy houses. Doris took me to his office early one morning."

"And that's when you took him in the back room?"

"Yeah, and she enjoyed watching. Even slapped him around a couple of times herself. She was angry as hell at him."

The pieces of the puzzle were falling in place. "So, you got the key to the locker from him?"

"What do you think?"

"And I was dumb enough to tell you what was on that slip of paper we found in the totem pole." Howie gritted his teeth. "How did you figure it was the bus depot?"

"After I told Beamer about it, his eyes lit up. Hell, I knew then he had made a connection so I convinced him that I'd spare his life if he told me what it meant." Margo chuckled. "He fell for it, too. Said it could be the depot since Johnny had a thing about riding Greyhound buses. Made sense to me."

"Why didn't you get the coins right away? Why did you wait?"

Margo frowned. "Hell, I thought they were in a safe place. Besides, I had another problem to take care of."

"You mean Squires?"

"He was getting too snoopy. I don't know how in hell he found out about me and Doris, but I wasn't taking any chances. Everything was going okay until you and your partners got too nosey." Margo leaned forward and thrust an accusing finger at Howie. "Because of your damn meddling I didn't get those coins."

"Tough luck. Cops have them now."

A black scowl crossed Margo's face. "I figured that."

"So what did you drop by for?" Howie asked sarcastically, his mind racing as he tried to figure out what his next move should be.

"Don't shit with me. I'm here to tie up some loose ends, if you know what I mean."

"You enjoy killing, don't you?"

"Yeah. I didn't know that about myself until I whacked Wentworth. And you should've heard Beamer beg for mercy. Bawled like a baby, and he was supposed to be such a tough guy."

"What are you going to do? Shoot me?" Howie asked in a mocking tone.

"Naw, that would too easy. I'm going to beat you bloody and then snap your neck." Margo offered a twisted half smile. "But go ahead and finish your coffee. Enjoy it. It'll be the last cup you'll ever have."

Howie stole a glance at the clock. Eight-fifteen. "Put it that way. I'd rather have a shot of bourbon. There's a bottle in my desk drawer. Can I get it?"

"Be my guest. I'll take a shot, too."

Eyes locked on Margo, Howie pulled the drawer partway open, fumbled for the gun that Wentworth had dropped at the Fun House, and pointed it at Margo.

"What the—" Margo's jaw muscles tightened for a moment. Then he relaxed and laughed. "Hell, I've seen those before. You press the damn trigger and a flag pops out."

Howie shrugged. "Can't blame me for trying." He tossed the prop gun on the desk, reached further into the back of the drawer and took out the Colt revolver Hatchaway had given him. Pushing himself out of his seat, he aimed the revolver at Margo. "This one doesn't come with a flag."

Chapter 84

Margo rose cautiously from the chair, his nostrils flaring, his massive chest heaving against his bib overalls. "Well, now. Maybe that thing is loaded and maybe it isn't."

Howie cocked the revolver.

"You're bluffing," Margo said. Still, he hesitated.

"You want to chance it?" Howie glanced at the clock. Eighty-thirty-five. *Where the hell is Mick?* He moved to keep his chair between them.

Margo shoved the barrier aside, but before taking another step the sound of tiny feet scampering down the hallway from the kitchen area distracted him.

Dashing into the room, Oscar leaped onto Margo's leg, sinking his razor-sharp teeth into his thigh.

Margo yowled in pain.

Seizing the opportunity, Howie whipped the gun's barrel across Margo's face.

A beastly cry erupted from within Margo. His eyes raged as he wiped the back of his hand across his nose and lips, smearing the side of his face with blood. A chunk of tooth floating in a dark crimson drop slid over his bottom lip, teetered for a moment, and tumbled onto his chest.

Oscar screeched in fury as he clung to Margo's leg, furiously attempting to shake it in an effort to topple the giant.

Margo grabbed Oscar by the tail, yanked him loose, and flung him across the room. The monkey hit the wall with a sickening thud and fell lifeless to the floor.

"Damn you!" Howie head-butted Margo in the chest as Margo tore the gun out of his hands and tossed it aside, then slammed the detective into the wall.

A bolt of pain screamed through Howie's body as his injured shoulder took the full force of the impact. Margo came at him again and grabbing hold of his sling, swung him on top of the desk. Howie slid across the mahogany surface, crashing onto the floor, taking with him the telephone and everything else. He lay there, struggling to fight past the vertigo of the damage Margo was inflicting.

"You're sure as hell not putting up much of a fight!" Margo taunted as he stood over his victim.

Infuriated by the smirk on Margo's face, Howie struggled to his knees, supporting himself with his good arm to keep from toppling over. Before he could get to his feet, Margo kicked him savagely in the side. The blow sent him sprawling face down on the floor, gasping for breath. His ribs burned like hot coals. Shoulder ligaments became shards of glass. He fought to stay conscious. With his attacker standing over him, he focused on Margo's shoes—black cowboy boots in need of a shine.

"What's the matter, Cummins? Not as tough as you think you are?"

Howie's disoriented gaze drifted from the boots to poor Oscar to a steel letter opener lying nearby. The eight-inch opener had an end as pointed at a knife. "Oscar!" he cried suddenly. "Attack!"

Margo jerked his head toward the monkey. Howie grabbed the opener and with all the strength he could muster, plunged it through the boot into the top of Margo's foot.

Margo screamed like a wounded animal, falling to the floor as he grabbed wildly for the opener imbedded in his foot.

Howie crawled toward his bathroom where he could lock himself in. He'd almost made it when Margo grabbed his legs and dragged him back into the office.

Pink spittle flew from Margo's mouth. Blood oozed from the gap in his boot. "I'm going to kill you inch by inch," he snarled, and raising his injured foot, stomped on Howie's shoulder as hard as he could.

White stars flashed before Howie eyes as the shards of glass shattered into even smaller pieces.

"You're going to beg for mercy before I'm done," Margo said as he picked up the letter opener. "I'll teach you to mess with me, you son-of—"

"Go to hell!" Howie cried.

The office door banged open and Mick burst in. He slammed into Margo, sending him crashing into the file cabinet, knocking over the floor lamp in the process. Margo struggled to get up, but a crunching blow to his face sent him sprawling. Bright red blood spurted from a nose now smashed to one side.

"Come on! Get up!" Mick yelled, his hands curled into fists. He kicked aside the letter opener Margo had dropped.

Margo lumbered to his feet. He took a wild swing, but Mick deflected it, landing a bruising blow to his jaw that sounded like the cracking of a whip. Margo's head snapped back and he hit the floor with a thud that was sure to bring Kass running.

Mick stood over his opponent for several moments before going to kneel by Howie. "Are you okay?" he asked as he helped him up into a chair.

"Wha...what time is it?"

"It's eight-forty-five. Why?"

A fragile smile crossed Howie's face. "You're late."

"Listen wise guy, you need to see a doctor."

"See how Oscar is, will you?"

"Okay, and then I'm calling JD." Still, Howie didn't relax until Mick reported that Oscar had his eyes open and appeared to be okay. He closed his eyes and leaned back in his chair as Mick placed the call to the police.

JD and four officers arrived within minutes.

Margo sat on the floor by the file cabinet, his back wedged between the cabinet and the wall, his hands tied behind his back with an extension cord. A dazed look of defeat had replaced the anger and fury he'd arrived with. JD had two of the officers take Margo away in handcuffs.

"He...he used me...the son-of-a—" Howie winced with pain.

"Save it," JD said. "You can tell me the whole story later."

"Ready to see that doctor now?" Mick asked.

"In a little while." Howie, determined to walk under his own power, needed time to gather his strength. "How's Oscar doing?" he asked Mick for the fourth time.

"Better than you," Mick replied for the fourth time.

Oscar sat huddled against the end of the couch, quietly nibbling on a banana Mick had given him. Every few seconds he eyed JD with suspicion.

An officer standing outside Howie's office door stuck his head in. "There's a fellow out here who wants to come in. He says he owns the drugstore downstairs."

"That's Kass," Mick said.

JD nodded to the officer. "Let him in."

Kass came rushing in, his eyes nearly doubling in size as he surveyed the scene. "Are you two all right?" he asked Mick and Howie.

"Howie's the one busted up," Mick said. "He's needs to go see a doctor."

"Let me help you." Kass reached out to Howie.

Howie waved him off. With great difficulty he pushed himself up out of the chair. He stood for a second before collapsing back into it. "I guess I'll take that help after all," he said, thinking, but unwilling to admit, that this was a hell of a way of making a living.

Chapter 85

Although it had been nearly a week since Howie's scrap with Margo, his bruised ribs still ached. As far as his shoulder, the doctor informed him that it would be a couple more weeks before he could lose the sling.

Oscar had faired better. According to a vet they had taken him to the next morning, the little monkey was remarkably fit for what he had been through. At the moment, Oscar was in the kitchen, enjoying a banana and a bowl of grapes.

Howie and his partners had just finished reviewing the LaBelle case when the door slammed downstairs and the stairs began to creak.

Adam cocked his head. "Who's that now?"

"Sounds like JD," Howie said.

Within moments the door opened and JD walked in. He strolled over and sat on the windowsill. "You need more chairs in here."

"You didn't come up to talk about my furniture needs, did you?"

"We picked up Les McGuire last night."

"Great!" Mick exclaimed. "Where did you find him?"

"Cheap motel in South Minneapolis. An officer responded to a complaint about someone staying but not paying. When the officer followed up, it turned out to be McGuire. He was so weak he could barely move. Kept mumbling something about having to get to the bus depot."

"Good work nabbing him," Adam said.

"Thanks, but it was a lucky break."

"What's he being charged with?" Howie asked.

"Accessory to murder, but with a good lawyer, he'll get off easy - especially since he's cooperating."

"What did he say about Beamer?"

"That Beamer used the monkey to get to Hatchaway. McGuire's story is that Beamer was supposed to put sleeping powder in Hatchaway's tea. When he found out that the old guy was poisoned, he said he almost went to the cops...or so he claims."

"What stopped him?"

"Afraid of what Beamer would do to him."

"How about Doris Beamer? Did you find her body yet?"

JD shook his head. "And Margo's not talking."

"Has he confessed to killing Squires and the other two guys?" Adam asked.

"No, but when we searched his bar, we found the murder weapon hidden in the back room. The gun's got his prints all over it."

Adam blew a stream of air past his lips. "This sure was some case."

"You can say that again," Mick said. "I hope we have some breathing room before our next one."

"You guys did a pretty good job on this one," JD said.

"Thanks," Howie said. "But I should've figured Margo out right from the beginning."

JD offered an incredulous smile. "Oh, yeah? Who in hell do you think you are—Bogart?"

Chapter 86

Howie looked up from his desk just as his office door opened. It was Bernadine. She had called him last evening to tell him she knew about her brother and was going to see him. However, she didn't mention anything about dropping by the office today to see him.

"Hi, Bernadine. Come on in and have a chair."

She made herself comfortable. "I stopped to thank you for all your help."

"Just part of the job."

"And please express my appreciation to Mick and Adam as well."

"I will. I'm just sorry that it turned out this way for your brother. It's too bad he got mixed up with Beamer."

"Yes, so am I, but it just may be for his own good. God works in mysterious ways," she said, fingering the slender cross she wore on a silver necklace.

"What do you mean?"

Bernadine looked more at peace than she had since the beginning of the case. "I'm praying that my brother will have an awakening while in prison so that he'll follow the straight and narrow once he's out."

Howie didn't think Les would ever follow the straight and narrow. "What's going to happen to his business?"

Her chest seemed to swell with pride. "I'm taking it over."

"You are?" Howie said, hoping his shock wasn't too evident.

"Yes, I think I've enough business sense and I believe people will come to know that I'll always give them an honest deal."

"Well, good for you, Bernadine!"

"With God's help I—" Bernadine's eyes suddenly widened as Oscar leaped onto the desk.

"Bernadine, don't be afraid of him. He's harmless." Howie watched in amusement as Oscar opened the right-hand desk drawer. "See, he just likes to get into a little mischief from time to time."

"Oh, my God!" Bernadine screamed. "He's got a gun!"

Oscar pointed the popgun at her and pulled the trigger.

The poor woman fainted just as the flag popped out.

"Oscar, that's not funny!" Howie chided, taking the gun from him.

292

Oscar screeched something in reply, bared his teeth, twirled around, and held out his hand for a treat.

Charles Tindell's writing career began one hot July day in 1995 while sitting in a canoe in the Boundary Waters Canoe Area in northern Minnesota. His first book *Seeing Beyond the Wrinkles* is the recipient of the National Mature Media's coveted GOLD AWARD designating it among "The Best in Educational Material for Older Adults."   His second book *The Enduring Human Spirit* is the recipient of the National Mature Media's Silver Award, symbolizing that the work is among the best of the best.

He and his wife, Carol, have three sons, four grandchildren, and two cats. Oil painting, ventriloquism, baking bread, canoeing, jigsaw puzzles, collecting hour glasses, and writing are among his interests. He serves as a volunteer police chaplain for his community. He also has had the privilege of speaking around the country on the subjects *Spirituality and Aging* as well as *The Courage to Be.*

This Angel Isn't Funny is his fourth mystery in the MAC Detective Agency series featuring Howie Cummins and his partners, Adam Trexler and Mick Brunner. His first three mysteries are: *This Angel Has No Wings; This Angel Doesn't like Chocolate; This Angel's Halo Is Crooked.* He is currently working on his fifth mystery in the series, *This Angel Has Blue Eyes.*

Made in the USA
San Bernardino, CA
16 December 2013